ALSO BY MIKE BOND

America

Snow

Assassins

Saving Paradise

Killing Maine

Goodbye Paris

The Last Savanna

Holy War

House of Jaguar

Tibetan Cross

The Drum That Beats Within Us

CRITICS' PRAISE

AMERICA

"*America* is a Coming-of-Age Masterpiece" – *St. Louis Post-Dispatch*

"*America* is an extraordinary and deftly crafted novel that combines interesting characters within the context of an historically detailed background… an inherently entertaining… fascinating read from cover to cover… highly recommended." – *Midwest Book Review*

"An adventure through America's rich and compelling history... a provocative and engaging read." – *Movies, Shows, & Books*

"Mike Bond has done it again, focusing his formidable talents on yet another genre: the historical novel." – *The Daily News*

"*America* brings to mind classic coming-of-age masterpieces such as "*Look Homeward, Angel*" by Thomas Wolfe." – *BookTrib*

"The characters are so vivid and alive, you think you're reading about old friends and recalling fond memories of youth." – *The Times-News Online*

"An involving, thoughtful tale that explores America's tectonic shifts leading to Vietnam." – *Kirkus*

"What I like most about this book it was personal, it had emotions, it had fear, and I learned many things… This book is a winner because it introduces our tumultuous history with characters we can identify with, admire and root for." – *Goodreads*

"If you love the history of the US then this one might be for you." – *Crossroad Reviews*

"I was intrigued and engrossed the entire time… a vivid world for the reader to get caught up in. – *Books and More*

"The most beautiful prose I have ever read… The author does not tell how others should think, but the beautiful story will help others to think. Each new book from Mike Bond seems to become better." – *NetGalley*

"I recommend this book to fans of historical fiction, coming of age stories, and readers who enjoy reading about the 1960s in America." – *A Dream Within A Dream*

"We wonder if the youth of today will have to fight the same fights for the same rights all over again. It would behoove them to read this book." – *Arizona Daily Star*

SNOW

"A captivating story of three friends on opposing sides of a betrayal… Bond tells his story in a crisp, propulsive prose that darts from sentence to sentence… He also has a sharp ear for dialogue and a knack for character development… Themes of the destructiveness of greed, both private and corporate; the sacredness of nature; and the primeval ways of mankind lend weight to a well-paced tale with intricate storylines." – *Kirkus*

"An action-packed adventure, but also a morality tale of what happens when two men who should know better get entangled in a crime from which they can't escape. " –*Denver Post*

"More than just a thriller, *Snow* lights up the complexities of American culture, the tensions of morality and obligation and the human search for love and freedom, all of which makes it clear Bond is a masterful storyteller." –*Sacramento Bee*

"A complex inter play of fascinating characters." –*Culture Buzz*

"Exploring the psyche and the depths of human reasoning and drive, *Snow* is a captivating story." –*BookTrib*

"An action-packed thriller that wouldn't let go. The heart-pounding scenes kept me on the edge of my seat." –*Goodreads*

"A simple story at its heart that warps into a splendid morality tale." –*Providence Sunday Journal*

GOODBYE PARIS
Pono Hawkins Book 3

"There's tension, turmoil and drama on every page that's hot enough to singe your fingers." – *New York Times* Bestseller, Steve Berry

"A rip-roaring page-turner , edgy and brilliantly realistic." – *Culture Buzz*

"Exhilarating ." – *Kirkus*

"Another non-stop thriller of a novel by a master of the genre." – *Midwest Book Review*

"A stunning thriller, entrancing love story and exciting account of anti-terror operations." – *BookTrib*

"Doesn't stop until it has delivered every possible ounce of intelligent excitement." – *Miami Times*

"Fast and twisty, and you don't know how it's going to end." – *Arizona Sun*

"Mike Bond is my favorite author... and his books are nothing short of works of art... I could not put this book down once I started reading it." – *Goodreads*

"A great book with normal special forces action and thrills, but what makes it great is the integration of Islamic terrorism." – *Basingtone Reviews*

"An action-packed story culminates in an exciting ending." – *The Bookworm*

"Thrills... crisp writing and intelligence." – *St. Louis Today*

ASSASSINS

"An exhilarating spy novel that offers equal amounts of ingenuity and intrigue." – *Kirkus*

"Bond is one of America's best thriller writers ... You need to get this book... It's an eye-opener, a page-turner... very strongly based in reality." – *Culture Buzz*

"An epic spy story... Bond often writes with a staccato beat, in sentence fragments with the effect of bullet fire. His dialogue is sharp and his description of combat is tactical and detached, professional as a soldier 's debriefing. Yet this terseness is rife with tension and feeling... A cohesive and compelling story of political intrigue, religious fanaticism, love, brotherhood and the ultimate pursuit of peace." – *Honolulu Star Advertiser*

"Packs one thrilling punch after the other... A first-rate thriller." – *Book Chase*

"Powerful, true to life, and explosive ... A story that could be ripped right out of the headlines." – *Just Reviews*

"Riveting, thrilling... so realistic and fast-paced that the reader felt as if they were actually there. " – *NetGalley*

"The action is outstanding and realistic. The suspense flows from page to page... The background is provided by recent events we have all lived through. The flow of the writing is almost musical as romance and horrors share equal billing... I wish everyone could read and understand this book." – *Goodreads*

"Assassins" starts out as a conventional book and then changes into a poem of pain, anger, and tragic existence...What sets this book apart from other thrillers by more famous authors is the deep character study of the protagonist. He is a patriot and does his work from that place. But the toll it takes on him can only be supported by a man of Herculean moral strength. – *Vine Voice*

KILLING MAINE
Pono Hawkins Book 2

FIRST PRIZE FOR FICTION, 2016, *New England Book Festival* : "A gripping tale of murders, manhunts and other crimes set amidst today's dirty politics and corporate graft, an unforgettable hero facing enormous dangers as he tries to save a friend, protect the women he loves, and defend a beautiful, endangered place."

"Another terrifically entertaining read from a master of the storytelling craft… A work of compelling fiction… Very highly recommended." – *Midwest Book Review*

"Quite a ride for those who love good crime thrillers... I can 't recommend this one strongly enough." – *Book Chase*

"Bond returns with another winner in *Killing Maine*. Bond's ability to infuse his real-world experiences into a fast-paced story is unequaled." – *Culture Buzz*

"A twisting mystery with enough suspicious characters and red herrings to keep you guessing. It's also a dire warning about the power of big industry and a commentary on our modern ecological responsibilities. A great read for the socially and environmentally conscious mystery lover." – *Honolulu Star-Advertiser*

"Sucks in the reader and makes it difficult to put the book down until the very last page… A winner of a thriller." – *Mystery Maven*

"Another stellar ride from Bond; checking out Pono's first adventure isn't a prerequisite, but this will make readers want to." – *Kirkus*

SAVING PARADISE
Pono Hawkins Book 1

"Bond is one of the 21 Century's most exciting authors… An action- packed, must read novel … taking readers behind the alluring façade of Hawaii's pristine beaches and tourist traps into a festering underworld of murder, intrigue and corruption." – *Washington Times*

"A complex, entertaining … lusciously convoluted story." – *Kirkus*

"Highly recommended." – *Midwest Book Review*

"A rousing crime thriller – but it is so much more… a highly atmospheric thriller focusing on a side of Hawaiian life that tourists seldom see." – *Book Chase*

"An intersection of fiction and real life." – *Hawaii Public Radio*

"An absolute page-turner." – *Ecotopia Radio*

"An unusual thriller and a must-read." – *Fresh Fiction*

"A complex murder mystery about political and corporate greed and corruption... Bond's vivid descriptions of Hawaii bring *Saving Paradise* vibrantly to life." – *Book Reviews and More*

"*Saving Paradise* will change you... It will call into question what little you really know, what people want you to believe you know and then hit you with a deep wave of dangerous truths." – *Where Truth Meets Fiction*

————

THE LAST SAVANNA

FIRST PRIZE FOR FICTION, 2016, *Los Angeles Book Festival* : "One of the best books yet on Africa, a stunning tale of love and loss amid a magnificent wilderness and its myriad animals, and a deadly manhunt through savage jungles, steep mountains and fierce deserts as an SAS commando tries to save the elephants, the woman he loves and the soul of Africa itself."

"A gripping thriller." – *Liverpool Daily Post (UK)*

"One of the most realistic portrayals of Africa yet… Dynamic, heart -breaking and timely to current events … a must-read." – *Yahoo Reviews*

"Sheer intensity, depicting the immense, arid land and never-ending scenes… but it's the volatile nature of nature itself that gives the story its greatest distinction." – *Kirkus*

"One of the most darkly beautiful books you will ever read." – *WordDreams*

"Exciting, action-packed ... A nightmarish vision of Africa." – *Manchester Evening News (UK)*

"A powerful love story set in the savage jungles and deserts of East Africa." – *Daily Examiner (UK)*

"The central figure is not human; it is the barren, terrifying landscape of Northern Kenya and the deadly creatures who inhabit it." – *Daily Telegraph (UK)*

"An entrancing, terrifying vision of Africa." – *BBC*

"The action is exciting, and a surprise awaits over each new page." – *NetGalley*

————

HOLY WAR

"Action-filled thriller. " – *Manchester Evening News (UK)*

"This suspense-laden novel has a never-ending sense of impending doom… An unyielding tension leaves a lasting impression." – *Kirkus*

"A profound tale of war … Impossible to stop reading. " – *British Armed Forces Broadcasting*

"A terrific book … The smells, taste, noise, dust, and fear are communicated so clearly." – *Great Book Escapes*

"A super charged thriller … A story to chill and haunt you." – *Peterborough Evening Telegraph (UK)*

"A tale of fear , hatred, revenge, and desire, flicking between bloody Beirut and the lesser battles of London and Paris." – *Evening Herald (UK)*

"If you are looking to get a driver's seat look at the landscape of modern conflict, holy wars, and the Middle East then this is the perfect book to do so." – *Masterful Book Reviews*

"A gripping tale of passion, hostage- taking and war, set against a war- ravaged Beirut." – *Evening News (UK)*

"A stunning novel of love and loss, good and evil, of real people who live in our hearts after the last page is done…Unusual and profound. " – *Greater London Radio*

———

HOUSE OF JAGUAR

"A riveting thriller of murder, politics, and lies. " – *London Broadcasting*

"Tough and tense thriller." – *Manchester Evening News (UK)*

"A high-octane story rife with action, from U.S. streets to Guatemalan jungles." – *Kirkus*

"A terrifying depiction of one man's battle against the CIA and Latin American death squads." – *BBC*

"Vicious thriller of drugs and revolution in the wilds of Guatemala." – *Liverpool Daily Post (UK)*

"With detailed descriptions of actual jungle battles and manhunts, vanishing rain forests and the ferocity of guerrilla war, *House of Jaguar* also reveals the CIA's role in both death squads and drug running, twin scourges of Central America. " – *Newton Chronicle (UK)*

"Grips the reader from the very first page. An ideal thriller for the beach, but be prepared to be there when the sun goes down." – *Herald Express (UK)*

———

TIBETAN CROSS

"Bond's deft thriller will reinforce your worst fears… A taut, tense tale of pursuit through exotic and unsavory locales. " – *Publishers Weekly*

"Grips the reader from the very first chapter until the climactic ending." – *UPI*

"One of the most exciting in recent fiction… An astonishing thriller." – *San Francisco Examiner*

"A tautly written study of one man's descent into living hell… a mood of near claustrophobic intensity." – *Spokane Chronicle*

"It *is* a thriller … Incredible, but also believable." – *Associated Press*

"A thriller that everyone should go out and buy right away. The writing is wonderful throughout… Bond working that fatalistic margin where life and death are one and the existential reality leaves one caring only to survive." – *Sunday Oregonian*

"Murderous intensity … A tense and graphically written story." – *Richmond Times*

"The most jaundiced adventure fan will be held by *Tibetan Cross*." – *Sacramento Bee*

"Grips the reader from the opening chapter and never lets go." – *Miami Herald*

———

THE DRUM THAT BEATS WITHIN US
Poetry

"Passionately felt emotional connections, particularly to Western landscapes and Native American culture... compellingly linking the great cycles of stars with little, common lives... to create a powerful sense of loss... a muscular poignancy." – *Kirkus*

"The poetry is sometimes raw, painful, exquisite but there is always the sense that it was written from the heart." – *LibraryThing*

"A collection of poetry that explores the elements of nature, what nature can provide, what nature can take away, and how humans are connected to it all." – *Book Review Bin*

"An exploration of self and nature... that asks us to look at our environment through the eyes of animals... and the poetry that has been with us since the dawn of time... comforting, challenging, and thought provoking." – *Bound2Books*

"His poetry courses, rhythmic and true through his works. His words serve as an important alarm for readers to wake from their contented slumber of self-absorbed thought and notice the changes around them. Eye-opening and a joy to read, the master of the existential thriller can add another winning title to his accolades." – *BookTrib*

"The language is beautiful, heartbreaking, romantic, sad, savvy, and nostalgic all at once. From longer poems to very short, thought-provoking poems, the lines of each take the reader to a world the poet has experienced or given much thought to. Truly beautiful." – *Goodreads*

"This is such a beautiful book of poetry ... the imagery is vibrant, devastating, and haunting... A thoroughly modern 21st century collection that revisits and revises classic themes. Highly recommended." – *NetGalley*

"The poems are beautiful and range from the long lyrical expressions of love and nature to the brief expressions of a moments insight into a sudden feeling, expressed with a few words that capture the moment and the feeling perfectly. " – *Metapsychology Reviews*

"*The Drum That Beats Within Us* presents us with a world gone awry, a world in which the warrior poet has fought, and a world in which only love survives." – *Vine Reviews*

FREEDOM

Published in the United States by Big City Press, New York.

ISBN paperback: 978-1-949751-24-6

ISBN ebook: 978-1-949751-25-3

ISBN Audiobook: 978-1-949751-26-0

Cover Design by Alan Dingman

Author photo by © PF Bentley/PFPix.com

https://mikebondbooks.com

PUBLISHER'S CATALOGING-IN-PUBLICATION DATA
Names: Bond, Mike, author.
Title: Freedom : volume 2 / Mike Bond.
Series: America.
Description: New York, NY: Big City Press, 2021.
Identifiers: ISBN: 9781949751246 (pbk.) | 9781949751253 (ebook) | 9781949751260 (audiobook)

Subjects: LCSH Friendship--Fiction. | United States--History--1961-1969--Fiction. | United States--Social conditions--1960-1980--Fiction. | United States--Social life and customs--1945-1970--Fiction. | United States--History--20th century--Fiction. | Bildungsroman. | BISAC FICTION / General | FICTION / Historical / General | FICTION / Coming of Age
Classification: LCC PS3619.O54 A64 v.2 | DDC 813.6--dc23

to
Lucas

The time is right for violent revolution.
– *The Rolling Stones*

Freedom's just another word
for nothing left to lose.
– *Kris Kristofferson*

Only the dead have seen the end of war.
– *George Santayana*

Don't follow leaders.
– *Bob Dylan*

MIKE BOND

FREEDOM

★★★★ BOOK 2 ★★★★
OF THE AMERICA SERIES

BIG CITY PRESS

CONTENTS

HOTEL KALI

THE 1776 HOUSE LIGHTS sparkled through diamond-paned windows onto the lawns and juniper hedges and the bough of the oak where the British spy Major André had been hung.

Mick went into the bar. Troy wasn't there yet, and it was Hal's night off. Mick ordered a beer and stood with his back to the bar, trying to imagine this room crowded with General Washington's officers that last desperate winter, the rushed meetings, the urgent planning of battles and resupply and provisions. The room was long and low, a ceiling of thick square oak beams with ancient plaster between them, oak-beamed walls, the maple floor shiny and worn, the creaking ancient irregular rooms and old mullioned windows, the massive fireplace, gray river granite from floor to ceiling. Was it in this room Major André was sentenced to death? How had this brilliant young English aristocrat ended up murdered in an American village? Should any man die for something as abstract as a king or nation? Mick's ancestor who had stood guard over André the last night had later written, *The prisoner was quiet except for a frequent need to micturate.*

The door slammed but it was a man with wavy dark hair and a

woman with a bleached bouffant and thick lipstick. *When I'm watchin my TV*, Mick Jagger snarled,

> *And a man comes on and tells me*
> *How white my shirts can be*

There was an old oil painting over the stone mantel, a pastoral scene, in the foreground a man with a straw hat and a wooden staff walking along a dirt road beside a split rail fence, beyond it a river easing through soft hills with a farmhouse atop one. He felt a terrible surge of envy and loneliness, wanting to walk that dirt road, back in the time before cars when the air was free and open, there was no separation between you and the world, and everything moved at a walking pace.

He racked the pool balls and broke, sinking them in order. How unlike Troy to be late; he thought of him in a Marine uniform like Dad's, of meeting him that first day in the deserted barracks, riding the rails, growing up together. How Troy had become the Marine that Mick had always thought he himself would be. But this was the wrong war. Like Sun Tzu said, you get to choose.

But weren't all wars evil? That was the goddamn problem.

Troy came in wearing a snap-button cowboy shirt and jeans. "Sorry." He shook Mick's hand, then hugged him. "Was there with Dad, he just kept talking."

Mick nodded. "Did he talk about my leaving?"

"Said you're driving him crazy, can't wait for you to go…"

"Old bastard," Mick grinned. "I hate to leave him."

"C'mon, you've worked all summer driving that Coke truck, it's time."

Mick smiled, thinking about it, that this eased his guilt for leaving. "What *you* drive up here in?"

"Fifty-seven Chevy with racing slicks, a two fifty-seven with two four-barrels and a four-speed. Lays rubber in every gear. Made it from Quantico in seven hours."

"And you're going back tonight?"

"Be there by five a.m., if I leave soon." Troy's face seemed harder, his reddish hair drained of color under the weak lights, his eyes pale gray.

"And then?"

"Next Wednesday. LA, Guam, Okinawa, Danang," Troy recited, as if off a map, out of a book.

"And then?"

"Up country somewhere, replace some other second loot."

Who's been killed, Mick thought.

"Some guy who finished his tour, probably," Troy said in that way they'd always had of knowing each other's thoughts.

It was unbearable that he'd saved Troy from the orphanage only to lead him to possible death a decade later. "What you going to do with that hot Chevy?" he said, to fill the silence.

"Leave it at Quantico."

Again it seemed to Mick that every thought was heavy with omens: what would happen to the car if Troy didn't come back? *Don't think like that.*

Troy chalked his cue and waited for Mick to break. "When *you* leavin?"

"Monday. Like I said on the phone, Seattle to Calcutta, then Katmandu."

"Who ever heard of it? Like that place, where was it, you went in the Sahara?"

Mick sank the six but drove the seven wide. "Timbuktu –"

"Notice they all end in 'u' –"

Like Pleiku, Mick wanted to say. "Wish you weren't going."

Troy snickered. "Climbing in the Himalayas you'll be in more danger than me."

Mick raised his cue, watching Troy. "It's horrible what we're doing in Vietnam. I wish you weren't part of it."

Troy glanced up, annoyed. "Can't you fuckin understand? It's what I *want* to do."

Mick realized the Marines had been taught how to deal with such issues by patient repetitive explanation. "You don't like the War either."

Troy let his cue slide down through his hands; the butt thumped the floor. "I can't back out on my country."

"Because I haven't joined up you think I am?"

Troy tipped his head back, looked Mick in the eyes. "Yes."

"But if this War is wrong, don't you hurt your country by doing it? If you'd been a German in 1938, what would've you done?"

Troy's ball skewed sideways. "You always make things sound so simple."

"Remember riding the rails with Molly'n Joe? What Joe said – freedom means not lying to yourself about what you do?"

"Oh yeah? Well, Joe was a Marine in Korea –"

"And he said it was insane, remember? That the soldier is the ultimate lemming, because no one else'd be stupid enough to run toward a machine gun, or die in some other horrible way, just because someone told him to! Is that what you want to be?"

Troy placed his beer carefully on the edge of the pool table. "You were always one for easy answers, Mick."

"This War's making me hate our country. And *that* makes me even angrier. I want us to be a good country, to back freedom not military dictators, to spread wealth not steal it, to give life not kill people –"

"You know how many guys *we've* lost already? Guys like you and me who loved their families and cared about their friends and tried to do what's right?"

"And *who* put them there in the first place? It's sickening to think of the lives they would've had. It's criminal we sent them there –"

"So their deaths were for nothing?"

"Yes, if we're wrong to be there. And more killing won't bring them back."

"And loyalty?"

"Is it more loyal to do wrong because your country tells you to, like the Germans in World War Two? Or is it more loyal to your country to insist that it do right?"

Troy took a breath, nodded. "When I look at Dien Bien Phu,"

he said finally, "how the French lost Vietnam in fifty-four, I'm not sure we *can* win this." Hands in pockets he looked at the floor. "Just like the French, we're underestimating Giap, their ability to resupply, their morale. You'd think we'd study how France lost, but instead we're saying, 'Oh those dumb French, who cares why they lost? We know how to fight wars better than they do –'"

"So don't go."

Troy snickered. "I'm a Marine. I don't get to say what I want."

"Can't you be a conscientious objector?"

Troy laughed. "Dope-smoking draft dodgers – you want me to be like them? Johnson just signed the law outlawing draft card burning – you want me to do that?" He shook his head as if all conversation were useless. "Hear from Tara lately?"

"Last week. I was going to fly through San Francisco to see her, but they're on tour in Texas."

"Touring all the time, what I hear."

"They've got a record out, but I can't find it."

"I write her but she don't write back."

"Last summer they did a show at the Crossroads, this famous place in New York, she said you were going to see her in Denver but you didn't come."

"Yeah, the Academy, it was during that cheating scandal. I was on an Honor Board judging those assholes. Can you imagine swearing not to cheat, then doing it?"

"Not everybody's like you, Troy."

Surprisingly Troy squeezed Mick's arm. "Or you."

They left the 1776 House and walked to separate cars. "Okay, man," Troy said. "G'bye." They hugged; it felt meaningless, mechanical. Troy gunned the Chevy, backed out fast and roared away, carbs snarling. Mick felt empty, alone.

He drove the old pickup the other way, along River Road toward Dad's place in Nyack, thinking how when they argued Troy's face had reddened, a flush up his neck under the red-gold hairs as he laid the cue along the edge for a side shot. Mick had sensed a new hostility, an anger he'd never seen before in Troy – the passion of someone defending the only thing he'd ever dared to love.

It was not the risk of death that made the War so bad, but the abdication of all rights to one's own life. To place oneself in the total power of someone else – whether it be an ignorant sergeant or the men in Washington – seemed insane. And doing it in obedience to an unjust, meaningless and ferociously brutal invasion of a faraway peasant country was so spiritually and morally damning that his body revolted from it.

I can't reach him, Mick thought. *He believes absolutely.* Maybe it was the only way Troy could deal with uncertainty. And anything that countered his belief had to be instantly rejected. Even Troy's letters displayed a certain attitude, nonchalance mixed with irony, a conscious distance. Hadn't he always been that way, though, from that first day in the deserted army barracks?

That first day Troy had wanted to fight because he'd been scared. Was that how we got into Vietnam? If so, what were we afraid of? Afraid of being taken over by Communists? Of losing to them, being forced to live their way? That some flaw in ourselves, our system, would cause us to fail? That the world's starving billions would not choose our way?

This was the real fear: that we weren't as good as we thought we were. The world he and Troy had grown up in had vanished, replaced by something cold and fatal. He suddenly feared he'd never see Troy again.

He thought of the Himals, cold, deadly, beautiful. *Maybe I'll be the one who dies.*

"**YOUR FAITHFUL** will drop you," Barney Dilson, the band's new agent, told Tara, "if you stop playing acoustic in concerts and play that damn electric guitar."

"If I go electric I can reach..." she halted, not finding the word... "more people. And the sound, it's *so* much more complex..." She turned away, conscious as always how hard it was to find words, that words weren't *enough*.

"I can reach more folks," she said finally, thinking of Luis's high, piercing solos, how they take you to another place in your brain. Where you *want* to be.

"My Fender can fill a stadium with sound," she said. "My 12-string Dreadnought can't."

"Amps."

"Bullshit."

"Fuck, Tara, you're going to lose everyone who loves you."

She cocked her head slightly, as if thinking. "Wouldn't be the first time."

"It's *not* the same music."

"Imagine an instrument that can make every single sound possible, can create the sweetest most beautiful harmonies and harmonics to delight the human soul…"

"Crap."

"My Fender does it. My Gibson. They're magical, what they can do, how they can fill the human heart. I'd no sooner give up my Fender than give up fucking."

"Holy shit," Barney said. "Okay. Okay then."

A month later of course Bob Dylan did it too, at Newport, and everybody jeered.

"The only fan you got out there," Barney told her morosely, is this guy Dylan."

"I've met him, he's cool."

"He's switching to electric too."

"Copycat!" she seethed. "Soon everybody'll be doing it."

LANDING IN DANANG Troy was struck by the wet fragrant heat, muck, rot, tropical plants and avgas – exciting, alien and dangerous, the indolent air loud with jets, choppers, jeeps, trucks, yelling voices and a distant rumble he first took for thunder. After processing he was assigned to a mixed fire and patrol base named Pretty Woman, up near the DMZ fifty klicks north of Danang, reporting to a Captain Cross.

On a chopper headed north he was one of eight new guys, their gear humped on the deck between them, seven other Hueys in the convoy slathering up through the wet claustrophobic air like swimmers clawing for the surface, the jungle heat through the open doors merging with the smells of sweat, fear, grease, jet fuel, guns, uniforms and the dark crust of old blood on the chopper's deck, a lingering metallic underscent. There was a grimace of weary pity on a door gunner's face as he scanned them briefly before turning to caress his gun with stained and callused hands – how many rounds, Troy wondered idly, had it fired? How many people had it killed? He recoiled from thinking of what it must feel like, the hard hot steel of a fifty cal bullet that could cut a man in half.

He'd grabbed a seat near the door to watch the green hills below. He was going to be the best officer he could be, and every detail, every awareness, would help.

As the Huey climbed higher the wind through the door cooled; sweat dried on his face. He noticed the gunner's worn filthy utilities and muddy wretched boots and felt embarrassed by his own newly washed creased trousers and gleaming boots. His rifle was too shiny; he was a *boot*; what would his platoon think – another Quantico baby to lead them stupidly into danger? He rubbed one boot sole over the other toe. The gunner grinned and winked at him and faced out the door again and the kindness of his grin made Troy feel better. *You're going to make it*, he told himself then wondered what exactly was he going to make.

You're going to make the best of it.

Distant pillars of blue-black smoke coiled up innocently from jungled hills; two Cobra gunships flitted nervously around the Hueys like birds round their nestlings' first flight. Now in places the earth below was blasted and pocked with craters half-full of brown water. Dirt roads meandered between iridescent swaths that might once have been paddies.

Now the land below had been burned, savagely beaten and

tormented. Uprooted, charred and shattered trees lay like kindling, the earth oozed red muddy sores, whole hillsides blasted and piled on each other amid tilting scraps of jungle. As the formation descended toward it, green and white tracers leaped up in distant lazy arcs suddenly whacking through the chopper's skin as it swung crazily to avoid them, the kid beside Troy threw up; disgustingly there was vomit down Troy's face and wiping it off he saw it was blood as the kid's head tipped forward, nearly severed. The gunner hung dead on his belt; the chopper rolled on its side falling faster and somebody screaming *We're going to hit* and the pilot's quiet steady voice saying *This is Delta Two Zero we are going down*, another screaming *Prepare to Crash Prepare to Crash* and the smashed flaming jungle crushed them in a wail of rotors, ripping metal, exploding ammo and a sudden *whoof* as the jet fuel caught, guys crushed together burning, the pilots mashed in the cockpit; he staggered to his feet trying to save them but the chopper exploded, a rotor smashing past him as he scrambled into the trees.

His head screamed with pain, the roar of rifles deafening. He had no gun. Black shapes darted among firelit trunks, bullets hissed at him. He ran back to the chopper and tried to pull an M-60 loose but couldn't. Bullets struck the dead gunner and bit through the hull and sucked at his head. He grabbed an M16 and ran into the jungle.

Everywhere voices, footsteps, yells, the hard crack of shots. He didn't dare move or stay still. *Flap-flap* of feet as a man in black shorts came running through the trees, skinny knees, narrow thighs, shocked eyes in a square flat face when Troy fired but the barrel hopped so he fired quick again and the little man spun and fell back.

A Cobra screamed overhead spraying the jungle, a hail of cartridges pattering down. Troy shot at two men running; his rifle jammed. A wounded man tried to fire back; Troy grabbed his gun, shot him and huddled behind a tree gasping for breath and shaking with terror. Eyes sweaty he checked the clip. Four shots maybe. Shrill voices neared. He squirmed through the fallen charred trunks and branches back to the chopper.

A Huey drifted down in a halo of silvery rotors, its door gunners hammering the trees as the two Cobras circled spraying the perimeter and Troy ran for the Huey, grabbed the harness and was yanked inside burning his cheek on an M-60 barrel. "How many?" the gunner yelled.

Troy rolled over gasping. "Just me."

"Fuck." The gunner turned back to his gun as the chopper leaped upward and flew north after the convoy toward a smoking hill, a clutch of nervous grunts watching him; the rotors dropped pitch, both gunners swung their guns like magic wands clearing the path; the chopper tipped on one side and dropped like a stone into an ear-crushing dive and Troy knew they'd die again but the Huey bellied out into a flare, the gunner yelling "*Go! Go! Go!*" as they leaped into knee-deep muck and stumbled hunched over for a barrier of mud and logs, and Troy realized the sucking whine around his head was bullets.

Captain Cross was a spare, wiry, angry guy about five-eight. "Sorry for what happened to you. Good thing is you won't have time to think about it. You're replacing Lieutenant Powell," he yelled back as he walked fast ahead of Troy through a muddy trench unsuccessfully floored with ammo crates. "Your platoon was pretty fond of him so watch your step."

For an instant Troy misunderstood, couldn't hear through the cacophony of Thunderbolts and machine guns, thought Cross meant in the trench. "How do you mean?" Troy yelled back, trying to catch up.

Captain Cross swung on Troy as if he were responsible for this bedlam. "Just because of what happened today doesn't mean you know anything. So don't try to tell *them* what to do till *you* know what to do." He ducked into a log- and sandbag-roofed bunker. "Sergeant!"

In the half-lit dusty bunker the noise was less deafening. A tall black man uncoiled from a bunk and saluted. "Here's your new Loot," Cross said, turned to Troy, "Eighteen hundred in the CP. Boone here'll show you where. Tonight's orders."

Sergeant Boone scanned Troy up and down. His uniform was torn and dirty, his look sarcastic. "Welcome to Pretty Woman."

Troy thought an instant then said it: "Welcome to Pretty Woman, *Sir.*"

Boone laughed, a huge wide grin. "Okay *Sir*! Let's round you up some kit."

LUIS PLAYED GUITAR with the same erotic, sinister rawness as Keith Richards, Tara realized. When he was *on* he was God. Took you to that high perfect place, touched your joy at its core.

Everything he did excited her: his brown Puerto Rican body with the coiled cobra tattoo across his chest. "Gives chicks an extra thrill when they're coming," he'd told her. The hard biceps with a knife scar down the right one. Amazing long, lithe fingers. What they could do to you. Silky fine black hair ponytailed down his back. Like a waterfall over your face when you fuck.

His reverence for Benicia, the Stratocaster he'd rebuilt with three humbuckers instead of two. This sacred, pure, scratched dented beast that could lull you and kill you and drive the stake of absolute beauty straight through your heart.

"Rock'n roll encourages you to live deep and be free," Luis said. "Like Hemingway says, with no bullshit." He went deeper than sound, backbeat and syncopation to get your body moving, back and forth in lilting melody, running straight blues licks in and out of soaring screaming solos, those lithe long fingers so fast up and down the neck hitting, bending, hammering, stretching the six howling strings, and the beauty of his playing so solid you could feel it against your face like the wind, filling your whole body with the sweet agony of truth.

"The secret to rock'n roll, Baby, is that ninety percent's left out. Your heart makes it up, fills it in, you fall in love . . . Music, Baby, is the holes *between* the sounds."

Now everybody was fussing about electric guitar coming in and messing up folk music. Couldn't they feel, didn't they realize, that rock'n roll was a pure mainline to God, that these magnificent and nearly impossible solos were simply *for* God? As Leonard Cohen had said it so perfectly,

Reaching for the sky just to surrender

Luis had lost both sisters and a brother in an East Harlem tenement fire. "Death," he said, "is nothing but an execution. A sin. A crime against us. A great evil, because it takes away life."

"Maybe it just transforms life –"

"I don't want to be transformed." His eyes burned. "I want to live."

FIRST MORNING IN KATMANDU Mick went up to the roof of the Hotel Kali, a climber's hostel, and watched the Himalayas all day, a place of mystery and adventure without end, so huge they cut off a third of the sky, a tall serene wall of rock and ice stretching beyond the horizon. The scintillating snow and soaring black cliffs and ridges, the steely sky, the vast clouds of snow and ice blown from the razor peaks all thrilled him in a way he had never known before, made him hunger to climb them.

He didn't want to stop looking, to eat, to go out and join the filthy starving multitude in the streets below. The mountains – it wasn't fair to call them that, for they were far greater – a mysterious, powerful and beautiful world, a place of dreams and eternity more deep and real.

He had no maps; all was new, all-revealing, a key to the universal door, a secret passage through the back of the closet into another, deeper life. Like when you met a beautiful girl you didn't wonder why you wanted her, you just had to have her. Nor did it seem strange to be captivated by this vast magical Himalayan wall.

For days he wandered Katmandu's dirty jumbled streets jammed with tilting latticework shops and houses, water buffaloes and dogs, crowds of elbowing skinny people and bicycle carts. The air stank of wet wood smoke, incense, strange spices, garbage and shit. Skeletal yellow dogs fought over wormy piles of human feces and howled all night in hunger while he lay beneath his mosquito net reading Tu Fu by a wavering candle,

Sleep does not come to me, for still

I worry about war, knowing I have
No way to set the world aright.

What was he doing wandering the world, climbing mountains, while Vietnam was getting worse? Shouldn't he be back there with the others trying to stop it?

But wasn't that falling into the same trap? Whether it was war or fighting against war, you were still losing your freedom. The War was insane and pointless but your country wanted you to die in it anyway. And if you fought against it your nights and days were an endless round of exhausted struggle with never a victory, for the War just grew and grew.

Problem was, how can you live easy and well when others are suffering?

Hotel Kali was a barracks of tiny rooms separated by thatched walls, in each a rope bed on four legs set in little pans of kerosene ostensibly to deter bedbugs. Further up the same crooked cobblestone alley was the Gobi Café, a sinister smoky room run by Tibetans where slabs of fly-covered water buffalo and yak hung curing before the stone fireplace, where you could buy a huge plate of yak stew and rice for six cents, and climbers met to buy and sell gear and link up with each other for new climbs.

One night he sat there talking with a tall sandy-haired New Zealander named Skip McDonald. He had a big bladed nose, long ears, and the hard-knuckled hands and lean powerful forearms of a rock climber. "So what're you climbing, mate?" Skip said.

"Just hiking. Might go up to Everest base camp, maybe try Mustang."

"Dodgy zone, Mustang. The CIA and the Tibetans're running weapons up the Kali Gandaki through Mustang into Tibet. Bloody Chinese're destroying all the Tibetan monasteries, killing tons of folks, burning everything, all the old manuscripts. The Tibetans are fighting a ruthless war against them but can't win. Bloody awful, mate."

Mick's only vision of Tibet was of Shangri-La, of rambling ancient monasteries locked in snowy valleys. "What the Hell do the Chinese care about Tibet?"

"They see it as a weak flank against a possible American invasion through India; they're trying to create a defensible border along the Himals."

"So what are you up to?"

Skip tamped hash into an Afghani lapis lazuli pipe and lit it from the candle on the table. "Like you, trying to get behind Annapurna, eh?" He passed Mick the pipe. "There's this mountain with no name. We call it Virgin Peak. Twenty-three five. Never been climbed."

Mick took a hit, soft and sweet; the room brightened; a curved *kukri* sword on the straw wall gleamed with sharpness. "Isn't Annapurna on the trail to Mustang?"

"Far as you're allowed to go. Where the Kali Gandaki canyon narrows you turn east. There's a site for a base camp in an ice valley at fifteen thousand. From there it's pitched camps."

"You've seen photos?"

"Willi Unsoeld took some from a few miles away. It's got some nice ridges and steady ascents, not a lot of gnarly shit. A wee cracker, could be."

Unsoeld had been on the first successful American Everest expedition. "Why isn't he going?"

"Bugger all I know." Skip took a hit. "Could be beaut, a Himalayan first ascent."

Mick's cheeks ached with pleasure. Everything was conspiratorially funny, that humans should climb steep dangerous mountains when life was so much fun down here. "Any western women around here?"

"A few Peace Corps sheilas out in the bush but most're with blokes. Local women'll give yer ferret a run for five pennies but you'll come down with the wrath of Genghis Khan, your pecker'll skizzle up like a pretzel and –" he flicked his fingers – "blow away on the evening breeze."

Mick found the idea discomforting. "You bring your own gear?"

"Most expeditions when they go home gives their gear to their

Sherpas, and they sell it in here. Yugoslavs just came off K2, the guy Goreng who comes in here, he's selling good insulated double boots with crampons for fifteen bucks, ten for an axe, fifty for a sub-fifty sleeping bag and double-wall tent. How I got mine."

Mick imagined the peak, sere and icily wind-blown, felt an urge to reach those white clear heights, find illumination, understand what went wrong. "How tough is it?"

Skip shrugged. "Can't tell from the photos. But should be a piece of piss to eighteen, then five thousand of slow slugging, couple of camps and Bob's your Uncle. If the ridges aren't too steep and the ice isn't nasty."

"Like I said, most of what I've done is rock climbing. I've only done a little high altitude, not much ice climbing."

"Good on ya, mate."

Two other climbers came in, tall and unshaven. "*Dobri vecher*," Skip called; they nodded and came over, shuddering the table as they sat, faces abraded by wind and sun, hands rough and scarred.

"This's Pavel and Sergei," Skip said. The two bearded monsters crushed Mick's hand. Pavel was tall, broad-shouldered and muscular, with short hair. Sergei was even taller, looser-limbed, a ponytail, crooked front teeth in a long narrow unshaven jaw.

"These blokes're from a team that just did Ama Dablam," Skip added. "They're going with me up Virgin Peak. We're looking for a fourth."

2

TEMPTING THE VOID

THEY TREKKED two weeks through emerald valleys and tall forests of exotic birds and lemurs and the blazing white flowers of rhododendrons. At night they slept in village *butthis*, stone or mud huts that for seven cents provided a meal of rice and lentils and a place on the stone floor for their sleeping bags or for the burlap bags their nine porters slept on, their worn blunted feet stretched toward the coals.

Mick enjoyed Skip's cheery, inclusive confidence, his "Good on ya, mate" attitude that made everyone a friend, how he ensured the porters and the others were comfortable before he thought about himself. He never complained, seemed to regard every setback as an opportunity to resolve, a new peak to climb. His standard response, "She'll be right", applied whether it was a missing tent, lost rations, or a porter who inexplicably went home one morning, adding fifteen more pounds to everyone else's load.

The two Russians joked and told stories in coarse English, one minute discussing rock 'n roll then whether Tolstoy was greater than Shakespeare – "No," the burly short-haired Pavel claimed loudly, "look how Shakespeare wrote poems, plays – he had more, what is it?" he turned to Sergei, "*raznobraziya?*"

"Variety," Sergei translated. "But Tolstoy is more deep, more understands the human tragedy. Think of *Ivan Ilyich*, or *Master and Man*; Shakespeare's people are always acting." He tugged back his long hair. "Even *Anna Karenina*, that is even more beautiful than *War and Peace*." He turned to Mick. "Don't you think?"

"Haven't read it," Mick said, feeling ignorant.

Sergei was from the Caucasus, and Pavel had grown up in Mongolia, one of many Russians whose families had emigrated there during the Stalin genocides. Both had climbed since their teens, Sergei in the paradise of Mount Elbrus, Pavel in the sacred peaks of western Mongolia. From his time in those holy mountains he had developed an introspective air foreign to the more jovial outgoing Sergei. "All Mongolians hates Soviets," he said one day, "for what they did to Mongolia."

Every day was sunny, the air cool, high and bright, the hiking wonderful. Mick felt inexplicably joyous, inebriated by the sun, the thin air, the brilliant greens of the hills and jungles and the stark Himalayan wall rising black and white halfway up the sharp blue sky. It was both scary and elating to be going up into these ethereal peaks, to enter their mysterious perfection.

In the hills the paths grew narrow, stony and often steep, but wide and easy across the terraced paddies and pastures. Yellow butterflies hovered over diamond rivulets that chuckled along the trail or crossed beneath it under flat stones. One early morning they came upon two cobras mating on the sun-warm trail with languorous erotic affection. "That's choice!" Skip crowed. "Make sure not to bother them, eh!"

Multicolored birds sang in the willows or swooped overhead through gossamer webs of light. Skinny barefoot boys ran after them; in villages little girls with braided ebony hair watched them silently from stone doorways. At night they sat on grassy hillsides smoking the intense Nepali *ganja* and watching the stars slide across the immense white peaks, and Mick felt he'd never seen anything so beautiful and true.

Often there was the pleasant steady *thunk* of a rice mill or the querulous bellow of a water buffalo. Red-scarfed women in the fields stared at them open-mouthed. "Never seen a white bloke before, they 'aven't," Skip commented.

"Lucky them," Pavel laughed.

They stopped to eat little oranges called *suntalas* under the wide boughs of two huge trees in an open valley. "This one's a *bo* tree," Skip said. "Buddha sat under one when he figured things out, eh? *Bo* means enlightenment. They always plant them with a *banyan* tree. It's sacred, and makes a beaut shelter for passersby."

They smoked more *ganja* and drank the water in the canteens they had treated with iodine. "No wonder the people're happy," Skip said. "No roads, no radio or TV, days and days of walking to get anywhere, no electricity –"

"I have this girl in Kazakhstan," Sergei said in English, "she electrocutes me."

"Codswollop," Skip snickered. "That means you're dead."

"No no *no*," Sergei waved a reproving finger. "She excites me so, it's like electricity under my skin –"

"Electrifies?" Mick hazarded.

"Yah, yah, that must be it. *Electrifizirovats*."

"*Da*," Pavel added, passing the pipe. "She lights right up."

"You know her too?" Mick said.

"Oh yah. Everybody does."

One night on a *butthi* wall he saw a photo torn from a magazine, JFK smiling, wind blowing his hair. "Ask them," Mick said, "why they have this picture."

Skip conferred in Nepali with the wrinkled old owner. "He says it's a great king from far away. Who got killed by evil men because he loved his people."

It's a knife in your chest, Mick thought, *JFK*. That never goes away.

THE TRAIL CLIMBED north up the huge Kali Gandaki canyon, snaking into tributary canyons where it narrowed to a foot's width against the cliffs, the barefoot porters climbing steadily under their loads, the white river crashing and booming two thousand feet below. "Four porters fell here last week," Skip called. "Be a bit careful."

Mountains towered over them, to the west the bleak spire of Dhaulagiri trailing its sari of windblown snow, to the east the massive spire of Annapurna and beyond it sacred Machapuchare the Fish Tail, bleak, vertical, unclimbable.

It took a week to reach Tatopani. "It means hot water," Skip explained, "there's hot springs there."

Death is the Great Divide, the words came as Mick stared westward across the huge canyon, a crack in the earth down to its core, *Mother of the Ganges*, cunt of the earth, and they were going up it to climb its virgin peak. It *was* sensual, beyond dangerous. As if they were intruding on a world far deeper and more intensely powerful than their own.

As they neared the climb the Russians changed; gone the jokes and self-mockery, the good-hearted chatter about women and booze. With Annapurna looming over them everyone grew quiet, a total focus, steely and intense. It sent shivers up Mick's spine, as if more than he'd intended he was going to face death.

Should I back out now he wondered one night sitting above a village of four stone houses with stone roofs on a wide windcut plateau, moonlight glistening on the silvery jumbled boulders, the river thundering in its canyon far below.

But without him they couldn't do it. *You don't go back on what you promise.* You don't "pike out," as Skip would say. But wasn't that what drove soldiers to fight, that they wouldn't desert their friends? And their friends wouldn't desert them. So they all died.

"They say you can tempt the sea but sooner or later it will get you," Skip had said. "Same with the mountains – keep tempting the void and sooner or later it gets you."

Mick scratched at his itchy two-week beard. Just because you're worried, that doesn't mean you're going to die. It just means be careful.

Dawn reddened the rumpled hills, glistening their terraces and wind-savaged ridges. To the north the soaring ice wall cut off the dying stars. *The myths of unity and separateness*, a voice said but he couldn't understand, let it go.

North of Tatopani the canyon grew even more sheer and steep, the trail narrowing even more, the cliffs under their feet gleaming with the promise of death. Twice they came up behind caravans of Tibetans leading horses packed heavily with guns and ammunition for the war against the Chinese. Dark-faced and fierce-looking as Cheyenne warriors, dressed in white sheepskin coats, leather leggings and tall sheepskin boots, their long swords hanging from their saddles and their rifles and cartridge belts slung across their chests, the Tibetans nodded stoically or ignored them altogether, their black slit eyes focused on the trail ahead.

"Chinese've killed thousands of them," Skip said. "Rifles supplied by the CIA against Chinese planes and tanks. But they won't give up. Last fall in Baglung I told a Tibetan I'd trade him a pair of Levis for a Chinese watch, eh? Three weeks later the bloke brings me one, still on some guy's arm cut off below the elbow. Took a week to get the smell of rotten flesh off the bloody watch."

"Sad thing is," Sergei said, "it's people dying for some geopolitical game."

"*Nyet*," Pavel snapped. "Like in Mongolia it's people defending their freedom and their homes against foreign invaders. Who don't belong there."

THEY SET UP BASE CAMP north of Annapurna at 15,800 feet on a wide ice slope. "Gives us four camps to go," Skip pointed at the peak. "Next is 19,000 feet, out on that arête, then two more, maybe, where we can't see." He prodded the photo with a dirty finger. "Bout here somewhere."

"What's it like, the climbing?" Mick said. "Can you tell?"

"There's the icefall to work through that'll take us here," Skip jabbed the photo. "And from there there's the long south ridge, straight ascent a little technical up to that col at about twenty-one, eh, then Bob's your Uncle, a straight slog up that ridge to the top."

"I think we should start carrying stuff up to the arête tomorrow," Pavel said. "While the weather is okay."

"Let's do another day at this altitude," Skip said, "before we start the thin stuff."

"Not necessary." Sergei shook his head. "I say like Pavel we go up right away." He looked at Mick. "What about you?"

"I'm winded already. A day will do me good. And Skip's the trip leader –"

"Pah!" Pavel said. "We will carry up the stuff tomorrow. Sergei and me."

Skip shook his head. "I'm taking a day."

Pavel stood. "I guess it will just be Sergei and me, then." He walked off across the slope and up into the boulders, climbed one and sat looking up at the icefield.

Skip turned to Sergei. "Fine if you want to. But after that we stick together. Or nobody gets to the top."

AT 21,000 FEET they made camp three days later. It had been a long steady climb up the ice face to the south ridge, kicking in the toes of their crampons and stepping up, driving the point of the axe into a new place on the face, raising the other foot and kicking in again, taking a breath, raising the other foot. Step by step the great vista of peaks and flowing ridges spread out below them.

At first he'd felt terror when he looked down at the endless sheet of steely blue-white ice dropping into infinity below him, but as he climbed one ragged crest to the next the fear left him, perhaps, he decided, only because he grew used to it.

Each toehold safely stood on, each tiny ledge gained, made it seem more likely that he'd make the next, that he wouldn't fall, could conquer this. Yet when he looked down he trembled, the void sucked his insides empty, called to him, *Fall now and get it over with. There'll be little pain.*

They set camp under a rock overhang high up the col. Avalanche chutes cut down both sides of the overhang like braids round a woman's neck, the two tents side by side over the abyss, a foot-wide ledge between them.

"Tomorrow," Skip yelled over the wind as they crawled into their two tents, "if the weather's good."

Mick woke, couldn't breathe, gasping and choking, the tent pressing down on his face. He squirmed sideways to reach for the zipper but it was jammed, Skip pushed up the tent roof and the snow atop it cascaded off. Mick yanked the zipper open; cold clear rushed in with a hail of snow.

"Blow me down!" Skip stuck his head out. "Looks like a long one, eh?"

For three days it snowed, a thick white screaming howl. They slept, talked about women and mountains and food. From the other tent came sometimes a vague rumble of Russian. "This is a good time," Skip said. "We need time to think, we humans."

"Silly to come way up here just to think."

"We're thinking higher, mate – much better."

After the first day of snow the avalanches started rumbling down both sides of their little ledge, the hurricane wind blinding with snow. Mick lay in his narrow sleeping bag, pinned in beside Skip, thinking of how easy it would have been to be caught out there, mangled and crushed and ripped to pieces all down the side of the mountain, or suffocated under forty feet of snow, and how many climbers had died this way.

It was like cave exploring, being in this tent pinned against a cliff at twenty-one thousand feet. Insane. In the cave the million tons of rock above can crush you; up here it just shrugs you off. And the moment you give into fear you die.

"After this," Mick said, "I'm going to Bali. Surfing on the north shore."

"The women are bloody lovely. And they all want to bonk you."

They passed the endless time talking and sleeping, trying not to hear the wailing wind, the cliff-shuddering avalanches, to ignore the deadly cold, the tiny cramped tent and each other's filthy odors, trying to wait out the diarrhea that forced them repeatedly into the freezing deadly storm.

"Climbing's freedom, eh?" Skip said. "But most blokes're happy to enslave themselves. You can't help them, it's how they are. Rather whinge than live free."

Only twenty-four, he had already climbed peaks on every continent including Antarctica. He'd grown up on New Zealand's South Island, had summited Mount Cook twice by the time he was fifteen. "She's not tall like the Himals. But what a beauty. More ways to kill you than a white shark, she has."

His favorites were the Andes. "The Torres del Paine, just like knife blades, straight up clean and white for thousands of feet. Not a toehold or handhold. And Fitzroy, named for the captain of the *Beagle*, Darwin's ship. A vertical beauty."

Skip was, Mick reflected, one of those people for whom one dimension overrode all others. The world was mountains, climbing: everything else was accessory or irrelevant. It must be good, he thought, to be so single-minded.

But it was hard to be so close. The stink of their bodies in the tiny tent, the catarrhal snoring, the immobility – when one person moved, the other had to scrunch against the tent wall holding his breath, and the moment you finally fell asleep the other would shove an elbow in your eye or a knee in your groin.

Tension grew between them, and between them and the two Russians. "Go to hell," Sergei yelled at Mick when he blundered into their tent asking for stove fuel. And Mick for no reason slapped at the snow hanging over the door knocking a cloud of it into the tent, then felt abysmally foolish. "Sorry, man," he called, but the damage was done.

The fourth morning at three-thirty Skip shoved him awake, "Up at the sparrow fart!" Mick tugged his flashlight from his sleeping bag and switched it on. Frost caked the inside of the tent and fell on them in sheets when he bumped it. The thermometer said thirty-eight below. "It's stopped snowing," Skip said. "No wind. Going to be a beaut day, mate." He pulled down the zipper, stuck his head outside.

"Shit!" Mick said as icy air poured in.

"Hey you communist assholes," Skip called.

"Already we have climbed her," Pavel yelled. "Already we are back."

They tried to make coffee but the stove gas was frozen. They ate crackers and peanut butter and jelly with handfuls of raisins. "Should we two-rope," Sergei called. "Or four?"

Skip stopped eating to consider. "We're half way up the col. It's all vertical and ice above. Four on one."

In pitch-blackness they roped up, shivering, teeth chattering, the wind picking up now, crashing chunks of ice past the tents and over the edge. Skip led, followed by Sergei and Mick, Pavel last, the silence between them heavy.

The sky was white with stars. As he kicked a toehold and saw the tiny flakes of ice scatter down the mountain, Mick reflected there were as many stars above them as molecules of snow on all the mountains of the world.

Dawn came reluctantly, a thin red edge against the eastern peaks, the slow fading of the stellar wonderland above. The wind blew harder, frigid screaming and buffeting. Far overhead he could barely see the peak against the thinning night.

At a sudden crunch of ice he looked up at Sergei falling at him. He drove his axe into the ice pinning himself to the mountain as Sergei crashed past, then Skip on his back sliding and twisting to arrest himself; Sergei's rope yanked taut choking Mick's waist, Mick's crampons slipping, his waist strangled by the rope, then Skip's weight hit and with a ping one of Mick's crampons gave way, a sheet of ice breaking loose beneath it, with a whack their bodies hit the cliff beneath him, their weight tearing him apart as his other crampon twanged loose, his boots scrambling for purchase against sheer rock, his arm breaking loose from his shoulder as Skip's huge force pulled him apart, and they were hanging there, two of them over the void, his arm in awful pain disconnected from the socket.

Frantically he kicked at the ice, dug in new toeholds, legs quivering as he put weight on them. He grabbed the axe with his other hand, let the dislocated arm hang, couldn't breathe with the pain, the altitude, the terror.

"That's good," Pavel's steady voice came through the wind's howl. "Hold little more." He drove a piton into the ice then another, belaying them.

"I climb the rope," Sergei called. "Pulling Skip." He caught a purchase with his axe and scrambled for a hold, then Skip. The rope round Mick's belly loosened, the weight gone. He leaned against the slope, pushed up the arm until it slid back into the socket. Pinioned on the mountain, shoulder in agony, he was free. They had not died.

Skip staggered up the ice sheet, gasping, bent over in pain, reached out and slapped Sergei's shoulder, "Cheers, mate!" – somehow conveying in those two words a universe of appreciation and respect, a vow that would last a lifetime.

They traversed to a shelf and pinned in, breathless, wind screaming and carving their faces. Mick's arm hung uselessly but he could raise it, use it if he had to. "One of us has to go down," Skip yelled over the wind. "With Mick. Or we all do."

"No way," Mick yelled back. "I'm going to beat this fucking peak."

"No you're not," Skip hollered.

Mick swung his injured arm, gritting teeth. "I can use it. We're wasting time."

The shelf brightened; the icy rock sparkled. To the southeast a white spot of sun had risen over the black ridges of Machapuchare. Mick turned to face it, its faint heat touching his eyelids. A good omen. He punched Skip's shoulder. "Let's go!"

Skip nodded, broke icicles from his moustache. "No time to fart about, mates."

The tension between them had flowed into a powerful feeling of love and kinship. The sun rose huge and orange over the frozen sawtoothed horizon as they toe-kicked their way up the col, each in his own rhythm, *kick, take a breath, step up, take a breath, kick*, then up the icy rockface, the two Russians alternating the lead with Skip. Mick came last, watching up the rope in fear of someone falling, knowing the slope was too steep now, he couldn't stop them, his boots so heavy that it seemed impossible to raise them up another step, no air – if only there was air – no air at all so you sucked in nothing, the body begging for it, the lungs empty.

And we're still low, he reminded himself. Twenty-one thousand. Everest is twenty-nine. He would never climb Everest, never climb any mountain again. What had Sergei said? – "If you're in love with death, be brave. So death can find you easier."

Get to the top and go home. He thought of Cynthia. She seemed far away, an abstraction. He wondered if he'd imagined her, up in this thin air. That she had never existed. What was real, anyway? What was really happening?

Cerebral edema: Get it you die.

The rock face ended in a chimney that they fixed-roped. Last out of the chimney, Mick stood bent over, hands on knees, trying to breathe, wind hammering him. Someone shook him – Pavel pointing up the steep ridge at a jagged point that glistened in the sun. "That's it!" Pavel yelled.

"Peak?" Mick yelled back.

Pavel nodded, turned and labored up the ridge, the rope arcing behind him in the wind. Mick followed up the long steep ridge toward the peak, and suddenly it was easier, the steady drive of his feet upward, the tempo of his breathing, of the steady hammer of his heart, and he felt the air come into his lungs, so cold, snatched up and driven into his blood, felt it reach his muscles and turn to strength.

Midmorning sun burned down on the black rock and its cornices and curlicues of snow. They were staggering in slow motion up a hideous burning desert, but what burned his lungs was not heat but a freezing vacuum like the pit of space so near above, making him fear his lungs were seared forever by cold.

He stumbled into someone. Skip. "What?" he yelled, meaning *What are you doing?*

Skip shook his head, pointed. "Top!"

Then he remembered, Skip wouldn't go to the top. Would never disgrace a peak by summiting it. The peak was *there*, wailing its wreath of windblown ice. Mick's heart swelled. He was going to make it, felt guilt for going to the top when Skip wouldn't.

From the top the world spread out as God had once made it, white and pure to the end of time. Sergei laughed and took pictures then Mick took one of them, then Sergei went down to Skip to take his. Mick felt like dancing, as if he could spring from this pinnacle and soar among the puffy cumulus so far below and up into the blue-black sky, beyond the world.

If I never do another thing in my life I've done this.

3

ROOF OF THE WORLD

FEARFULLY TARA watched Luis stir the brown mixture in the tarnished spoon bubbling over the candle. It terrified her, an approaching man-eater, the killer in the dream she could never escape. The evil needle, the brown fat sizzling, the pucker of Luis' skin where it went in, his sigh and sniffle of relaxation as it hit, lying back on the pillows and drifting into . . . what? Which was real?

He sat up on the side of the bed and gave a quick shiver. "Rapture." He rolled his shoulders, shook his head. "To see how it really is." He reached for her guitar. "Can I?"

At first his notes sounded almost random till they began to reappear and flow together, building into a perfect melody, familiar yet she'd never heard it before.

"Fuckin blues." He scratched at a sideburn with the D peg, reached out both hands, "C'mon Honey let's fuck," a wide happy smile, "before I get too wasted."

Afterwards they lay panting side by side, feet over the mattress edge. The madras fabric draped across the ceiling made her think of caravans on the Silk Road, the desert wind and cries of camels sifting with the dust under the tent wall. He laid his hand on her cunt, a warm feeling. "Play me something."

She held his prick, liking its damp softness, the stickiness of sperm. *Once you get used to it.* "Not after you."

"Damn it, Baby, play."

She sat over the guitar, conscious of her breasts and awkward arms and sticky skin, her voice flaccid, her fingering awkward and offbeat. He sang with her, on his back on the bed, hands under his head, his lean belly tensing and relaxing with his breaths, and her fear slid away, her never-ending fear of being no good. She sang simply with easy fingerings that made him smile, melodies bouncing off each other, joining and reaching with her words toward the same impenetrable magic place where words and sounds had absolute truth, *Sometimes I feel like a motherless child* – the words joining as they two had joined, strangers in a strange city this random night – *a long way from home* –

When she stopped he said nothing. Her skin felt cold. "Odetta," he said. "You sing like her. And Big Mama. You know her I'm talkin about, Big Mama Thornton?" Taking the guitar he played what she had, but cleaner, deeper. "Your voice is fantastic and you know it. But you're not living the music. It's too much in your head." He tapped her forehead with the heel of his palm. "Gotta let it take over your *whole* body."

Her cheeks ached with pleasure, her neck warm in her long hair as though she were framed by it. "Not many chicks can front a band," he added. "Like *you* can."

He cut a brown chunk in the spoon and held it over the candle. "Just this once. See the difference it makes. You no be the same person. It no be the same song. Like being twenty years old and for the first time you can see."

Just this once. If she didn't like it she could turn away.

If she didn't like it she'd give him up. *There,* that was the deal.

The needle stung. She imagined the brown sugar uncoiling through her blood to her brain, felt chilled. "I can die. I can die from this stuff."

"If it wasn't good I wouldn't let you do it." He slid callused fingertips up her belly. "You gonna sing like a goddess."

She lay back hearing the bang of heat pipes between the floors, the outside snarl of a car, a soft tinkle that became Mozart then a howling silence. "I am where you are," she said, surprised by her throatiness, then sang it, bluesy, naked on the bed singing to the madras fabric ceiling, to the world, hearing how perfect and beautiful it was.

His head on her belly made it hard to breathe. "You were just another white girl to fuck," he said. "Now I can't get you out of my heart."

She stroked his short rough hair. "You'll have infinity without me."

He glanced at her, his pained smile reminding her how easy it was to hurt him. "Death is evil. To give us this universe of life then take it away. That's plain evil."

DESCENDING VIRGIN PEAK grew easier; they pitched the tents at seventeen thousand and sat in soft snow as the sun dropped over Dhaulagiri. To Mick it seemed impossible so much could happen in one sun's rise and set, from the moment this morning when he'd felt it on his face after Sergei's fall, the long and dangerous climb to the top and the quicker more perilous descent.

"Try to see the mountains without focusing," Sergei said. "Keep your eyes wide open seeing the full half-circle and don't think."

The wind hushed over the universe of mountains and heavens, the darkening valleys darkening and still-golden peaks. "Like an animal sees the world," Skip said.

"Life's so simple up here," Mick said. "And so crazy down there."

"It's humans make it crazy," Skip said. "Politics, wars, money, revolutions."

"Before our Revolution," Sergei said, "there was much hope for change. But it all died in dictatorship, mass murder, poverty and sorrow."

"That's revolution for you," Pavel said. "Millions killed, everything destroyed – for this failure of freedom known as Communism? Mongolia was fine till them. The Communists killed all the Mongolians with brains, drive, education or independence –"

"Like in Russia," Sergei said, "so many of the young revolutionaries who died were fighting for the individual, for freedom, yet they created one of the most authoritarian, repressive, dictatorial, anti-freedom regimes ever – how is that?"

"Was the Revolution worth it?" Pavel said, ignoring him. "I still don't think so."

"Some things of the Revolution are very good. Others very evil. How many million people killed in Siberian work camps, the *kulaks*, the millions of murdered intellectuals –"

"But what we would have been without Revolution? That is the question."

"Sometimes when I'm taking the train from Irkutsk to Vladivostok, across that vast Siberian wasteland where so many young revolutionaries died –" Sergei turned to Mick – "fighting the White Russians who were backed by the Americans. and I wonder the same thing: was it worth it? Did they die, all those brave young men on both sides, did their deaths bring us anything? Anything at all? *Nyet* – I don't think so."

Half-listening as the last tinge of yellow left the high peaks Mick wondered where in Vietnam Troy was, feared for him, helpless to help him, hated the men in Washington who'd sent him there. Like the Russian revolutionaries so starved for power they'd kill thirty million people for what *they* wanted. They who have no private peace, no love but conquest and destruction.

Their evil seemed tied up with wrong-seeking. And people sought the wrong things like power because of some gap in themselves, some aching vacuum. If people could heal or prevent these gaps in children, could these sorrows be avoided?

"The superior person," the *I Ching* said, "curbs evil and furthers good, and thereby obeys the benevolent will of heaven, which desires only good and not evil." Here on this mountain, in this high cold air and vast blue distances, what seemed important was not political or financial power, but to live deeply and truthfully. To love and not fear being loved. Or not being loved. Knowing there can be no life without death.

The mountain shifted, exhilaration rushed up the back of his skull. *Why death?* Because it gives life form and value? Without death no life. And so to live every moment aware of death. Because it is the truth. Perhaps the only truth.

He tossed a handful of snow into the void. In the forest behind the family farm years ago he'd found an arrowhead, fine and white with tiny sawtoothed edges. He'd held it in his palm trying to reach the man who'd made it, failed and understood how limited, imprisoned, was his life, how little he could know. Yet on this mountain he'd stood where no one ever had before, looked from a peak where no human since the universe began had ever looked. Like in Skull Cave, he'd touched a timeless truth, stepped beyond the bounds of man.

But why did he never think, *I am happy?* He lived in his moods without understanding them. That had to stop. Or he would always be a victim.

DAISY MORAN stared out the schoolroom window at the sheets of rain coming down. They splattered wind-driven across the muddy courtyard where people caped in shiny raincoats ran barefooted from building to building. Rain so thick it hazed the view of forest, hills and sea beyond, and even though it was warm it made her cold.

She turned back as the next class, forty-eight boys and girls from nine to eleven, came clattering in. She smiled, thinking that she'd never expected to love them this much, loved them all, even the ones she didn't like. She bit back a grin, seeing the stubby-toed bare feet, the long skinny legs, muscular bodies and shining eyes, hair all glossy with rain, faces of grins and scowls, discord and laughter.

When she'd applied for the Peace Corps she'd had this image of Kenya as a warm and sunny place, but here in Kilifi it been raining steadily for weeks, mud everywhere, you couldn't even keep it out of your bed, your food.

But the teaching was wonderful, her students demanding and fun, and when she wearily climbed the stairs and opened the door to her own little hut, she always felt a rush of peace and happiness that had no explanation but of a day of giving and caring, and now the joy of being alone with her thoughts.

In those long nights alone she tried to understand how her mind worked, thought she was living too much *outside* her brain. Not aware, most of the time, that it was even there. As if *she*, this power of being, this *self* that she so facilely trusted, was independent of it, of anything, just existed. Somehow. Was that her *mind*?

How did she get in touch with her brain? If they were to know each other, could they do better? Or does my brain know me far better than I know it? Can we even imagine ourselves as separate, my brain and me?

Her brain remained separate, unknown, a hunk of blood and meat, impenetrable.

How do I reach you?

What is the mind?

THE LURE OF TIBET was scary but exciting, almost sexual. If he didn't try it, Mick knew, he'd always be sorry. Wasn't it what he'd always been seeking, the unknown, the walkabout down the rails with Troy so long ago, the hunger to reach Timbuktu? The yearning for the infinite, impossible, immaculate? Wasn't that what the knights were seeking in the Grail?

Roof of the world. The sacred land of eternal snows, of perfect beauty untouched by man. Like Virgin Peak, the Sahara, Skull Cave: the undiscovered.

If Skip was right the Chinese were burning thousands of Tibetan monasteries, their precious libraries of ancient manuscripts. What was this human hunger to destroy beauty, the past?

That night they reached the Kali Gandaki canyon and slept in a *butthi* full of Tibetans headed north across the border, their ponies tethered in a field, their loads of rifles stacked under canvas along one wall, seven men crouched round the fire cooking chunks of yak meat on pointed sticks. One Tibetan spoke some English and seemed friendlier. "I like you, America," he said to Mick. "You give us guns."

"To kill Chinese?"

The man smiled square white teeth. "We kill many Chinese. You come? We show to you."

In the morning the wind down the canyon was icy and bitter. It was crazy, the idea of going to Tibet. "It's a forbidden zone," Skip admonished. "You get caught you'll wish you hadn't."

Mick had never met a westerner who'd seen Tibet. "Who's going to catch me?"

It was nerve-wracking to ride a horse after so many years. The old mare Apache he'd ridden as a boy had been gentle and devoted to the family; a child could sit on her back without fear. This long-maned, long-tailed Tibetan pony was nervous, fast, jerky and hostile; she swung her head trying to nip his knees, to shake him off when the trail got narrow and the fall dangerously gut-wrenching.

The mountains were stark, moonlike, huge dark crests to which lone pines clung like shipwrecked sailors. All was barren; a banshee wind howled down Mustang Pass driving all before it: rocks, dust, and the frail possessions of men. The Tibetans' leathery faces seemed hardened by it, as if after so many years, wrapped in their thick sheep-skins, they could no longer feel it, their hands toughened by cold and horsehide to steel so they seemed inhuman, fingers strong as tree roots.

They rode for three days higher into the mountains, the peaks rising over them like waves of a frozen sea. He had time to think, nothing but think, too uncomfortable in the wooden saddle and jabbing ride to drift, bored yet intimidated by the scenery that never changed, always austere, wind-scoured, beautiful and terrifying in its immense loneliness. Squalls of snow blew down the canyon, the unshod ponies slipped on the icy trail and almost fell into the abyss; in the wailing blizzards he could barely see the rump of the horse before him, could not stop shivering as the wind drove down his neck and up his sleeves and cuffs.

At night they piled together in the Tibetans' horsehide tents in the stink of unwashed bodies, tainted yak grease, gun oil, and the stench of cold half-rotten mutton they ate by handfuls from leather satchels.

In the morning if there were twigs nearby they brewed tea with rancid yak butter and ate dried barley rolls. If not they wordlessly rolled the tents and laid them over the heavy pack saddles of rifles and cartridge boxes balanced on the weary ponies and started up the trail.

Gorath, the one Tibetan who spoke some English, grew more reticent as they neared his country; Mick wondered why he'd been so foolish as to join them, and what awaited him across the border. "Border?" Gorath said, surprised. "We there yesterday!" He slammed the ground with a fist, "*Here! Here* Tibet!"

Mick glanced around at the jagged spires of snow and ice, the plateau where the savage wind drove billowing clouds of ice needles before it. "How soon we go back down?" he asked offhandedly.

"Down?" Gorath scoffed.

THIS WAS INSANE. He hated himself. Why had he done it? If he died up here no one would ever know. He saw his body on some icy slope covered with snow for twenty thousand years. Gift to some fucking archaeologist – the thought made him laugh.

Nothing's so bad when you can laugh about it.

Next morning the Tibetans were sharing out ammunition, the clink of metal, the grunt of voices planning something. "What is it?" he asked Gorath.

Gorath smiled at him with Genghis Khan eyes. "We kill Chinese."

"Now?"

"Now."

They rode single file across a wide valley between incandescent crags, the wind a frigid whip. Ice built up on his eyebrows and the wind razored it away.

His pony gasped as it plowed through the deep drifts up a ridge with a rocky slope descending from it to a valley with a road of beaten snow and three brown trucks and a line of tiny men in puffy brown uniforms moving along it. The Tibetans tethered the ponies behind the ridge, leaving one older man with them. "America!" Gorath pointed at the ground. "You here!"

Mick felt dizzy, scared. Gorath was shaking, nervous, the others tense and hostile as they checked their rifles and the extra magazines they tucked into the pockets of their sheepskin coats. It seemed unreal these men would kill those others down below in their fat brown uniforms. Those others about to die and didn't know it.

One by one the Tibetans edged downslope staying in the shelter of the outcrops. Hidden in the snow on the ridge Mick watched them take up positions behind the lower rocks.

The wind brought the sound of engines and gnashing gears as the trucks slithered up the road toward a pass on the right, the soldiers trudging steadily behind them. Crazily Mick wanted to warn them, to call down to the Tibetans *Don't Shoot!* – to reverse the time and make the Tibetans go elsewhere. He imagined one of the soldiers thinking of home and a girlfriend as he plodded closer, boots squeaking on the icy road, rifle sling biting into his shoulder.

The trucks and soldiers had almost passed and still the Tibetans didn't shoot. There's too many, Mick decided with relief, they're not going to risk it. Then the sudden roar of guns in the frigid air, the soldiers crumpling, crawling or running for the trucks, more soldiers leaping from them with nowhere to hide but behind the trucks shuddering in the hail of bullets, one's engine afire.

Something cracked past his head and Mick realized it was a bullet, the Chinese firing steadily now, and rock by rock the Tibetans were retreating. Gorath crawled toward him leaving a trail of blood in the snow. Not thinking Mick dashed through the rocks, grabbed Gorath under the shoulders and dragged him back uphill, the bullets going *spat spat spat* against the rocks and twinging away like angry angels, like they were unsatisfied and still wanted him and would keep coming till they got him. There was no air in his lungs but he ran on, Gorath's blood trail showing the bullets where to follow and he knew he'd be hit before he reached the ridge, the bullets singing harder as he got closer, making him fear the bullets would wait till the last second then smash him.

A Tibetan shoved him and Gorath toward the ponies, the bullets crackling past his head and a pony fell screaming, blood spraying, the

Tibetans returning fire in a cacophony with little golden cartridges flying, the ponies trying to gallop through the snow and again he sensed the bullets would hit him then they were over the top of the ridge and down a long icy valley, hooves clattering on ice of a frozen lake as a huge whack blew apart the snow ahead then another and the Tibetans turned aside and Mick realized it was mortars, mortars raining down on them as they galloped into a slot canyon of black stone narrowing on both sides and his ribs were afire from a match or something burning in his coat, but when he batted at the coat to put the fire out it hurt much more and he realized he was hurt, screaming with pain and anger and fear and joy and the vicious hunger to kill.

They rode very fast for miles down this canyon, Gorath's body bouncing up and down on the mare in front of Mick. Night fell like a guillotine; they huddled against a cliff shivering while the ponies stamped and whinnied trying to stay alive. Mick's ribs hurt so much he tried not to breathe; when he opened his coat the icy air made him shiver uncontrollably. His shirt was hard with frozen blood; something sharp had sliced along the front of his ribs and out under the armpit.

Now that he saw how bad it was it began to hurt worse.

One of the Tibetans lit a match cupping it in his hands against the wind and looked at the wound. He said something Mick didn't understand, made a noise mimicking a mortar hitting the lake. He touched the wound in front then felt under Mick's arm and dug something from the flesh, making Mick drop to his knees with pain.

The Tibetan held up something in the darkness as if it were a talisman, a chalice, dropped it into Mick's hand. A tiny flower of metal sharper than glass and sticky with blood.

"Fuck," Mick said. "Shrapnel."

The Tibetan gave him a questioning look, wiped at Mick's bloody chest with a fistful of snow and nodded for him to close his coat again.

They bunched together against the cliff, the keening wind so cold it seemed from outer space. It bit through clothes as if they weren't there, cut straight to the bone and turned it to ice. No matter how

Mick moved the pain of his wound got worse; he could not sit, lie, turn or stand. Blood trickled from it, warm for an instant on his cold flesh, then turned to ice.

If it had been shrapnel from the mortar explosion, maybe because it was so hot the wound wouldn't infect.

If it did infect he was in very serious trouble because it would take him five days to Tatopani but there wasn't any medical help till the UN clinic at Tansen, ten days away.

At first pale light they shoved Gorath's body under a rock and rode on; when the tiny sun had reached mid-sky they pulled up at a crossing with another path that Mick recognized as the trail they had ridden from Mustang into Tibet.

"America!" The old man who had watched the ponies on the ridge grabbed Mick's arm. He pointed south, back down the trail. "Tatopani!"

For an instant Mick didn't want to leave them. But he and they had no common language now Gorath was dead; Mick was injured, a hindrance not a help. The old man pointed at Mick's pony. "Tatopani!"

"Tatopani," Mick nodded. "I'll leave him in Tatopani."

When he looked back fifty yards down the trail the Tibetans had vanished and wind-driven snow was covering their tracks.

4

BALI

LOVINA BEACH gleamed black under the dying stars, its onshore breezes warm and enthralling. Mick stepped from his hut onto the cool damp sand. Mynahs and doves were chanting in the palms, the first coals of dawn were glowing above the eastern sea.

He waded into the soft waves. A gull flapped away before him. He dove and came up like a porpoise, laughing at the freedom of it, the joy, swam far out until the land was a low line on the horizon with the palm crowns tiny above it, and lay floating on the swell.

Bizarre, he thought as he swam shoreward, that in three weeks you could go from fifty below zero atop Virgin Peak or in Tibet where death waited for you every instant, to this innocent sea nearly warm as blood. And for four dollars a week rent a hut and swim all day and lie in the sun and drink beer and eat coconuts and grilled fish.

The mortar wound in his ribs barely hurt now, more like a pleasant reminder of adventure. It had never infected nor hurt badly. Because of deep snow it had taken him a week on foot down the Kali Gandaki canyon to Bhutwal and a flight to Katmandu. The plane had been an ancient C-47 from World War Two, wooden benches down each side of the fuselage, a rope from front to back as a seat belt, and hog-tied goats and crates of oranges, vegetables and clucking chickens all piled in the middle.

Five days later he found Lovina Beach.

Mr. and Mrs. Surawaya owned the huts and the little palm-frond café where they served *nasi goreng* – fried rice with egg – and chicken cooked in coconut milk, *satay* meat with peanut sauce, fresh fish right off the brazier, warm Bintang beer, and all the coconut and papayas you could eat. There were maybe ten huts in all but he was the only client. "Everyone stays away," Mr. Surawaya had said the first morning morosely over his green tea. "Because of troubles."

"What troubles?" They had seemed unlikely in such a place.

"America is very angry at President Sukarno because he doesn't agree with them about Vietnam. Now our generals try to use that to push him out. There is much fear."

Mick had downed his beer and glanced over Mr. Surawaya's shoulder at the surf crimsoned by the setting sun: there was time for one more ride. "I wouldn't worry about the States," he'd said getting up. "We're too damn busy in Vietnam."

Now he swam toward shore, his sore ribs tugging. The sky had lightened, the stars gone. He dove deep till all was black. Not knowing which way was up he hung there till he began to rise, surfaced and swam toward shore, sucking in oxygen.

Gulls were feeding on something in the waist-deep surf, a log maybe; as the wave carried it past it looked almost like a person – a skinny man in tan shorts and thin undershirt. Mick splashed to him and pulled him up; the man's head flopped back, throat cut to the spine. Mick dropped him gagging and washed his hands in the reddish water.

Gulls had eaten the man's eyes. Mick dragged him ashore, seeing in the shallows another body in a white sari, a white-haired woman with a serene face and a hole in her forehead, tiny fish feeding on blood trailing from the back of her head.

More bodies bobbed in the surf, their throats cut or intestines trailing. He ran to the office; Mrs. Surawaya lay face down in a pool of blood. He knelt gripping her cool hand, nauseated by fear and the reek of her blood, thinking her killers could still be here, would kill him too, that he'd survived only because he'd gone for an early swim.

His bungalow door hung open, his backpack gone. Standing in the silent din of terror, barefoot in a bathing suit, he had no passport, no money and no clothes.

Guns were firing erratically in town. He ran upstairs to the Surawayas' apartment, found a shirt and trousers too small so he tore open the waist and retied it, shrugged into the paisley shirt that would not button. All the men's shoes were way too small; he grabbed the biggest flipflops and dashed downstairs.

Gunfire exploded in the next street. He snatched a knife from a kitchen counter and ran into the palm groves and west along the sea, away from the village and toward the ferry terminal forty miles away at Gilimanuk.

The flipflops soon disintegrated and he ran barefoot. After several miles he fell on hands and knees in the scrub, gasping with exhaustion. Guns rattled in the distance. Where could possibly be safe when every move risked being seen? What had *happened*? Why were they *dead*?

Who were the killers? Where were they now?

The palm grove was silent but for the susurration of fronds, a far rush of sea, his rapid gasp and thundering blood. His feet were ripped by roots and rocks, their bleeding soles sand-crusted, Mr. Surawaya's shirt and trousers torn and muddy. Crouching below the scrub he headed west, sometimes on all fours, knife in his teeth, not knowing where he was going but not daring to stay.

All day jeeps and trucks rumbled along the roads; now and again gunfire erupted. Once circling a thatched-roof village he heard a yelled command then the roar of rifles, again a minute later, then again. Slinking deeper into the bush he felt misery and fear for the poor people awaiting their turns to die.

Night fell. Nauseous and empty-hearted he stumbled toward the port town of Gilimanuk, keeping to the brush, drinking from ditches, wiping mosquitoes from his arms and face, deafened by their whine. By a silent hut he found a bicycle and because his feet were so sore he chanced riding it on the road, dismayed by the squeak of its chain. The road was rocky and potholed; in the dark he fell three times, scraping and banging knees and elbows, got up and hurried on.

A distant puttering became a motor scooter behind him; he dragged the bike into the bush and hid. The scooter rattled past, no light, the shadow of a man on the seat with a woman in a white scarf behind him.

He got back on the bike and pedaled after them, the scooter's sputter diminishing into the darkness ahead. If he could follow them to Gilimanuk he could maybe get on the ferry back to Java. But with no money for a ticket?

Solve one problem at a time. Stay alive now, worry about the ferry if you get there.

Lights flickered ahead. He ducked into the bush, heard voices then a woman's scream, a man's yell, the bang of a pistol, then bang again.

Men laughing, a man imitating the woman's scream. Laughter again. He wanted to kill them. Something slithered over his arm and he tossed it aside, raised the bike on his shoulder and circled through the jungle. In gaps in the branches he saw flashlights flicker on the faces of four men in Muslim headscarves. Chatting animatedly, they pushed the motor scooter into the brush then dragged the two bodies farther into the trees. One scuffed dirt over the streaks of blood and they moved back into the bush and put out the flashlights.

Trucks were coming. Headlights popped from the jungle and down the road. The men in the headscarves stood in the road waving. The trucks pulled to a stop, a jeep behind them. In the headlights the men were talking with an officer from one of the trucks and with a big blond man in a white shirt. The officer turned and spoke to him, then to one of the killers, then back to the blond man as if translating.

The jeep and trucks went on toward Lovina, the motor scooter tied to the back of one truck, the killers staying in the brush by the road. Mick did not dare to continue on the road so he left the bike and hobbled through the scrub, silently swearing at the rocks tearing his feet.

When it rained he lay sucking it from leaves and crevices. It stopped; tree frogs were cheeping and raindrops spattering down from the trees. He slept a few minutes then limped toward the lights that became the empty haphazard streets of Gilimanuk.

Ducking through shadowed muddy alleys and across silent intersections he headed downhill toward the terminal. Dogs were barking everywhere; Army trucks rumbled through the sodden streets with people in the back lashed by their wrists to the pickets, toward the distance from whence came the irregular crackle of rifles as if from a shooting range. A jeep with a loudspeaker wandered the town, its loudspeaker blaring the same incomprehensible message over and over.

At a noise behind him he spun round to see death itself in the shadows of men filling the street, the gleam of machetes. He sprinted down the street around the corner despite the agony in his feet, down another street, then another, the race of life, the men's footsteps distancing behind him. Ahead was a low wall, seven feet maybe, he leaped it grabbing the top, hands ripped by the broken glass cemented into it, squirmed over and fell into a garden as the men rounded the corner and clattered past.

Hissing with pain from his hands he crawled into deep bushes and squeezed his palms together to slow the bleeding. After a long silence he crawled from the wall to the thickest corner of the garden and lay under a pile of leaves where he could see the house and garden but could not be seen.

DAWN CAME lushly with the riotous cackle of mynahs, wailing dogs, crowing cocks and cooing doves. The firing had slowed but trucks still rumbled through the streets.

The house was two-story, white stucco, a red tile roof. No one went in or out, its back door half-open. He found a rotten mango in the leaf pile and ate it. The day grew warm; he wished he had thought to find water.

All day no one moved inside or out. Footsteps sounded rarely in the street; few cars passed. Three times the loudspeaker jeep passed ranting the same message.

After dark he crossed the garden and entered the house. Downstairs was a kitchen, washing room, storage area, bathroom with a tin tub, and a living room with a small television. Upstairs were three bedrooms with gauzy curtains and an office with a desk and typewriter.

The back door was still half-open. If he closed it someone in nearby houses might notice. If he left it open they might notice also, wonder who had broken in. Finally he left it as it was.

In the kitchen a jug of water he drained gasping. Cans of food and a can opener. Not able to read the labels he opened one, a spicy sauce, opened another, a rice and nut paste he ate quickly, downing more cans of strange food till his stomach lurched. He hid the opened cans and upstairs found clothes that almost fit, and socks that went on over his wrecked feet. In the back of the upstairs office was a closet; he took two blankets from another drawer, crawled into the closet and fell into a half-awake doze.

At dusk he left the closet, used the toilet but it would not flush. Eating more cans of food in the kitchen he noticed what he'd thought was dirt on the floor was blood that trailed out the half-open door to large dark patches on the dirt. The people who'd lived here weren't coming back.

Two days he hid in the closet and came out at night. His feet and hands were healing. He searched the house but found no money, nothing to pay the ferry to Java.

At day he watched the street from the back of an upstairs bedroom. Few people passed, hurried and nervous, mostly men. Now and then a car, usually a sole driver. The soldiers and the killers in the Muslim hats were still patrolling.

Once they stopped a man in glasses carrying a plastic bag of oranges, knocked him against a wall and beat him with rifles; the man fell raising his hands pleadingly but they kept smashing his glasses into his face as Mick stood in the darkness with clenched fists, frantic to help the man but knowing they'd just kill him too. All afternoon the man's body lay there; after dark a truck pulled up and soldiers tossed it in the back.

Next morning a young woman in a blue sari came walking fast up the far side of the street, glancing back and tripping and running on ahead. A jeep was coming up the next block below, its soldiers scanning the street. When it neared the top she ducked behind a jasmine bush below his window, peering between the branches. Soldiers dismounted from the jeep and began walking up both sides of the street.

He dashed downstairs across the garden to the front gate and yanked it open. She leaped up in terror, tried to dart past but he grabbed her arm and pulled her inside. "Soldiers!" he pointed down the street.

She had a western face, pale skin, golden hair under the sari he'd knocked loose. "Who?" she gasped in English, "who are you?"

"American. In the house! Hurry!" They ran across the garden and upstairs and watched from the window as the jeep puttered away, the soldiers with it.

She knelt on the floor panting, her hair dirty and tangled, her blouse torn. "Oh God," she gasped. "Oh God." She swallowed. "They almost got me." She raised her eyes to him in sudden shock. "How? Why are you here?"

He told her. "But what's happening? Who are they?"

"The Army and the Muslims. A coup. Killing everyone! Everyone who can read or think – teachers, nurses, union members, doctors, shopkeepers . . . " She bowed her head, deep-breathing. "Truck drivers even. Because they travel, see too much."

"Why are you here?"

"Peace Corps teacher. High school. Math and science." She shook her head miserably.

He brought her water from the cistern and opened cans of food. "There's clean clothes upstairs. There was a mother and daughter – there'll be something."

"Dangerous to look hunted." She glanced at her filthy blouse. "Or afraid."

"Don't show yourself in a window."

She came down in a green silk blouse and long green skirt, a middle-class Indonesian but for her golden hair in a kerchief. Her still-haggard face was wide and full-lipped with large blue eyes, her tanned arms slender and strong. "Where were you trying to go?" he said.

"Like you, the ferry." She shivered, looked up. "Bastards!" She paced again. "Bastards."

"What's your name?"

"Erica." She bit her lip again. "Erica Whalen." Her voice, husky and deep, seemed to go with her assertive chin, strong cheekbones and high forehead, made him fear she'd bolt on her own like a cornered cat.

"I was hiding in a house behind the Police Station," she said. "Day and night they kept bringing people in trucks. Torturing them and lighting them with gasoline in front of their families. Going on right now, thousands of people . . . " She stared away as if trying to see through the stone wall the horrors happening right now.

A steady cadence of rifle fire began down by the port, stopped then started again. He felt immeasurably sorrowed, helpless. "When you last sleep?"

"Don't know. Before this all started? How long's that?"

"Three days, maybe. I've been sleeping in a closet upstairs. You sleep and I'll keep guard here. If anything happens I'll wake you."

She was pacing again. "At my school the teachers had to decide which of us should die. Had to denounce the principal. Or we'd all be killed. Such a lovely man."

He kissed her forehead, felt her take a breath and relax slightly. "Things'll calm down," he said, feeling guilty for the lie. "Then we can get out. Got any money?"

She shook her head against his shoulder. "The soldiers took my bag. When they raped me."

"Oh Jesus." He held her tighter.

She pushed away, glanced out the window. "Just show me where to sleep."

. . .

TROY WATCHED THE FACES of the squad gathering round him. Blacks standing together, hostile. Sweaty white boys with dirty faces and hard hands, bored or cynical, all of them lean and relaxed in their faded utilities, some naked to the waist or wearing only shorts and boots.

"I realize you've been here a while," Troy said, "and –"

"More'n we wants," one said.

"– and you've been in the shit and now you've got this new guy straight out of OCS and he don't know shit. So I'll tell you what I want to do." He saw one grin at another who made a kissing face and shook his head.

"My goal is to take care of you guys. Yes we're going to do our duty but we aren't going to do it stupidly. I've got a steep learning curve here, and I'm going to depend on Boone and Dillon –"

He glanced round at all of them, trying to catch their eyes. "We're never going to take the easy trail when that's what Charlie wants. We're going to stick to the trees and the hills and the stuff that's hard to move through. I may be a new officer but both my father and adopted father were Marines. And all I care about is you guys."

"D'as what the last loot said, 'fore he got waxed," one offered. "'N lost five guys."

YET VIETNAM WAS BEAUTIFUL, a rolling land of gleaming glades and paddies, banana trees canopied over thick green scrub, paths meandering through flowered and grassy meadows, cloud forests veiled in mist, the chuckle of streams under log bridges, terraced hills rising in all directions like lustrous Mayan temples.

White egrets roosted on the low dirt berms between fluorescent paddies where women and men with rolled-up trousers bent in water to their knees slicing the resilient stalks, others threshing the rice into wooden crates by beating the stalks against them.

In the villages bamboo fences separated the huts; naked children, black pigs, multicolored ducks and chickens filled the alleys. In pastures flanked by treelines boys with sticks rode somber splay-hoofed buffaloes with gray-black flanks and great curved horns, and graceful young women trod delicately between the dung piles with straw baskets of fruits and flowers atop their heads.

I could love it here, Troy thought, sliding fingers up the oiled breech of his gun. *This place could change my life.*

5

SEARCH AND DESTROY

WHILE ERICA SLEPT Mick watched the street, a few times tiptoeing to the closet to check on her. Her pale, exhausted face snuggled in the rough blankets filled him with a fierce protective fear. Even if he didn't survive she must. It made him weary and angry not being able to decide what to do, afraid of deciding wrong and killing them both.

After dark the rain came pelting the streets and houses, the sky jagged with lightning. "When I woke up," she said, "I didn't know where I was. Then I remembered but thought it wasn't true."

"You hungry?"

"Now it's dark we *have* get to the ferry."

"Not till things calm down."

"What if they don't? If they keep getting worse?"

"They'll check everyone getting on the ferry, then we're both dead. We've got no money so we can't buy tickets anyway, have to sneak on."

The rain roared louder, hammering the roof and gurgling down the gutters. She glared at him, her strong face silhouetted by lightning. "When things collapse you have to get out fast."

He took her hand, feeling the pulse flutter in her wrist, blamed himself for being craven. What if he was wrong? What if she died because of him?

"It took three of them to hold me down," she said. "While the fourth raped me. They took turns. I bit at them, got one real bad. I can still taste his blood." She turned on him. "Tonight this rain will help us! We could be in Java tomorrow –"

He held her closer, kneading the muscles of her back and shoulders. "If we even reach the bus to Jakarta the Army'll kill us."

"Then I'll go without you! I don't even know you –"

"Erica, Erica!"

She broke away and started pacing again. "I'll kill them."

"Let's focus on getting out of here. If we're very careful maybe we can."

"Oh Christ. I wish I knew." She took off her clothes and went into the hidden back garden and stood naked in the rain. For a moment he glanced at her, rain-sleek and high-breasted, arching her back to shake out her hair. He turned away, ashamed to have looked, and that he'd been distracted from watching out for danger.

Next afternoon while he was watching the street from a shadowed room she came down from upstairs and suddenly yanked the window open. "What are you *doing*?" he hissed furiously, snatching her back.

"It's Jensen –" In the street a tan Army jeep with a huge blond man riding in the back, an Indonesian military driver and officer in the front. "He's from the consulate – I saw him once. He'll help us!" She twisted away. "Let *go* of me!"

"I've seen him too," he held her tighter, "the other night at a checkpoint, helping the Muslims and the Army kill people!"

Her shoulders slumped. "Whatever we do," he whispered, holding her, "we have to do on our own."

"I came down to tell you." She gripped him tighter, then pushed away. "I found money upstairs, in a woman's shoe, six hundred rupiahs. Enough for the Jakarta bus."

Next night in a hard rain he scouted the dark spattering streets around the terminal. The ferry sat at the pier, half-lit and hazy, smoke coiling from its rusty stack. He returned for Erica and they went down together, soaked, cold and frightened, and hid in a bottle-strewn alley watching the few Indonesians huddled in the misty waiting room. A gangway lay against the ferry's side, rising and falling with the faint swell, a chain across it. After waiting a long time they ducked under the chain into the ferry's main salon and hid behind a wall of curtains at the end of the room.

At dawn the ferry began to throb with erratic vibrations; voices called; feet tramped the deck above. Through a porthole he saw people queuing at the gangway barred by soldiers with rifles. The rain had ended; day broke orange-bright. The ferry's whistle blew; one by one the people showed their papers and tickets to the soldiers and came on board. Soon the salon was filled with people and the odor of damp clothes and clove cigarettes; Mick and Erica slowly moved from the curtains to the edge of the room, people noticing them but saying nothing.

The ferry's engines rumbled louder; it broke from the pier and waddled out into the swell. He caught a glimpse in a mirror of himself, tall and gaunt in his too-small Indonesian shirt and trousers, Erica taller too than the Indonesians, strands of her blonde hair gleaming from under her kerchief, her face weary and rigid with fear.

In late afternoon they docked at Ketapang and an hour later got on a bus to Jakarta. It was jammed with brightly dressed women and dirty barefoot children, with sacks of vegetables, papayas and mangoes, with chickens tied by their feet clucking sorrowfully. An old man was snoring in his seat, and the tiny ancient woman beside him kept shaking his shoulder to stop him. Twice there were checkpoints; each time soldiers walked up and down the bus aisle staring into faces but let the bus go on. "They're looking for people," Erica said.

It was after midnight when they risked a taxi from the Jakarta bus station to the US Embassy. Two Marines came out of the guard huts on either side of the Embassy gate, guns leveled. "We're American," Mick said wearily. "Let us in."

. . .

THE EMBASSY MAN was lean and athletic, late forties, a blue pinstripe shirt and red tie, thin graying hairs tonsuring a polished skull. "We have no idea," he said, "what's going on."

"What's going on is slaughter," Mick said. "Genocide."

"We're so happy you got out." The man leaned across his desk to straighten a little paper American flag on a plastic stand. "So tell me, what have you seen?"

Erica bit her lip, glanced at Mick. "Like I said, we hid out most of the time."

The man nodded, turned smiling to Mick and it stunned Mick to realize that the man was thinking he'd slept with her, was envious. "You've been lucky," the man said.

"So where's Jensen?" Mick said.

The Embassy man flinched, scratched his skull. "Who's Jensen?"

"He was on Bali. I've seen him. With the Army."

"Nobody I've heard of. What's he look like?"

Mick told him. "Could be anybody," the Embassy man said. "German, Dutch, Russian? Actually, could be Russian. Whole thing's a Communist plot you know."

"Like Vietnam?"

"You could say that." The Embassy man stood. "We're getting you kids some new clothes and passports and tickets home." He smiled. "Sooner you go the safer you'll be."

JUST AN AFTERNOON PATROL through hills of tall trees. The canopy splintered the sunlight into brilliant shards that ran like lizards up and down the trunks, the ground lay deep-shadowed, the soil soft and silent, birds chanting and monkeys giggling in the high branches, spider webs tickling Troy's face.

Above them towered walls of trunks, boughs, branches, leaves, vines and creepers. Knee-high pungent wide-leaved shrubs hissed across his legs soaking them with dew. Flickers of sunlight like a welder's torch cut through the treetops and danced around them, a blinding kaleidoscope of darkness and light.

Like a cathedral Troy thought as he watched everywhere for a flash of motion or a fracture in the pattern, checking the ground in all directions and underfoot for that tiny little wire that blows a man apart, the misplaced twig, inhaling through his nose for even the tiniest odor of fish oil, sweat, feces, gun oil or any other human thing that might mean death, listening with mouth half-open for alien sound in this medieval chant of birds, bumbling buzzing insects, and monkeys chattering and shaking the boughs far overhead.

The high light glittering through the forest's clerestory windows, the dark trunks tapering upward like Gothic columns into the fretwork of boughs above – the feeling you got sometimes, in church at the Boys' Home. That your heart is connected to something.

He raised his hand and the men behind him halted. Dew pattered down as a breeze rustled the canopy. The chant of birds and insects loudened, the susurrating leaves and whisper of wind on bark, once or twice a clink of metal from the men behind him, the soft rustle of a utility, a sigh. Even his own breathing was far too loud.

He heard it again. Far ahead, filtered through the trees, a cock's crow. That would be the village. The target. He nodded to the men, pointed forward.

Half an hour later they came out of the forest above a wide paddy gleaming in the sun. Along one side a man in a straw cone hat was plowing the muddy earth with a wooden plow behind a water buffalo, the buffalo's reins around his neck. Beyond him a slope of banana trees rose two hundred feet to the edge of the forest. Low ridges of banana trees ran along both sides of the paddy, dropping down into open pasture at the far end where a huge banyan tree flung its boughs wide over a cluster of straw-walled tin-roofed huts.

He sent three men to check the low ridges along each side of the paddy all the way to the village. "We're supposed to meet Captain Cross's patrol at 13:10, so we have plenty of time."

They watched him, curious and judgmental. "Stay in the trees," he said, "fifteen yards apart, one guy watching the paddy, one guy watching ahead, one on the slope, checking the far side." He turned to the others. "Spread out, up the hill. You watch our rear, for any motion above or behind us. We wait till our scouts come back. Then if it's clear we move in, wait for Captain Cross and his patrol. Got it?"

The men spread out. He crouched in the deep shadow of a huge tree on the soft fragrant earth between its huge buttress roots, smelling the spicy detritus and cinnamon odor of the tree whose great roots sheltered him, hearing the crowing of the rooster and the mournful bellow of the water buffalo, watching ahead, to the sides, listening. His wrists were trembling, he realized, his stomach taut and nauseous.

In twenty minutes the scouts returned. Nothing on either side of either ridge all the way to the village. "In the village?" Troy said.

"Old guy cleaning something, a harness maybe. Coupla mamasans pounding some rice in a pit. Straggly chickens, bare-ass babies, three geese, one dog. Old mamasan just took a shit in the paddy."

"*Nice!*" a Marine said. "And we gonna *walk* through that?"

"No sign of Captain Cross?"

"No sir."

"Any men in the village?"

"No men, no older boys."

Troy settled his pack on his shoulders, scratching the itchy sweaty skin. "Why don't we go down both sides. Groups of five, low, midslope and high. Meet where the forest ends on both sides, spread out beyond and come in, real quiet-like to meet Captain Cross's two squads. Got that?"

"Groups of five?" Sergeant Boone snickered. "Where's *that* show up in the Marine Manual?"

"It don't," Troy said, waited a second. "Get it?"

Boone said nothing. "Yeah. I get it." He looked at the men. "Loot is right. Do what he fuckin says."

A weird warmth shot up Troy's spine, of having been right, not for himself but for them. He led them along the right side of the paddy into the banana grove. Midmorning sunlight angled down between the wide long banana leaves, their spiry peeling trunks like columns in a temple dedicated to the sun.

A distant rumble leaped to a banshee roar as three planes

screamed over low making him almost hit the dirt. "Tornados!" a Marine yelled. A few raised clenched fists. "Death from above, Motherfucker!" one called. "Death from *above!*"

The jets echoed away. "Sarge!" someone screamed. "Logan's hit! Sarge!"

He ran with Boone back to the Marine crumpled on the red dirt, bright blood down his forehead from a hole just behind the temple. "From where?" Troy yelled, furiously scanning the forest beyond the banana trees.

"Don't know, planes made too much noise!" a Marine screamed, glancing nervously around. "He just keeled over."

"They waited for the noise. So we couldn't tell." Again Troy scanned the forest edge, feeling vulnerable, imagining the sniper watching them, seeing his lieutenant's bars. "Let's get him to the village and call in a dustoff."

He wanted to throw up, barely remembered Logan, just an impression of a tall sincere kid with auburn hair and eyebrows and bony elbows, a short-timer. He wiped the boy's blood from his hands and turned toward the village.

Captain Cross met them under the banyan. "Kill the little shits!" he screamed when Troy told him. Short, wiry, trembling with rage, he glared at the small fearful people huddled before their huts. "Okay you little yellow assholes, who did it?"

The people flinched, eyes widening. Cross strutted toward them racking his forty-five, waved it in their faces as if it were a magic wand that would make them speak.

He made them lay Logan's body in its bloody poncho in front of the people, and gripping each villager by the arm he made them look down at the dead boy's face in its raiment of blood. "You tell me, you fucking yellow shit, who killed my Marine!"

The people tried to back away; Troy wondered what they felt like, this terrifying man screaming at them in an unfathomable language, waving his gun, the other Marines watching them emotionlessly, the patent evil and danger. A young woman with ebony hair, pale face, wide lips and wide narrow eyes set far apart, absolutely beautiful, came forward. "I am a teacher. I speak little English," she said. "Can help?"

She wore a pale blue gown with a heart-shaped hem at her neck. Her lips were trembling, the skin of her neck pulsing, her fingers clenched in terror. "Don't worry," Cross half-smiled. "We just need to know who shot our man."

"I am sorry," she said. "Please say slowly –"

Cross said it again. "No person here," she waved at the village, "no person here hurt you. We live here. We no fight no person."

"Our man died." Cross stared at her fiercely, muscles in his jaw working. "Who shot him?"

"It came when the planes came over, Captain," Troy said. "From the jungle. We can't be sure from where. That's the problem."

"This girl here," Cross yanked her elbow hard as if to frighten an answer from her, "knows what the fuck I'm talking about."

"Sir, she's just a teacher, speaks a little English."

Cross settled his shoulders under his flak vest. "Fuck her. I got a dead Marine." He twisted her elbow. "Who did it?"

She choked, staring at him wide-eyed, open-mouthed. "Please American Sir, we not hurt any person. We not hurt –"

Troy moved closer. "I've called in a dustoff, Sir."

Cross shoved her hard; she tripped backwards and fell. He held the gun over her. "Now goddamit you tell me!"

Troy grabbed Captain Cross's arm. "You kill her, Sir," he felt his chest go hollow with fear, "and I'll report you."

Cross tilted his head back, scanned Troy through mirror sunglasses. "And who are you, little pissant of a boot, to be –" as a dark shape leaped at him, an old man in black peasant shirt and trousers, hand raised to strike, and Cross shot him square in the face, the man's neck snapping back, body collapsing. The girl screamed and leapt at Cross and he shot her too, in the neck above the heart-shaped hem, and she fell spraying blood and grabbing for the pistol, the others screaming and running through the huts toward the forest. "Oh fuck," a Marine said.

"You asshole!" Cross swung on Troy. "You made me shoot her!"

"I did not!" He could barely talk.

"She was the only one spoke English you stupid shit." Cross turned to Lieutenant Kovacs. "Take it out."

"The whole place?" Kovacs said.

Cross glanced at his watch. "Soon's we dustoff our dead Marine we move out, then I want Willie Peter, five hundreds, napalm, the whole deal. The houses, the paddy, them bananas, every damn thing. Tell them," he stared at the remaining people, "they got ten minutes to leave town –"

"Sir!" Troy choked, "they didn't *do* anything!"

"– and due to enemy activity," Cross continued, "resulting in one Marine KIA and a body count of two VC this area is now a free-fire zone." He turned on Troy. "One more word'n you'll be court-martialed." He spat. "For refusal to follow orders during combat."

"This isn't combat."

Cross snatched his arm, talking up close. "We *all* start with good intentions, Lieutenant. But you want to *win* this war, avenge our dead Marine and all the other dead Marines, then you *have* to be tough, Lieutenant, you have to *learn* to be *tough*! They shoot at us, we destroy their damn village, kill their damn water buffaloes, sometimes some of them die, like today, and they learn not to let anybody take a shot at us because it costs them more'n it costs us."

Troy thought of Logan, the girl in the blue gown, the old man. "The Waffen SS did that."

"Damn right," Cross shook his arm. "Best soldiers world's ever seen. It was politicians brought them down –"

THE DUSTOFF CAME escorted by two gunships that circled while it touched down flailing dust and poncho halves, its rotors flicking viciously as four Marines carried Logan's body to it, his blood and brains spattering their legs as they tilted it up. Troy had a vision of the Huey as a giant insect being fed sacrificial dead. *You are an integer*, the words came to him. *You are no longer a person.*

As they climbed the ridge above the village there came a rumble from the south, F-4s wailing in low, so fast they seemed a vision, a film accelerated, their innocent silver canisters tumbling down and streaking a black-orange inferno through the village, the banyan tree a torch, the houses skeletal red then gone, fire ripping at the sky, the water buffalo running, aflame.

A Marine raised his fist as the tumbling canisters exploded in fiery streaks across the village. "Get some, Motherfucker! *Get some!*"

"BC don't mean *Before Christ* anymore!" Captain Cross yelled. "It means *Body Count.* Jesus *hates* Communists! Jesus *wants* Body Count! I want you to think on this, Lieutenant: Do you really want the Army to beat us Marines on Body Count?"

Steadily the planes worked it over till the village vanished, the banana groves and paddy, the forest ablaze in black-white phosphorous. The whole valley was burning as they crossed the ridge, a vast flaming pit, a volcanic caldron. It had only taken minutes, a few planes. If this was what it was, Troy thought, he'd go insane. He couldn't do this.

But he was in it now. He had to make it work.

"Any God allows this," a Marine muttered, "deserves to be crucified."

"Cut it, Finkelstein!" Captain Cross yelled. "That's sacrilegious for Chrissake."

ON THE PAN AM 707 to Seattle Mick stared unsleeping at the dark sparkling sea and tall moonlit cumulus, his face half-reflected in the Perspex, as if by looking outward he could almost see himself, could almost understand.

But there was no way to understand what humans did to each other. He shouldn't feel guilty for escaping when so many were dying. Indonesia wasn't his country. They weren't his people. It wasn't his fault.

But if you paid taxes and called yourself American you were responsible for what it did.

Out the window, to the northwest beyond the billowy clouds, was Vietnam.

What was he doing about that?

In Seattle airport he called his father to tell him he was back, but Tara answered the phone. "I tried to call you," she said softly, through tears. "But you weren't any*where* ..."

"Tell me *what*?"

"Dad died last Tuesday. Yesterday was the funeral."

"*Heart attack*," Mick repeated stupidly, stunned. "I'll be there tomorrow."

"I have to leave tonight, back on tour. Had to cancel two concerts."

Mick leaned against the payphone, couldn't breathe. He'd left Dad to go to the Himals and now Dad had died and he hadn't been with him. "You were there?"

"When he died? I was on tour in Memphis."

"I was going to tell him," Mick stuttered, "what happened in Bali..."

"Bali? Compared to Vietnam, Bali's a paradise."

6

—

SEA OF LOVE

ICY WINDS prowled New York's streets. Taxis called to each other through concrete canyons like lost sheep. Mick trod the pavements seeking a job, any job, startled by every footfall behind him, by the abrupt horns, engine roars and shouting voices, the snarl of a jackhammer, the rumble of a subway underfoot.

Dad's death had steeled him, he realized, that everything bad will happen, so get used to it. Dad was gone and though he thought about him constantly that wouldn't bring him back.

Having lost all his gear in Indonesia, all he had was what he'd stored at Hal and Sylvia's house, plus the outfit from the embassy in Jakarta. So after landing at Kennedy he'd gone to Tappan. "You should stay here awhile," Uncle Hal said, "get a job with Coke … I can use you part-time at the bar. Relax here a while, get over this."

Get over what? How could he tell Hal and Sylvia that with Dad gone he couldn't *be* here? Maybe it was revulsion – against what? Sorrow? Or was it this bowing down before death's blade, this resignation? He didn't know what it was.

But couldn't breathe here.

He pulled down the folding staircase that went up to the attic of Hal and Sylvia's house where his and Troy's gear was stored, found a backpack and clothes and the Fender Mustang he'd named Black Beauty, and took the bus to Manhattan.

Peter Weisman was doing a master's in economics at NYU and lived with his girlfriend Lois on the second floor of an East Sixth Street tenement. "Never thought you'd come back," he hugged Mick, "once you reached the Himals –"

When Mick told him about Indonesia, Peter sat silent a long time. "I can't believe it." He stood and gazed out his kitchen window. "This fucking country."

When Lois came home from City College, Peter told her. "Jesus," Lois said. "Oh my God."

"God apparently doesn't care," Peter said.

"I've called *The Times*," Mick said. "*The Herald Trib, The Post*, everybody. Nobody wants an interview, or thinks anything happened."

"Just like Vietnam," Lois said. "Have you seen the pictures – what we're doing to that poor little country?"

"Nobody wants to know," Peter said.

"You know what they told me about Indonesia at *The Times?*" Mick said. "This guy, he laughs apologetically and says he's sorry but he can't touch it unless they've already reported on it."

Peter sighed, shook his head.

"Like this War," Lois said. "They don't report on that either. Like for instance so who is this Walt Rostow? And what's a National Security Advisor anyway? What right does that give him to kill thousands of people?"

"Hear about that guy last week?" Peter said, "Burned his draft card? Crazy idea."

Peter opened a wine jug and filled three jars. "Here's to grad school, easiest way to avoid Vietnam. Like your old buddy Seth Calhoun's doing. You should try it."

While they cooked spaghetti Mick went for a new jug of wine. Streetlights sparkled in puddles; cars slept like bears along the curb. The dim corner market smelled of Puerto Rican spices and roach spray.

"It's sickening to eat and drink while people are dying," Peter said.

"People are always dying," Lois said.

"Remember those old photos from World War One," Mick said, "guys running in ranks toward machine guns? You know why? Because they were *told* to. Why would anyone ever put himself in a position where somebody can *order* him to die?"

"My father did," Peter said offhandedly. "A little coral island in the Pacific. Place called Palau. They had to wade waist-deep six hundred yards against some of the most concentrated machine gun, artillery, and rifle fire in human history. You know why?"

"It's okay," Lois said.

"Because the admirals didn't bother to go around it. They didn't notice the tides would be too low for landing craft to get over the reef. They could've gone around the island, the Japs couldn't be resupplied. It wasn't on the way to anything." He shrugged. "Because the lives of these men wading ashore really, you know, didn't matter. We were winning the War, what difference was a few extra lives to an admiral trying to work his way up the line?

"Okay," Lois said. "Okay."

"On the troop transport the night before they went ashore, he wrote my Mom a letter. This is a guy, she tells me, so full of life – archaeology and music and classics and fixing cars – and in this letter he tells her he knows he's going to die tomorrow and wants her to make peace with it. That he's spent every second thinking about her and me. I wasn't even born yet. He never saw me."

"My Dad," Mick said, "he told us that everyone already knew, even when the War started, that this was about the Jews. That you can't allow that kind of thing to happen without fighting it, if you want to call yourself a human being. He came home with bullet holes in his jacket, many dead friends, medals he disdained, and screaming nightmares for years. But he never said he shouldn't have done it."

Mick knocked on wood thinking how his life would have been without his father. And there wouldn't have been a Tara. He wondered at all the children who'd never been conceived because their fathers hadn't come back from the War.

"The Warsaw Ghetto," Peter said. "That was a just war."

"For most Vietnamese," Lois said, "this one is too."

HE STAYED TWO NIGHTS with them but it was far too small, Peter and Lois on a foam single mattress on a plywood platform and Mick on the floor beside the stove, roaches running over his face.

But he had no money to rent a place of his own, no job.

Late at night, by the light of a flashlight or a streetlight through a rain-streaked window, he tried to write it down. Indonesia. But as if a huge glutinous monster held his hand he could not write, could not remember it, would not except in dreams, in nightmares.

He'd wake sweating, vomit in his throat, standing with the huddled masses before the machine guns.

After the second night he gathered his few things and Black Beauty, hugged Peter and Lois goodbye and headed uptown to stay with Seth and Miranda Calhoun.

Seth was CIA. Seth would know.

SETH was doing his masters at Columbia; he and Miranda had an elegant Upper West Side apartment overlooking the Hudson. If the Lower East Side had been desperate half-lit streets of junked cars, junkies, trash, danger and carnivorous despair, the Upper West Side was a well-lit haven, busy and prosperous, and therefore educated and liberal. Walking the distance between them, Mick reflected, you crossed from the poorest to the richest of a whole nation, from the filthy deserted doorways where drunks and junkies huddled to the gleaming chandeliers in tall polished windows, from the scampering rats and roaches to the svelte harmony of restaurants with caped doormen whistling imperiously for cabs.

Their apartment had a double living room, dining room, library, a large shiny kitchen, and three large bedrooms. There were Orientals on the hardwood floors and oak fires in the marble fireplaces and French antiques and paintings. He was given a room with a Shaker bedstead and writing desk, two silk Oriental rugs and a slivered view of the river.

Miranda was cold but cheery; beautiful and unapproachable as Dhaulagiri. "That can't be true about Indonesia," she said. "We don't *do* that kind of thing."

"Then what's Vietnam?"

Seth took a puff of cigarillo that with the blazer and cravat gave him a Prince Rainier look which perhaps he coveted. "If you were Russian, you wouldn't have the freedom to oppose things. You'd have to do what your government told you."

"I *do* have to do what it tells me. Or I go to prison."

Miranda uncrossed her legs, got up and went into the kitchen. "Seth," she called, "where's that Montrachet?"

"You're in graduate school to escape the draft," Mick said, "but you support the War?"

Seth took a long drag, dropped ash in a crystal saucer, glanced at the ornate ceiling. "I don't support it or not support it. I just think it's inevitable."

"That's an easy out."

"It's a proxy war. Better than us and the Soviets fighting each other."

"*Their* soldiers aren't dying in the paddies." Mick thought of Troy, leaned forward to knock on the ebony coffee table.

"What have you heard from your brother, anyway?"

"They're guarding some firebase in the middle of nowhere. Says he spends his days reading and his nights playing poker."

"A gentleman's war?"

"Ten months till his tour's up. I just want him home safe."

"You're against this War because you're worried about him?"

"Most Americans are against this War. You'd be too if you had to go."

"But your brother isn't against it –"

"He has this weird thing about the Marines, because Dad was a Marine. His real dad was a Marine too."

"I'm sorry about your dad dying. I never met him, but he must have been extraordinary."

The mention of Dad was like a knife. "Extraordinary? How so?"

"Well, I mean the tales of your family. There seems to have been so much happiness, the farm, all that ... Your sister, I have all her records. Amazing." Seth took out a joint. "I trust you'll have some of this."

Mick parted the thick curtains. Rain slid down the pane, wobbling the headlights far below. The Hudson gleamed black. He thought of the Manhattoe Indians and what this river had been like then, when you could kneel on its forested banks and drink its sparkling purity, and Paradise was here on earth. "How's Columbia?"

"Nobody has a single new thought. All politics and anal intrigues. But," Seth leaned forward with a conspiratorial grin, "it keeps me out of Vietnam."

Miranda came in with the wine and three glasses. She looked beautiful and deadly. "I'm so delighted you can stay –"

"Just a few days," Mick said, embarrassed. "Till I get a job, can afford a place –"

She stood between them and the fire, a wine glass in her hand, spread-legged, a fiery-haired shadow edged in red. "Tonight at art class" she said, "we had a live model."

"What was she like?" Mick said, imagining a slender pretty girl, being able to watch her naked without shame or involvement.

"He was very muscular and handsome," she tossed off her glass. "And had a big you-know-what. And with that I'm going to bed." Leaving her glass on the mantle for the maid, she pecked Mick's cheek, patted Seth's head and swung her hips through the doorway down the hall.

Ants were racing back and forth on a log Seth had just set in the fire. Mick moved to get up and remove it, realized there was nowhere to put it, that he couldn't save the ants. He thought of Troy. "With all your ROTC you don't have to go?"

"Everard tells me to finish course work this spring, go into the Company in June." Everard was Seth's father, a CIA station chief whom he called only by his first name. "Kirk's in Nam," he added of his brother. "Already a captain."

"And you support it?"

Seth turned away with an exasperated hiss, meaning that the situation, or perhaps Mick, was idiotic. "Maybe we shouldn't have gotten in –"

"You've never before admitted that–"

"But we did. So there's no way, given our history, the history of that place, this war to the death we're fighting with the Communists." Seth reclined a bit in the maroon leather chair, hands behind his head, his plush body relaxed, "that we can walk out *now*."

"But you're not *there*," Mick said. "*You're* not at risk! What right do you have to say other people should die just because of some idea in *your* head?"

Seth was getting drunk, expansive. "Once you're in a war, you have to hurt them more than they hurt you. Then they won't tangle with you again. They leave you in peace."

"They?"

Seth drained his glass. "You know it's them, the Communists, beneath this all."

"Everybody in Vietnam is against us, except the ones we pay."

"Even some of them are against us." Seth chuckled. "But it doesn't matter." He had a way of flattening his lips to dismiss something, a near-sneer. "Our generals – you know how *long* they've been waiting? This's what they've lived for all these years. Senior promotions, more ribbons and medals, new toys, real battles to try out your tactical skills with real soldiers and real enemies. The chance to shoot people, bomb them, burn them alive. You might as well try to pull a stallion off a mare as pull these generals out of it."

"Kennedy was getting out –"

"They shot him the day after he gave the National Security Council order to start pulling our troops out. You know that."

"*They?*"

Seth shrugged. "You know that too – and that in his first day in office Lyndon Johnson reversed the order."

Surgically, ruthlessly, the deed had been done. So powerfully it didn't matter that you could see right through the official explanation.

At seven the next morning the Byrds on the clock radio woke Mick from more nightmares of Bali,

A time for peace, I swear it's not too late.

MIRANDA HATED HIM as hard as she pretended not to. Hated him because they'd once been too intimate, she'd been too hungry for sex, had given herself away, because he'd chosen her sister Cynthia over her, and, most of all, because he knew her too well. This hatred she began to turn on Seth, so Mick took his gear one evening and hiked up to Harlem to move in with Cousin Johnny. Thinking if things got really bad maybe he could pawn Black Beauty for a week or two, till he got a job.

The Harlem wind was sharp, stirring cinders in the alleys. On 151st and Amsterdam the streetlights leaned along the sidewalks like hookers. People rushed past, keeping to themselves. There were no lights over the doorways and no numbers he could see. The reek of garbage and urine was everywhere; there was garbage on the sidewalk he couldn't see, soft and squishy when he stepped on it, and bottles that banged loudly into the gutter if he bumped them. He felt afraid of angering someone by his alien presence as he peered for numbers, feeling for them against the weathered grimy wood.

A line of doorbells ran down one side of the door but there were no names and the front door was open. Mick climbed to the third floor, listening for Johnny's voice. Four doors faced each other under a dim bulb, a colorless scrap of rug between them. Behind one a TV gibbered; behind another a man was yelling, "Don't be likely anybody's gonna be waitin on *you* –"

He knocked at the third, fearing the sound. It opened to the astonished face of a small unshaven man with grizzled hair. "Git outta here!" he yelled, and shut it.

Johnny was in the fourth. Thin and ragged, he seemed to lean on the open door for support, followed Mick into the room with a weary ease. "What you want?"

Mick glanced at the soiled walls, the floor. "Can I stay, a couple days?"

"Shit no. Shit no I don't care." Johnny paced, came back. "You want to work?"

"Deliveries?"

"Yeah."

"I got some job offers already. Don't need more."

"Where you been?"

Mick told him about the Himals and Indonesia but Johnny's eyes were straying.

Antic laughter burst forth from the floor above, a crash of glass. "Remember one time," Johnny said, "we were about eight, had a crabapple fight in the orchard? You hit me in the eye."

"Sorry," Mick said. "But why are you still here?" He nodded at the bedraggled apartment, the stained mattress and cracked windows, the sad neighborhood.

"The revolution starts here," Johnny snickered.

"These people don't give a shit."

"They're poor, they're angry. With little to lose."

"This War'll stop soon. It has to."

"No way, the politicians love it. The defense industry, the military, the unions, the patriots. Getting hardons for death. The bomb and bullet makers – *you that build the big guns, you that build the death planes,* like Dylan says. Even if it does end," he smiled, "what difference would that make in Harlem?"

"They wouldn't be getting drafted," Mick said. "Killed."

"And learnin' *how* to kill. You and me, Mick, we're just average whiteboys. The world's our oyster and this War an inconvenience. We can duck it with a college degree or some whiteboy deferment, but what about the kid upstairs, a high school dropout getting jazzed on heroin to make up for all that's missing in his life?"

"Fuck those who fuck themselves."

"This War's just a metaphor, like Malcolm said –"

"That's exaggeration. These people've never been napalmed, bombed by B-52s."

"– the Negroes, like the Vietnamese, are a subjugated people."

"Well *you're* not, unless you choose to be."

"*And I'll stand over your grave,*" Johnny laughed, "*'Til I'm sure that you're dead.*"

Draino came in, a skinny guy with an ineffective little moustache and a balding Afro. He was a street runner like Johnny, but far more gone, a walking addiction whose existence focused solely on acquiring and injecting smack. His name came from his tendency to mix that product into his bags to stretch some extra for himself.

At all hours people staggered in and out; there was loud angry talk about Whitey and the War, or smack deals with shivering dancy young men. Draino wandered like a blind albatross seeking some chemical clue far back in his brain. Hookers were working downstairs and some of their tricks didn't like white boys. Twice when guys tried to hold Mick up with knives he outran them, but worried about the ones with guns.

One night when he got back to Johnny's, "*Come with me, my love,*" was playing on the radio and Draino was sitting in the corner shooting up. The chord progressions in "*to the sea, the sea of love –*" made Mick want to play it and he went into the bedroom. Black Beauty was gone.

"Draino you dumb fuck," he raged, "where'd you pawn it?" Draino looked aggrieved then put his head down on his folded arms and nodded out. Mick grabbed his wrist, surprised by its feebleness, and twisted it till Draino admitted he'd taken it down to the fat man's pawnshop at 135th and Amsterdam. But he'd lost the ticket.

"Can't buy it back," the fat man said next morning. "Wid'out I git the ticket."

"It's stolen goods. You know it's mine. You gave Draino ten bucks for it and I'll give you ten back. You don't like it I'll go to the cops."

"Cops? You some kinda natural born idiot? Don' say that word round here."

Mick dropped his last ten dollars on the counter and walked out with Black Beauty, half-expecting the fat man's bullet in his spine.

SMILEY LYNCH had been a bodyguard for Malcolm X; Mick had met him two years ago in a Harlem church basement. He was a huge blue-skinned man who'd been a boxer and fixer and convict who now ran security for Harlem bars, dealers and parking lots. He'd never got over Malcolm's death, and although he'd been in Newark when it happened he blamed himself.

"I don't want to kill people in Vietnam," Mick said.

"Barbados," Smiley said. "Where I come from. Down there nobody find you."

"I'd stick out like a white thumb."

"They be lotsa white boys. Heh, heh, go down'n sail, huh?"

"With what money?"

"You short, come work for me, nex coupla weeks."

"You don't want a white boy up here –"

"Be nice, a white boy workin for us. Usual the other way round."

Mick started at four-fifty an hour, and for the next two weeks watched over parking lots, private parties and a rancorous blues bar called Memphis Uptown, where after hours he learned the Delta blues walking thumb base from Grover Till –

You think you lookin good, honey
But you can't see yoself at all –

Grover was all bourbon breath, smoky gnarled fingers, gray brillo hair, and graveyard snicker. "Don't let it catch you, Mick, all this busy-doin stuff. People stayin in contact, callin each other up, bein friends? Jus' consolin themselves for the death they see comin down the tracks. Better you play music, keep your *soul* alive."

Smiley paid him for the first night's work so he could buy food, and paid him again Saturday. A week later Mick had almost a hundred dollars. "Sorry I got no more work for you," Smiley said. "But you come see me anytime, you wann' go down Barbados way. I set you up."

TRYING NOT TO VOMIT, Tara stood waiting on the dark stage, bile up her throat, her knees trembling, voice quivery.

In the darkness behind her Luis hit the first notes, Blade coming in on the piano, real slow, then the soft *tick tick* of Sybil on the high hat.

She was going to throw up. Right on this stage, the lights coming up, this wild New Jersey crowd jammed into the hall and down the aisles and stacked against the back wall, roaring as they saw her, the band, the lights blinding her, people clapping roaring cheering as she walked to the mike swishing her hips in her trademark short silky thing with no underpants, yanked the mike from its stand, afraid she'd fall down, terror draining her heart. *"If I mistreat you, honey,"* she slid into their opening song, strong as she could,

> *I sure don't mean no harm,*
> *I'm a motherless child*
> *And I don't know right from wrong.*

For hours the crowd roared and cheered and stamped the floor for more; afterwards she was emptied, shriven, dissolved, throat raw, beyond fatigue. All was false, she didn't care, but when she'd been out there there'd been that bond between her and those people, the band, a weird symbiotic beauty, a truth.

Luis came in with an early edition of *The Post*, crosslegged on the bed waving his cigarette and reading, "This scrawny Rockland County farm girl who dumped a piano scholarship at Juilliard to join the Blade Jones Blues Band, this hundred and ten skinny pounds of pure vocal magic that soars to the ceiling and cuts you like a knife. No, I wasn't impressed by Tara O'Brien. *I WAS JUST BLOWN AWAY . . .*"

"Hey, Baby," Luis said, "like I told you –"

Exhausted, disinterested, she looked at him. "What'd you tell me?"

"You thank the Brown Sugar, Baby. For comin sing with you."

. . .

"A HORRIBLE WAY TO DIE," Saul Finkelstein said. "Ripped apart by a 50-caliber machine gun – can you imagine?"

"Quicker'n an AK," Outlaw countered, "'less it hits you in the head."

"Fuckin bullet four inches long and half an inch thick that mushrooms as it hits you into a softball of hot steel ripping around inside you then punches a basketball hole out the other side. You're eviscerated, man – know what I mean? Gutted."

"AK in the gut, tha's the worse," Sergeant Boone said. "You see what happen, that new kid, what was his name?"

"Fratelli," Outlaw said, "Fraterny, something like that –"

"Rips through you but you live two or three more days begging to die till finally the blood poison kill you. "

"But still, the fifty cal – this wall of steel rips you apart. Think about it."

"Finkelstein," Sergeant Boone said, "you gotta stop worryin. If a bullet's goin gityou it's goin gityou, and ain't nothin you can do about it."

7

BEFORE THE FALL

"AFRAID OF HEIGHTS?" the Dinofrio Construction foreman said, a taciturn half-Mohawk named Ephraim. "Done steeple-jack before?"

"Just construction, but some of it pretty high." Mick thought of walking a girder with eighty pounds of cable looped over one shoulder and trying not to look into the aching void below. "I've climbed a lot of mountains –"

"Mountain don' mean shit. Job pay five eighty-five for hour. Sign to union hall, pay dues. You be working high so dress warm. You be carryin loads on thin wet girders so if you don't like that idea back out now."

Mick took a slow breath. "I said it's fine."

"Last guy died. So watch your step. I can't afford another goddamn insurance claim."

DON'T TAKE THIS JOB," Peter said. "It's in*sanely* dangerous. Guys get killed all the time – what was it I read in the *Times*, six killed making some building."

"If it gets too dangerous I'll quit."

That first day looking down on the city from a steel skeleton thirty-four stories up he thought of Virgin Peak and wondered why he was drawn to impossible heights. On Virgin Peak there were vast vertical sheets of black ice to fall from, the ground so tiny it would take forever to hit. Here one slip and twenty stories straight down to concrete and hard steel.

One of several laborers lugging I-beams and steel angle beams and crates of bolts across narrow windy ridges of steel, he was usually clipped in, which meant unless the cable broke he could fall only a floor or two, down through red rusty ribs of steel toward concrete-stacked platforms far below. But when the wind grabbed him or his foot skidded or the load of metal on his back made him stumble, terror would leap in his throat and his body congealed with horror of the imagined fall, of smashing down from beam to beam, tiny cars and pavement rushing up.

He *had* to stop obsessing about this. Or he *would* fall. He should think about Indonesia. Had to get it revealed, but even in the antiwar movement no one wanted to hear. "It's awful, man," they said. "But we have to stop *this* War first –"

He was totally out of money, hungry every night when he went up to Johnny's place in Harlem, his shoulders bruised and sore, knees weak with fatigue, an empty aching belly that no amount of brown rice could fill. At night he couldn't sleep with the torn soreness in his bad shoulder; by Thursday he was walking both ways from Harlem to Wall Street to save on the subway.

Friday he got no paycheck. "What do you mean?" he screamed at Ephraim.

"Work week done today. Checks cut Wednesday. Payday Friday."

"Today's Friday!"

"*Next* Friday. First you work one week." Ephraim's eyes seemed fixed downriver, above the office rooftops and Battery Park, past the ferry docks and Statue of Liberty, somewhere out on the ocean where all the sewage went. "You don't get much anyway."

"I get a week's pay!"

"First week deduct your union signup. Take most of check."

Mick wanted to hit him. "How much do I get?"

Ephraim had already turned away. "Twenty dollar. Maybe."

Walking up Amsterdam Avenue Mick's rage at himself filled the hungry hole in his stomach with the furious self-castigation of one who has screwed himself once more, will never think smart enough to protect himself from the tricks and traps of his fellow men. That his money for a week of exhausting and dangerous work would be stolen by the AFL-CIO's war-rabid, flag-waving, peacenik-hating, hardhat mafia that cheered each body count and each new charred village made him seem to himself even more a dunce.

He was a fool and fools never get it right, condemned to repeat their disasters all their lives. Dizzy with the odors of hamburger counters and Italian restaurants and hot dog stands and delicatessens, his shoulders aching from another hundred tons of steel lugged across airy nothingness, he traipsed through the smog-silted Friday evening from Wall Street to Harlem. The bars, taxis, hotels, and restaurants were jammed with happy people; limousines swam the broad avenues like sated sharks.

"Had dinner?" he asked Johnny.

Johnny turned from staring out the window at the gathering dark. "Not hungry."

"Bastards stiffed me at work. I'm so hungry. You got no money at all?"

Johnny said nothing and for a moment Mick had hope. But Johnny had just forgotten him. "You have any money?" Mick yelled.

Johnny's eyes flicked toward him. "Do my rounds Monday. Till then – *nada.*"

Roaches sprinted for the corners when Mick opened the cupboards. Only thing left was salt, rat poison, and an open box of bouillon cubes the roaches had been eating. He put them in a pan with water but the gas had been shut off. The cubes wouldn't mix in the cold water so he broke up a shelf from the bathroom and made a fire in the sink and held the pot over it till it boiled.

In the morning he was nauseous with hunger. He took Black Beauty downstairs past the screaming babies and laughing televisions, the doughnut counters along the sidewalk casting their hypnotic aromas, the breakfast counters with their opium of bacon, fried eggs, toast and coffee, the shut bars with their litanies of sweetish liquor and rancid beer, back to the fat man's pawnshop on 135th and Amsterdam.

The huge bearded black man in a beaded cap was sipping coffee and eating a cherry Danish. "I 'member thet guitar."

Mick didn't look at the pastry in the man's hand, not wanting him to see how hungry he was. But if he wasn't hungry why would he be here? "I was thinking of pawning it for a couple weeks. Girlfriend's coming. Need a little extra cash."

"Mojo money, huh?" The man fiddled with it inexpertly. "Like I tell your frien'. Ten dollah."

"For pawn? That's way not enough! You could sell it right now, over a hundred!"

The man put it back in the case. "Ten is to *buy* right now. No pawn."

The thought of losing Black Beauty sprang tears to Mick's eyes. He wanted to beat in the man's face, from disappointment and because he did not respect the guitar.

He tried several more pawnshops, and finally at a place near Columbia a worn pessimistic old man with a nicotined moustache gave him twenty-two dollars and lodged Black Beauty carefully in its case between two violins. "Come back by ten days," he warned, "or I must sell." Unexpectedly he smiled. "I can see you don't want that."

"I'll come back for you," Mick promised Black Beauty under his breath. He stood on the sticky sidewalk, stunned by his loss and the money in his hand.

He bought rice and frozen peas and cheap hamburger already rufous with age – it was true, you couldn't buy decent food in Harlem – and went back to Johnny's, his mind on the guitar. Johnny wasn't there but Draino was sleeping in his bed.

It was difficult not to hate himself. His moods soared and plunged like a junkie's. He was unable to succeed at anything. His life would be a string of failures, a self-induced inability to accomplish what he wanted.

The hamburger was too rotten to eat.

TROY WATCHED THE BEADS of water on the leaves but none had spilled. There were no snapped stems or upturned leaves on the untouched earth.

The jungle was silent; yet there was a steady throb, of life, of insects, birds, leaves, stems, boughs and breeze, the distant chortle of water.

The chant of life came to him as he parted two stems, seeing how the dew dropped down making tiny circles in the mud – and that there'd been no circles before, thinking not of the words but only of death, the dangers of this place. Each instant seeing death from so many places: bullets from a place he'd never see, a tripwire too fine, stepped on only because he wasn't watching *exactly* where he was stepping, listening for any changes in the birdsong or monkey fussing or the warm wind through thick leaves, sniffing constantly for odors out of place: gun oil, sweat, kerosene, rotten fish.

It terrified him every second – a deep-seated terror that spread to the far fabric of his being – terror of smashing agonizing death. And yet he couldn't stop this, this walking point – far beyond the excuse that an officer *leads* his men. "Loot likes it," Sergeant Boone said, "walking point. So we let him."

"He gonna get his white ass killed," Isaiah Norton said.

Sergeant Boone had said nothing, then, "Somebody got to."

WITH HIS FIRST PAYCHECK Mick reclaimed Black Beauty and rented a fourth-floor apartment on East 4th between A and B on the Lower East Side for thirty-five dollars a month. Its metal-sheathed door opened into a low kitchen with a bathtub to the left, and ahead a square room with a brick wall and fireplace and two windows looking over a fire escape down four stories onto a trashy patch of dirt and the brick wall of another building. Behind the door was a narrow slot filled by a single bed and beyond it a toilet in a small closet.

There was a mattress the landlady, Mrs. Romeo, said he could use. He and Peter found a sticky couch and a cable-spool table on the sidewalk, and he bought two plates and silverware in a Puerto Rican second-hand shop, an aluminum pan in the Five and Ten, and hamburger, raisin bread, peanut butter, milk, and wine at the corner bodega.

The apartment must have been empty a long time, for the roaches were starved. They came out in millions, some so hungry they scuttled along the wall above the stove and leaped into the pan. Each time he put down his glass a roach scrambled up it and scurried along the edge trying to reach the wine.

"This's New York," Peter said. "What do you want?"

"What can I do?" Mrs. Romeo gave him a cornered look. "These people," she waved her hand to indicate the other tenants, all Puerto Rican, "they bring cockroaches with them. The hard-working Italian people, Irish people, Russians – all moved away – now nobody rents here, just *them*. On welfare." She glared at two brown-eyed skinny children hovering in the stairwell, both in sleeveless undershirts, barefoot in the April wind. "Be sure keep your door locked, or they steal everything."

HE MET TUCKER RUSSELL at a midtown antiwar meeting. A Vietnam veteran, Tucker was pushing antiwar issues onto the agenda of regular veterans' groups, speaking at American Legion meetings, building a network of returned vets to work on phone banks calling other vets. He had been wounded twice, had three medals and a glass eye that he would take out and put in his mouth to clean and then pop back in the socket. He worked construction now, and sometimes he came to Mick's with scrap wood for the fireplace.

"I don't think we can stop this War," he said, "It's too big. They're making too much money killing people."

Mick stared into the flames. "I've started doing all this antiwar work. Mailings, phone calls, talking to community groups, all that shit."

Slim yet very strong, handsome but shy, brilliant and passionate, Tucker was a cauldron of opposites. He was placid, irascible, kind and furious. Amid a burst of laughter his face would harden, his features darken, and he'd hunch down defensively ready to hit someone. "Don't underrate it," he told Mick. "People listen to you. You've got that *thing* – they trust you."

"But it seems to make no difference: have I lost faith or am I just lazy and defeatist?"

"It's like Pascal. If you *could* make a change but don't? *That's* the sin."

"I get so weary of it. Then I think of the new deaths every day, of what it's like to be blown up or burned alive by napalm or torn apart by bullets. When you lie there and it takes five hours to die."

Tucker fiddled with the fire, leaned back on his elbows on the rug. "Do you think it can be burnt out of you, what happens? Exorcised?"

"My Dad used to wake up at night with horrible nightmares of Tarawa. Two decades after it happened."

Beyond the window sirens wailed, a child was calling. "We'd been choppered into an LZ in the highlands in Cambodia," Tucker said. "Don't believe them, the bastards, when they tell you we're not in Cambodia."

"Who said I believed them?"

With his knife Tucker slit a sliver from a piece of wood and lit it to restart the joint. "We hike up this long ridge through rain forest. A squad, maybe fourteen of us. Pines along the top. We stop to eat, set out a perimeter. Quiet as a sleeping baby. Just the buzzing of a fly or two attracted – God knows why – to our C-rats. A flock of little birds comes through, singing in the pine tops. I was always very tough with the guys, no noise, no cigarettes, kept them spread out, radio silence, the works. *Noise is death*, I told them.

"We were always nervous, but this was a quiet sector, wasn't near Charlie's routes out of Cambodia. We'd been in a horror a few weeks before, lost four guys, and I was happy to be out here. Make it last, I told myself. Just wander this country quietly, keep your guys out of trouble."

"What did you all think of the War, back then?"

"Most of us thought it sucked even back then, except a few gung-ho guys who got people killed, and the officers in the rear. The lifers out of danger, man, they love this War." Tucker stopped to listen to a plane rumbling toward LaGuardia. "Still strange to realize those planes aren't carrying bombs."

They listened to the fading engines. A light rain was tinkling down the metal of the fire escape, drip drip dripping from the window. "I get them moving," Tucker went on. "I have a guy fifty yards ahead on point. I take slack – that's the second guy – thirty yards behind him, twenty yards ahead of my team. I got another guy dropped back behind us and keeping my guys twenty yards apart.

"What in Vermont we call a bluebird day. The pines have that lovely resin smell. The breeze just a little chilly, and you can see clearly through the tree trunks down the ridge on both sides. There were red rocks sticking out of the earth, and I remember thinking they'd be cover too if we needed.

"You're always doing that, every instant watching for danger and looking for solutions if danger comes – where to take cover, where enemy fire will come from, where to call in strikes, how to get your people out. But today it seems so artificial, like kids playing war in a park. And any moment our moms would call us home for dinner." Tucker tensed at a rustling in the hall.

"Just rats," Mick said. "Or junkies, checking if I'm here."

Tucker kept listening, his single eye flat. "So after an hour the ridge slopes southwest. We take a spur down into a thick brushy forest. The sun so bright you can't see through the trees. Sometimes you hear water trickling, on the breeze. We spread out through the trees, moving a hundred feet every five minutes, each guy estimating his distance and stepping silent as he can, finger on the trigger guard, looking out for death –"

He said nothing for a while, then, "The ridge descends, to the loveliest valley. A narrow meadow with a trail down the middle, on the edges bamboo then palms and jungle. Where the trail curves into the jungle there's some banana trees, their leaves just gleaming, the yellow little bananas showing through. There's flowers in the meadow and the buzz of all these insects and the calls of birds, the breeze rubbing the leaves together and the sound of water splashing down rocks somewhere out in the valley."

Sirens roared uptown on First Avenue, echoing off the buildings. "It never stops, does it?" Tucker said. "I'm wasting your time, this?" then added quickly, "I want so fuckin much to understand. It goes around in my mind all the time and I can't answer."

His voice close to tears made Mick nervous. "Answer what?"

"Why were we there?" His eyes glistened in the firelight. "Why *any* of it?"

He got up resolutely, as if leaving, put more kindling on the coals. "I hated all this, being responsible for their lives, that I could fail, get people killed."

The sirens faded. It kept raining. "No one takes the path. We infiltrate the jungle on both sides, the bamboos at the edge, the palms, watching for trip wires and punji pits and snakes and anything ahead or on the side or back that might be people, guns, movement. The air smells sweet like bananas, almost rotten. The soil like spring rain, everything green. Even the light was fuckin green. We come to a stream, four feet maybe, shallow. Water grass in it, rippling like a girl's hair, you know, long, in the wind . . ." He tossed wine dregs on the coals. "Then it starts."

"What?" Not wanting to interfere, half not wanting to hear, Mick watched the blue flames from the creosoted wood shiver up the chimney.

"A baby cries. I wave the guys down. We wait a while then I go forward." Tucker's hands moved as if pushing a gun through branches. "Keeping in the trees by the stream, cross another path, no wires, just tracks of bare feet. Come to a little paddy flashing in the sun and beyond a bamboo shelter, a guy in black pants sitting there. He's cleaning a rifle, broken down, the sun's in my eyes but I can see the curved clip, an AK. I get this cold feeling knowing I have to take him out.

"Another one comes around the shelter, in black, wearing a pack. Looks right at me, points. The other one's swinging up the gun and the first one's grabbing in the hut for something and I squeeze on them both, the one going into the hut spins around with arms swung wide and I know it's a death hit and the second one scrambling toward him, my bullets kicking dust around him and I know I've got him too."

They sat silent, the tang of creosote from the fire like the stench of cordite, the rumble of a subway like artillery. "They fall like dolls," he said. "Time to empty a clip, automatic. I take cover in the paddy trying to reload, worried about return fire, about bullets hitting my chest like I had just hit these VC.

"Nobody returns fire. The frogs start to croak again, birds calling. I'm stunned, never killed anybody before, not for sure. My point guy whistles our three-note whistle and I whistle back. He and two others come up and we circle the hut and move in.

"The one who was cleaning the AK has fallen sideways in a ditch. His chest's all smashed, blood everywhere. One of my guys puts a boot in his eye, gives us the thumbs up. I move in on the hut.

"The other one has no face but long black hair full of blood. A woman. On her back what I thought was a backpack was a baby. The baby's dead too. Little fists, chubby baby arms stretched out straight."

He took a breath. "The AK clip's just some kind of hoe he was sharpening, to hoe the rice. There's no guns, nothing. Just a guy and a girl and a baby and cooked rice in the hut and dry rice in a clay bowl, some dishes and a candle."

He shook his head, holding back. "I sit outside, don't care if VC kill me. The guys keep saying you did the right thing, man, don't sweat it, I'd have done the same, can't take a chance. It washes right off me. I know I've murdered them. In that valley, that beautiful valley, they were like . . . the first family. The first human family. Adam and Eve and their child. Before the Fall." He stood, looked out the window, down the lightwell. "I am the Fall," he said quietly, "I am the evil. I'm what the Bible's about."

Tucker had been raised, Mick remembered, in a conservative Methodist family, serious Sunday morning churchgoers who prayed at every meal and believed in a Heaven or a Hell at the end of one's journey. "I am," Tucker repeated, "and deserve to be, doomed."

"That's silly." Mick tried not to think of the family in the banana valley.

Tucker shook his head. "I knew right then nothing would make up for what I'd done. For the rest of my life I'd pay."

"But look what you're doing now."

Tucker smiled the same sad smile as when a pro-War Rear-echelon motherfucker called him a coward or a traitor. "God is obvious, but not what we think."

Mick eyed his watch. After midnight. Aimless thoughts ran through his head, of calling a girl, going to Ratner's, going climbing on the weekend. He put on *Yesterday and Today*, very low, thinking *it's therapeutic*. He was ducking Tucker and knew it, tried to force his mind back to him, but every time he saw the boy sharpening his hoe, the girl with the baby on her back, the sun-golden hut in the paradise valley in a sudden horrid hail of steel. "Once you go there," Tucker said, "you can't ever come back."

"Sure you can, you . . ."

"There's nothing in the rest of my life can make up, for what I did."

"I keep having nightmares," Mick said finally. "Of my brother being wounded or blown up or crushed in something. Driving me nuts."

"A vets' meeting last night, this big blond-haired guy with a beard in an old Levi vest, you know the type, starts yelling about how we have to blow up Selective Service offices, telling all these stories about what our men do to VC prisoners, and he weirds me out, man, I don't like it. And I'm thinking we have to get rid of this guy, and Tinley says no – you know Tinley, the Air Force guy, flew all those missions?"

"Yeah."

"Tinley recognizes this guy, says he does this at other meetings, he's an FBI plant, trying to make us look more radical. So I say let's beat the shit out of him but Tinley says like with all these guys, don' let them know we know."

Mick opened the window. *Nowhere man,* the record said, *please listen.* Cold air rushed in stirring the cinders. *You don't know what you're missing.* He wanted to climb onto the fire escape, stand in the rain. Wanted Tucker to go away so he could get back to his own life. It's not my fault, Mick told him silently, that you went to Vietnam.

I'm not half the man I used to be, the Beatles sang, *there's a shadow hanging over me.* "Right on," Tucker laughed, reached for the joint and took up Mick's guitar, singing Phil Ochs,

> *It's always the old to lead us to the war*
> *It's always the young to fall*
> *Now look at all we've won with the saber and the gun*
> *Tell me is it worth it all.*

"Of course it's not worth it," Tucker looked at Mick. "But when you talk to people, man, it's worth it: they understand." Tucker stood, shrugged into this coat, staring out the window at the facing walls, the dark sky, this crazy world. "It's worth it all."

He stopped at the door, saluted. "Just wait and see."

POLICE BROKE UP THE PEACE demonstration on Fifth Avenue by riding horses sideways into the crowds and pushing people through plate-glass windows. "Pig!" Mick leaped from the speakers' podium at a cop who swung at him with his club then chased him on horseback through the crowd, swinging his club.

Mick ran down a narrow alley, the horse clattering after him, the policeman's club swishing, dashed in the back door of a bar and through it out the front at the corner as the cop came clattering round to the front with the club in his hand, the horse huffing, its breath steaming in the bar's lights.

He reversed his jacket and returned to the demonstration but it was all broken up, clumps of people here and there moving away fast, posters flattened and filthy on the street or flitting along the gutter in the sharp wind, a police truck receding up Fifth Avenue flashing garish shadows on the canyon walls.

Peace marches did no good. There had been huge ones in every major city – millions of people in the streets. But even if everyone in the country marched, the men in Washington weren't going to stop bombing and killing Vietnamese.

He was speaking at two meetings a week. Big ones. The city throbbed with protest. The nation.

There had to be some way to *make* a difference. To stop this War.

"YOU'RE WASTING your time," Seth told Mick. "Speaking to all these peace groups. All these speeches, these protests, make no bloody difference. We're going to do this Indochina War seven more years, that's the plan."

"Plan?"

"At that point we'll have pushed it far as it can go. Sold all the weaponry to DOD they can ever find the taxpayers' money for. Time runs out on wars . . . it always does."

Not understanding, he told Seth about Tucker's story of the banana valley. "You once said Cambodia was the most exquisite place on earth. Remember, the cities of carved stone temples, deer grazing at the edge of the jungle, amazing birds – you never *saw* so many birds? The sense of peace? You meet a girl in a water taxi or on the street and she wants to make love. They love making love: it's not a sin. There's no crime, you leave your bicycle when you go in a place, it's there when you come out."

"These people," Seth leaned back in his leather armchair and inhaled thoughtfully on his cigarillo, his face hurt by what Mick had said, "they're ripe for Communism. Poor and hungry, with no chance to get ahead –"

"If it's better for them?"

"Doesn't matter what's better for *them*," Seth said. "But what's better for *us*. That's *real*politik. These Negroes rioting in the cities? Mick, you *know* it's Communist-inspired."

"So it's okay to send our Green Berets into Cambodia, into that peaceful beautiful place, to kill these people and destroy their country?"

"If Johnson gets thrown out in three years maybe we'll stop."

Allowing such slaughter and destruction to endure any longer seemed insanely evil. "You once said, 'the *men* who killed Kennedy,' but you wouldn't explain."

"Hell, everybody knows it. The Agency's Mafia Cubans, but now Agency's deflecting it, saying they weren't under our control, we didn't approve it."

"So who approved it?"

Seth gave him the grin one gives an idiot. "I just told you."

HE BACKED INTO LONNIE in a used clothing store, a short girl in a navy beret, a scar behind one dimple like a laugh mark that made her smile a little sinister. They had beers in a bar and more back at his place and she said she didn't mind the roaches and as they were kissing on the couch he realized she was going to make love, that after so long he hadn't lost the love of girls forever.

They made love again and again, roaches scurrying for cover, and again in the morning. She had a bag of Maui Wowie and they went half-through it, smoking and making love. "I don't understand their problem," Lonnie said.

"They?"

"The Feds. Grass is so *lovely*. It widens your awareness, makes you feel warm toward other people. Helps you understand yourself, so you can live better in this world, be more productive and caring. Why do they hate *that*?"

"Because when people are aware, they refuse to be led like sheep, to die in Vietnam because they're told to, or pay taxes to napalm people in rice paddies. Won't work all their lives at a job they hate. What'd happen to our economy then?"

"When I started smoking grass my grades went up. Things I was studying became fascinating because I understood them better –"

"They've started using B-52s to bomb North Vietnam. Can you imagine, millions of tons of bombs raining down from invisible heights on rice farmers?" He knew he shouldn't talk about it but it was in his mind constantly, couldn't ignore it. Night and day, up on the high steel or down under in the subway, seeing it all, happening right now, the pain and death, the horrible burns, the fierce shredding of bombs – why? Why couldn't he, in all these meeting and speeches, find a way to stop it? *Why?*

She lay back, her supple body along his, exhaled and handed him the joint. "Even Walter Lippmann has turned against the War, says we can't win. It'll have to stop soon."

He didn't believe that. After a few nights he no longer wanted to see her; there was something too eager and simple in her, a stark enjoyment that bothered him, a lack of torment. Since the War had begun he wanted sex to be an ecstasy of guilt, not cheery and light-hearted or too easily enjoyed, couldn't imagine happiness in the presence of the War.

But when he was alone again he hated it. Often he wanted to see Peter and Lois, Seth and Miranda, to call anyone, wash away Indonesia or he'd go crazy. But he feared bothering everyone, revealing the shame of his loneliness. Didn't you have to seem the opposite of what you were, to get what you wanted?

In the day, carrying cable and bolts and cement and pneumatic drills across networks of high steel, sitting on a beam with legs wrapped around it, he was happy, forgot Indonesia, never felt alone. But when he went home the aching hollowness crept in like the darkness, like the fear of shadows, like a beast waiting for night to feed on you, so you'd be his, and no longer you. Time and time again he saw the Indonesian dead, the couple on the motor scooter shot by the Muslim killers, the people beaten to death, Mrs. Surawaya in a pool of blood.

Loneliness, he told himself, is nothing but fear of death. *You can't live with anyone else till you can live with yourself.*

Unless you stop this War you will never be free.

Never be happy.

No matter what he did, it wouldn't be enough.

When he met a new girl he'd want to make love then not want to be with her, would wander the empty streets or sit in his cold dark apartment, lonely again. He feared he might never love or be loved.

He would go home after work, out of the subway in cold darkness, slush soaking his worn boots, arms wretched with fatigue, the East 4th sidewalk grim, pale patches of light here and there where an entry light had not been smashed, into his doorway taking the few bills from the broken mailbox then up the creaking half-lit stairs with their splintered linoleum and the little balls of bloody cotton where Puerto Rican kids had been shooting heroin, wondering as he climbed to the fourth floor if they'd broken into his flat again and if they'd found Black Beauty's hiding place under the floorboards.

And tonight what meetings to chair, to show by his presence – who the hell was he? – that yes we can stop this War. Together we can stop this.

There must be a way.

Tonight his broken mailbox had two letters in it. One was from Tara, "I'm doing fine and the tour went well and we're getting real studio time. Can you come out some time and see me? P.S. I'm *in love* – you'll like him."

The other letter was just a scrap of paper, almost a parking ticket, ordering him to report next week to Whitehall Induction Center for a pre-induction physical.

8

IF IT FEELS GOOD

"**I**F IT *FEELS* **GOOD**," Rebecca Griswold said, "I do it." Tugging back a coil of chestnut hair, she raised up on one elbow, lovely breast against his arm. "It sounds too simple and easy, right? But what if it *is* right?"

"What if it hurts someone else?" Mick said.

"Hurting someone else *doesn't* feel good. So we don't do it." She had left Harvard Law to organize for SDS, Students for a Democratic Society, pushing them toward street action, thus siding with Mick in the antiwar political battles. Short and slim with long coils of chestnut hair, she had helped organize the first antiwar teach-in at the University of Michigan and broadened it to nearly forty campuses across the country, reaching hundreds of thousands of students.

"Some people," Mick answered, "don't feel good unless they *are* hurting others."

She snickered, squeezed his prick in a ring between her thumb and forefinger. "I don't *think* so."

Next day, high up on the steel girders, he thought about it. If something felt good, did no harm to others or ourselves, why *not* do it? Was it wrong to listen to the body, the heart?

He slid four inch-thick bolts through a plate of metal at the end of

93

a wall strut then through a steel wall column, spun on the nuts and air-drilled them tight. In not doing what we wanted, weren't we being subjugated by the culture, the herd, into doing what we *should* do according to the herd – what *it* wanted? Even when it made us unhappy?

If it feels good. Weren't our deep feelings the wisest, most moral way to live? A natural way not overridden by our culture? If we could consistently follow them would our lives not be enriched? Wouldn't we be naturally moral, because to hurt others was to not feel good? Was there a whole way of living to be found here?

Do unto others was a good moral law but a rather selfish one, so complex in its potential applications that it seemed rarely followed. *If it feels good do it* was far more moral. *If it feels good* led to joy, truth, power and achievement, was far fairer to others and far easier to follow.

The bolt holes of the next strut wouldn't line up and he had to lean outwards to lift the strut and turn it a quarter turn, as he stood balanced on a ten-inch girder over the netted void. It settled perfectly against the column and he bolted it home. It was the same with thinking, sometimes you had to turn things upside down or sideways, then they fit perfectly. You had to think things over again, anew.

And it was easy to see that to do good was simply to lessen suffering, and to do evil to increase it. True, suffering was relative: Food for hungry humans is death for the lamb – but you try to avoid unnecessary suffering, and help others when you can. An example would be to never kill for pleasure, only as needed for food. Whenever possible avoid inflicting pain.

And *if it feels good do it* negates domination by the culture, the herd. The culture fears and hates pleasure. It told you *if it feels bad, do it. It's good for you.* Minimizing this life and baiting us with promises of better ones later.

The herd tells you it's brave and masculine to run off to attack some country and get your brains blown out. Then it weeps over your casket and licks its lips for the next one.

If it doesn't feel good don't do it was the corollary. That knocked all religions out of the batter's box of veracity, showed them for what they were: diatribes against pleasure, joy, freedom, knowledge and women.

"And clothes," Rebecca said. "Why do we hide the sexual parts of our bodies? What's wrong with genitals, the difference between us that drives sexual evolution?"

He laughed, snuggled into the warm deliciousness of her crotch. "I like you far better *without* clothes."

She leaned back, opening to his tongue inside her. "When I'm making love," she said half-breathlessly, "it feels *so* good. So of *course* it's right. As long as you're sure, *oh Jesus yes do that*, as long as you're sure you won't get knocked up, *yes don't stop*, fucking is lovely. Why *not* do it? What's the constraint? *Oh yes do that...* Who's up there saying *NO, YOU CAN'T DO THAT? Oh God yes ...* "

"All the things we bury," he answered from the beautiful fragrance between her thighs. "But can't get rid of."

TROY'S PLATOON patrolled for three weeks of heavy rain through the foothills and paddies in an arc thirty klicks northeast of Pretty Woman. Sometimes the rain fell straight down in sheets, sometimes from the side when the wind was blowing, but it almost never stopped. The knee-high sawgrass was soggy and sharp and sliced their sodden utilities and skin, the ground so muddy they slipped under the weight of their packs and guns, the M-60s and mortar tubes, radios and ammo. Fat brown leeches climbed all the way to their crotches and the mosquitoes ate at them unabatedly.

"We're bullet magnets," Finkelstein said gloomily. "They send us out here to attract bullets so they can locate the VC. We're just bait."

"Will you shut up Finkelstein." Outlaw squirmed to a new position under his poncho halves, a puddle of rain coursing down his neck.

"Same thing last November," Finkelstein went on. "First Cav getting blown away at Ia Drang –"

"That was the fuckin Army not the Marines –"

"Westmoreland," Isaiah Norton said. "Somebody say he on the

cover of *Time* magazine? Man of the year – him what walked us into Ia Drang?"

"Don't think about it," Outlaw said. "It doesn't matter."

"It's too quiet, this sector," Finkelstein said. "It worries me."

"Everything worries you," Outlaw readjusted his poncho halves and shook water out of his ear.

They were dug in with the rest of the platoon across a moonlike hilltop blasted and cratered by bombs, a soaking greasy red mud the rain didn't sink into. "Don't think," Outlaw repeated in his flat Maine accent. "Or think about something else."

"I have. About plant and animal families," Finkelstein said. "How to improve on Linnaeus."

Outlaw half-snickered. "What the fuck's that?"

"Instead of having all these Latin names for species'n shit, what if every vegetable is in the same family as all others that start with the same letter? So you got redwood and rose, for example, tulip and tomato, bacteria and bamboo. Animal names work the same way – elephant and eel, for instance . . ."

"But everybody don't speak English," Isaiah said, tipping rain off his helmet.

"Easy. Every country, every language, has its own classification system. It'd be so much simpler –"

"I don't know, man." Outlaw scratched his ear. "Sounds like trouble."

"It's all sound and fury," Corey Dillon said. "Signifying nothing."

"Man, that sounds familiar," Finkelstein said. "Who said that?"

"Faulkner," Dillon answered. "Emily Faulkner."

Watching through the dark rain Troy grinned. Same kind of bullshit Mick would throw at you, when we was kids. Remembering the Tom Paxton song that was all over the radio, back in the world,

What did you learn in school today, dear little boy of mine?
I learned our government must be strong
It's always right and never wrong
Our leaders are the finest men

And we elect them again and again

"IF WE ALL REFUSE THE DRAFT," Mick argued in a midtown hotel meeting of all the antiwar groups, "then they have no army, can't fight the war."

"The government doesn't care what people want," Tucker added. "Taking away their soldiers might be the only way to stop them."

"Peaceful protest is as far as we should go," the Quakers argued.

"Five years in jail," Rebecca Griswold said. "If you burn your draft card."

"No, we've got to blow up the Selective Service offices," the FBI undercover infiltrators said.

"Instead of burning your card," Mick argued, "you're just refusing induction. Forcing them to prosecute you."

"Ten years in jail," George Wharton of Clergy United said.

"Not if *every*body does it," Mick countered. "If we can reach critical mass. They're not going to jail a hundred thousand guys."

"They'll jail the leaders. That's what they always do. Then no one else dares."

"It could work," Dr. Benjamin Spock said. The world-famous pediatrician who had written the book many children had been raised on, he was a leader of the Committee for a Sane Nuclear Policy. "In World War One the only reason the generals could massacre their men at the rate of ten to fifty thousand a day was because of conscription."

"For now it's too radical," Al Lowenstein said to Mick an hour later in the elevator going down. It was full of reporters trying to interview him, but he ignored them. "I wish," Al continued, "you'd build some ties between draft resistance and college students –"

"They don't care," Mick said. "They're not at risk till they graduate."

Lowenstein was a brilliant Yale lawyer and wealthy New Yorker who had worked eighteen hours a day for years in liberal politics and civil rights, and who believed in due process, in not fighting crime with crime. "The trouble with pessimism," he would say, "is that it leads to inaction." His immense wealth drove him to seek for everyone the same opportunities he had had, his motivation simply that no one can be free if anyone is not, that no one is free of guilt when another dies from hunger or injustice.

"I wish you'd work with me instead of this draft organizing," Al said.

"I'm a street fighter," Mick answered, not sure what he meant.

"This Resistance is pussy stuff," Rebecca said.

"A war needs money and soldiers," Mick answered. "We can't cut off the money, but maybe we can cut off the soldiers."

"Every day more people turn against the War," Lowenstein said.

"Every day hundreds of people are dying," Mick answered. "Sometimes thousands."

President Johnson had started the bombing of North Vietnam again, after a 37-day halt, to which Bobby Kennedy warned that the country was going down "a road from where there is no turning back, a road that leads to catastrophe for all mankind."

The most respected of American political observers, Walter Lippmann, wrote that unless stopped the War would tear the US apart. "Gestures, propaganda, public relations, and bombing and more bombing," he added, "will not work."

A group of a hundred twenty vets had just tried to return their medals to the White House. Antagonism against the War was hardening everywhere. In newspapers, the sorrowed television coverage of napalm strikes and bloodened bodies, the *Fuck War* graffiti and anti-Vietnam posters everywhere on walls, the constant protests filling the streets –

Hey, hey, LBJ, how many kids did you kill today?

In the notices of meetings pinned to telephone poles, the bumper stickers and protests and drugs and sex and talk of freedom, the change was growing fast. In the rallies and meetings and in talking on the street there was the intensity and excitement of battle –

One two three four, we don't want your fucking war –

If they *could* organize, convince, and work together, they *could* stop the War.

"These young guys about to be drafted," Tucker said, "I tell them, hey brother, you got a choice. Either you can screw all the girls you want, take these wonderful drugs and listen to magnificent music, enjoy life to the fullest, or you can enslave yourself in a heartless deadly organization, give it life and death power over you, go to a beautiful place on the other side of the world and destroy it, live in mud and heat and filth and snakes, leeches, scorpions, shrapnel, bullets, rockets, artillery and land mines, and run a good risk of having your head blown off. Hey brother, it's your choice."

"Most guys," Rebecca said, "don't have the balls to see it that way."

"If you're going to ask young people to die," Tucker answered, "you better have a damn good reason."

A WEEK BEFORE MICK'S INDUCTION they took Peter's old blue Lincoln to go climbing in the Shawangunks. It was a morning for living deeply, the leaves brilliant, the first taste of winter in the air, the cliffs like black marble against the bitter sky.

There had been a letter from Cynthia in Vienna that Mick had pocketed unopened. When they got to a set of cliffs that weren't too crowded he sat under a maple to read it.

*Last week I went to Durnstein and walked the walls where Richard
the Lion-Hearted must have paced, looked through crossbow slots at
the curve in the Danube and the forested mountains on the other side
and tried to imagine what he thought, waiting to be ransomed.*

*From where I sit as I write this I can see out my narrow window to
the stone façade across the alley and down to the heads of the people
with their string shopping bags and red caps and loden coats and dark
boots squelching in the snow. A man just passed smoking a pipe and I
can smell it here, five floors up.*

*I'm happy but so lonely. Nietzsche is a sour old man, so is Kafka. I'm
tired of gerunds and genders and Goethe. As you suggested I've taken
a lover, a shy boy with long dark hair named Luther. The sex is satisfying but it's annoying having his puppy eyes following me around.
When I'd rather be with you.*

Peter tossed a coiled rope on the ground and went back to scanning the cliff. Mick put the letter in his pocket, imagined Cynthia
making love with this dark-haired boy. *The sex is satisfying.*

Sun gleamed on the rock face. It soared straight up, its silver
black-laced sheen towering over them into the bright sky. It seemed
impossibly hard and dangerous. "There's a nice seam up there," Peter
pointed. "Let's go up a ways and see where it goes."

"We should grab some pins, rope up."

"Nah, let's just free climb it a little, see what it is. Then we'll come
down for the gear."

Mick followed Peter up the seam, vaguely aware of a dissonance
inside. A little pissed at Peter for showing off. But this seam was easy,
so that wasn't it.

The seam went straight up about a hundred feet then angled left.
At first there were good fingertip holds and rough spots in the wall
for toes, but as the rock climbed it smoothed, perhaps due to more
exposure to the wind and rain, and all they had was the seam,
narrowing and granite-slippery, fingertip-wide and inch-deep. It was
nice to be up in the open, sun on your back, and so far it was easy. His
hands, tough with carrying steel, hardened with dirt and grease and
rough with weather, felt glued to the rock.

He fought a sudden unexpected need to look down, thought of
how exposed they were, for an instant trembled, forced it away. "Go
down now," said the voice in the back of his skull. "Before it's too late."

The sense of safety began to pour out of him like water from a
torn plastic bag.

"Please," the voice begged. "Go down now."

He took a good grip and looked down. The maple tree under
which he'd read Cynthia's letter was two hundred feet down, its

canopy wide as a basketball at hand's length. If he fell he'd land in that, not in the boulders beneath. He imagined his body smashing down through the boughs onto the rocks.

But this was an easy climb. The seam would open up ahead and the face would tilt back. He imagined the last few elated steps to the top. Sitting up there in the sun. The pride of looking down on other climbers, having free-climbed it while they were roped. "How is it?" he called up.

The words came down echolike though Peter was only fifteen feet above. "Still quite clean." He waited for a breath. "Should spread out soon."

At this point it would be worse to go down so Mick kept moving up the cliff. The seam was like a snake, a lightning bolt. The rock had a blackish patina, had grown more crumbly – or was he imagining it? Wind blew dust from the seam into his eyes; his football-dislocated shoulder ached from holding himself up by pulling at the sides of the crack.

Just ahead must be the place. Where the seam widened and deepened and they could get a toehold in this fucking rock. Fingers jammed into the crease he clung to it like an exhausted lover, trying not to think that they should've used a rope and pitons, how much better it would've been.

Never again would he do this. That didn't help now. Never might be very soon. He tried not to think of hitting the rocks, the awful aching terror the moment you fall.

But with no gear they couldn't go down.

Peter's boots were right above him, gritting the rock. "Got some options here."

Mick was in a bad place, one finger, one edge of toe. "What?"

"Go left, hope it widens. Go right up a thin seam. No protection. Hope it opens." Peter's boot toe scraped as it sought contact with the rock. "What we thought, was the seam, going straight up – just a stain. On the rock."

"There's no seam?"

"No seam."

"Fuck."

"We can't go down."

"Fuck." Mick imagined Peter falling, knocking him off the rock.

"Up left looks better . . ." There was a wait while Peter moved his face a bit off the rock for a better look. "Deeper. Better angle."

"Toeholds?"

"No."

"Other one?"

"No."

Mick began to think how to get down. Unlike squirrels humans can't go down face first, can't see where they're going, have to try to remember from the way up and feel with toes and use fingers for purchase. But the seam was too thin in places to go down.

They would fall.

This horrible fact hit him, the aching terror of death at two hundred miles an hour. What it would feel like.

He imagined stepping over the top, emptied his lungs and sucked them full to clean CO_2 from his blood. This made him dizzy and he almost fell.

"Swinging up to the left," Peter called nonchalantly.

When he got to the fork Peter was now four feet up that way, toes begging at the rock. The right fork was deeper, at least at the start. Again Mick thought of Peter falling on him, how they'd both go.

"Going right," he gasped.

"Nasty, that way."

Absurdly, he thought of Cynthia looking down from her window at the shoppers in the faded medieval alley five floors below, the trampled snow. If he could only be that close to the ground it would almost be okay to fall.

The crack stayed consistent ten feet at an eighty-degree angle then went vertical and crazily was slick with water, had to be a tiny seep somewhere but that couldn't be, not this kind of rock, not here. But his fingertips were wet and the rock slippery. And nowhere to put his toes.

He carefully moved his cheek away from the rock so as to look the other way. Though he wanted not to he saw down. Far down the slick rock wall the maple was tiny as a dime. Below him the cliff was steeper than vertical, glistened and shivered in the heat, waiting to shrug them off. "Shit!" he called.

"Shit?" Peter sounded as if they were at home, just talking. Mick had a tinge of comfort hearing him then the awful sorrow of knowing there was nothing either of them could do.

"Nothing."

"Getting shitty here, too."

He had no touch for his toes, just eight fingers jammed in a slippery crack, could not feel his fingertips.

His life was over. It could be seconds, minutes, maybe an hour. But he was going to fall off this cliff.

The trembling started in his right Achilles tendon, spread up his calves. His ankles grew weak, powerless, his thighs numb against the rock. His knees began to shiver and bang against the cliff. He shut his eyes to avoid looking down, to keep the sweat out.

The mountain yawed. He held on, gasping, arms aching to fall. He couldn't stand the terror, shoulders shaking, wrists so limp he couldn't wedge his fingers in the crease. His fingertips began to slip. When he tried to shove his fingers in deeper it only pushed him further from the cliff. *You're going to die now. If you don't get a hold.*

He found a nub of stone beneath one toe; it held. He dug four fingers of his right hand deeper, slid down his left till it found a dry point in the crease, dug these in and waited.

"Fuck!" Peter whispered.

"Yeah?"

"How you doing?"

"Stuck."

"We have to go down."

"Fuck."

It felt good to hear Peter's voice though he too was doomed. For an instant they seemed strangely human, linked by fate. Different from the rest: about to die.

"Step at a time," Mick said, "I'm going down. You follow."

There was no thinking, no discussion, he just said it. It came from deep in the rock. His fingers felt part of the mountain, not different; his skin touched the same skin. "Easier," he called, "than it seems."

Peter did not answer. Mick wondered was he having the same moment of terror he'd just survived. Or was he losing it, starting to fall? Getting ready to go.

The fingertips of Mick's down-stretched left hand felt down to the juncture of his crack with Peter's. "Where are you?" Mick called.

"Coming down," Peter grunted.

"Got a hold?"

"Uhn."

"One of us has to go down first."

"Uhn."

"Which do you want?"

For a moment nothing, the rasp of leather on rock. "Neither."

It was scary, the urge to laugh. "Take your pick."

"You go down, Mick. I'll follow."

It was like two friends in jail trying to decide which one will be shot. If the lower one fell the top one might still make it. But if the top one fell they'd both die, unless in falling the top one pushed himself away from the rock to avoid hitting the other on the way down. But in that last terrified slip who would have the courage or mind to do that?

Peter's boot brushed Mick's wrist. "Fuck," Peter said. "Sorry."

"I'll go down first."

"No," Peter said, but Mick had slid to the seam, Peter's gritty sole above him. For an instant he almost lost it, distracted by Peter's boot. He held for a minute while he readjusted his holds. "Wait a bit," he whispered. "Give me some space."

"No problem."

The seam was steady for a while then swung right, very dangerous because you had to switch from right hand high to right hand low. To do this you had to jam the left fingers slightly inversed as tight as possible into the seam then hang on those fingers, bring the right hand down to the left. Then you had to let go with the right hand and, hanging on the left, swing the right round it to snatch the seam again.

The hot dry rock sucked the moisture from his throat; his fingertips and wrists and arms and ankles were slack with exhaustion. Above him Peter's boots seemed to be skidding and slipping and his gasping was terrifying.

The hold broke, he slid, fingernails scraping rock, caught a hold and felt his bad shoulder tear as the arm dislocated. The pain was atrocious; he wanted to scream, tried to pull the arm back into the socket but it was too extended, he was hanging on it. He was going to die.

Slowly, very slowly, he pushed up with his toes, jamming against the hold with his good hand. But if he let go with the dislocated arm he'd fall; if he didn't get it back into the socket he was caught here, would fall too. *Let go*, the terror begged him, *get it over with*.

Inhaling the dry mineral taste of granite – his last moments of life – he slowly let go of the right hold, slid, caught, wavering on the void. Inch at a time he lowered his right arm till it slid into the socket. Minutes passed as he eased the hand, wedded to the rock, out and found another hold, then below it a seam wide enough to jam two fingertips.

The seam deepened and there were places to wedge his toes. When he dared to look down the maple was bigger. The sun had passed the cliff top and they were in shade. Once he began to hope he grew stronger, more resourceful. When he could not find the next move he went slowly, trying till he found the best, never committed early.

He was down to the top of the maple, its cool damp smell, the wind whispering in its leaves. The rock easy now, the last few feet, as he staggered back away from the cliff Peter broke loose sliding scraping spinning upright in midair and landed on his feet and tumbled onto the ground between the maple roots.

Peter stood up swearing and laughing, scraped and bleeding. Mick's dislocated shoulder throbbed angrily, his wrists and biceps shivered. The world spun, the fatal deep was still beneath him, the sheer raw stone, the tiny treetops, the implacable rock against his face, the pulsing of terror through his muscles, the ache to let go. He feared he wasn't down, that this was a dream, happening after death.

He sat under maples by a stream. It was cool and the mossy rocks smelled good. For a while he didn't tremble and then it started again with a sickness in his stomach and a vacant chest. Blood heated the back of his neck. He kept saying *Thank you and how could I be so stupid and thank you thank God thank you Jesus.* He the atheist, the scoffer, drowned in horrified release from death.

"Climbing's like life," Skip had said on Virgin Peak. "Have to always be aware of the moment, where you *are* on the rock, but also where it's taking you, and do you want to be there."

Mick's hand brushed his pocket, felt Cynthia's letter. It was sweat-sodden; rubbing on the rock had shredded the envelope and the bottoms of both pages.

> *. . . love the impossible because you know you cannot have it. You love*
> *best, Darling Boy, when love's most doomed. Is it just because it's*
> *safest or are you really that afraid of death? I think you . . .*

The rest was gone. He couldn't remember what she'd said there, nor any of it from before the climb. He could not stop trembling. Other climbers walked by; with their alien ropes and jangling pins and carabiners they were a different species, insensate, robotic and dumb.

Don't do it, he called to them silently. But he was still too afraid, too ashamed, to speak. He imagined going up to one climber on the stony path beneath the leafy maples, saying *Don't do it you could get killed.* As others passed he saw them falling, heard their sharp screams, saw their entrails on the rocks. And he called out silently to them, knowing it was as much in vain as calling out to all the young men lined up at Whitehall to pledge their lives to death.

9

TEN YEARS

WHITEHALL was a smog-coated brick building near Wall Street. They sent him to a little room where other inductees waited. The chairs were all taken so he sat on the floor. "Once you say the words you're in," a chunky black kid was saying. "Then if you try to get out they can shoot you. For de-*sert*ion."

"If you think the War's wrong don't go in," Mick said, trying to reach each of them but sensing they would not listen.

"What's *that* got to do wit it?" the black kid said.

"It doesn't mean we're afraid of dying. We're not chicken. But do we have a right to kill the Vietnamese? Their hero's Abraham Lincoln, because he set people free. You want to kill them for that?"

"They're Communist," said an earnest curly-haired kid, self-consciously scratching his arms as he spoke. "If we don't stop them now we'll have to in Hawaii –"

"That's so untrue." Mick felt despair that this lie told by those in power was so readily accepted.

"The govenmint's the govenmint." The black kid nodded to himself as if he'd said something profound. The double doors clanged open and someone was called out, then someone else. Again the doors banged open, a tall spare man in a brown uniform and scrambled-egg cap. "You there!" he yelled at Mick. "Get off the floor! Sit on a chair."

Two of the chairs had become empty. "I'm not in your Army," Mick said, "so you can't order me. Go sit on a chair yourself."

The man's eyes widened, his face contorted. He started to speak, backed out and shut the door.

The room was silent. People edged away from Mick. "*Whoa!*" said the black kid.

Mick looked at them, feeling deserted. "We're not in the Army. They can't order us around."

"We're about to be and, *whoa*, look what you jes' said."

"They can't make us join." To Mick his own voice sounded hollow, impotent. "Like you *said*," he added, "till you say the words."

"You *have* to make the pledge, man," said a skinny bearded guy with a New England accent. "Or they arrest you."

Mick stood. "You don't *have* to go in! You can refuse."

"Five years in jail," the bearded guy said, and in an instant Mick saw what would happen to him, dead face down in a bloody ditch. He wanted to grab his skinny teenager's wrists and save him. The doors banged open and two Federal Marshals in black uniforms grabbed Mick and yanked him into the hall.

"You know who you jes' insulted?" one spat into Mick's face. "Colonel Ax. Who's the officer in charge of this whole *Seelective* Service part of the cuntree? The one who decides who gits drafted and who don'? And I don' be*lieve* you're the little pissant what jes' talked shit to him."

They cuffed his wrists behind him. "Don't make a sound," the second spit into Mick's ear. Mick tilted his head to wipe it on his shoulder and the marshal hit him in the gut and he doubled over choking as they shoved him up metal stairs into a cramped room with four gray metal chairs and a steel bar along one wall where they attached his cuffs. "Gonna 'poligize?" The first hit Mick while the other held him. "Goin out there and swear to protec yer cuntree?" With his hands cuffed Mick couldn't protect himself, didn't dare kick back for that would make them worse.

The marshals switched places. The second was smaller, a narrow face with a broken nose, a west Texas accent. "Y'all goin out there, ain' you son, and step up to the white line like a 'merican. Like you're not some yellow Commie-loving homersexal." He grabbed Mick's hair above each ear with his hands and smashed his forehead into Mick's nose. Electric pain darted through Mick's skull. "You oughtta be more careful, son, before you attack a federal officer. That could get you *truly* hurt –"

"He's gotta 'poligize," the first said.

Blood was running down Mick's face and the back of his throat. "Christ I apologize."

"That's better," the Texan chuckled, and swung his nightstick up into Mick's crotch laughing as Mick collapsed. They pulled him up and hustled him down a different corridor to a little gray office where Colonel Ax sat behind a metal desk. "I 'poligize," Mick gasped.

Colonel Ax smiled. "Induct him."

Back they went past the closed doors of the waiting room to a larger low room with a flag at one end. Young men were standing behind a white line, hands on their hearts. The marshals led Mick to the white line, one on either side of him. The Texan twisted his arm. "Say it!"

He was sick with pain but would not say it. The other inductees, skinny pimply white boys, wide-eyed nervous blacks, turned-off angry Puerto Ricans, all pretended not to see him, except the bearded kid with the New England accent who glanced at him sympathetically. "They'll kill you," Mick called to him but he faced away.

The Texan was trying to twist his injured arm out of the shoulder but he fought it, twisted the arm back. "We're gonna *truly* beat you up," the other hissed, quiet-like as if urging Mick to make some plausible choice.

"My father's a big lawyer," Mick lied. "He'll sue you."

"Sue? Poor little boy, shoulda named him Sue." They walked him from the induction room down the corridor into a men's room. "We should make you suck us, faggot. But we don't wanna catch your disease."

"Now git out'n here," the Texan said. "And shut up about what happened, 'cause you're gonna see us again real soon, when we pick you up at your hearing and take you to jail. You don't want us to be angry wit' you." He shoved him. "An doan you ever, ever, try to beat up on a Federal Marshal again." He slid off the cuffs and they were gone.

The blood running from his nose was a flag of cowardice, defeat. He limped down the long stairs and stood outside by a newsstand till his eyes adjusted to the day's brightness and the roar in his ears dimmed. The gray-haried news vendor looked him over, a sharp, appraising face. "I just got attacked," Mick said, "by Federal Marshals."

"You musta deserved it. Protests, drugs, sex, you young people. Nothing's sacred anymore."

"I just refused induction, too," a wiry, dark-haired kid standing nearby said.

"What'll they do?" It hurt to talk.

"Now?" The kid's eyebrows arched. "For now, nothing. In two-three weeks they finish your paperwork and try to induct you one last time, and when you refuse they throw you in jail till your trial. Your trial will take five minutes then you're off to Leavenworth."

He made it sound like a vacation destination, Acapulco or the Riviera. "Are you going?" Mick hazarded.

"You crazy? I'm going to Israel."

"You'll have to fight there."

"Israel's threatened by deadly enemies. America's in no danger from Vietnam. It's a premeditated massacre. Same as what was judged inhuman at Nuremberg."

"I won't go to jail for five years."

"So," the kid shrugged bony shoulders, "you have two weeks to disappear."

"GO TO CANADA," Peter said.

"Where he should go," Lois snapped, "is a lawyer."

"What can he prove?" Peter said. "Those guys'll say *he* attacked *them.* No one even saw him except some kids who are now on a bus to boot camp somewhere."

"Sure he attacked them," Lois said, "with his hands cuffed behind his back."

"Go to Canada," Peter said.

"I won't be pushed out. Who are these people, to ruin my country?"

"If my parents hadn't been chased out of Lithuania," Lois said, "they and I wouldn't be alive now."

"YOU'LL DO TEN YEARS," Lou Graziano said. A *pro bono* attorney for several peace groups, he'd been wounded twice while a Marine in Korea. "They're hunting down all you antiwar leaders. Listen, Sweetheart, with all these meetings you've been doing about turning in draft cards, they *really* want you."

"I won't go to Canada."

"Instead of ten years in Leavenworth? Of course not, be a scrupulous asshole and see how it feels. Enjoy your hair shirt, your crown of thorns, getting cornholed by every lifer gang in Leavenworth . . ."

"I won't go to Leavenworth either."

Lou eyed him, put down his pipe. "So disappear. No more antiwar speeches, change your name, all that... I ain't recommending it, mind you. But if you do . . ."

"Fuck that," Mick said.

". . . if you *do* disappear, the Feebies will hunt you. And soon so will every cop and sheriff and deputy and every other kind of dick in this nation." He leaned forward for emphasis. "You can get arrested and put in jail with no bail till like I said you get ten years."

"THINK OF ALL THOSE NICE GIRLS in Canada," Tucker said that night, "aching to open their pearly thighs to a brave draft resister." He picked up Mick's new black Yamaha acoustic. *"I'm a jackhammer, Baby, gonna hammer it to you* – Hey, I got some acid. Ever tried it?"

"No."

"Me neither. Shall we?"

Mick thought of riding the freights with Troy. "Fuck the War. Why not?"

They took two tabs each, drank more wine and smoked more weed and went out into the steamy, sticky night. "God I'm getting high already," Tucker laughed.

Girls passed, lithe and sensual as leopards. Sirens called to each other through the lonely streets. "Don't worry, Montaigne said, which way you're going," Tucker expounded, "till you get to the crossroads." He took out his glass eye, popped it into his mouth to clean it and put it back in the socket.

They leaped down subway stairs to a platform, its walls undulating softly, the warmish air ripe with sewage and incense. The rhinoceros worm of the train chewed out of the tunnel, hissed to a stop, doors banging open, and lurched them back down its burrow into the clattering night.

Garish ochre faces melted into blue cadavers while rats danced down the aisle in tune with the screaming metal wheels and hot sewer winds. A man with blazing green eyes unzipped his pants, pulled out a gun and shot a woman who raised her dress and writhed against him. The seat chuckled and nipped; Mick felt the whipcords of the earth straining, the agony of time. The subway roared on, going nowhere, coming from nowhere, an asteroid wandering deep space *out of the cradle endlessly rocking*. He saw through the women's clothes their upswung aureoled breasts and down their bellies, stretched his tongue through the throbbing air to their sweaty reek of sex and the cool breath of death waiting in their cells.

A girl's face of pink rubber over red oval mouth, arched black spiderweb eyelids. A rat climbed her naked leg and snuggled in her black crotch, leaped to a pole, eyed him, tittered and in Nixon's hideous voice said, "How can you want *that*? You don't eat *roaches*, do you? They're cleaner than pussy . . ." Stations howled past, protoplasmic statues cavorting on their platforms.

He and Tucker couldn't stop laughing, tried not to look at each other because that made it worse, people staring angrily, which was even funnier, how they peered and leered, yanked fingers from their pockets, cocked them and fired, how the bullets came twirling; there was always time to duck and the bullets spun emptily out the roaring windows through which the cinders and shit of New York's night boiled in. Between the advertisements for temp jobs and cold remedies and hair treatments gargoyles jutted, and in their acerbic vicious faces there was more kindness and beauty than in men.

He pushed through the end door of the subway car and stood on the coupling in the wailing thunderous electrified night and the filthy hot wind between the clanking rattling cars. The coupling twisted and yanked as if trying to throw him under the wheels; the car shuddered, slowing, burst from the tunnel into a bright station. He jumped onto the platform and banged on Tucker's window.

Tucker came out. "How'd you get out here?"

JOY SPREAD INSIDE him like a warm sea. All was insane, made perfect sense. At Sheridan Square they ate Chinese food, the flavors fantastically intensified by the LSD, then walked down Christopher Street singing in the lovely exuberant fullness of life that you could feel in every cell,

You must leave now, take what you need you think will last

A poster on a head shop window of two ducks flying, a horny-looking drake licking his chops atop a grinning female, and underneath it,

Fly United

and another poster of an orgy of all the Disney characters – Donald Duck happily humping Daisy, Snow White giving head to the Seven Dwarfs, Mickey balling Minnie, a big grin on his face.

Nothing's more fun, he realized, *than discovering the lie under every sacred truth.*

At the White Horse a skinny girl with long spangled hair invited them to a party off Washington Square, a low wide apartment looking out on the Arch, a throbbing HiFi, *I look inside myself and see my heart is black*, the air thick with hash smoke and young female animals on the prowl.

He could see them naked through their blouses and short skirts and smell their hungry silken sex. Power flowed from him and enveloped them, every word and look had meaning, a knowing he could do anything, could reach anyone, ask her anything and she would say yes. "Life is everything," the skinny spangle-haired girl said, and he wondered did she mean *every thing*? She was stoned, too, the room shifting shape with wild hash and the sweet aftermath of acid and mushrooms,

Somethin is happenin and you don't know what it is

They did not speak; down one corridor was a kitchen and bath and beside it a bedroom but there were too many people screwing there so they went into the bathroom and she pulled down her Levis and underpants and leaned back against the sink wrapping her legs around his neck as he shoved her blouse up, cupping her small breasts then lifting her ass in his hands drove into her and she kept whispering *fuck fuck fuck oh oh oh* and he kept fucking harder and with the acid it went on forever, each second deeper and more completely true till they were the room and the building and pulsating city and all the couples fucking in it, thousands in this moment fucking and they were them all, hairy pubic bone to bone, sweaty hungry flesh to flesh, nameless to each other and memorably together, while people were banging on the bathroom door yelling they had to use the bathroom and Mick yelled *Go piss in the sink.*

Shriven and exhausted, legs quivering and sweat running down, they leaned against each other panting then went out into the room full of noisy people,

Hello darkness, my old friend,
I've come to talk with you again

THE DIAMOND RING SPARKLED in the man's bloody hand. He had a tilted hat and a narrow junkie dance. "Busted it right out, the window. Jewlry sto'. Wit' my fist. Why it's bleedin. Biggest diamon' I *sure* ever see."

A quarter inch across, it glittered in his reddened palm like a star. "I need money bad," he said. "You boys want this?"

His bloodshot yellow eyes watched Mick and Tucker look at the ring. It kept expanding and contracting, sometimes white, sometimes red. "How much?" Mick said.

"Five hundred?"

Tucker laughed. "Let's go."

"I don't have any money," Mick said, "just a few bucks."

"Lessee," the man nodded at Mick's pocket, "lessee how much."

"C'mon," Tucker said. "Let's get more pussy."

"Could be worth two thousand," Mick whispered. "This guy needs a fix." He showed the man the ten dollars in his wallet.

"You can't spend that," Tucker whispered, "we need it to get laid more. Man I'm *hungerry*," he added, drawing out the word.

They were almost to Harlem. In ten minutes Tucker could be home, eat, get laid. But if Mick spent his last ten dollars on this ring he'd have to walk all the way to the East Village – a hundred blocks down and across town.

He lodged the diamond in the watch pocket of his jeans. "You shit," Tucker said.

"You'll be sorry in the morning when I sell it."

"Cops'll get you."

"*To live outside the law*," Mick sang as they walked, "*you must be honest.*"

"You can't sing," Tucker said, "plus you'll attract cops. They'll think you're dying." He headed uptown and Mick walked on, thinking of Seth and Miranda, she warm and naked and spread out before him as once she had been. "You were mine first," Cynthia had said, "so what right does *she* have to be jealous?" *I should've fucked Miranda more*, he told himself in his acid haze, *while I could.* Her claws and teeth, her hard clasping flesh.

The walk home was long and cold. The LSD wore thin and the hard pavement ached his legs. He kept checking his watch pocket, fearing the ring might leap out by itself or be forced out by the motion of his hips.

Salmon dawn tinged the greasy sky between the downtown high rises. Coffee, bacon, and cinnamon roll smells drifted from delicatessens and coffee shops. It was Saturday morning and he had no money till Monday. Unless he sold the ring.

And in a week, two maybe, the Federal Marshals would come. Where to escape them? Canada, start a new life? Or Paris. But once you leave you can't come back. And they can find you there.

Exhausted, he climbed his tenement stairs. His door hung open, the jamb splintered, his apartment ransacked. "Dirty fucking junkies!" he yelled, ran into the bedroom and looked under the bed. His new black Yamaha acoustic was gone.

At nine he knocked on the barred glass door of the pawnshop on Second Avenue and West Houston Street. The old man was so small his armpits barely reached the counter. He didn't even look at Mick's ring with his jeweler's glass. "It's fake," he hissed. "Zircon."

"How much is it worth?"

"Nothing." He looked up at Mick. "How you get it, this thing?"

"A guy, he gave it to me."

"A gift." The little old man puffed. "A fine gift."

10

ACID

TO AVOID THE FBI Mick moved to another apartment under the name David Collins, up four flights in another brick tenement, East Sixth between First and Second. A slightly better neighborhood, Jewish restaurants on Second Avenue, the B&H Dairy Delicatessen and a Russian bakery that made fantastic black bread around the corner.

His new place had a kitchen with a stove full of roaches, a sink and bathtub, a corridor wide enough for a bed, a toilet at the end, a living room with a bare brick wall and fireplace and two grated windows to a fire escape, and across the cindery yard another fire escape, brick wall, and window. He left early and came home late.

Indonesia's "success in defeating Communist rebels" was a large article in the latest *Life* magazine, a compendium of lies and misinformation that had he not been in Indonesia he would have accepted as truth. In the Public Library he went through a year's worth of *Life*, finding an increasing crescendo of anti-Sukarno stories culminating in this "Economic Reforms in the Aftermath of the Violent Overthrow of the Indonesian Communist Party."

"Time Life belongs to the Agency," Seth snickered, as if continually stunned by the credulity of Mick and his fellow-humans. "Lock, stock and barrel."

"So how do we get honest news?"

Seth raised his eyebrows mockingly. "Overseas we have all these radio stations and newspapers to blanket the world with our viewpoint. Apparently one in ten journalists on international issues gets a stipend from the Agency –"

"There must be some way to make a difference," he said to Peter. "No matter how many protests we make, how many speeches, how many people get arrested, how many ads we run in the *Times*, that most Americans have serious reservations about or completely oppose this War, nothing makes any difference."

"You see that full-page ad Dave Brower put in the *Times*?" Peter said. "About damming Grand Canyon?"

"Who's that?" Seth said.

"President of the Sierra Club. The dam builders have been pushing the dam by saying tourists will be able to float close to the top of the cliffs, so Brower's ad says *Should we also flood the Sistine Chapel so tourists can get nearer the ceiling?*" He turned to Mick and Tucker. "You antiwar guys should copy something like that."

"A group of antiwar groups just ran three full pages in the *Times*," Mick said. "Signed by almost seven thousand professors and teachers. It made no difference."

"Bastards that run this country," Tucker said, "don't care what the people want. Funny thing, most folks still think this's a democracy."

"That's called denial," Peter grinned.

"Even burning draft cards doesn't make a difference, because then the Selective Service doesn't know who it was that burned it. We have to make a stand."

Tucker shook his head. "Go to Canada."

"Most guys don't want to fight. If they refused, the War would stop."

"And?" Peter said.

"What if everybody who didn't want to go just sent his draft card back to the Selective Service? Said *Hey man, I've decided not to do this?*"

Tucker shrugged. "They can't arrest everybody."

Mick slapped his hand on the table. "That's it! They can't arrest everybody. If we can get it coordinated, so we all opt out together, they're screwed."

"Maybe," Peter said.

"The War would be stopped," Tucker added. "In a year."

"After the Nazis invaded France in World War Two," Mick said, the French created the Resistance. At first only a few people, then lots more."

"So," Tucker said, "this movement, you guys should call it The Resistance."

"Ben Spock once said that without the draft the World War One generals couldn't have wasted those millions of lives. The draft is the key."

"People will die," Peter said, "before they'll join a revolution –"

"The ancient Chinese character for revolution was an animal's pelt," Tucker said. "Because it changes with the seasons."

A FINGER TAPPED that night on his door. He took out his knife, tiptoed to the door and opened it fast expecting a teenage junkie but it was Rachel from across the hall. "You hear?" she whispered, as if not to wake this tenement full of sleepless despair, "they're burning Atlanta."

"Who?"

"The Negroes. It's crazy, just like Chicago, Cleveland – what's happening to this country? American cities are war zones, just like Hanoi –"

"For the same reason."

Rachel was a small girl, very pretty with a wide smile ruined by grayish teeth – too much fluoride, she'd said, when she was little – and it took away her confidence, made her too anxious to please. She had a sharp nose and straight long hair the color of raw honey, almost umber, and fine as silk that the slightest breeze would ruffle. She wore a man's button-down pinstripe shirt and nothing underneath, had really come to make love, first on the couch then on his squeaky single bed. They lost track of time, there was no time but this, this ceaseless going in and out, this lovely ache every instant fulfilled and every instant wanting. And all the time another American city going up in flames, people hurt and dying.

The rioters were living Al Lowenstein's theory: to change the world you must lose your fear of consequences. If they were burning all these cities, wouldn't New York be next? Burn it all to ash and cinders – what rose up might be better than what was here.

Revolution meant renewal, shedding the old skin, molting. But how could you keep the good and lose only the bad?

DAISY MORAN STOOD IN THE BLISTERING heat in the shade of her Kilifi porch roof with the letter from Stanford in her hand. She'd applied four months ago, never hoped to be accepted, but Stanford was doing the kind of research she wanted. She'd written an impassioned essay about living on the savanna and trying to understand how people had lived here a hundred thousand years ago, a million years. Night after night in her little hut with the desert-hot wind under the eaves and the annoyed roars of lions beyond the thorn fences, she'd tried to imagine being here when it was still wild, when people scavenged for marrow and traveled in clans. And what were their stories?

She realized her face was dirty when her tears ran brown on the letter. Full scholarship, a letter from Leon Jacobson, the head of the anthropology department. "We are delighted to have you as a future student." And another from Dr. Vargas, the head of the neuroscience department, "It will be a pleasure to have you with us."

She looked out at the clustered, heat-soaked trees, the hovels of rondavels, a distant dust devil, the bare blue sky. I must not forget this place. I must take it with me.

. . .

"I GET CRAZY tryna figure things out," Corey Dillon whispered as he sat with Troy in the LP. "Sometimes I think what matters is to have a family and create new life. Then I think what counts is to follow your own road, deep into the mystery of life, take no one with you, because we all go our own way." With his sleeve he wiped dew off his rifle barrel. "But either way I don't understand why we're here. Unless it's a lesson. A joke on us."

He turned toward Troy in the darkness. "You think it's a lesson, Lieutenant?"

Troy listened to a mosquito circling, waited till it landed by his ear and slapped it. "I see it in political terms. What we have to do to keep the world from going Communist."

Dillon removed his helmet, scratched his scalp. "Okay, but here's the riddle: if each person can experience only his own perceptions, right?"

"Right."

"Then when you die everything you were part of disappears, to *you* anyway – so you're dying for something that no longer exists."

"That's too deep for me."

"Shit," Dillon wiped sweat from his face. "I got a million things racing through my head, tryna figure them out –"

Troy spit on his kerchief and wiped the dust and sweat from his face, liking its cool feel in the hollows round his eyes. "Don't think too much, the football coach always told my brother, it hurts the team."

Dillon chuckled. "You got a brother, huh?"

"A sister too. I'm adopted."

"Me I got five brothers'n four sisters. Advantage of bein Catholic." For a while Dillon said nothing, then added, "You did the right thing today, Sir."

Since when is killing someone the right choice? Troy had led an attack on a treeline and had killed three VC but also two old women. "I should've maybe yelled, covered them, they might've *chieu hoi'd*."

"Rule One from the Marine Corps Manual: *Do not kill innocent people.* Rule Two: *No one is innocent.*"

"Then we're going to have to kill them all."

TARA WOKE to find her forehead against the airplane window. Below, a hazy view of clouds and earth. Soon another city, another ravaging, exhausting concert, another frantic spilling of her guts into the vast smoky den of God's music, then a hotel, too much booze and coke and smack and way too much fucking and tomorrow another plane ride to another concert in another city, then another and another . . .

The gritty walls, the yellowed Kliegs, the chanting foot-stomping clapping cheering mob, their hunger to devour her, grind her in their screaming gnashing teeth, the sorrow and solitude afterwards of a fancy hotel room at five a.m., watching the sacred sun rise over another filthy city.

Why me, so many times she'd asked them, her fans – why do you want *me*? What have *I* done to you? All I want is to fill my lungs and throat with song, to bring this beauty up out of my heart into the world.

I'm not here for you, she'd wanted so many times to tell them. *I'm here for music*. For the magnificent, impeccable untouchable great God of Music.

There was no way they could know, she'd realized, how touring brutalizes, betrays, and destroys us – me and Blade and Luis and all of us. For eight months straight . . . How can we survive this?

You want top Billboard, their managers kept telling them, you gotta tour. The Stones have been touring a year and a half. Lots of bands tour all the time. So shut up and do it.

At least the guys get to fuck all the girls. Every night half-naked girls climbing all over them. Me I'm tired of fucking. I'm tired of men.

If I have to fuck another man I'll throw up.

Please, a cabin in the country somewhere. Green grass, chickens, a view of mountains, forests and the sea. It has to be out there somewhere.

Please.

Before I go crazy.

THE NIGHT BEFORE INDUCTION Mick met Sabrina at an East Village party. Dark lashes, big white teeth, curly dark hair and black eyes, black satiny dress. Holding a glass of wine and watching the crowd, her smell very sexy, both of them standing there pretending not to notice the other while passing a joint. Knowing no one, ignored by the crowd.

"Linguistics?" he yelled over the noise, thinking cunnilingus. "Like Margaret Meade?"

She laughed. "The structure of languages –" They danced drinking her wine, her cheek soft against his neck, her curls tickling his nose. They went out on the back porch sharing somebody's joint under a jaundiced moon. Here it was quieter, a New York tenement back porch, four stories on four-by-fours, skinny boards underfoot, a cindery airwell beyond the wobbly wooden rail. Above them a yellow-black horizon of smokestacks, vents, and walls, and over it an aqueous midnight and the lights of a jet drifting over.

You know that it would be untrue, Jim Morrison was singing, *you know that I would be a liar,*

If I was to say to you
Girl we couldn't get much higher –

Hands on the rail she peered into the darkness. "It's so crummy," she said in a soft drawl. "Is this *all* there is?"

"You mean here, this building? Or the Lower East Side?"

"I mean everything! Is this *it?*"

"You can make it what you want it to be –" he said sententiously.

She laughed, caustic. "Blind as bats. Bumping round in the light."

The porch rail creaked. "Don't lean on that –"

"How can being imagine non-being?" She laughed again, low and throaty.

He kissed her, hands under her skirt up her smooth cool thigh into the hot silkiness of her cunt. "If life isn't enough, what more do you want?"

"True desire," she smiled. "Unblemished fire, to the center of the heart –"

"You're stoned."

"And you," she giggled, "let the joint go out."

"S'in my pocket."

She slipped a hand into his jeans. "I can't feel it," kissed him, her tongue wet and carnal. Delicious ecstasy washed through him. Moving against him to the music she slid up the black satin dress and threw her white underpants over the rail and they made love with her back against the brick wall and splintery post, and someone came out on the porch and said "Excuse me" and went back in, the porch jiggling, making him fear it would crash down four stories. So exciting the flicker of her eyelashes against his cheek, her lips along his jaw, her slithering tongue, her wiry body as she slid up and down him like a cobra then wrapped him in strong slender thighs, her small tight ass in his hands, riding up and down him, so hot it seemed to last forever, no matter the people coming in and out talking by the rail, the coarse laughter in the room, the raw music, the deck jiggling and groaning. "You make my cock," he gasped, "sing with joy."

"God," she gasped, "Christ," bit his ear till he pulled away and saw blood on her lip. "Christ," she sighed, "how wonderful."

"You damn near . . . bit off my ear."

"You hurt my back, shoving me into the bricks like that." She pushed him. "Go, get some wine."

"*Jeez*," Dylan was singing, "*I can't find my knees*," the marijuana-smoky room full of dancing people, Sabrina's smell on his face, her taste on his lips. On the kitchen table were scraps of cheese and olive pits but no wine or glasses. In a box under the table he found a bottle of Lancers, guarding it like a baby as he weaved back through the crowd. She raised cupped hands to him. "Guess."

He imagined a spider, or a moth battering its wings. "Don't –"

Like stigmata in her palm two little purple pills. "Larry's handing them out. He's got a friend who makes it, some Yale chemist."

"Larry?"

"It's his party."

"And he can cry if he wants to," he sang falsetto. Then like a *memento mori* tomorrow came back to him. "I've got a draft induction physical in the morning."

She drank long from the bottle, looked at him across it. "You're not *going?*"

"To the induction physical? If I don't I go to Leavenworth."

"No, silly. To the War." She slid a tab between his lips.

Like a church wafer. It stuck in his throat; even after he swallowed it still seemed there. "No." Dancing with her was like making love again, moving skin to skin, breathing each other, the supple way they fit.

When the acid began to hit it was wonderful. The room swelled, glowed with deep color and meaning, laughter and promise, warm as a hearth, erotic as fire. A flame pulsed in everything, sex the door between body and soul.

Every thing throbbed with fire and blood. A girl sideways on the couch, wine glass in her hand, pale arm resting along the back of the couch, her split-sided dress an arrow pointing up her thigh – he could see right into her, her belly and coiled gut, her arched spine and pale bones and tendons, her lonely brachia clattering her ribs, the skull baring teeth in a come-on smile, her blood-hot brain.

An ashtray throbbed like a mule's heart, a gray windworn coral island shell – he heard the waves echo in it – a wolf's head and a spur of granite mountain, an old man's heel protruding from the dirt. The peeling walls blazed with golden constellations, the filthy carpet undulated on a cloud. The electricity of women's bodies flashed in the air, their fertile scents and perfumed flesh, and inside them the same lascivious gracious ache, the wet heated core of life.

Sabrina wasn't there, instead a short-haired blonde with a broad Dutch face. She wore a long-sleeved gray sweater and gray wool dress. They went into the bedroom, but there were two couples on the bed so they sat in the corner by the closet. She had a nice, full-lipped mouth and a little tongue darting in and out like a hummingbird and her underpants were wet making him wonder how many guys she'd already done it with and she came down on top of him hidden in the tent of her dress, slow at first then faster making it exquisite till they both came and she fell forward on him and then slid aside, the gray wool dress around her waist.

He was very thirsty and went to find wine but when he got back she was gone, or he'd gone to the wrong room. Maybe he'd been away too long and she'd tired of waiting.

Sabrina was with someone, arm round his waist. "This's Larry," she said.

"Larry of the acid?"

"Yeah." He had sunglasses and slicked black hair and Mick wanted to hit him.

"Larry's nice," she said as he drifted away. "He's got a big dick."

"You fucked him?"

"Just now. Me and Lacey."

"What for?" Mick started to ask then laughed at himself.

A couple came up, naked. He was tall with a thin hairy chest. "Would you like to change?" he said. She was skinny too, sweaty, with blonde braids and teardrop breasts. "We'll do it first," she said to Mick, "and they can watch us."

More of Larry's acid came around and he got higher. He could go on fucking forever and it felt more fantastic each time. People were lying in indolent piles. The record player needle kept scratching; he lifted and put it to the side but it just came out and stopped then went down in the middle again, *All the lonely people, where do they all come from?*

He found his jeans and barefooted downstairs to the damp smelly sticky street, stepping round broken bottles and windshield glass. Four a.m., the waking clatter and snarl of trash trucks, hiss of steam grates, the chill windy stink of the East River. He ran, tireless and fleet, cool air in his face, bare feet whipping the cold pavement.

When he came back the apartment door was locked and he had to bang on it. The Dutch-faced girl opened. They made love again on the little kitchen table knocking over empty bottles that rattled at his feet, her ankles round his neck, then in the bathtub a dark girl named Mia, then two others, the girls so full of come and wet and slippery inside, each one so uniquely exciting and delightful till they all became one, the great goddess of sex, beauty, creation, motherhood and love.

And it was joyful to love each one and to love them all.

He sat up looking for his clothes. Bright day outside. There was something he had to do but he couldn't remember. A red-headed teenager snored softly beside him, her small tits tilting outwards, narrow belly puffing up and down, her little crotch fuzzy in the sunlight. With his head on her thighs he began to lick her; she tasted salty and tart and sweet too, like vinegar honey.

There was something he was supposed to do.

She woke up and took him in her mouth, girlish fingers up and down till she quivered and pulled away. "Christ I'm beat," she sighed, "Can't you come?"

"I'm going to . . . don't stop –"

Larry came from the bedroom holding his pants. "Okay folks fun's over."

Mick rubbed his face. "What time's it?"

Larry made a show of looking at his wrist. "Nine-thirty."

"I mean what day's it?"

"Monday." He nudged them with his toe. "Time to go."

The red-haired girl was pulling on pink panties. Mick couldn't remember where he'd left his clothes, walked around till he found them – the jeans behind a chair in the living room, the shirt in the bedroom where he'd taken it off for the Dutch-faced girl, his shoes in the sink, a cigarette butt and an expired stick of incense in one, beer in the other.

Sabrina was sleeping on one edge of the bed, two guys and a girl beside her. She'd put the black dress back on but it had rucked up around her waist. One guy's hand lay on her thigh. Mick moved it off. Her eyes opened. "Hey you," she said.

"How you feel?"

"Great." She pulled him down and kissed him. "Good luck."

"Huh?"

"Aren't you going to the draft board?"

I'm screwed. He dashed downstairs, shoe sloshing. *Ten years in jail.*

11

BABY KILLER

NO CABS on Second Avenue. He ran down subway stairs leaping a turnstile but the train was pulling out. "Hey you!" a cop yelled, chased him up the stairs through the crowded sidewalk across the street, cars swerving and screeching as he dashed into Woolworth's past the jewelry counter, a girl holding up a shiny necklace said "Oh!" as he knocked over mannequins and bras and girdles and ran out the back door and a big black cop reached out of the next doorway and grabbed his arm. "Where's the fire?"

"Late for my draft board –"

"Better tie that shoe. Before you trip'n break your face."

He got a cab but the traffic jammed. The LSD returned, waves of visions and terrors and pleasures, weird faces leering, sirens and rock songs and the cab's rattling fender and cigarette-soiled leather, an Arrow meat truck, men's suits in windows, a Chinese man with a bowl of rice, skyscrapers undulating in oily exhaust.

Paranoia strikes deep, the radio said, *Step out of line, the man come and take you away.*

Today they could send him to Leavenworth. He looked out on the myriad city and tried to take it in. *For years you might not see this.* If they arrested him at Whitehall he'd never get another chance. Better to leave now. Then he'd be a fugitive forever. But wasn't it better to be a fugitive because you missed a physical than because you'd been arrested and jumped bail?

He got out of the cab and it pulled away, the last part of his last life leaving him. Whitehall towered over him, wavering in a mirage, as if heat were rising from it.

Go in there your life is changed forever.

He didn't have to. A new life in Paris, French girlfriends, a French home.

Numbly he climbed the stairs. "You like this War?" he said to the Marine at the door who just stared straight and didn't answer. The Marine's face turned green, skin rotting and sliding from the bone, making Mick laugh. "Sorry, man. I wasn't laughing at you."

In the LSD's rampant elation everything was funny and tragic, the naked boys in lines with hands clasped over their groins, their stench of sweat and cold fear, the peeling brown trim and yellowed walls, weary typewriters, sagging flags soiled by years of cigarettes, the filth in the cracks between the floorboards.

"You been running to here?" the doctor said. "Your blood pressure it's too high." Hunched and balding, not a doctor but an ancient monkey.

Mick bit his tongue trying not to laugh. "How high?"

"One hundred eighty over one ten. Is far too high."

"I've been higher than that."

"Higher than that you are dead. I take again."

Mick could see inside his own arm the pulsing red artery, the arterioles, capillaries and cells. He increased pressure and the artery walls contracted. "One-ninety over one-fifteen," the monkey-doctor grimaced. "You take some drugs or something?"

"Don't even take aspirin." *Ha Ha*, he laughed at his crazy self. *It's the only thing I don't take.* His crazy self laughed back and ducked around a corner. There were other crazy selves sitting on a bench under a window, swinging their feet. They giggled and pointed at him and he gave them the finger.

"You're rejected," the monkey-doctor said. "You'll get a letter. In

June you come back. Maybe your pressure will be down then." He nodded at the next boy. "Bend over."

Stunned, dizzy and unbelieving, he walked along the sunny sidewalk, elation like a volcano inside him. He wanted to laugh, grab people saying *Can't you see how lovely life is? Why are we living in a box, racing from place to place? Why are we killing each other?* Let's just sit down and pray in thanks and live in peace.

He grinned at the news vendor, the same gray face, the same blue smock and black fingers. "You're free! You don't have to spend your life on this corner!" But the man didn't look up, didn't answer. A cop approached nonchalantly swinging his stick; Mick couldn't remember why he'd been afraid of cops and walked past him singing, took the subway to go looking for Sabrina.

The LSD grew even more explosively wonderful, the erotic throbbing beauty of every thing, blazing colors and ethereal laughter, the tempest of life in the blue pit of death. Rats ran through the subway tickling his ankles and giggling.

Sabrina Sabrina, he sang walking down Second Avenue, *where you been so long? I almos' got drafted, while you was gone,* and backed into an old man with a cane.

"Shitfuck!" the old man snarled, stamped his foot, a malodorous goat blocking traffic in front of Levinsky's Corned Beef at First Street and Second Avenue, with his droopy chin and withers and deep mournful eyes, his little pointed ears back-tilted under curly white fur.

"Sorry, sir," Mick said.

"Shitfuck!" The old man shoved past. *He's what we become,* Mick thought, *if we don't give thanks. If we don't get laid.*

Hundreds of scents in the filthy air, Sabrina's coarse chuckle, her lavender taste, her fine long hair tickling his lips, the delicate dark moss of her cunt, her dancer's slim tight belly. Sabrina in her rucked-up dress on the edge of the bed. If she was gone Larry'd tell him where to find her. But when he reached Ninth Street and Second Avenue he couldn't find the building.

It had been *there* – fifth from the corner. But it wasn't the same. He pushed doorbells till someone buzzed, and climbed to the top floor but the yellow-tiled landing was wrong. A strange man peered out a door. The buildings on Eleventh were wrong too. And on Twelfth and Eighth, Thirteenth, then the same streets between First and Second.

He called every university in New York but found no grad student in linguistics named Sabrina. He looked for her on every street but never found her, never saw the Dutch-faced girl or dark-breasted Mia nor the red-haired teenager nor any of the others, never found Larry's.

Work on the New Bank Building had reached the thirty-eighth floor. It was warm in the streets below but high up on the steel was a cold dangerous wind. Uptown through silvery haze you could see the Chrysler, the Empire State, the broad blade of the Pan Am building, thousands of buildings, Central Park's green swath, a latticework of bridges up the Hudson and East Rivers, the other way down to Wall Street, the Battery and Staten Island, the New Jersey coast slipping away into the mist. He would not wonder how many lives had been lost building these towers. The rooftops of smaller buildings were so far below they seemed unreal – you could dive out into that space, fall almost forever. It made him shudder.

WHEN PEOPLE WERE DYING every minute how could you not try to stop the War? Even America's ally De Gaulle had condemned it and said the US should leave Southeast Asia. Wouldn't people understand?

Instead Johnson had doubled troop levels to nearly four hundred thousand. "We're gonna nail that coonskin to the wall," he told the American people, and Mick thought sadly of the night long ago with Clem and Carl, the doomed raccoon's battle against a dozen dogs. "It weren't worth it," Clem had said afterward, a dying dog in his arms.

As the War grew and grew, the illusion faded that Americans had control over their government. A travesty of what Mick's father and so many other Americans had risked their lives for, that half a million had died for, a nightmare where one cannot raise a hand to defend what one loves.

"And Lyndon Johnson told the nation," Tom Paxton sang,

Though it isn't really war
We're sending fifty thousand more
To help save Vietnam from the Vietnamese

Days Mick was working high up on steel, and nights and weekends fighting the War. Expanding the Resistance, creating bridges with other groups, trying to convince them a more radical approach was needed. Night after weary night of planning demonstrations, organizing students and canvassing, writing and printing leaflets, more speeches and frustrations.

He hated doing it, hated the forced phone conversations with strangers, trying to change them, reach them. Tired of feeling overwhelmed by an enemy far stronger than he, but that he had to fight because of the horror it was doing. The burnt children and devastated landscapes, the evil . . .

He'd seen film from an F-4 flying low over a line of farmhouses along a lovely sinuous river, children playing among chickens in the courtyards, the water buffalo coming in for the evening, sun turning them to gold across the golden paddies.

Hitting every one with a 500-pound phosphorous bomb exactly between the house and barn – the whole place – kids, animals, beautiful old house with its carved lintels, weary farmers and weary wives, wrenched into horrified searing death by the huge blast and awful heat of a phosphorous bomb made in Ohio, back in the US of A.

How could he stop this?

If he didn't stop this, he was as guilty as the rest.

So even though he didn't want to do this he had to. Because it turned his gut and left him no peace, no time he could stop thinking about it, about who had died just in these last ten minutes he'd been trying not to think about it.

Sometimes in the meetings long-haired bearded husky men stood up and ranted about offing the man and bombing banks and recruiting offices.

"They're crazy, those guys," he said to Tucker.

"They're FBI. Like I keep telling you. Trying to split the movement."

He thought of punching them, knocking them to the sidewalk. It would be so easy. "We should shut them out."

"Why? They still think we don't know. It's a gift."

Dark fell earlier now, the evenings cooler. At dusk his window darkened from translucent to reflective, from a view outside of blackened brick walls and dark smoky sky to a mirror of his apartment, its red brick wall and fireplace, the seedy couch, the table with its candle and wine, the kitchen bathtub and sink beyond. As if evening had turned him to inner thoughts, had banished the outside world.

But nothing banished the War. How many bullets had *he* bought with his ninety-seven dollars in taxes this month? How many people had those bullets killed?

"I grew up thinking of America as a good, loving country," he told Tucker. "But to be honest, how are we better than Hitler's Germany, killing millions with no moral justification? What do they think, the people who support the War? Are they so stupid they believe the lies?"

"Stupidity," Tucker said, "is not innocent. Particularly not *intentional* stupidity. Clinging to a lie when they know the truth – that's evil, because it causes evil. Stupid people who believe slogans, lies and flag-waving, they're not just dumb, to be pitied. They're actually evil."

"My country right or wrong? They say that – can you imagine?"

"Trouble is, if you know you're country's wrong, and if you love it, you *have* to want to change it. Or you don't really love it."

Mick stretched out on the floor. "Sex, drugs'n rock'n roll – the new national anthem. No more killing by the rockets' red glare, the bombs bursting in air."

Tucker strummed the guitar softly. "All comes down to one thing. Free love."

"YOU SHOULD WORK full-time for the peace movement," Al Lowenstein said.

"I can't," Mick said. "I need money."

"There'd be enough to live on."

Now that he was making good money steeplejacking, the idea of earning a pittance in the movement felt reprehensible. And they would control him. "What I make now's barely enough. And I don't pay my rent and electricity –"

"Don't they cut the power off?"

"I just go down to the basement, undo the meter and turn it on again."

"Oh." Al pushed his thick glasses up his thin nose. "Still, as a full-time organizer, going around to campuses . . ."

"Al, I'm doing more *here*. If we can spread the anti-draft message to all the other peace groups, the black power groups, to all these young guys all over the country like the ones I was with at Whitehall. They didn't *want* to go. They knew the War's wrong! They just didn't *dare* refuse. If we show them all they don't *have* to go, that *we're* not going, the more *they'll* dare not to."

"I think Mick's right," William Sloane Coffin said. The chaplain at Yale, he had been chaplain at Williams when Mick was there. As an undergrad at Yale in World War Two, he'd quit to join the OSS as an American agent linking the French and Russian undergrounds, and had somehow survived. He'd been a CIA agent in East Germany during Korea, had quit the Agency when it veered to the right under Eisenhower and began murdering moderate leaders in places like Iran, Guatemala, and the Congo. He'd worked with Martin Luther King, knew Desmond Tutu and Nelson Mandela, been arrested in many southern sit-ins and was now leading the national ecumenical resistance groups against the War. Tall, gangly and handsome, he was brilliant, gracious, and frequently sarcastic. "Even if you win the rat race," Mick remembered him saying one Sunday in Williams Chapel, "you'll still be a rat."

It was two a.m. in Bella Abzug's living room. The co-founder of Women Strike for Peace, Bella was a brilliant lawyer and activist, outspoken, aggressive yet kindly and warm, soon to be a Congress-woman from New York. A few others were there, Bella's husband

Martin, Al Lowenstein, muscular, burly, balding, with thick glasses sliding down his nose, in a rumpled tailored suit and sweaty shirt, tie twisted and askew, talking at the speed of light.

"Mick," Bella said angrily, "If you do this Resistance thing you're going to jail! What good will you be then? How can you organize?"

"Inside the jail, maybe."

"You'll be there for *years*! They'll isolate you!" She leaned forward. "Anyways you think these young men will choose *five or ten years in jail* over two in the Army?"

"They can't jail everybody."

"Most people are followers." She slapped her knee. "*Sheep!* Once you jail the leaders the rest do what they're told."

"What's the alternative!" He felt angry, isolated. "I work with other groups too, like the returned Peace Corps volunteers, retired federal employees, thousands and thousands of them. We're sending every one a letter, asking them to sign a letter to the *Times* – some of them'll do that but they won't break laws. The government'll grumble about them but they're not doing it any harm."

"Draft resistance *might* be a better alternative," Reverend Coffin said. "Maybe we *should* be confrontational. And like Mick says, the Peace Corps volunteers, the retired federal employees, the church groups are fine, but they won't take a strong position."

"The country," Al said wearily, "is not ready for draft resistance. We alienate the people we're trying to reach. The people in the middle."

"As long as we keep being good Americans –" Mick snapped, "they'll just keep ignoring us and expanding the War. We have to *focus* the War in everyone's minds till they can't avoid it anymore."

"If you do something people perceive as un-American –"

"Like burning the flag," Bella said. "Or your draft card –"

"– then you lose their support." Al paced, waving his hands. "They *reject* your position because they reject *you*!"

"In Vietnam!" Mick yelled, "Where's *their* due process? You're like someone watching a murder and saying no I can't intervene, that'd abrogate the killer's rights!"

"That's too much, Mick," Bella growled. "That's not true."

"Of course it isn't!" He turned back to Al. "We *need* to break the law. To make the big guys realize they have trouble on their hands. Now they're bombing the shit out of Laos too – the War just keeps expanding! The big guys need to understand that if they keep expanding Vietnam they're going to lose what they own here."

"So what do you think they'll do? They'll clamp down *here*. And when they do they'll bear down harder in Vietnam too, go nuclear like Goldwater wants."

Mick grabbed his jacket. It enraged him that the disagreement was always the same. "If they try to expand the War any more the American people won't take it."

"So what do *you* think 'the people' will do? This's *not* a democratic process."

"The big guys respect only power."

"You mean revolution?" Reverend Coffin said.

"If it comes to a revolution, so be it."

Outside the night air was cool and damp. If he walked fast he'd be home by three-thirty. Nearly four hours' sleep before a day on high steel.

Revolution. Sounded exciting but made no sense. Would be a horror. a war to stop this War? To stop all wars – against the earth, against the poor and different. A war to give everyone an even chance. And equal freedom.

But wasn't freedom something you had to get for yourself? What Pavel and Sergei had said on Virgin Peak – the horrors of the Soviet Revolution had not been worth it. And what about the French Revolution, or the misery in Algeria? Was any revolution worth it?

Every answer led to further questions. The other steeplejack guys he worked with were part of the "power structure" but they were good caring people – why overthrow them?

In his building entry he stepped around a dead rat and tiredly climbed the stairs. The bulb was out at the top and he tripped on the last step, swearing softly.

"Mick!" Rachel whispered from her door across the hall. "Some guys're in your apartment. Guys in gray suits." She tugged him into her apartment and quietly shut the door. "FBI, Mick. They looked *just* like the movies."

"Shit! They've found me."

"Want coffee? I've got some monster hash."

"Christ Rachel, it's three-thirty. I have to leave for work at seven."

"I've finished my project." She scowled at an easel by the window, a red splurge across a yellow canvas.

"It's nice," he said halfheartedly.

"It's horrible. I don't believe in non-representational art." She glanced at the door. "They must want you pretty bad."

"I thought I'd lost them." He sat on her sheepskin rug. She brought wine and hash, sitting cross-legged before him, her girlish panties and golden thighs wide, and after a while he lay with his head on her thigh kissing her through the panties and soon the War was far away, the deaths and sorrows, even the FBI didn't matter when this felt so good.

Afterwards he lay thinking that on the other side of the world people were being shot, blown up and burned alive by the same country that was giving him an easy life. How easy to side with the winners, not think about the single American mother whose only son dies in Vietnam, the young Americans terrified in foxholes, the Vietnamese farmers whose children are burned alive. But if you wanted to understand life you had to consider those whose lives were hell no matter how good and loving they were.

In the morning through her keyhole he watched the three men leave his apartment and clump downstairs in their heavy shoes. "I bet they bugged it," Rachel said.

"We'll fuck over there, then, and you moan a lot. It'll drive them crazy."

For the next few days he called Rachel's before he went upstairs, but the three suits never returned. One night late as he was sneaking upstairs there was a rustle of steps above him, but the voices were speaking Spanish so he went up past them, three young boys shooting up, watching him with faraway hostile eyes.

Every day after work he took the subway home, ate something

quickly then raced back uptown to an antiwar meeting or a café or church to talk to people about the War. Sometimes it was just a few older folks at a community center, paper shopping bags by their feet. Sometimes he'd have two hundred people at a rally, tried to reach them about the Resistance, about refusing to carry a draft card. Sometimes everything looked impossible, the future a defeat, the present lonely as a coffin. Then he'd be possessed by fiery endless energy – speaking, writing, arguing against the War.

But the Democrats were wary of antiwar groups and the unions were terrified of redneck backlash. And the unions wanted the jobs the War provided – *you that build the big guns* – and the Democrats would do nothing without the unions – *I'll stand over your grave till I'm sure that you're dead* – Wasn't that what had happened in Indonesia?

The big guys had the government, they had industry, they had labor. They would keep this War going till they'd sucked every drop of blood and money they could.

Or was that just his excuse for not doing more? Pretending it made no difference?

"We're reaching the students," Al Lowenstein said. "They're more empathetic and open-minded, concerned with moral and ethical questions." As a former president of the National Student Association, he had been meeting with student body governments in colleges and universities all over the country, educating them on the War and civil rights, energizing them to reach out to their own students, to other campuses. It was working. He was turning America's colleges against the War.

"So whom do we reach next?" Al looked round at them, the intensity of the question burning in his eyes: *We have to end this War, it is destroying our country and others, like a fire burning our house – how do we stop it?*

"You move further left," Mick said. "We're carpet-bombing an entire nation – you do whatever it takes to stop that."

They went to Bobby Kennedy's place in the United Nations Plaza. Bobby was slender and whipcord tough, had a heartwarming boyish smile and a fighter's stance. He had been elected Senator from New

York in '64 and everyone was hoping he'd run against Johnson in '68. "No, Mick," he said in his flat Boston accent. "I have no plans to run against the President."

"Even though he's secretly expanding the War while preaching peace? Was President Kennedy going to send ground troops to Vietnam?"

"President Kennedy had no intention of enlarging the War. He never had any intention of committing ground troops." Bobby glanced down, remembering. "He started force reductions the week he was killed, and intended to be out of all of Vietnam except the Delta by sixty-four and out of there by sixty-five."

And that's why he was killed, Mick wanted to say, remembering Seth Calhoun's CIA insider talk. But Bobby would know that too.

Going home the radio played the same song, you could hear it twenty times a day,

The eastern world, it is explodin'
Violence flarin', bullets loadin'
We're on the eve of destruction

A GIRL WAS UNDRESSING in a window across his lightwell. Tall and long-boned with black braids down her breasts, she slid out of her underpants, raised up on her toes and twisted her hips side to side, slid her palms up the insides of her thighs, rocking her pelvis. She cupped her hands round her pubic hair making the outline of a heart, tucked her hands behind her neck and danced slowly, breasts high.

"Jesus fucking Christ," Tucker said.

"She does this every night."

"You haven't fucked her?"

"Just watch."

She slid into the bathtub and lay there undulating in the water, got out. Swinging her hair back over one shoulder she took up a white towel, dried off and began to pat herself with talcum powder.

"I can't *believe* you haven't fucked her."

"She's got a guy. She's doing all this for him. See, there he is, by the bed."

"Sex," Tucker sighed, "is the fucking antidote to war."

"When you think about it," Mick said, "Vietnam's a metaphor. What living thing would *intentionally* develop a weapon to destroy themselves and all other life?"

The girl had climbed over the man, rubbing herself up and down against him. Tucker snickered. "All those charming virtues we're so proud of – defending and caring for others, sharing – hell, most animals do all those better than we do." He looked from the window, shook his head. "We're insane," he sighed. "Criminally insane."

Mick laughed. "I'm hungry. Let's go down to B&H."

They walked along the sidewalk in the cool October sun. "Jesus will you look at her," Tucker whispered, nodding at a girl ahead, "imagine her naked on top of you?"

"Easily."

"I'm thinking of becoming a monk. One of those Benedictines, that don't talk."

"Benedictine's booze. My sister loves it. Drink too much you don't need to talk."

"I need to sort my mind out, man. Got myself coming and going. Doing too much phone bank. When you call these vets, the American Legion guys, say you're a Nam combat vet and you'd like to talk to them about the War. *Right away* they want to know what branch, where you served, all that. Want to talk about their military career, no matter how short or uneventful. You tell them about Vets Against the War and instantly they're yelling screaming you're a pinko fag and if they could find where you live they'd come beat the shit out of you, that kind of stuff. When you did thirteen months in the paddies and they did supply on some Air Force base in Texas."

In the B&H Dairy Delicatessen they joined the line along the back wall. At a loud noise Tucker jumped, but it was just the cook whacking a bakery tray against the sink. "You see," Tucker scanned the room angrily, "everything's dangerous." He watched the cook. "Have to be ready for an ambush. Had to stop carrying my knife, afraid I'd do somebody in the subway – they get too close."

"You need to get away from the vets. It's just digging it all up inside you again."

Tucker watched people coming in the door. "You walk around all day telling yourself *Cool it, Baby, Be Peaceful,* but sometimes you can't take it anymore. You got to let go." He smacked the man behind him into the wall and shoved out the door.

Mick had to run to catch him. "You fucking nuts?"

"Gotta keep movin." Mick stayed with him till East Houston Street but he wouldn't stop. When Mick got back to the B&H the guy Tucker had shoved eyed him irritatedly.

"He got fucked up defending your country," Mick said.

A fork of scrambled eggs in midair, an Italian guy, thirty maybe, *Aamco Industrials* in white letters on his blue jacket. "You want I should feel sorry for him? A fuckin baby killer?"

CAPTAIN CROSS WAS A LIFER but not one of those Rear-echelon motherfuckers like most lifers, who all they'd learned from the Marine Corps was discipline and keeping your boots clean and your utilities pressed and looking sharp on parade. No, Captain Cross was determined, intense, and insanely seemed to believe we could win this upside-down horrible bloodletting no matter how many lives it took.

He was a movie Marine but this wasn't the movies.

Since the day when Cross shot the teacher and the old man Troy had tried to keep his distance, which was difficult because Cross *was* CO, and when Troy brought his platoon back from some horrible stinking patrol with his guys exhausted and sick with diarrhea from drinking paddy water and eating C-rats and from sawgrass cuts and leech holes that got infected into feculent boiling sores, the skin stripped off their feet and ankles, and sometimes a man or two not with them because he got to ride home early on the big medevac in the sky, or at least pieces of him did – and right away Captain Cross wanted a full report even though Troy called them in every day when there was radio and all the other shit Cross yelled about and sometimes Troy was tempted to tell Isaiah Norton and a couple other bucks, *you frag the motherfucker I don't care.*

"Sometime I like to frag him," Norton said. "But I can' do that."

"It's bullshit," Finkelstein said, "hurting your own team."

"Since *when*," Dreyfus, another black Marine, said, "is the lifers on *my* team?"

The black Marines were slipping away, not staying in touch with what was going down. They clanned up together smoking weed and listening to their own music, cleaning their rifles and looking at you meaningfully when you gave them orders. To Troy it didn't matter because they knew he would defend them with his life, any Marine he would defend no matter what, and so they stuck to him and did what he said and looked to him when the shit was bad. But it wasn't good, what was happening to the Marines, they weren't like Dad at Tarawa, pushing through deep surf toward the hungry machine guns. *They weren't happily dying just because you told them to.*

The first day at Pretty Woman in the mortar barrage after Troy's chopper had been shot down and he was in the numb terror and insanity of being the only survivor, Cross had been wordless, cold, disinterested. But now Troy knew that Cross like many commanders lived with it every day, a chopper lost with eleven souls, or three more kids in a firefight, a medic stepping on a mine. To be a CO was like a father watching his children die one by one or in clumps, and you tried to protect them while you sent them to their deaths.

When Cross killed the teacher and the old man there'd been no explanation except utter evil. Troy had seen Cross machine-gun VC prisoners to make others talk. He was a killing machine placed on earth to destroy the good wherever he could find it. But to Troy he'd grown more complex – still cold-hearted, but as if for deeper reasons.

"It's a mystery," Cross said one day as they counted stinking VC corpses on a carbonized hillside. "Yesterday these guys were alive, and where are they now?"

And where will we be, Troy wanted to say. *In an hour? A week?*

Now Cross wanted him in Hué. "First Marines HQ is looking for guys can talk gook. I told them you'd been studyin it and they said send him."

"I want to stay with my men, Sir."

"You don't have a say, Lieutenant."

"I'd be deserting them after we worked for months together, can slide through the boonies without Charlie knowing. Some new guy, Sir, he could get them killed."

"You're a fine Marine. I hope you stay in, because we need men like you."

"Thank you, Sir." Troy stepped back.

"But what HQ wants, it gets." He punched Troy's shoulder. "It's a promotion, Lieutenant. So do like those hippies say, *go with the flow –*"

Was Cross getting rid of him to avoid his testimony in some imagined future court martial? There'd never be one. As he packed his duffel in the hissing lantern light Troy tried to stem the excitement and relief of the transfer with the guilt of leaving his men.

12

DUMP JOHNSON

HUÉ WAS A TROPICAL PARIS, the loveliest city Troy had ever seen. Its ornate boulevards and wide French homes in expansive gardens and palm groves, its classic stone buildings, its bistros, sidewalk cafés, parks and open-air markets all seemed part of a civilized and stable union of east and west far wiser than either by itself.

Like the Seine, the Perfume River cut the city's middle, the ancient stone Citadel and its more ancient Imperial Palace and the Palace of Perfect Peace on one bank, and on the other bank a younger city with a French-designed capitol building, resplendent university, wide-lawned country club, and tree-shaded streets of red, orange, white and yellows roses, purple bougainvillea, lotus and orchids.

Along the many canals the straw-roofed huts clustered under papaya and mango trees with boughs spread over the water. Blue age-silvered sampans floated in their silver-gold reflections; on the streets and alleys the myriad bicycles clanged constantly, with baskets on the front or over the rear wheels, and ridden by lovely girls in white gowns or by grizzled old women selling oranges.

Statues of meditating Buddhas smiled like Mona Lisas over yellow-robed barefoot monks holding out brass begging bowls on sidewalks where uniformed school children filed solemnly, each clutching the back of the shirt of the one ahead, shepherded by slender lovely teachers in *ao dais*. Old women with wide earrings and betel-nut teeth, their faces maps of many lives and places, chatted with him toothlessly and cackled at his pronunciations.

Even the birds' cries seemed familiar. People here seemed freer, as if the War were far away. Often he felt pointless guilt for being here while his platoon waded through paddies and humped through leafless forests stinking of Agent Orange that made them nauseous and gave them harsh headaches. Even after a week in Hué the ache had persisted in the middle of his forehead, a chemical tartness on his tongue.

His Vietnamese was still rudimentary but people could understand, were shocked he'd tried to speak it. And each day he was getting better. How could you win their hearts and minds if you didn't speak their language?

In a shady street a girl was trying to start a Vespa, her sandaled heel angrily banging the starter, her yellow straw hat sideways. It puttered helplessly and died; she thumped her fist on the handlebar. "Can I help to you?" he said in Vietnamese.

She glanced up shocked then faced away, an impassive perfect face with almond slanted eyes and thin deep lips, little ski-jump nose and long neck down into a willowy body with high small breasts under a pale pink blouse, slender arms and long fingers. She shook her head not looking at him. "It's your *carburateur*," he said, the French word. "It's under water."

She giggled, then looked away and wouldn't speak or acknowledge he was there. He knelt beside her and turned off the key. "Give it some minutes." He popped open the engine compartment and wiped the carburetor down with the tail of his shirt and blew it dry. He shut the clutch and started the engine. "To not go fast."

"I'm late –"

"Hurrying makes you later."

She gave him a foreign glance as if surprised by some species of insect that had shown a hint of vestigial intelligence, then twisted the throttle and spun away, her yellow hat vanishing in the crowd.

He stood on a bridge over a canal remembering the curve of her back and her slim buttocks, her long rangy arms and wind-trailing ebony hair, how she leaned the Vespa into a corner like a jockey on a fast horse. A sampan full of long green stalks slid under the bridge, the man's dark bony knees apart, the leaves of his conical hat visible from above, his long slender pole trailing drops along the water.

The Vespa had only gone a few streets. He walked toward the last sound he'd heard, past thick-trunked massive trees and high stucco walls with little front gardens and two-story houses behind them. She was pushing the Vespa, head down, forcing it. "I'm glad I came back," he said in French.

"You didn't fix it very good," she said in English.

"WE'RE GOING TO DUMP Lyndon Johnson," Al Lowenstein said. "With a student movement. Based *on* the campuses. To stop him from running next year."

"I don't think anybody can stop Lyndon," Bobby Kennedy said. "The War's still approved by fifty-nine percent of Americans. Sure, there's Wayne Morse and Bill Fulbright and Gene McCarthy and a few other senators speaking out. But who's listening? Come on, Al, you don't depose a sitting president within his own party."

"Even Martin Luther King has *finally* come out against the War. Says it's immoral, and risks revolution at home. These young black men who don't get a fair shake here then face death over there supposedly for freedoms they don't have at home – it's true."

They sat on gilded couches in the vast, corniced library of oriental rugs and oak herringbone floors in Lowenstein's apartment on Central Park West. Al made his pitch, pacing, leading with his Yale lawyer's logic to an irrefutable conclusion: the antiwar movement had the strength and the energy to depose a sitting president. But it needed an alternative candidate.

Bobby had been Senator for over two years. He had hardened against the War but didn't know how to stop it. "If you decide to," Al said, "you can do it."

"Me?" Bobby chuckled. "I couldn't touch Lyndon next year. If I had any thoughts of running it'd have to be in seventy-two. *If* I had such thoughts."

"In the meantime," Al said softly, "how many thousand American boys are going to die who wouldn't if you won in sixty-eight? How many million Indochinese?"

"Al," Bobby snapped, "don't throw that shit at me."

AT SIX A.M. the alarm rang, the girl beside Mick mumbling. Furious he'd set it so early, he reset it for six-fifteen and fell asleep. An instant later it buzzed. He forced himself awake thinking if he was late Ephraim would make him do something dangerous, out on a beam with no tie-in.

Barefooting round roaches he washed his face and brushed his teeth in the tub, not bothering to shave, doused his dirty underwear and the armpit of yesterday's blue work shirt with deodorant, asked the girl to leave the key under the doormat and raced to the subway.

He hung to the strap half-seeing the ads for secretarial schools, life insurance and breath mints, the downturned faces of the other passengers wasting their precious lives by marching clockwork from one hive to another. And he too. *Termites, rats in a cage* – is that what Sabrina had meant? Where *was* she?

Life so short even if you lived to old age. And he could die now – anyone could – any second. A quick slip off a beam and twenty stories down. *This amazing mystery of consciousness,* how crazy to squander it. And a major way of squandering was mindless labor, lugging concrete all day, setting bolts into steel to create more air-conditioned boxes for people to get trapped in. *Why* was he doing this?

Most of the other people traveling this subway seemed resigned to squandering their lives. He imagined them sitting all day at their desks then going home to watch television. They complained about having to work but went shopping for things they didn't need and so had to keep working. *Half-lives,* the walking dead.

But the antiwar effort was wasting time too, the constant meetings chewing over the same issues till the more reluctant groups came aboard, the constant need to grow through unity by bringing in more people, diluting the message to include all.

The problem was he was alone while others had a fabric to their lives, nice apartments and friends. He was a failure: didn't have relationships, structure and meaning. Just like Cousin Johnny – caustic and indifferent, vaunting solitude because it was all he had? Was there more than one kind of heroin?

Peter and Lois, Seth and Miranda, other couples he knew had all found each other, sexually alive, casual nakedness and breakfasts together – when would he stop refusing love, running away? He envisioned a girl, long dark hair, slender face and body, a fine and sensitive awareness, someone with whom meaning could be discovered. Somebody like Daisy Moran had been, once.

Yet the girls he met he wanted to leave once they'd made love. Till then he'd feel full of interest and charm, wanting them with the deep unpurged hunger of a monk. Then he'd find himself beside a sticky disheveled stranger, conscious of her emanations and distasteful odors, her moles and imperfections. The breasts that only minutes ago had so excited him now seemed ungainly, or the nipples too large or too dark. Her lovely soft-haired pubis and the deep hot slit within her now seemed less interesting. He wanted to be alone but the intimacy he'd been so hungry to create was now fraught with duties of affection and respect.

He'd pace the floor naked, get dressed, not wanting to hurt her, castigating himself for lacking tenderness. He'd always be alone, too immature for deep, enduring love. "I have to be at work in four hours," he'd say, or pretending some suddenly remembered task, kissed her unwillingly and descended into the damp echoing midnight filling his lungs with the fetid reek of freedom.

The next night he wanted her again, or another. He'd meet her in a bar or playing guitar or on the street. If she smoked grass with him she'd sleep with him – grass a little sin to loosen the feelings, excite the body, open the thighs to greater sins and excitements. With grass she lowered her guard, was intimate already in another way, and its sensuality made her want to fuck. Priming the pump, lubricating the piston of love.

"Damn you," Rachel said, "you dance the best, take the best drugs, climb the nastiest mountains, fuck the hardest, fight out there in the night alone . . ." she smiled, looking down at him, his prick in her hand. "And you have the body of Michelangelo's David. So of course we *want* you. And you're hot because we can't really have you, not like we want. Your damn freedom enslaves us –"

Sex throbbed in him with the steady heavy thrum of an electric guitar and he had to purge it as the guitarist does with every song. The girls with spread thighs and aching breasts, slippery in their own lust and sweat, their hair in his lips and their nipples supple hard as he plunged into their volcano of life. Then the dream unsatisfied, the grail lost, he awakened in a stranger's arms.

But a day or two without sex and he'd burn inside. In political meetings or in the streets and bars he ached for every lissome girl. All the supposed raptures of religion, he now understood, were claimed by those who feared or hated sex. Religious passion was nothing more than ersatz sex, a blowup doll for the soul.

And sex was a good religion, built on the naked flesh of girls and women, on lovely salacious pleasure and deep aching joy. The lovely moment when a girl slid off her clothes – slender and silvery in streetlight through the window, kissing her fragrant body and sinking into her slim velvet heat, her cries and moans as she drove her body against his – was the deepest, loveliest, most fulfilling joy he knew. The closest you could get to God, why so many people said *Jesus* or *Oh God* when they came. And the deep glow inside afterwards, as if closer to the hearth of life, the eternal fire. Door to the spirit world, the body's pulse, the love of mystery and adventure.

Each girl a new country, some long-legged, narrow-bellied and too deep to reach completely, some wilder with a thick red bush, others blonde, distracted and sylphlike. Each unique and infinite, the taste and texture of her hair, and scent of crotch and skin and underarms, the softness behind her ear and the roughness of her soles, the way her breasts hung and how she bit her lip or moaned or swore, her undisclosed thoughts and reservations, a half-candid laugh or flash of anger – how was the great city of the world seen through her windows? What was it like inside her skin?

This most essential act for life, Rachel had once said. A perfect Darwinism: the greater the urge for sex the more likely the species survives. Why then did we so shame and denigrate it? As Miranda had said long ago, one dusty afternoon in Mick's dentist's office in Williamstown – why do they *hate* it? Why do they *fear* it? When it's so much *fun*?

Why fear and shun it when it was one of life's deepest joys, brought happiness, serenity and health? There seemed no answer other than a rote Freudian: it's only by controlling lust that we've evolved. Or that humans take more joy in pain than pleasure.

One night late on Second Avenue the woman of his dreams came toward him – tall, slender, dark-haired, pretty, but weeping. Instantly he wanted her to know her, comfort her. Her weeping made her more approachable, vulnerable, making him ache to talk with her, hold her, love her. "Hey," he halted in mid-street. "You okay?"

She tossed her head and kept going, an unmanned vessel heedless of shores. He walked with her for two blocks, begged her to talk, trying to show he'd give her more than she'd lost. But in her total absorption in her own pain he did not exist but for the furious heart-broken shake of her head signifying he was another pretender, another predator so far below the man for whom she sorrowed as to be unworthy of response.

THE GIRL WITH THE VESPA was named Su Li. She was a teacher in Bach Dang, a quarter of Hué between the northeast wall of the Citadel and the river, and lived with her mother and two younger brothers in a two-room house with a storefront where her mother sold rice, dried fish, vegetables, Coca Cola, coconut candy and anything else she could find. Su Li's father was dead and her income as a teacher was the major support for her family.

At first she had almost refused to speak. When her Vespa had broken down again he had cleaned the carburetor again and told her to empty the gas tank. "*Nu-oc*," he said, then in English, "You have water in your gas tank. You have to empty it and fill it with good petrol."

She nodded tugging aside a wisp of sable hair, watched him without expression as he tipped the Vespa and let the gas run iridescent into the mud, then walked silently beside him as he pushed it to a godown where an old man sold gas out of five-gallon tins. Refilled it ran perfectly.

She faced him, distant, nearly hostile. "*Cam on*" – Thanks.

He held the handlebar. "I should go with you, make sure it doesn't stop again."

"No." A sideways shake of the head, cold utter refusal.

He gripped the handlebar, afraid, indecisive, then dared: "Have tea with me?"

She lifted her chin in a brief laugh as if he'd asked something foolish and illicit. Emboldened he added, "If you don't, the scooter won't run."

She cocked her head sideways, not understanding.

"*Si vous n'avez pas tra avec moi, la machine ne va pas –*"

She giggled, slim fingers over her lips, eyes suddenly black. Fearing to do it he took the key from the ignition and put it in his pocket, nodded at a café tilting on rotten posts over the Perfume River. "*Hai tra?*" – two teas?

She scanned the roofs of shacks and shanties and the low white clouds and piercing blue sky, him. "You are officer?"

"Second lieutenant."

"Oh-kay," she smiled, face bright as the sun.

He felt outlandish in the little café with its tiny tables and tipsy stools, the thin-whiskered old men tipping faces into their cups, the proprietor's wife staring at him with undisguised hate then grinning gold teeth when he caught her glance. His pistol felt ungainly on his belt, his uniform too hot, the girl across from him more beautiful than a lotus, than the sky itself, and more remote. He was trembling – why? *I can have ten of you in a whorehouse for a hundred bucks*, he told her silently but that didn't change his excitement, his fear she'd walk away and he'd never see her again.

At first he talked foolishly of wanting peace, seeing as he spoke the napalmed bodies and phosphorized villages, realized he was being an idiot. Her long fingers laced round her cup, her small breasts beneath her pink blouse, her full lips like some flower about to open, the arc of dimple on each cheek as she smiled – he was stunned by them all. Again she flitted from somber hostility to a kind of teasing grace, as if trying out attitudes with him to find the right one, sometimes bantering in Vietnamese he couldn't follow then translating in schoolgirl English with here and there a word of French, "We have *bonne chance*, that you Americans save us from Communists."

It's not that simple, he wanted to say. *I'd be a Communist too if I was a peasant here, a factory worker*, shocking himself with the thought.

His tea reflected a fighter group crossing the blue sky, their roar eclipsing her words. In her simple cotton blouse and black trousers she seemed proof of all he'd lost, never had. Insanely he wanted to ask her *will you marry me*, knowing in some deep place if they did marry he'd never regret it. He resettled the pistol on his belt. She rose. "I go now," held out her hand. "*Tam biet*" – Goodbye.

Suddenly nothing seemed more important than not losing her. His mind scrambled for ideas. "I must go with you, if Vespa is lazy again."

Slender as bamboo she seemed taller than she was. "If you go my house, Communists make trouble my family."

He tried not to tower over her. "Please, come with me to finest dinner in Hué," aware of speaking pidgin, easy to understand. "Tonight, tomorrow?"

Again she looked away, as if calculating a sum. She looked into his eyes with that distant nearly hostile gaze. "Where?"

He didn't know, had never eaten here, knew only C-rations gulped down between patrols. "Where is best place in Hué?"

She grinned at his innocence. "Tomorrow, six in night? We meet here? Then we go Chez Henri – you like French food?"

He felt she was slipping away but had no room to argue. "Please come. Please don't stay away."

She smiled pure white teeth. "If I say, I do."

"IT'S PISSING ON YOUR COUNTRY," Al Murillo said as they sat on an I-beam thirty-six stories up eating lunch, "to turn in your draft card."

"If the War was right I'd be the first to fight," Mick answered. "But I won't kill people for no reason."

Murillo balled up a tinfoil wrapper and dropped it into the void. "What kinda freedom you think these Vietnamese will have, them Communists win?"

"Al, are *you* ready to die for their freedom? If you're a grunt with a girl and a '57 Chevy waiting for you back home, are you willing to die in a mudhole, your chest or balls or head blown apart? When it's a lie and you know it?"

Murillo spit. "When you put it like that –"

Looking down on gray Manhattan it occurred to Mick his country had become the specter of itself, *I Want to Hold Your Hand* replaced by *Eve of Destruction* – a new dark vision of *Amerika* where automatons goose-step to mindless verities and steel bombers unleash fiery death on distant peasants. But what if we'd always been this way? Though too young, too much a product of it, or too damn dumb, to realize?

"You and me riskin our lives," Al Murillo swung one leg over the girder and sat sideways. "On these skyscrapers, to push them up into the blue, huh?"

"Yeah?" Mick waited.

"You start with a piece of land then these architects plan how to squeeze the last bit of space onto each floor, push higher till the damn things bend in the wind like bamboo, huh? And the bankers change the zoning so you can go even higher and make more money squeezing more and more people into less and less space, huh?"

Murillo adjusted his seat on the cold girder. "Well, it's you and me riskin death so the big guys can make money. So I think, how is that different than this War, huh?"

. . .

ON JUDGEMENT DAY Mick woke early, took two tabs of acid and lay beside Rachel waiting for it to hit but it didn't. He'd had night-mares again of Troy wounded, of himself hunted in Bali. Rain hammered the window-panes and sloshed down the downspout. Rachel fumbled for her watch in her clothes on the floor. "Hey it's eight-forty."

In the Lex train going downtown he couldn't tell if he was stoned or not. The weird advertisements, the drum and shriek of wheels, the gently rocking passengers, were clearly hallucinations. But there was no disconnect between what he thought and did: he wasn't stoned. *Damn.* He tried to think how to raise his blood pressure.

The doctor sat at his metal Selective Service desk scorning peti-tions of malady from a line of supplicants. Implacable and lethal, he had literal power of life or death over his cringing naked subjects. He said you were 4-F and you were out on the street, free forever. He said you were 1-A and you climbed on a bus to Fort Benning and in three months could leave your brains and guts on some Vietnamese hill.

He scanned Mick's file, took his blood pressure. "You don't have hypertension."

"It says right there –"

"*I* said you don't have it. You're headed to Vietnam." He stuffed Mick's file back in its folder, cocked a thumb at the induction room. "Get in line."

Mick stood in a line of young men in a dark corridor, all naked, feet cold, soles dirty, clasping their folders before them like fig leaves. Not sure why, he stepped into the john. It had two stalls, one with no door. Holding his breath against the smell of shit he waited for the one with the door, locked it and scanned his file. Everything was there.

Terrified at what he was doing he ripped the first three pages to small pieces then the rest, then the folder too, flushed and flushed again till all were gone. Sure that abject terror would show in his face, he stepped into the corridor and joined the line going the other way of young men who had been rejected and had their files turned in.

Wouldn't the Selective Service know it was gone? Or would its absence simply make him invisible? When they checked on the draft status of Resistance leaders wouldn't they see it was missing? With shaking knees and a hollow stomach he dressed and stepped dizzily out the heavy door into bright midmorning sun.

"IF YOU'RE NOT WORKING," Thierry Gascon's voice crackled across the undersea cable, "why not come to Paris and work on Gisèle's campaign?"

"I can't hear you," Mick said.

"There – is that better?"

"You don't have to yell!"

"If you have no work on skyscrapers in winter, and you've decided not to join the War . . ."

After two years teaching at Williams, Thierry had returned to Paris to teach medieval lit at the Sorbonne. Gisèle Halimi was running for the French Senate, a brilliant and beautiful Socialist lawyer, a friend of Sartre and de Beauvoir. A defender of the poor and oppressed, she had represented Algerian revolutionaries in military courts and had become notorious and widely praised for exposing the Army's torture programs.

Mick had saved good money from steelworking all summer and fall. Al Lowenstein wanted him to work full time for the antiwar movement, live on what he'd saved.

Or he could take some time off from the meetings, rallies, phone banks, all the intensity.

Plus he'd just torn up his draft file. If they came after him, he'd be a lot harder to find in Paris.

"Election's next March," Thierry said. "Gisèle could win. Imagine, the first woman senator in France . . ."

13

JESUS WHERE WERE YOU

THE FIGHTING NEARED Hué, artillery thudding and rumbling in the distance, a far glow of napalm in the nights, crackling radio traffic of Marines pinned down, wasted.

The North Vietnamese Army was trying to shut Highway One north from Hué toward the DMZ. It made Troy worry for his former platoon and for Su Li, and fearing he might die and never see her again. Three times now they'd come to Chez Henri, he'd even kissed her once in a godown alley slipping on chicken shit, she giggling then slapping him softly then angry for some reason she wouldn't explain. The kiss was still on his lips, he could summon it any moment, see her lovely chiseled face, hear her entrancing half-taunting voice.

The first night she'd been friendly, asking him about life in the States, his regiment and what they thought of the War, did he think the Americans would win, with funny questions about growing up on the farm, why his brother was not fighting. "He's a leader of the opposition against the War," Troy said.

"So he is coward."

"He's just doing what he thinks is right." It bothered him saying this.

She shook her head. "He should come here too, help save us."

157

Her doctrinaire opposition to the Communists was more intense than other Vietnamese he talked to, even the ARVN officers who had the most to lose. But if she hates the Communists, he told himself, then many other Vietnamese must too; we must be doing the right thing. "Why do you hate the VC so much?" he said the second night.

"They kill my father, destroy everything."

"Why did they kill your father?"

She looked away as she always did when avoiding emotion. "Want to make everyone same-same them."

Cantilevered over the Perfume River, Chez Henri had been prosperous before the War but was now serving only the simplest meals, when it could get food. The patron was from Vichy, with its echoes of defeat and betrayal, and had a Vietnamese wife. The piano player sat at a tuneless piano tinkling at movie love songs that somehow did not seem out of place.

For a slender person Su Li ate like a tigress; the far rifle fire and sucking thud of bombs the third night did not bother her, "I love this French food – better from Viet Nam food," finishing his plate after she'd cleaned every scrap of fish and duck from her own.

He took her hand. "We'll go to Paris, then. You can have real French food."

She stared at him. "I not go anywhere with you. You thinking I simple Viet Nam girl, make *làm tình* like other Viet Nam girls."

He smiled happily at her, took her hand. "Just kissing your hand is better than *làm tình* with any other girl."

She snatched it away. "You say anything to get what you want."

He could not stop smiling, she was so lovely. "What *do* I want?"

She hunched her shoulders, looked at the Perfume River green fast and smooth beyond the rail, glanced at him darkly. "I think you like just bother me."

"Do you want to go to Paris? As soon as my tour's done?"

She shook her head. "You make fun. And my students? Who teach them if I go? Who take care my family? And you make talk only, not real."

"Would you marry me?"

Her eyes were a deep spring, unfathomable. They widened, glistened. She stood, threw down her napkin. "You leave me alone. Forever!" She crossed the patio and he leaped up to follow her, remembered he hadn't paid, went back and threw ten bucks on the table. When he reached the street she'd vanished.

DAISY WAS TORN between cognitive neuroscience and paleoanthropology. It drove her crazy day and night that she wanted to do both and felt a kind of divine link between them, but she had to choose one discipline for her PhD.

"You have to be selective, my dear," said Leon Jacobson, the bearded elderly head of the anthropology department. "I trust," he pushed his rimless glasses up his long narrow nose, "you'll select us?"

"Don't listen to them," Dr. Vargas, the head of the neurosciences department, told her. "Those guys, what they do is like religion. What we do is facts."

The paleoanthropology was exciting because you were looking at human behavior from twenty-five thousand years ago. Or a half million years. You picked a time and concentrated on it. And for her it was the emergence of *Homo sapiens* on the European continent, followed by the eventual die-off of the existing humans, the Neanderthals.

And the *real* question was, were our paleolithic ancestors less warlike than the agriculturalists who supplanted them?

In the end, however, she chose cognitive neuroscience because it allowed her to pursue this deep inner inquest she couldn't get rid of, into how the brain works. Her brain. *The* brain.

Know thyself, inscribed on the Temple at Delphi. From all the way back to Luxor and even before. Because, as Socrates wasn't the first to point out, *till you do you can't know anything else*.

Can I see my brain work?

To map the places in the brain responding to certain stimuli, and to note the effect of altering those stimuli?

Like alcohol does.

It was true, she knew already, that she was looking for a way to save her Pa. To bring him back to what Mom said was "a fine man" before this bizarre drug called alcohol took him down. True, as Mom said, he'd had a tough early life, beat up all the time by *his* dad, et cetera.

We know what causes such behavior on the environmental level. But what does it do to the brain?

Can environment change DNA?

And is there a way, a chemical, that can help to reverse it?

Or make it better?

"IF YOU'RE GOING TO PARIS," Seth told Mick, "you should register for grad work at the Sorbonne. It'll get you out of the draft."

Mick shook his head. "I thought you supported the War."

"Not enough to die in it."

"Aren't wars always waged by the powerful and died in by the poor? Ducking the draft with a deferment is just leaving the poor in the trap. It's the draft itself that has to be defeated. Without it the War can't go on."

"You get a deferment and you can keep working against the War. Without one you're either in jail or hiding: either way there's nothing you can do to stop the War."

"My skyscraper's done – my tiny part of it anyways. I've made good money and I'm going to France to have fun. Not to duck the draft."

TUCKER SHOWED UP at Mick's that night with a half gallon of Chianti in a paper bag. "Went out to Coney Island. That Ferris wheel, roller coaster, the one with the wings – prehistoric monsters crouching over the beach, coming toward you, and you've got your back to the water. So I went way out to the Bronx Zoo, you know, as far from Coney Island as I could."

He opened the Chianti with the corkscrew of his Swiss Army

knife. "Lions and tigers pacing their cells, caged wolves. Everybody doing time. All of them innocent. But they never finish their time, not till they die. Ocelots that can run seventy miles an hour across those endless savannas – what was *their* crime?"

Mick washed two jelly jars. "Just like on a firebase," Tucker said, "in life you have to lay down your free-fire zone. Napalm your perimeters till everything's ash. So you don't get ambushed."

He put down Mick's new guitar to take his jar of Chianti. "In Vietnam we don't *have* any territory. The Vietnamese people *are* the enemy. There's no rear lines. So for an infantry operation we have to set up artillery bases to support us, and soon's we withdraw those firebases are sitting ducks." He raised his wine jar. "To the gods of war."

"I won't drink to that."

"Come on now, where'd we be without them? We'd be chewing on leaves in some swamp like chimpanzees." He struck a G on the guitar. "Besides, if you revere them enough, maybe the war gods won't kill you." He hit a D and it hovered, expectant. "Operation Paul Revere, this huge new attack on Pleiku province." He fingerpicked an A minor, moving his left little finger up and down the top E string. "Imagine what Paul Revere would think of us naming the slaughter of thousands of farmers after him? He who helped to free the farmers of America."

He sang, "*The Farmers of America*," a song he'd made up, to the tune of "Stewball," "*keep our country strong. So we always do good, and we never do wrong.*"

"You sound worse than shit," Mick said.

"All day in Coney Island I've been afraid of going crazy. Hoping if I distracted myself enough." He sat back, the guitar's neck against his forehead. "The War just keeps coming back. I don't *want* to remember. At night I wake up in some hutch somewhere, hear the bullets, smell burning thatch – acrid and sweet at the same time – the dung in fields and paddies. A little girl crying, an old man weeping –"

"You ever try to talk it through?"

"Can't, man." Tucker smiled, took a hit. "It's into your bones."

"Why was she crying, the little girl?"

"Just her family, all shot and thrown into the hut and set on fire. Started last summer."

"The dreams?"

"No, the program. Search and Destroy. Find the enemy and destroy him and his supplies. At first we patrolled with Marvin ARVN, that vicious little chickenshit, wandering the countryside and every village we came to they'd go in and kill everyone and burn the place down while we stayed on the perimeter and pretended nothing happened. Then we got into it too, you see, we *had* to, because every Vietnamese – every farmer, every baby on his mother's back – was the *enemy*."

Mick felt worn down, nauseous with Vietnam. "You shouldn't drink so much."

Tucker drained his wine, poured more. "Coney fucking Island. My first patrol, in the Central Highlands. Mountains like the Poconos but steeper, thick forest. In the valleys villages with farm fields. I was so afraid, tried to stay in the middle of the column, you know, step where the others did. One guy laughed at me. 'You won't lose your cherry today,' he told me. 'This place been pacified.'"

His fingers sliding up the strings made a faraway whine. "In the first village maybe fifty people dead, in the burnt huts, on the terraced fields going up to the hills. Like some magazine advertisement of this beautiful tropical place except there's teenage girls with their intestines spread out on the ground and bearded old men all torn apart by fifty cals. Funny," he hit an E minor, a soft strum, "how we humans do things so automatically – those women trying to shield their babies with their own bodies, when they musta known the bullets were gonna blow right through them."

Again Mick felt like throwing up, wanting to turn the thoughts away as if one could avert one's eyes. The War was no longer a vast and horrible mistake we would soon recognize and halt. No, the slaughter of civilians, like the War itself, was deliberate and intentional, and the self-absorbed righteousness with which it was enforced was its greatest evil. The scorn of the SS officer for the girl kneeling before his pistol, the generals and politicians with their body counts and tactical programs.

It was just a simple melody Tucker played, a C to A minor to D and then G, with a walking thumb line, hammering on the inside string, singing

"Jesus, who watches over everything we do,
Have you seen the slaughter, is it true?
So tell us, Jesus, what to do,
And when it happened, Jesus, where were you?"

Baby Moses, down by the river born,
Have you seen these children burned and torn?
These people all cut down like corn,
So tell us, Baby Moses, do you mourn?

"My answer," Tucker grinned, "to 'Ballad of the Green Berets.' Don't have a chorus or bridge. Can't find the next verse. And some of the lines, man, they suck – like the one about corn."

"It's good, the one, *When it happened, Jesus, where were you?*"

"That 'Ballad of the Green Berets' – how it goes?" He sang falsetto, *"Back at home a young wife waits, Her Green Beret has met his fate, He has died for those oppressed, Leaving her his last request –"*

"That his son should grow up to be a Green Beret too, and die just like his dad –"

Tucker laughed, shook his head. "What kind of a father is that? But it's sold more records this year than the Beatles or Stones. How you going to reach people like that?"

He ran through a few chords. "I thought it was Marvin ARVN – our brave Vietnamese allies – had killed those people. But it wasn't ARVN." Tucker slammed his wine jar on the table, it shattered and he held up his right hand in surprise with the shard of glass sticking out the side of his palm. "Sorry, man." With one hand he swept broken glass from the table into his other palm and dumped it in Mick's trash.

"You dumb fuck." Mick tied off Tucker's hand with a torn T-shirt and scotch tape.

Tucker shook his bandaged hand a few times, picked up the guitar. "It was our guys. First Cav, on search and destroy. Part of our strategy now in II Corps is to wipe out the villages so they can't shelter and feed the VC. Like Ferlinghetti's 'Coney Island of the Mind',

Heaped up groaning with babies and bayonets under cement skies,
in an abstract landscape of blasted trees . . .

"He already knew, didn't he, ten years before it started?"

"You suppose," Mick said softly, "someday Vietnam'll be all forgotten, forgiven?"

"This kind of sin, it lasts a thousand years –"

"I think most humans are dangerously stupid. When grouped together they'll run to war and religion and hatred and ignorance intentionally, determinedly, and will destroy you in the process. To live wisely it's essential not to trust or have faith in one's fellow humans, to watch out for them as one might a rabid bear. At the same time to not hurt or degrade or denigrate them, to push forward toward the light, toward friendship, understanding, love and peace, but never be so foolish as to expect what you hope for –"

The telephone rang, harsh and insistent, a girl named Beverly. "You sleepy?" she said.

"Talking with a friend," Mick said.

"Oh."

She sounded hurt and he realized she'd think he was with another girl. "Guy from Vermont." *Back from Nam,* he started to say, then remembered her husband out there somewhere, blown apart.

"Can I come over," she said half apologetically. "For a while?"

He glanced at Tucker who with a frown of concentration was busily rolling another joint. "I'd love to see you."

"She's a nice, crazy girl," he told Tucker.

"When he get it, her husband?"

"About a year ago. Never got out of his plane and there was nothing but a crater where it hit. She tells me that, straight-faced."

"Poor kid."

"Then she gets feeling guilty, that he might still be alive and she should be keeping the faith."

"And not balling you?"

She was wearing a long red scarf down the front of a golden raccoon coat, her hair full of dampness and electricity from the street, her lips chilled with mist. She circled Tucker keeping her distance, taking the joint and fingertipping it back. She swung on Mick. "I never know if you're going to call or not."

Neither do I, he wanted to say, annoyed at her, himself. She wore small oval glasses and had to tilt her head back slightly and peer down her nose to see through them, and this, combined with her irritated coily hair, gave her a peremptory inquisitive air that made him angry.

"You work with him?" she snapped at Tucker. "You're wasting time. This bastard's not reliable. He never calls."

Mick found another fruit jar, washed it and filled it with Tucker's Chianti and gave it to her. "When I do you're always out."

She opened the reefer. "Nothing but hypothermic roaches. Mick, you should clean them out. You're wasting your time," she repeated. "Never will you stop this War."

Tucker grinned, cradling his bandaged hand. "We have a fucking oracle here."

"Mick you should clean your floor." She scuffed the carpet with her boot, swirled her skirts and flounced down cross-legged, wine jar by her knee. "Everything's so easy for you. So you think it is for everyone." She huffed her blouse up round her shoulders.

"Think so?" Tucker said.

"You don't trust anybody," she added. "Maybe from how you were brought up. But don't you see how easy it is for you not to trust the War? Your government?"

"Shit," Tucker said. "I don't trust it either –"

"So you look down on my husband Tim," she said, "and on Tucker here, for getting into the War – but that was easy for them to fall into – they're nicer than you."

"That's not true," Tucker said. "I'm not nicer than him."

"They trusted their government, were willing to risk the supreme sacrifice . . ."

"You mean die," Tucker said.

". . . to protect their country." She bit her lip hard, her eyes shiny. "You shouldn't look down on normal people, Mick."

"And what were they –" Mick tried to keep irritation out of his voice, "protecting the country from?"

"There you go again," she said. "Can't you see it doesn't matter? That the thought was, I love my country so much I'll die if it asks."

"Now I wouldn't." Tucker pulled out his glass eye, popped it in his mouth.

"That's gross," Beverly hissed.

"Gift of our government –"

"Before I risk losing this ecstatic mystery of life," Mick said, "I want to know *what* I'm losing it for. What's everybody, or somebody, going to get in return for my being erased from the rest of my life? For my not having a family, and kids and growing old with my grand-children around me, a lifetime of days?"

"For you, Mick, maybe life's too important."

"Otherwise we can get a scenario where there's little booths on the street and if you want to show your love for your country – or your wife, for that matter, or Macy's or Howard Johnson – you go in and shut the door and it executes you."

"That's absurd!"

"You can even do it painfully, if you want, maybe get the Congressional Medal of Honor." He glared at her. "Or, how about if you can choose to go in there and just get wounded – lose a leg, or a bullet in the balls – and then you get a Purple Heart?"

"Mick you're sick."

"If you buy someone a gun, knowing he will use it to kill people, by law you're as guilty as he. Americans are buying weapons for an Army that has to commit war crimes every day just to follow orders."

"That's true." Tucker put back his glass eye and gulped his wine.

"In a pig's ass!" she turned on him. "You, who were paid and trained to defend your country, who *enlisted* to –"

"You know how easy it is to kill someone?" Tucker stood, put Mick's capo and tuning fork on a shelf. "The human body's soft as protoplasm – bullets go right through us." He reattached the guitar strap and shut the guitar in its case. "You know what children look like after people like your husband burned them alive?"

"Fuck you, coward."

He smiled at Mick as he stood in the door. "Tomorrow's a phone bank night."

"Oh shit." Mick said. It was awful talking to strangers on the phone, trying to motivate them against the War.

Tucker turned to Beverly. "You don't really want to fuck me so don't say it. I'm probably not a coward, as I got three Purple Hearts and two Bronze Stars. I think we should use words accurately or they lose their value. Like when I say, *you* are a dumb bitch, I mean two true things: you're stupid, and you're a nasty vicious woman."

Her mouth opened. She said nothing, then, "You're a goddamn Benedict Arnold."

He saluted her and his voice faded down the stairs singing "Onward Christian Soldiers," making Mick worry about his neighbors.

She dug fingernails into Mick's wrist. "I'm sorry. I just can't live with people."

"Neither can Tucker."

"I get lost in ideas, nothing's what it seems. All my ideas are wrong, don't represent what *is*."

"But what's *is*?"

"That's what ideas are for – to find out what *is*. But they go astray like horses, like bullets that hit someone else."

He held her closer. "Stop thinking about this."

She kissed him hastily, pulled back. "Mick I don't want to sleep with you tonight."

"That's fine."

"How come you always make such a sex thing between us? Why can't you just once, for *one* night, be my friend?"

"I said that's fine."

"Yeah but you didn't *mean* it. And now I came all the way down here to see you and you just want to fuck me!"

"Hey, I'll sleep on the couch."

"You'd sleep on that couch? It's filthy, Mick – what's wrong with you?"

He pulled her near, feeling her tense against him. "You know," she murmured, "you were the first guy I slept with after Tim? That bar where you gave me your Guinness because they'd run out. I was alone but I didn't want you to know. So I pretended to be looking around –"

"For your brother –"

"I was really looking for Tim. In a dream the night before that bar was where I found him – so I looked around and he wasn't there and I said okay I admit you're dead, Tim. And as I sat down beside you – there was that open stool – my tit brushed your arm and it was like stepping on a twelve-volt battery. You ever have a cattle fence? Bare wire connected to car batteries – wow I was *zapped*. And I said to myself I was going to fuck you that night whether you wanted to or not. I was going to fuck your brains out."

"I swear you did. I've been stupid ever since."

"You were before." She shifted her legs, a thigh bronzed by firelight. "I didn't like that song you sang."

"Yeah, you told me. 'Masters of War.'"

"That's why I got so mad at your friend, just now. Because that song's true." She brushed a tear from her cheek with the side of a finger. He took her hand feeling the tear's cool damp streak and the sharp edge of her engagement ring. "If I admit he died for nothing," she said, "it's like losing him all over again."

"It was random as a car accident. Stop digging it up."

"Ever since he was little he wanted to fly. Sent away to all the plane companies for pictures and manuals, did ROTC at Bowling Green and went straight into the Air Force in '64. Never heard of Vietnam, thought he'd be flying over Europe."

She looked straight at him, holding in the tears. Mick glanced down, found himself turning her engagement ring round her thin finger, its sapphire the color of the sky at forty thousand feet. "And then he finds himself," she said hoarsely, "flying F-105s napalming peasants."

"How'd he deal with that?"

"He finally talked about it in Waikiki. I told you that was the last time I had sex before you, but Tim and I in those four days' leave we only fucked twice. He was so *crazed* by this War. He sat on the edge of the bed with his elbows on his knees and his head down between his shoulders like a condemned man – I can see it now, the pink scalp under his short blond hair. He had to keep the TV on, said he needed the voices."

With a palm she angrily rubbed tears from her cheeks. "People on fire, running out of their homes . . . That's why I got so mad at Tucker – because Tim's dead, and he did bad things, things that drove him crazy, this lovely sweet boy like you, and now I know too he died for absolutely nothing."

Mick felt weighed down by incorrigible loss. Since the beginning of time what had there been but sorrow? He touched her forehead with his, kissed her wet cheek. "Honey you've got to let your heart rest." He tugged a pillow from the couch for their heads and pulled her down beside him. "Got to stop wounding yourself."

"He wanted to look down on the pretty little fields and villages of Germany, to see what God sees."

"God doesn't see."

"I tried so hard to understand. Did God love Tim so much He *had* to have him? But wasn't that selfish? Doesn't God care about the sorrow of all the loved ones? Or does God think sorrow's good for us?"

He kissed her tears, holding her close. "Forget God."

"Then I thought maybe Tim was a sinner, that's why he had to die. But if he was, it was the War that made him a sinner. God made him a sinner then punished him. Why?"

Perhaps because it's only through pain that we learn, but he couldn't tell her that. For a long time he held her watching the fire's glow till it cooled and he pulled her raccoon coat over them and the glow of the coals faded on the ceiling into the dawn, voices and radios and arguments in Spanish and food smells rising up the lightwell.

In three days he'd be in Paris. And all this far behind.

14

IN GOD'S EYES

SHE CAME TOWARD HIM down the aisle of the Air France 707, more beautiful than pretty, a wide mouth, long nose and silky almond hair. Oh if she'd only sit here, Mick begged, but no, that never happened. The rule was you always got the fat smelly guy from Idaho who snored all night.

Halting she checked her ticket. Her orange silk blouse lifted above her jeans showing a perfect navel as she tossed her shoulder bag into the overhead bin. She saw him look away, smiled and slipped into the seat beside him. "How are we supposed to sleep," she said in English, "in these little chairs?"

"We're not supposed to," he said in French.

She gave him an appraising glance. In her early thirties, a wedding ring, blouse open to the tops of small breasts that made his heart race, long legs in black jeans, black open-strapped high heels, an under-scent of roses and lavender that made him dizzy. She nodded at the Nikon in his lap. "Another American taking a camera to France? Putting us in a box to enjoy later, like *herbes de Provence?*"

"You French do it too. In New York, shooting the Empire State Building . . ."

"Cameras rob the soul," she said as a stewardess filled their champagne glasses. "That's what an old Tibetan told me."

The champagne tasted of iced peaches and lime, magnificent. "You always believe what old Tibetans tell you?"

"Oh always."

"I actually was there, last year, in Tibet."

"No you weren't. It's not allowed."

"I didn't say it was." He told her about the long hike through the Himals, climbing Virgin Peak with Skip, Pavel and Sergei, the Tibetan pony trains of guns and ammunition, the battle on the Tibetan steppe, the Chinese watch on the truncated arm.

"I see –"

"You don't believe me."

"Of course I do."

He laughed. "No, you're making fun."

"Someone told me Tibet has the world's best hash. Is that true?"

"I have some with me." He'd been going to tell her what had happened after Tibet, the holocaust in Bali, but that was a downer and they were getting high on champagne and what did it matter as long as you hid it all inside?

Eyebrows raised, she pretended to be shocked. "On this very plane?"

"In this very pocket. Not hash but weed. Two joints. Actually it's not Tibetan but just as good. Almost."

"Why not wait to buy it in Paris?"

He nodded toward the lavatories. "I was going for a smoke – want some?"

She smiled, too well bred to be offended. "I saw enough of that in New York."

"How long were you there?"

"Just a week. Business."

"Can I ask what kind?"

"You are too curious. Anyway it was to visit my publishers. I write women's novels – you Americans call them bodice rippers."

He laughed, a little drunk. "I love that idea, torn bodices. I hate clothes."

"It would be boring if we all go naked."

"You believe that?"

She smiled, glanced away. "What's it like," he said, "being a novelist?"

"Very boring also. Get up early, have coffee, try to write, have breakfast, write terribly for a few hours, have more coffee, tear it up, try again. And again and again."

"What makes it terrible? So that you tear it up?"

"When it's false. When it doesn't say what you're seeing."

He imagined her in a negligee getting out of bed. "Is your husband a writer too?"

"No Frenchman would ask this, about family. No, my husband's a politician."

The stewardess was lovely too, her slender tanned wrist slipping from the blue Air France uniform as she poured more golden champagne into their crystal glasses, her chiseled face framed in dark curly hair in the dim cabin lights. Mick felt on a magical ship of beautiful wise people taking him to a sacred place. "If you had to live a year alone on a desert island and could bring three books?"

"Maybe I wouldn't bring any books."

"You have one there –"

She flipped over *Tropic of Cancer*. "It's not a book, it's life. Here's what he says about the Seine." She scanned the pages: "'*I am a sentient being stabbed by the miracle of these waters that reflect a forgotten world*' – how perfect –"

Salad came, then steak. They finished a bottle of Air France Bordeaux and the stewardess brought them another. "It's tourist class, this wine," she said.

"Better than Gallo Hearty Burgundy."

"What is that?"

It was inevitable to talk about the War. "We too made the mistake of Vietnam," she said. "But at least we had an excuse; it was our colony and many thousands of French people lived there, and we had many investments there and had modernized the country and brought them the French way of life. I was in university; we protested but it did no good. Governments do what they want till they are thrown out. Maybe that will happen in America?"

"America should have a revolution every fifty years, Thomas Jefferson said."

"Revolution's a lovely idea but it always turns to hell. Look at ours, how we murdered hundreds of thousands. Even worse, the Russian, the Chinese. Millions of people die for some ideal that never happens. What if America and Britain had stayed together, a single world empire? Instead, the American Revolution started the decline of the world's greatest power since Rome."

"But aren't *we* now the world power?"

"Not for long. America's never tried to unite and teach the world like the Romans did, the British, or us French, for that matter. All you ever want is money and power."

He raised his champagne. "If I have to choose between them I'll take money."

"They're the same."

They finished the Bordeaux and the stewardess brought a third one. He was mildly drunk, high on this woman's exciting eyes and throaty accent, her fragrance and warm nearness. They spoke softly now as everyone was sleeping, her face near his, her lips against his ear. "You are not afraid to carry it, that grass?"

"Of course not. Ever smoke it on a plane?"

"Of course not."

"It's even better than on the ground. Up here you're already high." Not giving her time to refuse he got up. "Meet you back there." He walked the darkened corridor to the lavatory and waited with the door cracked open. After a moment she came to the door. "I don't believe I'm doing this."

With barely room for two, the lavatory had an unpleasant chemical odor, soapy water in the sink and a crumpled tissue on the floor. He lit the joint and they smoked watching each other in the spattered mirror. The ceiling vent blew the smoke in all directions. "Why are you going to Paris?" she said. "To see some girl?"

"You know Gisèle Halimi? I'm going to work on –"

"Do I *know* her? I don't like her. Those revolutionaries she defended killed many innocent people. You should not do this."

"Okay I won't." He kissed the soft down between her eyebrows, her nose, the lovely crevice of her cheek and her wide strong lips. "Whatever you say."

"*This* is very strong grass."

It was wonderful, as if it were the last kiss either would ever have, her long waist and slender ass in his hands, her lovely tits perfect fruit with small hard nipples and lovely soft undersides. He undid her belt and started to slide down her jeans.

"*Non!*" She bit his lip gently. "Idiot!"

"Sorry." He moved his hand up and down her crotch, softly massaging, opened his fly so she could hold him, her breath coming deep and fast. "You know what I've always wanted to do?"

She squeezed his prick. "I won't."

"On a plane? Have you ever?"

"Of course not."

Her kisses sucked him into a frenzy of mystery and pleasure, her fingernails down his back as he kissed her breasts and tugged down the tight Levis and slim underpants and holding her against the wall went into her, her legs round him with her heels against the sink, her teeth in his neck. He drove harder making her gasp and bite till she gripped his buttocks hard making him slowly ease in and out, riding waves of orgasm and after a while he let her down, knees quivering, and knelt to kiss her tangled pubic hair. She pulled him up. "We must go back."

"Already I want you again."

"Go out!" She pushed him. "I want to pee."

Reluctantly he slid up his jeans and buttoned his shirt. "Maybe later?"

"Out!" She sat on the toilet. "First look no one is seeing."

He went back to his seat suffused in her perfume, her sex smell, sat looking at the black shimmering ocean and thinking how hard it would feel to hit, how cold. It was impossible to imagine them as they really were: a little village in a tin capsule seven miles high going six hundred miles an hour. When Virgin Peak had been less than five miles high and had nearly killed him.

She came back and tugged blankets over them. "I always fly first class but it was full. Instead I got you."

With the sex and weed and champagne and wine he felt very happy, squeezed her thigh. "I'm very lucky."

"At first I was angry to myself then I realize though what we did was crazy, in God's eyes what was the harm? Is life so long we can refuse pleasure? Isn't it true, what Anatole France said: A missed orgasm is a sin against God?"

He felt a warm and happy closeness. "I don't even know your name."

"Lily."

"Lily what?"

"Just Lily."

Too soon the cabin lights glared on. The sea was turning gold against the rising sun. He raised the elbow rest between them; she folded the blankets and put them in the overhead bin. The stewardess came with coffee, croissants, butter and wild cherry jam.

He took her hand, amazed at its sleekness. "When can I see you?"

"Never. I have a husband and kids." She tugged a paperback from her bag. "Take it. It's you."

"I've read it. Which one am I, Zorba or the other guy?"

"Read it again, remember what we did. Then you'll know."

PARIS WAS cold and rainy. He found a cheap hotel on Boulevard de Raspail for nine dollars a week. His steeplejack savings would last four months but not if he stayed in Paris. But by May there'd be steelworker jobs back in New York, girders over the void.

Gisèle Halimi's Senate campaign was an explosive cauldron of the Parisian intellectual left at a time when Charles de Gaulle ruled as inexorably as Louis XIV, and from the students' and workers' quarters spread sharp seeds of revolution. Meetings were parties and parties meetings, sex and wine and food everywhere, stunning new movies and late-night revels in whisky bars, Saturdays wandering rainy *paysages* on foot and in Monique Manon's Renault 4, and always ideas, the battle of ideas, of how best create a new and better world.

Monique was a Socialist Party organizer, skinny, tall and volcanic. With her cherub's lips, wide far-seeing eyes and curl of boyish chestnut hair at each high cheekbone she looked like a Renaissance angel and used it to her advantage. She chain-smoked, drank Irish whisky straight, loved jazz and lived in the workers' district of Issy-les-Moulineaux – a name evoking the wooden windmills that once graced the quiet countryside beyond the medieval Paris walls and gave a bucolic tinge to the grinding industrial air. She loved to make love all night, exhausting him with her skinny sexuality and endless desire. "Can we do again?" she would gasp, "I want to come more . . ."

Gisèle Halimi was a sensuous Socialist lawyer with fiery eyes and ferocious determination. In her forties, she'd defended Algerian revolutionaries, led feminist movements, and was as opposed to US wars in Vietnam, Cambodia, Cuba, Africa, and Central and South America as she was to the *apparatchik* domination and sheeplike submission of the masses in China and the USSR. To her the individual stood tall, the boy at the barricades in 1848, the eternal human dissatisfaction with eroded liberty, and the resolution to recover it. "You're not happy with things?" she would say. "Change them. You see people suffering or oppressed? Help them."

As this was the first Senate campaign of a woman in France, and as Gisèle was so fiercely loved by the best and brightest, the campaign and her home were jammed with fascinating argumentative people, young exciting writers just back from Peking, Cuba, or the Congo, revolutionary thinkers like Régis Debray and others trying to create a valid structure by which humans could live in liberty, equality, peace and progress.

Nights became days and days nights. As in American antiwar politics there were mimeographs to print and distribute, meetings to attend, of factory workers in blue coveralls, Métro employees, trash truck drivers, school teachers, refinery workers and librarians. The Sorbonne was in ferment; the girls in short skirts despite the winter wind were hungry for sex, the food was intense, always intense, and the wine was *veritas*.

Vietnam colored everything; by some people Mick was suspected of being a CIA agent and would be drawn into insane discussions where he argued, as a good German might have in 1941, that his country was not what it did. One morning about three a.m. as Monique and he were crossing the Pont des Arts and he was singing in English they were attacked by a band of radicals for being American. He pointed out that the French had killed more people in Vietnam than the Americans, and the French had just finished a vicious colonial war in Algeria. The resulting fight felt ludicrous, for he agreed with them about Vietnam but he would not tolerate them attacking his country, nor did they have the right to criticize America for the same thing their country had done.

Among the French this truth was never far from their minds, and any criticism of the US was usually prefaced by a "Sadly we are equally guilty. But we learned, why can't America? Also, it was our colony. And you, the Americans, why are *you* there?"

"THE REVOLUTION'S ALMOST HERE!" Monique drove left-handed, gesturing with her right. "I can *feel* it!"

"Watch that truck!"

The truck roared past shaking her little car. "*This car* nearly had a revolution," Thierry called from the back seat.

"Monique's a Marxist," Thierry's girlfriend Romana said. "Don't aggravate her."

"Marx was right!" Monique turned round, skewing the wheel. "Capitalism *imprisons* people. He wanted to *free* them. Is that a crime?"

"Are you crazy?" Thierry said. "*Of course* that's a crime."

"The best thing about sex is it's anti-capitalist," she added.

"Will you drive straight!" Mick yelled.

"She's a double agent," Romana said. "Trying to kill us."

"Even your Dos Passos," she turned to Mick, "says the only person who profits from capitalism is the con man and swindler."

"Jesus will you watch the road!"

After weeks of intense campaigning for Gisèle they were headed south for a long weekend off, four of them in Monique's tiny Renault and nine more people squeezed into an ancient black Citroën driven by a friend of Gisèle's, Alexandre de Beaurepart, an impecunious baron with a castle on the Dordogne River.

"The Russians I knew in Nepal," Mick said, "said their revolution was a failure. Thousands of young revolutionaries died for individual freedom, a better life for everyone, yet they created one of the most dictatorial, murderous regimes in history –"

Monique honked as she passed a bus on the inside. "But Marx wasn't *wrong*, it's how he's being *used* by Russia and China!"

"I don't dare disagree," he said, watching the road.

"Look at it this way: the worker sells his labor to the capitalist for a wage, but it's less than the value of what the worker puts into the product. And the total of all the wages to make this product," she spun the wheel to avoid a panicked squirrel, spraying a shrapnel of road-side gravel, "is less than what the capitalist makes selling it. So workers produce wealth but aren't paid their full share. The product they make is more valued than their work!"

"But Marx isn't counting the economic value of investment money," Mick argued, "or initiative, entrepreneurship, risk-taking, all that stuff the capitalist provides."

She slipped into second gear for a hill. "The rich get richer and the worker gets poorer because the capitalist wants the greatest possible return on his investment."

"I'm so poor I'm sure to get richer. I can't get any poorer."

She ignored this. "So the capitalist wants to pay the worker the lowest possible wage and sell the goods at the highest possible price –" the car shuddered as she jammed it into first "– but the worker wants the highest possible wage and to pay the lowest possible price for what *he* buys. They're forever in conflict, and people grow alienated from each other because they're forced to *use* each other, compete for survival, like the jungle –"

"You should slow down –"

"– and people end up fighting for wealth and possessions, standing on each other's heads to reach higher, take more. When this productivity could better the human condition!"

"– there might be a policeman," Mick said hopefully.

"There are no *flics*, ever, on this road."

"No matter your system, the same people will get to the top. Look at the Soviet Union, run by the same hustlers that run America –"

"– or France," Romana offered from the back.

"But Marx," Thierry interjected, "said that capitalism can be overthrown only by revolution, because the ruling class owns and runs most of the state and its courts, police, and other lawmaking agencies. So non-revolutionary change doesn't work, because the state always protects its ruling class."

The car shuddered to a stop part way up a steep hill and a big silver Peugeot blasted past them. "Somebody has to get out," Monique snapped. "Or we can't get up this hill."

"Ah the capitalist approach to labor," Thierry laughed. "Who gets left behind?"

"We all do," Romana added sarcastically. "It's *la condition humaine*."

"Didn't Malraux say," Thierry puffed as they trudged up the shoulder, "awareness of our own deaths is the source of all our fears? Shit, I've got to stop smoking."

"If we could live forever would we still make war?"

"Shit, I don't know. Is the individual inviolate and free? Or does he owe his life to society, must he pay taxes, obey laws and die if told to?"

"Only answer I can come up with," Mick said, "is do no harm –"

"Every time we breathe we do harm. To somebody or something."

They drove across the Limousin plateau and descended the Périgord's vibrant pastures of black and white cows and undulating oak forests under a sapphire sky, white stone villages with church towers and ruined battlements blazing in the southern sun. In a bright bistro with Françoise Hardy on the jukebox they had sandwiches and beer, and it seemed to Mick he was living a deeper truth, a more honest life, in this coarse sunny loud smoky café glaring at the midday sun, surrounded by farmers and truck drivers hunched over their wine and smiling with broad dirty contented faces.

My heart is nearly naked, Françoise Hardy whispered, *my feet are in the tomb*, as her cool sensual tones sank into the sunny room with the perfect simple truth from the heart that's nearly naked, the lovely *double-entendres* that are the heart of France, the rose dying, the girl dying of love.

The Dordogne valley below, the river reflecting puffball clouds and white castles, rows of poplars in iridescent leaf, the streamside willows budding red, the grass already surging from the rich dark soil like green wildfire.

Monique drove with the self-assurance of a race-car pilot, screaming the little R4 through the sunny Bordeaux curves while singing dirty songs with the others as Mick tried to catch their twists of meaning, the puns turning back on themselves, the French joy in words and in knowing that just as all roads lead to Rome all meanings lead to sex.

Every curve in the road brought new vistas over blooming trees and bright hills down to glistening rivers and streams. It was easy to fall back eight centuries as each castle loomed up with shining towers and sleek slate roofs. "It's because of the Arabs there's so many castles here," Monique said. "They were always invading from Spain, destroying everything, killing everyone, and the Dordogne is where we whipped them."

"Can you imagine France," Thierry said, "controlled by Muslims?"

"All of Europe, if the Muslims had won, the veiled women, the stonings –"

"You see," Monique turned to Mick, "some wars *have* to be fought."

"Watch the road!"

"Last thing Pascal wrote," she downshifted, biting her lower lip in concentration. "As he was dying –"

Her quick changes of subject, like the fast curves in the road, never ceased to floor him. "What?"

"*Fire, God of Abraham, God of Jacob, of Isaac. Not of the philosophers and savants.*' You think it's true?"

"Truth's in the spirit, not the mind?"

She pulled up for cows ambling across the road. A boy stood at the side, willow whip in hand, chewing a grass stalk and watching them from under a dark cap. "That was Pascal's question all along," Thierry said. "It's better to take the path with God, because if God exists you're safe, rather than risk the alternative."

"If I were this alleged God," she snorted, "those are the first ones I throw into the hole – the ones who think like that. After the Muslims."

"In Algeria the Muslims were good to me," Mick said. "They saved my life. Even the poor shared the food they had."

"I don't mind them *there*. But think what they're doing *here* – crime's way up in Paris, the broken families, the lack of cohesion. They're not French and refuse to be. Our country is a race and a religion, not a political entity. They're changing it for the worse."

"France is a religion but you don't believe?"

"It's bipolar: worship of Mary on one hand and of atheistic rationalism on the other. Nobody gives a shit about the Pope; it's in perfect balance, the electron and nucleus, yin and yang. We are the most conservative and radical people on earth."

"Most moral and immoral?"

She grinned. "Let's hope."

The village of Lanquais was a few farmhouses hunched over the road. Alexandre's castle rose above a hill of young poplars. A cobblestone track snaked through a broad stone gate in the castle wall and into a wide paved courtyard.

"The right side," Alexandre pointed to the battlements and towers of weathered white stone, "is eleventh century, the middle part thirteenth, the left sixteenth. By then the Muslims were gone, so you can see the evolution from the crossbow slots on the right toward the showy cut stone windows of the Renaissance on the left."

Inside the great halls extended into a shadowed perspective of tapestries, forty-foot tall elaborately carved oak ceilings, ancient rugs, and vast fireplaces. It was five stories up a corkscrew stone staircase of an eleventh century tower to a little room overlooking the moat and valley bathed in sunset, the newly green poplar tops like toys beneath the *meurtrière*.

It was a word he loved, *meurtrière*, the feminine of deadly, a cross-shaped slot in the stone wall through which a crossbow could be fired with accuracy, yet so narrow there was little danger of arrows from below. Like Camus' Meursault, a name also rooted in death – the leap of death, Kierkegaard's *seliger Sprung in die Ewigkeit*. Standing on this cold stone floor you could almost live in the hearts of the men who'd showered bolts of death on other men five stories below.

At a farmhouse they bought jugs of local red, bread, cheese and a huge rooster whom they trussed like a Muslim captive and brought to the castle in the back of the R4. Looking into his eyes it was clear he knew he was doomed, and the sharp beak he sank into the back of Mick's hand only made Mick like him more. One moment he'd been king among his hens, the next Louis the Sixteenth on the guillotine. But they were hungry and Mick brought the axe down on his neck with a show of insouciance he didn't feel.

The castle kitchen was the size of a train station; in the smallest of several huge fireplaces they skewered the rooster over an oak fire. In the soccer field-sized dining room the finely carved four-hundred-year-old oak table alone was half a basketball court, with carved chairs for over two hundred of one's closest friends. The glittering chandeliers hung on silver chains twenty feet below the carved oak ceiling and twenty feet above the table. In a limestone fireplace in which Monique's R4's could have hidden, a thick oak log burned fiercely but never took the chill off the cavernous corner in which they huddled, thirteen young people having fun yet conscious of the feudal centuries of sorrow, joy, love and fear that had been lived here.

The rooster was so tough Mick thought he'd broken a tooth getting him down, while the others gave him up for a meal of wine and bread. Mick reflected on the rooster's useless sacrifice as he picked out "Talking Blues," and regretting even more they'd wasted him.

Was down in the henhouse, down on my knees
When I thought I heard a chicken sneeze,
But it was just the rooster saying his prayers,
Thankin the Lord for all the hens upstairs

Playing at being young and gallant they'd robbed the rooster's irreplaceable life for nothing; it vinegared the wine that cast red diamonds through cut glass on white linen, rendered illusory the bright herringbone floorboards retreating toward an infinity they could imagine but never reach.

Thinking of Lily it was easy to pick up another song, gentler and more eloquent,

She's the kind of girl you want so much
It makes you sorry,
But you don't regret a single day –

Though he'd never even had a day with her. And never would.

15

THE ENCHANTED CASTLE

DAISY TRIED TO UNDERSTAND the word *sacred*.

Its roots went back to ancient Middle Eastern languages six thousand years ago: *to make holy, consecrate*. But what does that mean, to *make holy*?

What was *holy*, anyway? What made it different from anything else?

Sacred was out of fashion now in the world of universities and research, replaced by a new religion, science. What bothered her was this new religion disavowed recognition of instinct, subconscious, dreams and all the unknown psychological dimensions beyond the textbook.

LSD brought you in direct touch with the sacred. It reminded you that the sacred exists, a vital force that asks you is there a power, an emotion, awareness, linking all these universes? Is there a God? *Gods?* Who do *they* answer to?

For a year she had been studying the human brain and the brains of monkeys, mice, rats, fruit flies, and nematodes, as well as the neurology of single-cell invertebrates, plant cells and very simple life forms, seeking the moment that the brain is formed, a locus in addition to the body's other sensory networks, that links them. The brain that gave rise to the mind. But did it? When?

The virtue to LSD was that you could ask these questions all the way back to the source, to their true meaning, to what she'd before been unable to discover. In this year of brain studies she'd memorized most of it in every detail, understood what the best researchers at Stanford thought about how it worked, on the chemical, cellular, electrical, and mathematical levels.

She sat back in her easy chair, loving the silky fabric, the resilient soft cushions, swung her feet up on the footstool, raised her mug of black coffee from the wooden side table, rejoicing in its many clashing odors and tastes, turned to watch the Cezanne print on the brick wall dance and glitter with life.

The amazing thing about what she'd learned about the brain in laboratories, books and lectures, was exactly what she *saw* on LSD. But what if she was just imagining what she'd already learned? She'd tested it one midnight on acid, looked into a corner of the Purkinje layer, a part of the cerebellum she'd not yet studied, and wandered through its tiny, branched dendrites like a cave explorer under a new mountain. They were called *arbor vitae*, the tree of life, and she could see why, how they climb inside the cortex like branches of a tree.

She'd written it all down while high, made sketches and colored them. Then two days later she'd gone to the library and looked up the Purkinje layer and it was nearly the same, the only difference being that what she'd seen was more detailed than the dissection photos and drawings. Even the microscope slides were fuzzier, less accurate, than what she'd seen on LSD.

She got a container of chocolate ice cream from the fridge and ate it all. It said 8:13 pm on the kitchen clock, sheets of November rain down the sliding doors onto her tiny balcony, car headlights glittering in the street below.

Before she'd come to Stanford, she'd thought California winters were dry and sunny, but here it rained all winter, and sometimes the puddles misted with ice. She thought of rain falling on the dairy farm far back in her childhood, how it froze in the cattle hoofprints, her father's drunken rages, the selling and moving, then moving again – what parts of the brain had determined that?

"White Rabbit" on KMPX; she turned it louder, way louder, entranced by the power of the song, its soaring melodies, the explosive ending. *Feed your head*: for an instant she understood everything – her brain, this kitchen, the rainy world outside with its streets and buildings, grass and people, the vast gangling universe, unending.

That this what she was doing, *feeding her head*.

And thereby feed the world.

With a tinny, alien sound the phone rang. She ate her last spoonful of ice cream and answered it. "Daisy?" a man said.

"You can't tell, by now, my voice?"

"Listen, Daisy, you're a psychologist –"

"Studying to be."

"– I've got a psychological problem."

"You *are* a psychological problem."

"I need some help."

"I'm studying."

"Women won't make love with me."

"Get lost, Tony."

"Just a half hour, really going at it? You'll be able to study better afterward, I promise. You'll be more *on*. And I've got some really good Afghani hash . . ."

She watched inside her brain as the decision was made. A discussion between the amygdala (*Oh please yes*), the nucleus accumbens (*he's right, you can get right back to work*), the hypothalamus (*it might even intensify your perceptions*), though the good old PFC, the prefrontal cortex, that Puritan of our mind, warned that being high on LSD and smoking Afghani hash and making love was likely to take more than thirty minutes, and she might not get back to work for hours.

"You got any chocolate ice cream?"

"No but I'll get some."

Give it an hour, she told herself. *Then back to work.*

. . .

HANDS CUPPED over candles in the wind, Mick and Monique climbed the castle tower's stone spiral stairs five stories to the top. In bed they kept their clothes on till it warmed, and her kisses, fiery and unprincipled as she, drove the dead rooster from his thoughts.

Afterwards they lay cuddling and happy with each other. "My legs are too thin," she said. "Don't you think?"

He slid his palm up the inside of a slender muscular thigh. "Most women'd kill for your legs. You know it."

"You'd say anything –"

"– that's true too."

The icy wind blew through the *meurtrières*, the cross-shaped crossbow slots, reminiscent of dead centuries and people who had lived here. Candle shadows darted over the pitted stone. How long before this skinny sexy girl and he would be dead too, two more shades in this room of shadows? Tomorrow was his birthday, Troy's too, and the terrible fear returned that Troy was in danger. That he had no way to help him didn't make it any easier, just made him feel guilty.

Almost dying in the Sahara he'd learned to follow the path with heart however irrational, going with the blue-painted camel thieves rather than waiting by the sandy track for a ride that would never come. Not to take seriously the human circus and to remember the constant proximity of death as a means of trueing one's path.

Now in this frigid martial tower, this ancient dispenser of death, his infatuation with Lily seemed silly as a radio love song, New York unreal as a bad novel, Virgin Peak imaginary as *Lost Horizons*. Only *here* was real, only *now*, like the throb in his hand from the rooster's beak.

Monique breathed softly in her sleep, her warm bony back against his ribs. Wind keened in the *meurtrières*; candle shadows shivered on the walls and a huge ancient clock struck midnight in the canyoned hallways far below.

At dawn standing naked on the icy stones he scratched bug bites and watched the eastern sky pale from bright orange to pink till the yellow sun edged from far hills of forests, castles and vineyards. From here all was feudal: a dirt track over a Roman stone bridge, a field of new flowers where five horses grazed, slate-roofed stone huts with their wells in stone courtyards where early chickens pecked.

It was easy to see this place a thousand years ago, a young knight watching the same sun rise at the same point in the forested castled hills and thinking of his life to come and what he'd already lived. Just as in the future another person might stand here imagining those here now, and Monique and Mick would be as gone to him as the young knight was to them.

Sun through the *meurtrières* cast flaming arrows down the walls; steadily they sank toward the bed where she slept innocent in her tousled hair and parted lips. He felt tender and fearful for her, that even her tough brilliance would not protect her, no more than it could from these arrows of sun through the *meurtrières*.

This morning he was twenty-four, and it seemed a promise, a totem of life to come, to explore and live deeply, a banquet where he'd already tasted many fine things and the future might offer more. To have this morning in this castle tower on his birthday seemed to herald that life would be equally as unusual, exciting and revelatory.

All day they wandered the castle, hills and forests. The others lowered him on a rope into the *oubliettes*, the forgotten dungeons deep below the castle cellars where English captives from the Hundred Years' War had been chained to the walls to die. The dirt was soft, composed of ancient flesh and nightmares, the air cold and rancid; dust clogged the beam of his flashlight. The walls were stained where chains had rusted away, but of the English knights nothing remained, not a ring or piece of metal nor tooth or fleck of bone.

In the fleshy dirt he found a wine bottle, tied it inside his shirt and climbed the rope, exultant as a diver surfacing with an unopened amphora. The spidery notation on the yellowed label said *Chateau de Lanquais 1867*; through the green handblown glass the wine was golden.

They hung it in the well for dinner but it proved worse than vinegar, as if distilled from the flesh of the long-dead English knights. Instead they drank the local red, danced and sang and wandered late and happily to their quarters with new partners, his the dark-haired Romana, a friendly, athletic, disciplined soul who kept him awake very late, when still drunk they listened to an eerie clink of chains along the stone floors below.

"Oh that's my ancestors killed by Saracens in the battle of Jerusalem," Alexandre explained over a breakfast of bread, honey and coffee. "Their bodies were never brought back, so their souls keep searching, waiting for them to return."

"You don't really believe this?"

"They've never stopped dragging their chains. Night after night, generation after generation of my family, century after century."

In the spirit of such things they tried the last night to levitate a table or make the spirits knock, but a lack of success soon led to laughter, more songs and drunkenness, and wandering the hallways with candles looking for Alexandre's chained ancestors.

In the morning he woke beside Monique, both covered with red itching sores, peppered with them, and as the cold air hit their skin the itch turned to torment.

"*Merde*, it's bedbugs," she said, hopping one-footed to yank on her underpants.

They scrambled down the tower stairs scratching and swearing. To the others it was hilarious. By the time they pulled out of the Dordogne valley the itches had increased ferociously. Mick sat in the Renault's passenger seat unable to move without aggravating them, while Monique drove fanatically, scratching with one hand as she downshifted, upshifted, and steered with the other, except when over-come with a paroxysm of itching that demanded two hands, so steered with her knees while chafing them together in a vain attempt to reduce the stinging there, all which caused the tiny top-heavy car to swerve from side to side like a packhorse chased by wasps, while Romana and Thierry in the rear yelled, "Watch the road!" But watching the road was far beyond Monique's concerns, and the more she itched the faster they went till the dotted line down the middle was a flashing blur and the engine roared like a maddened sewing machine.

There was no position that did not further antagonize and inflame the itches. In a one-café town Monique bought a jug of vinegar and as she drove frantically onward they pulled off their clothes and he rubbed handfuls of vinegar over their bites.

The car's trajectory suffered but they were in ecstasy – no hallucination, not sex, not even sex under the benign influence of mushrooms and champagne, nothing could parallel the rapture and beatitude of acidic vinegar on the fiery itches scraped so intensely raw. The hotter the vinegar burned the faster Monique drove till the wind howled under the windshield like a singed dog and the roadside trees zipped backward like a film accelerating in reverse.

It came up behind from nowhere, a huge motorcycle with flashing blue lights and wailing siren and the unfortunate word *Gendarme* across the front. Mick was naked, Monique in underpants rolled down to her knees. "Go faster!" Romana yelled, but the little Renault had already far exceeded its manufacturer's specifications.

Grabbing for her clothes Monique hit the brakes. As full braking at this speed had also never been considered in the car's design, it immediately swung sideways like a horse in an old western, all four hooves skidding across the pavement, its pack-saddled body tilting toward the oncoming trees. Nearly strangled by the bra round her neck Monique was shoving both feet into one leg of Mick's Levis as she pushed down on the brakes, downshifted and twisted the wheel against the car's spin.

In the stench of aggrieved rubber and dust they came to rest under the spreading boughs of a chestnut tree. For a while the gendarme lingered by his motorcycle as if fearing to approach, a time Mick and Monique spent unsuccessfully untangling clothes and applying them to the naked parts of their bodies. That his and Monique's Levis were indistinguishable led to a mini-tug of war and a few unkind epithets at the unpropitious moment the gendarme reached her window.

"You've committed so many crimes," he sighed, "I don't know where to start."

"It's the bedbugs," Romana said.

He glanced at Thierry and Romana in the back. "You, at least, are dressed."

"We all were," Monique said reasonably, "but . . ."

"I imagine you were." He pulled out a pad and began writing. "At one time or another."

"I can explain," Mick said.

The gendarme's nose wrinkled at Mick's unpalatable accent. "An immigrant." He wrote faster.

"I'm a student –"

His nose wrinkled harder as if Mick had just confessed to the serial rape of elderly widows. He bent down to peer in Monique's window, making her yank Mick's shirt to cover her breasts, which was untimely in that he'd been using it to cover his crotch. "And," he sniffed, "you've been drinking."

"That's vinegar."

"Most local wine is –"

"It's for the itches." She pointed at her chest. "Avert your eyes!"

"*Faire l'amour c'est bien*," he said, "but while driving? I'm sure there's a law against it." He scratched his head under his helmet and peered at Mick. "You Americans do it with other people watching?"

"They weren't," Romana repeated. "It's the bedbugs!"

He peered closer. "I see no bedbugs. Unless it's these two, doing what they should be doing in bed."

Regrettably, putting on clothes made the bites worse. Thus while the gendarme continued to write up Monique for everything he could think of, she and Mick hopped round like demented porcupines, he going so far as to rub his back felicitously up and down the delicious bark of the chestnut tree. Although the gendarme raised his eyes it was clear now nothing would surprise him. He nonetheless refused Monique's pleas to inspect their bites. "I'm no epidemiologist, but if you've got the plague I'm happy to quarantine you." He reflected a moment. "Yes," he smiled for the first time, "for the safety of everyone."

"We got them in bed, last night," Mick said, "it was an old bed, in the tower of a castle, the bedbugs were hungry, they must've been waiting a long time."

"Yes," he nodded, "no doubt."

It was three a.m. when they reached Monique's apartment. It had a bathroom the size of a broom closet with a shower narrow as a gun barrel that they wormed into together and turned the scalding water on full and passed out afoot in the sheer orgasm of it searing their itching inflamed skins.

MILTON GREENE was about five-ten, lean and lithe, scholarly-looking in his steel-rim glasses and balding pate, more an African intellectual than AWOL American. He worked nights as a guard at the Louvre and was getting a PhD in biochemistry at the Sorbonne during the day. A friend of Thierry's, he also worked with American antiwar veterans' groups finding other AWOL Americans places to stay and jobs.

"I miss it, America. I do." He clasped his beer mug in both hands, glanced down at it. "But," he looked at Mick, "I wasn't going to die in that horror for nothing."

"I wouldn't either. That's why I refused."

"Refused? There wasn't a *Refuse* option when I got drafted."

"There is now."

"If you dare use it."

"Yeah, like anything else."

"You have to face yourself, Brother. You have to say *am I just a coward and fleeing, and letting somebody else die in my place*? Or am I refusing because the War's insane and crazy, like asking all young American guys to play Russian roulette, and one in ten of them is going to die? Am *I* crazy, a coward, to refuse *that*? That I won't die for some silliness just to show I love my country?"

Mick chuckled. "You know the answer."

Milton gripped Mick's arm, smiled, let go. "I grew up in Tennessee – you been there? Those lovely rolling hills you see in *National Geographic*?

They go on for miles and miles, in the fall with all the colors it aches your heart, or in the spring shimmering green. Then in Vietnam I watched us destroying this beautiful place just like Tennessee. Man, there were tiger tracks in those hills, and deer and monkeys and boar and a hundred different birds all singing. And in one month we turned it into a charred wasteland, Man, saturated it with thousands and thousands of thousand-pound bombs, there were impact craters on top of impact craters, each one as big as a baseball diamond, miles and miles in all directions. Wasn't a live tree standing, no streams, no animals, no villages."

"That why you quit?"

Milton shook his head slightly. "Six months later, a hill we took." He swallowed. "It took us a month and we lost eighty-seven KIA including my three best friends and over three hundred wounded. Day and night the Air Force bombed that hill and napalmed it and our artillery hit it with everything in Quang Nam Province while we gutted our way up it from blasted tree to shell hole, using our dead buddies as cover, over downed trunks and burning brush and VC mines. D'you know that one in every five American KIA is friendly fire? They won't admit it but it's true. Ask any grunt who's been in a few firefights. Sometimes I was in five firefights a day."

Milton turned to watch two girls coming up from the Métro, tall and thin in very short skirts and leggings and high boots. "Such beautiful women, man." He glanced up at the Panthéon, "what a beautiful place."

Mick grinned. "Fucking best place on earth."

"After we finally took that hill we found twenty-eight dead Charlies. And we'd lost all those guys. Worse thing is we pulled out three weeks later. And Charlie took it back."

"Why?"

"Why'd we pull out? Because nothing in Nam has any strategic value. You just try to gather as many enemy as you can in one place and then try to kill them. Like the Marines say about themselves, it's true of the Army, too – we're *all* bullet sponges." He listened as a church bell rang five. "What a sound, Man – ain't that communion?"

"Then what happened?"

"After we pulled out I got ten days R&R in Melbourne. There's lots of Australians helping our guys get away. I'd been saving my combat pay, my Ma didn't need it, just bought herself a brand-new Buick, so I used the false passport the Aussies gave me to fly to London and took the ferry across and here I am."

"You staying here?"

"In France? Absolutely. This place has given me a new life. And I think what do I owe America? The place that kidnapped and enslaved my ancestors and holds my people down today. That kills great leaders like Jack Kennedy and destroys our neighborhoods and gives us terrible schools then makes a joke of our stupidity, our poverty. That sends us to kill innocent people in useless places – why do I need *that*?"

"When Kosygin went to Hanoi to try and negotiate a peace, we bombed it on purpose. Did you know that?"

"Fuck no." Milton rubbed his shorn head in frustration. "No, I didn't know."

"Nixon's trying hard as he can to destroy peace. And that evil little troll Kissinger. It's coming out now, that in the '68 elections Nixon convinced the South Vietnamese to sabotage Lyndon Johnson's peace effort. Nixon didn't want peace, it would lower his chances of being elected."

Milton drew a ten-franc note from his pocket, put it on the table. "In Tennessee I couldn't eat in the same room as white people. Couldn't ride the same part of the bus, go to the same hotel, piss in the same toilet. What I *did* have a right to do was go somewhere else to kill people and get killed." He shrugged. "What I *do* owe my country is the deepest moral response I can make."

"And the Revolution?"

"Ain't comin, Brother. Forget it."

"C'mon – how many riots last year? Two hundred? The Army coming apart, drugs 'n rock'n roll are telling all these young guys to stay alive. Maybe it's time."

Milton gave him an exasperated glance. "The Revolution won't come till the average working man doesn't have a job." He sat back, palms wide on the café table. "In this life, what I care about is my girl-friend Lamia just like she cares about me, and I try to help every person I see, and I'm getting my degree in biochem because I love it, I love how the world fits together on the molecular level. And that and marrying Lamia and having kids are all that matters to me. I decided not to die for nothing in Nam, and I'm not dying for nothing in some revolution either."

Mick grinned. "Not even for the betterment of man?"

Milton chuckled deeply. "Yeah, Brother. Not even for the better-ment of man. Or of women either." He nodded at the Panthéon's golden globe in the late afternoon light. "From our bedroom window I can look out on that beautiful building – where all these wise people are enshrined. France is a society that tries to live by wisdom, justice and love – how can you not dig that?"

MICK OPENED LILY'S *Zorba* the next night. The Paris rain had made him hungry for Crete's ardent sea and wild mountains, a synthesis of the ancient dialectic between the timorous introverted engineer and wild Macedonian genius, the fearful mind versus wine women and song, The Thinker versus Dionysius. Inside the back cover she had written, *Ce livre appartient à Lily de Lanzac, 21 rue de Grenelle, Paris 7ème*.

It was two-ten a.m. He walked through the rain to the 7th and down Rue de Grenelle to number 21, a high iron gate in a stone wall. Soaked, he walked back to the hotel and returned at seven to Lily's and sat in a corner café drinking *grandes crèmes* with brandy till he warmed up. After eight the iron gate swung open on a tall manor house beyond a cobbled courtyard. A silver Mercedes slid out, Lily in the passenger seat, a man driving, two kids in back. The gate shut.

That afternoon and the next he returned to the café. He was angry with himself for ignoring Paris; he should be going to museums, seeing the monuments, was ashamed he cared for neither. Instead he was bugging a married woman ten years older he barely knew. To her what could he be but a callow American? The café was full of busy people living full lives and he was a purposeless outsider.

When she passed on the sidewalk he leaped up knocking over his beer. She was ahead, a woven shopping bag over one shoulder. She went into a cheese shop; he went further and turned back, waited till she came out. She stopped, open-mouthed, caught herself, angry. "Follow me," she said in English. "Not too near."

She turned down a side street, entered an apartment building and stood in the shadowed lobby facing him, eyes black with fury. "Can't you be happy with what you got? Do you always want more?"

"Lily I've missed you –"

"Missed *what*? Your fantasy? You don't *know* me!"

Under her anger was something intangible, kindness or understanding. "I want to see you, talk with you. What harm can it do?"

"You don't care about *me*, that I could have trouble with my husband –"

"On the plane you didn't care either," he said nastily.

She bit her lip. "I was stupid, the plane."

"It was lovely. Please?"

She laughed scornfully. "And if I don't you'll pester me?"

"If you tell me no, I won't ever come to you again."

She glanced at the empty doorway. "You are going soon?"

"To Crete, as instructed."

She half-smiled, squeezed his hand. "Where do you stay?"

"Hotel Montesquieu, seventy-two Boulevard Raspail. Room eleven."

"Tomorrow, after two. I'll come for a few minutes. But that's it." Darting forward she kissed him hard and backed away. "Don't ever follow me again."

"**WHEN THE RICH** no longer need you," Thierry dunked a sugar cube in his espresso and chewed it, "they throw you away."

"But she's *there*, beneath it all, I care about her."

"Would you," Thierry smiled, "if she were Monique? A factory girl?"

"Monique went to the Sorbonne. She's better educated than I."

"Admit it, with Lily there's something you'll never have. She'll never give."

Mick waited for a bus to rumble past the café. "We can never give ourselves completely."

"But most of us try. People like Lily, they make sure we never have them all."

"To make us want them more?"

"Because they never spend their principle. Only their interest. Because they'll never risk their hearts."

"The rich don't gamble, that's what you're saying."

"Why should they? They have everything to lose, and nothing to gain they don't already have."

SHE CAME at two o'clock exactly, smiled at his cramped bare room, the metal-frame single bed with its skinny mattress. "How romantic. You should write poetry." Her body lithe and tight as a dancer's came into his arms, her pelvis hard against him. She bit his chin. "No falling in love, all that *merde*! Just *fuck* me!"

They lay sweaty and panting on the squeaky bed, her body golden in the late afternoon light. There was so much to say, to ask, so little time. With a fingertip he traced a bead of sweat between her breasts. "I can't tell you how lovely you are."

"No," she said, "you can't."

He grinned. "You are so lovely you spin my head with joy. I want to stay in Paris, see you every week –"

"No, this is *it*, my beautiful boy. The last time."

"I want you so much –"

"You keep talking of what *you* want. As if that was all."

"So what do *you* want?"

"Of course I'd love to see you, often, often. I would love to teach you how to make love, not this quick boyish humping like a rabbit.

And that making love without oral sex is like dinner without wine. But never again. You are absolutely delectable, like *foie gras*. But one cannot live on *foie gras*. It will kill you."

"Can't I be your lover?"

"Lovers are discreet, my darling."

"I can be discreet."

She laughed. "Maybe I will put you in a book. The delectable boy who tried to be discreet. Women love that."

Angry, he pulled back. "Don't act so damn superior –"

"I'm just a little girl who married who her family wanted, and he married who his family wanted. What is it you Americans say – it is my bed so I must lay on it?"

"*Why?*" Fury choked him.

"What I was trained to do: marry someone from an old family like mine."

"Trained by *who?*"

"We're the Old Guard, darling boy. We survived the Revolution and got our castles back. We run the government and big companies and best schools and we don't let outsiders in unless they have power too. Some people buy a fake '*de*' for their names when they've made a fortune, but that never changes who they are. Ours is real."

He pulled her tighter. "You sound so lonely."

She seemed to listen to the traffic outside. "That is mean, to say."

"Because I say it? Or because it's true?"

"Both."

He kissed the edge of her lips. "I'm sorry."

"For what you said? Or for me?"

"Both."

"You bastard." She sat up, hand on his thigh. "You have so much to learn."

"Teach me."

"Life will." She reached across his chest to check her watch on the bedside table, rolled atop him. "We can do it once more, then I go. But slower this time, enjoying every touch, every second. I will show you how to make love without moving . . ."

When she had gone he sat for a long time in his tacky room, his body drained, rain beating on the ancient single panes, the heat pipes banging, the sounds and lights of evening traffic outside, a chill setting in.

Her fragrance filled the room, his tousled bed; on her *Zorba* he could smell her; tangled in his sheets were the crimson underpants she'd worn beneath her cream-white tights, he could taste her cunt in them.

The timbre of her voice against his throat, the taste of her in orgasm and joy, the long slow loving she had taught, her intense abandon and opening to him, a caring for him and a sharing of her most honest self. How could she not want him again?

She *did* want him, she'd said so. And said she never would.

It was only because he couldn't have her that he wanted her so much. No, that wasn't true, for even the thought of her hollowed his heart. "Lily," he kept saying to bring her back, pacing the cold room and glancing through the rainy window, seeing nothing. He was being silly. Hardly knew her. *Hated* this place.

That night while he and Monique and two others were putting up Gisèle posters in a street behind Montparnasse Station a gang of de Gaulle's enforcers attacked them with steel pipes, smashing Monique's car and sending him and Monique to the emergency room for stitches. In the hospital the police arrested him for disorderly conduct and gave him twenty-four hours to leave France. He cleared out his room, threw away his bloody shirt and caught the midnight train to Belgrade.

16

CAGED WOLF

TROY CAUGHT SU LI leaving her school, clad in a simple white *ao dai*, books piled in her arms, barefoot children capering round her and calling in singsong voices. Her face went from shock to anger when she saw him. "I no want with you," she said when the children moved away. "Not no more."

"Why?" He ached to hold her. "What did I do?"

"Nothing you didn't do." The wind wisped her sable hair at her cheek; her face was the epitome of life, loveliness and love: if she would love him he'd be happy for life, *they* would be happy for life. Her beauty made him tremble, powerless – not her physical beauty for it was simply a metaphor for the beauty *of* her. "It's me," she added. "Not good for me with you."

He held her hand, wouldn't let go. "Because I might get killed?"

Tugging her hair aside she smiled, as if death were not the issue. "Anybody get killed, these days. Everybody die all time. But I no like you no more."

It wasn't possible. For weeks when they were together her eyes had followed his every motion; she'd smiled when he smiled, squeezed his hand in happiness just because he looked at her. Was he *crazy*? Because he'd been an orphan maybe he didn't know how people show love? But growing up in Mick's family he'd seen lots of love; when people love each other they can't hide it, and in Su Li's dark eyes he'd seen so much love. "Your family, they don't want you with an American?"

She shook her head, almost tearful. "No. Not my family."

She tried to pull away; he gripped her. "I *won't* let you go."

She took a soft breath. "Wasting your time with me when someday I am killed."

He ached to snatch her from whatever might hurt her. "I'll send you to the States, your whole family – I've got money saved, you can stay with my brother, my sister, till my tour's up. Please, Su Li, be honest: don't you love me?"

"No." She looked at him across a great distance. "I hate you. Never you come here again or to my mother's house. Never look to find me again. Or I will tell the bad people to shoot you."

"Bad people?"

"Viet Cong. I hate them too. But I hate you more."

YUGOSLAVIA was wild and beautiful, the people warm. "We're mixed cultures, races, and religions," a man said to Mick in Belgrade, "so we get along. A symbol of what the world should be –"

Lily drove him onward; there was nowhere to stop that he didn't think of her, nowhere far enough away. At night he could think of nothing but her in bed with her husband. He'd never seen one of her books, or tried to find it in the bookstore – why? Did he care for her at all? Or as she'd said was he just caught up in his own fantasy of love?

Hitching south from Belgrade there was rain and wind and crazy drivers, a trucker who missed a tree by maybe an inch, knocking off the mirror by Mick's elbow, a German motorcyclist who kept yelling back at him, "You are *not* leaning enough" on the insane hundred mile-an-hour curves he took nearly horizontal to the asphalt. There were gap-toothed peasants who had come down from the hills to earthquake-toppled Skopje, women with huge loads of sickle-cut hay on their backs, old men in wooden shoes gambling and smoking hookahs, some people so poor its fear burned in their eyes along with a stupefaction at cars and roads and the smell of food everywhere.

Skirting Albania the road snaked through the conifered peaks of northern Greece. It was snowing hard and getting dark; a farmer let him out and turned west on a dirt road. With disquiet Mick watched his taillights fade into the slanting snow and wink out. He was alone in the near-silent hiss of snowfall and an icy wind from the peaks.

For an hour he stood hoping someone would come up the dirt road. His feet were numb. He cursed himself for not asking the farmer if he could stay with him. As the snow deepened above his knees he realized no more cars would pass that night.

He could see only about fifty yards yet everything seemed half-visible in the moonlight behind the clouds. After hours of walking the road began to climb. To the right was a valley of pure white that sloped down to a rim of dark firs and a stone building with deep snow on its roof.

It was a small sheep barn smelling of clean straw. The roof was five feet at the highest, the stone walls two feet thick. In a moonlit window he ate his last roll and candy bar and lay half-awake in the soft warm straw watching the misty snow fill up the universe. This, he thought, was the happiest night of his life, and he wished every other being on earth could be safe and warm as he.

Late the next day he reached Salonika, full of diesel fumes and noise. On his way to a cheap hotel he cut through the zoo. Out of a cage two yellow eyes caught his.

A wolf, huge and chocolate brown. His cage was too small to turn around, and fouled with his shit. A few chunks of spoilt meat lay in a puddle of urine by the door. Although it was late afternoon it was still hot; he stood panting, tongue hanging, long-haired belly huffing.

Likos, the plastic sign beneath the cage said. *Jugoslavia*.

Mick knelt before the cage and talked to him. He looked straight back into Mick's eyes, and in his eyes burned all the bitter irony of seeing humans not only as they thought they were, but as they were.

Mick bought three hot dogs at a nearby stand and when no one was looking slid them through the wire. The wolf ate them instantly and kept watching him. *Are you alive?* his eyes challenged. *Are you different from the others? Will you do it?*

He bought a crowbar in a plumbing store and stuffed it down his backpack. Near the port he ate in a cheap restaurant full of aging whores then waited in his room till ten. There were still people in the street; a tourist with a backpack would not be out of place. When the sidewalk was empty he climbed the wall into the zoo, crossed between the lion and tiger cages. A big cat rumbled deep in its throat. *I'd like to let you out too.*

The wolf stood. Mick put his hand against the wire, letting him sniff it. The wolf huffed once, waiting.

The door had a large padlock bolted into the frame. Mick slid the crowbar under it and levered the hasp free. When it popped the wolf backed up, growling. Holding the crowbar in defense Mick moved to the side of the cage and swung the door open.

For a moment the wolf did not move. Then he scrambled out and landed with a grunt on his belly. He staggered a little, caught his balance, limped across the open ground between the cages, broke into a lope then a run, and vanished northwards toward the mountains he had watched so long and hopelessly through his cage.

Later in bed Mick worried where the wolf was. Had he been hit by a car? Did he know the way home? Could he feed himself on the way?

Was it better to be free at risk of death than locked in a cage? Wasn't this the dilemma of all humans everywhere?

At dawn there was little traffic; the south wind beat the ocean to whitecaps and made the yellow and gold roadside flowers swing crazily. A gray Mercedes decelerated; the driver leaned over and lowered the passenger window. "*E kaliste?*"

"Athens."

"I am going part way," the man said in French. "To Larissa."

The interior of the car was warm and bright from the sun and smelled of leather, wool and cigarettes. Scents of dry stones, green sage and countless flowers blew through the open window. "It is your first time to Athens?" the man said. "How lucky you are! My first time was in the War. But I have never forgotten how it felt."

"To see the ruins?"

"No, *kyrios*, the life. The city is alive, and the first time, is entrancing."

"But you don't live there?"

"I live in Salonika because of my business. I am a wine merchant to foreign countries. I must stay close to the vineyards."

He wanted to talk about Vietnam and what was wrong with America. "France is not a democracy either," Mick said, thinking of de Gaulle's police.

"It's a Greek word, *democratia:* 'the people rule'. But we don't have it either in Greece. How can we speak of the people's rule when so many live in poverty? In ignorance and fear?"

"Won't Papandreou make a change?"

"Believe me, they won't let him."

"Who?"

"There will be no elections. Instead a police state. Backed by you Americans."

"That's bullshit."

The road crossed a stream. To the left the land opened in a delta to the flat far sea. To the right the stream came down a barren rocky canyon. "It's the Vale of Tempe," the man said. "Famous from the ancient poets as the home of Apollo the Sun. Now is very different. Just like democracy. Once there were many pine trees and the poets said the scent of flowers was entrancing."

They stopped at a small café for coffee and retsina. The man raised his glass, a quick toast, the sun casting pink prisms. "You like this wine?"

"It's bitter."

"Once it was this way because we used pine pitch to caulk the casks. Now we make it in stainless steel tanks and add resin flavor to pretend it's still the old days."

"Like democracy?"

He smiled. "I'm freer than most Greeks, have a car, some money.

It's possible for me to find freedom, but when the CIA takes over, I will be among the first imprisoned."

"Why?"

"In World War Two I fought against the Italians, then the Germans. When the War was over I joined the Resistance and fought against the Army, the British and Americans. I am a Socialist." He leaned forward. "I believe in Greece!"

His name was Karides. Georgiou Karides. He drove twice a month from Salonika to Larissa. "You don't tire of it?" Mick said.

"I *live* for it. Each trip the land is not the same, the earth and sky change color, the wind tastes different. And I have my friend who comes from Athens to meet me in Larissa. I'm lucky to have such things to live for."

"Only for these things?"

"A few hours a month? We are lucky to have that."

"Sometimes I try to make every moment count; other times there's nothing."

"When you're older you'll understand that when you were young you had everything to live for but didn't live enough. But with age only a few things remain. You want to know why people pray? Because everything's insufficient. Everything we have serves only to show us what we lack. We're always wanting."

"What?"

"What is unavailable." Karides pointed at the road ahead. "If a truck comes at us now, straight at us, wouldn't you pray it didn't hit us?"

The railroad station was in the center of Larissa, a brutally loud and filthy city. "I'll get my friend," Karides said, returning with a young dark-haired woman with full lips and lowering eyes who spoke no English. "Sophy wants to know do you like Greece," he said. "She says come with us to Olympus. It's on your way to Athens."

Where the road climbed into the mountains Karides stopped to buy dates and wine. The car radio was playing bouzouki music; the sun's heat made the colors of the flowers dance against the bone-white rocks and dusty greens. Like the land, time expanded in an all-engulfing animal moment.

The road ended at a crumbling yellowed church half-buried in the rocks. Brush climbed its walls; dusty trees leaned over its door. Stone walls circled an overgrown orchard of stooped wrinkled apple trees bright with blossoms.

Inside the church was springlike and cool. It was empty and poorly lit by spider-webbed clerestory windows. Mike opened an oak door into the orchard and sun poured in. The air vibrated with flies and bees and the *churr* of cicadas. He walked to the end of the orchard where a yellow stone wall ran along a cliff and the mountain dropped to a maze of treetops and white boulders and shimmering sea.

Karides walked away along the yellow stone wall dappled gold beyond the white and pink blossoms and green leaves. Soon the heavy grass and low boughs hid him and silenced his steps. The sun beat on Mick's back and on the church wall and heated the perfume of the flowers to a gold intensity.

Sophy came up behind him, half-shadowed by leaves, sun splashing fire on her hair and white blouse. She held out her hand, her palm cool as the inside of the church. She moved against him, breasts against his shoulder. "What about Karides?" he said. She smiled and tossed a glance downhill, toward the sea wall.

In the ardent sun and flowers and vibrant perfumed hum of bird and insect life, desire pulsed in the air and throbbed in the music and wind and smelled like apple blossoms and was pure bursting heat inside his body, a coma of passion brought on by Greece, by Aphrodite's omnipresent musk perfuming the white-hot soil and wine-dark sea, by the heady drunkenness of ouzo, retsina and sun. It felt so wonderful to kiss her, her body hard against him, her tongue deep in his throat.

Karides came back through the apple trees smiling at them. They drove down from Olympus in a pollen haze, Sophy in the middle, her thigh against Mick's. He felt excited by her and guilty to Karides for having kissed her. For an unknown reason the words in Spanish came into his head, *con rumbo desconocido* – with destination unknown, bringing a sudden promise and joy in floating free of goals, free to live.

Karides stopped at a ruined castle cantilevered over the sea. As they wandered the toppled walls alive with bright green fragrances, white flowers, yellow lizards and singing insects Mick tried but could not imagine the lives of those who once had paced these battlements staring out to sea for danger or deliverance, in winter's chill and summer's heat, dreaming of home and loved ones, of a past that would not come again.

They drove on, southeast. Athens was now too far to reach tonight. Karides offered dinner and a room in the little hotel where they were staying by the sea. They had fish fresh from the boats, fine white cold retsina, tomatoes, feta, olives, rough dark bread, peaches and Greek coffee. Sophy was moody and silent, Karides fatigued from speaking French. Mick left them on the terrace under the stars and went to bed.

An hour later Karides knocked at Mick's door. "Sophy wants you." He spoke in a tone of defeat. "I try to satisfy her, but she insists . . ."

In the windowed moonlight he could make out her form on the bed. Under the sheets she was nearly naked, just a little white shift. He dropped his clothes and slipped in beside her, Karides on her far side. She gripped him like a drowning swimmer and in moments he was inside her, riding an enraged explosive desire that had heated him for hours. She was moaning and crying in Greek and he could hold back no more, seeing as he came the muscles of her outstretched neck marbled by moonlight. He fell aside and Karides mounted her, his rear twitching fast under the sheets, and it made Mick nearly laugh at how small and ludicrous this motion seemed against the earthshaking rhapsody of the feelings it induced. Soon she yelled out in glorious despair and Mick grabbed his clothes and barefooted it to his room.

It was hard to sleep. He felt transgressed, guilty. What he'd done seemed vulgar. Nausea undulated in his gut; he tried not to think. Sex was an affair of jiggling rear ends, lurid as its secretions, pathetically Pavlovian. As he fell asleep the words came and stayed with him all night: *That which you have is not what you must have.*

Lily was dead to him now; what he'd done made him less worthy somehow. But why? What had been wrong with it?

She'd probably done it too.

NO POINT IN LOVING a musician, Tara told herself. Because no matter how much he loves you he'll never be faithful. Not even close.

She leaned up on one elbow to look at Luis, hairy and muscular, naked and big-cocked spread out on her bed. How he warmed her, not only the hot sex but more how he cared for her, respected her, was awed but not overwhelmed by her talent.

But no matter how much they loved each other they were never going to make it longtime. Music uses you up and spits you out – jazzed out, raw, weary, addicted and alone. Never together. It would never be a forty-year marriage in the suburbs. Which was better? She didn't know. Probably this.

"I can love you all I want, Baby," he'd told her, "but I ain't gonna turn down all these gorgeous babes come wantin to fuck me after a show. All these that comes to the warehouse door while we're practicing, these long blonde reporters come seekin me out, want to talk about what it's like growin up in East Harlem and how did I get turned on to the guitar and can they slip down their panties and fuck me? You think I crazy? A chance to eat blonde pussy and red-haired pussy and every other kind a glorious pussy, when someday soon I'm gonna be some old guy was famous once and no chick's gonna want to ball me – so till then how can you blame me?"

She laughed at the comedy of it. "I love you anyway. We just aren't going places –"

He gripped her, almost angrily. "Hell, Baby, ain't nowhere to go. Just *this* minute, *this* hour, you and me on *this* bed, that's all we have. Or you and me in some crazy concert, you and me in the airplane going to the next concert, in that fuckin bus, snorting coke with Blade and days and nights of practice and studio and sometimes I think I going crazy, why no go back to East Harlem, make good money selling goods on the street, why do I bother this shit? I can play guitar at home – nobody needs to hear me!"

She clasped his arms, nuzzled into him thinking *okay I'll fuck other guys too. Even if I don't want to.* "Everybody needs to hear you, Honey. Everybody."

"There's two roads in life: classical or rock'n roll: are you going to map it all out and read the notes, or let the music drive you and live and learn through it? You know which road is right. I'm going down the right road, Babe. Till I die."

She had just turned twenty-two and was going down the right road too, though not the same as Luis. I'm way too young, she kept telling herself, for anything permanent. Not that she wanted that. But it *was* hot, this love with Luis, and with Blade too when it happened.

She was going to have to do better at separating sex and love. Have fun with one, avoid the other.

For a while now she'd been realizing, after she'd sung and wasn't happy with it: you're bridling yourself, girl. You're holding something in, not letting go. If music really is your God, you're going to have to get more into it.

Get deeper.

Get true.

Luis' soaring solos reaching for God.

If God would only listen.

17

———

DEMOCRATIA

TEN DOLLARS bought a third-class ticket from Piraeus to Crete, same as Mick had paid for fourth class from Oran to Marseille five years before. The waves ran alongside the ferry like phosphorescent porpoises, the wake spread out behind to infinity, his destination dark and invisible before him. He woke early to the late-night lights of Heraklion like a burning ship on the horizon.

It took all day to hitch to the east end of Crete. After Sitia the road became two cart ruts through fields of blood poppies. Fifteen kilometers to Vai, the last driver had said, pointing to the eastern mountains and making an up-and-over motion with his hand.

The sun was luxurious, poppies dancing in a fragrant wind. He followed the cart ruts for miles then crossed toward a saddle in the bony mountains, sat on a rock ledge and played guitar for hours. He now understood that he was seeking, and that *that* was the purpose which had driven him here so erratically. But *what* was he seeking?

The war of life could end only in defeat. Yet he could not stop trying to understand, find the right way, for himself and the world. Was *that* life's purpose?

At dusk he reached a clump of weathered huts that a raw-faced old woman said was Vai. She sold him some rough cheese, dry bread, and

211

two bottles of retsina. Two miles further, goat trails led to a short beach backed by palm trees ragged in the wind.

It was dark and spitting rain. He tented his two ponchos under a palm, lit a fire of fronds, feasted on bread, cheese, and wine, rolled up in his sleeping bag, and listened to the waves thunder on the beach and the wind gnash the palms. Every time he felt lonely he reminded himself how many times he'd been alone and come out fine.

Next day the body surfing was lovely, six-foot waves that rose three hundred yards out and fell apart at the shore. At night the stars rose straight out of the depths, dulled by no lights except the occasional firefly glow of a freighter far at sea.

One afternoon in the hills, sleeping and reading in a hollow of honeysuckle and sage, the warm sky striped with taffeta clouds, he came on a passage in *Under Fire* of a French soldier in World War I who got leave from the trenches to be with his wife for the first time in a year and a half. But she couldn't get a travel permit so they barely saw each other, having only one night in a room full of soldiers, and on the next assault he was killed.

What had persuaded that poor soldier to relinquish his freedom so completely? Anyone who went to Vietnam equally lost his freedom. With a shock he sat up, it suddenly seemed so clear: *the sovereignty of the individual can be guaranteed and protected only by the individual.* And any reliance of the individual on the group to ensure his or her own freedom is doomed. *Because the group doesn't want you to be free.*

A whole philosophy could spin from this thought: assure your own freedom first, being sure in the process not to lessen the freedom of others. John Stuart Mill again. But what of those who cannot get free – the caged wolves, the disenfranchised, the poor? The Nepali porters who labor like Sisyphus till they die, never free of other peoples' burdens that they must carry over the mountains – what chance did *they* have to be free?

But another person's slavery was no reason to enslave yourself. Try to help them but not join them. Or did *democratia* mean the rule of the people *over* the individual? If so, what value was it?

Not that most humans seemed free. They traveled in a little ambit like a prisoner's exercise routine from a home owned by a bank, in a car owned by a bank, to work for someone else, to home, to work, with other duties thrown in – meetings, church, shopping – to home, to work *ad nauseam*, with just enough variety thrown in – weekends, television, vacations – to convince them they were not truly slaves.

And wasn't the purpose of school to teach them to lower their dulled heads into the yoke? In Calcutta mothers maimed their children so they'd always have an income as beggars – so did not parents elsewhere maim their children with soul-crippling school so they'd always have a chance to fit into the heart-numbing drudgery of work?

It was early April; that he'd soon be out of money filled him with despair. To be free to wander, follow the surf, screw lovely women, climb mountains, play music, travel unknown paths, explore the mystery of life. Instead of being buffeted from job to job, trying to eke out private freedom in the wash of imposed tasks and events. Was there a path that was free, where time was your own to wander and live?

One thing was clear: to be free you could not live like other people.

The wolf. *You gave him his freedom, and now he's trying to give you yours.*

FROM THE SPINE of the Cretan peaks he could see the fishing village of Sitia, tiny white boats moored in the bay. He hiked down and ate fresh tomatoes with feta, octopus, and lamb stew in a café on the harbor as the sun set, drinking retsina and trying to understand the freedom that had seemed so clear at Vai.

The café owner, short and wiry, spoke some English. He nodded at Mick's guitar. "You play some music?"

"I don't know any Greek music –"

"We already know Greek music." He put a bottle of ouzo on the table. "Can you play Beatles?"

The café filled. Men kept coming up and toasting him as he played and he had to toast them back, and some people were dancing and others telling stories and singing in Greek along with him. Someone brought out a bouzouki and tried to teach him Greek songs on the guitar but he was too drunk to remember so they taught him Greek dances, going dizzily round in a circle arm in arm, someone waving a red kerchief.

There was a word for it, this deep vein of fun that tickled your bones and made you grin so hard your jaw ached, the fellowship with others, the commonness. You understood others and they understood you and you all valued and cared for each other. You were all human.

The starry night faded over the eastern hills. "We all come to my house," the café owner said. Mick climbed with others into the back of his red Datsun pickup and fell asleep on a living room couch.

Someone was shaking his shoulder, speaking fast. The café owner. "Wake up! The Army's grabbed the government. Soldiers coming."

Mick sat up thick-headed, still drunk, looking for Troy. The sunny living room with its bright icons, Formica table, and plain pine furniture spun nauseously. The café owner shook him. "Hurry! Hurry!" he hissed. "The soldiers are arresting everyone!"

Mick stumbled to his feet. "What will *you* do?"

"Take my family to the mountains. Like the time of the Germans. You go on the bus to Heraklion. Is better for you. Ten minutes!"

Mick caught the bus as it was pulling out. The driver waved his hand away when he pulled out drachmas. Everyone sat stony-faced. The bus chugged slowly across the countryside of rocky hill farms, prairies of poppies, bony-white cliffs and ridges notched with steep valleys opening on the sea. Still drunk, he fell asleep.

Something jabbed his shoulder. A black rifle. A soldier. "Passport!"

The bus had stopped. Other soldiers stood in the aisles taking people's papers. Mick fumbled for his passport. It was American, after all – what was to fear?

On the rifle's barrel was stamped *Bridgeport, Connecticut*. The soldier handed back his passport. "You airport. Go away."

Mick nodded. Facing the deadly hole in the rifle barrel he would have agreed to anything. Other soldiers pushed four people off the bus and stood them at the side of the road by a puddle of shiny new blood.

Twice more soldiers stopped the bus and took people off. On the boat going from Heraklion to Piraeus people stayed in their cabins or clustered below in silence. At Piraeus soldiers took away a truckload of passengers. Not daring to risk the youth hostel, he took a bus to the Plaka and found a hotel on Odos Apollonos, street of the Sun God.

The streets were jammed with people protesting the coup. He went down Odos Apollonos to Syntagma Square where people were dancing and singing the songs the new military government had banned. A young man named Nikos borrowed Mick's guitar and sang for the crowd songs about *eleutheria*, freedom, and love, till cars with flashing lights drove into the crowd, big white Chevys with shotguns bracketed on the dashboards and caged rear windows, cops swinging clubs into people trapped by the crowd, everyone screaming and running. One cop knocked Nikos down and smashed Mick's guitar on ancient marble steps and as Mick grabbed it the cop swung his club straight into Mick's mouth. They drove away beating up Nikos in the back seat of the police car, and Mick stood spitting blood, the broken guitar neck in his hand, strings dangling.

Someone grabbed his arm. "Let's go!" A stocky guy with tangled russet hair and beard, three cameras hanging from his neck.

Mick spit blood. "Bastard broke my guitar. Broke my goddamn tooth."

"Hurry or they'll break your forkin neck. And they'll take my film!" They ran through the back streets to the Plaka and stopped in an open café. "I'm Johann," he panted, holding out a roughened muscular hand.

"You Brit?"

Johann looked offended. "Netherlands. Who was that guy they took?"

Mick ordered four ouzos. "Nikos, said his name was."

"They're going to kill him –"

They downed their ouzos and went to the police station. "I'm a photographer from *Life*," Johann told the cops. The cops checked downstairs but said there was no Nikos.

"You work for *Life*?" Mick said as they stepped into the street.

"Nah. Sent them pictures once, bastards didn take em. The only thing'll save Nikos now is they think we're going to publicize it."

"It's an internal Greek affair," said the man with a crewcut and a tie with little purple ducks at the US Embassy. "We don't meddle in other countries' politics."

"You bastards set up this whole coup," Mick snapped, swollen-mouthed. "At least let one innocent person go –"

"May I see your passport?"

Mick stood. "Fuck you. And fuck your fucking coup."

They ran back to the police station. In the basement they could hear a woman screaming. "Tonight," a soldier said. "You can talk to him tonight."

"I'm filing my story this afternoon," Johann said.

"Fuck your story," the soldier said.

AFTER MIDNIGHT a guard brought Nikos in handcuffs. His face was beaten and swollen. He didn't want to see them, as if their visit could make things worse. Johann told him about *Life*. "There's so many people in here," Nikos said. "Don't worry for me."

"You've got the wrong guy," Mick told an officer. "He's very pro-American, translates for *Life* magazine. We're the biggest anti-Communist publication in the United States. You've made a mistake – let him go and we'll forget about it. But if you keep him any longer I'll ask the owner of *Life* to call President Johnson."

"We have that magazine here," the officer said, suddenly conciliatory.

A little after two a.m. they left the station with Nikos and sent him home in a cab. "Find another place to stay," Johann told him, "till this blows over."

"Without freedom we have nothing," Nikos said. "The ancients called this *katastasis* – the moment before the catastrophe."

"I'll get the bastards back," Mick said. "For my guitar."

"Once you kill music," Nikos said, "fascism is next."

"If I fly out they'll take my film at the airport," Johann said. "So I'm going by train to Istanbul, stay at the Hilton, send the film to Amsterdam from there."

"I'll go with you to Salonika," Mick said. "Someone there I want to see."

CROWDS WERE RIOTING in Salonika, running the streets ahead of the soldiers, breaking windows and overturning cars. Police were beating photographers and people they grabbed off the sidewalks. There were blood smears on walls and sticky red puddles on the sidewalks.

Georgiou Karides' address and number was in the Salonika phone book but his phone didn't answer. The memory of him in his gray pinstripe, his caring politics and sad kindness, his existentialist awareness of tragedy, his hunger for honor and freedom that seemed as organic to him as the scrub hinterlands of his native land, all made Mick fear he was dead, that like the warriors at Thermopylae he too would place principal over life.

Rifles were firing, their echoes clattering through the streets. A car horn was honking, loud and steady like an aggrieved animal. Karides' gate was locked and the broken glass stuck in the top of his wall made it difficult to climb. Mick knocked at a neighbor's, a short man about fifty-five with a halo of long gray hair round a bald pate.

"They went to the country. They're safe. Now you – go away!" the man said in English with a quick glance at the canvas-sided US Army trucks disgorging soldiers down both sides of the street.

He tried to shut the door but Mick blocked it. He yanked Mick inside. "I don't want trouble. I'm a surgeon. I just want to do my job."

Rifles hammered on the door. The man opened it and three soldiers shoved in, followed by an officer. "Why you here?" he asked Mick in English.

"I'm going to Istanbul. I was afraid of the rioting, knocked at this man's door."

The officer yelled something in Greek. "What'd he say?" Mick asked the surgeon who did not look at him or answer. Two soldiers pulled him out to a truck. A soldier sitting on the truck's back bumper pointed a rifle at his face. "I'm American!" Mick yelled, raising a hand as if to deflect the bullet and trying not to look scared. The soldier laughed and pulled the trigger. It made a little *snick*, a firing pin on an empty chamber.

In the back of the truck two men in blue working clothes with bleeding faces lay unconscious. A teenage girl huddled in the corner. Through the open back Mick could see the soldiers working down both sides of the street.

The soldiers got in the truck. It drove east, afternoon sun bright through the canvas. "Where are we going?" Mick said in English but no one looked at him or answered. He tried to slow his heart. He was American – why would they shoot him?

The truck stopped. The door slammed and the officer came to the rear. He called out something and the girl silently climbed down. "You!" he said in English. "Out!"

A lonely field of half-barren furrows, a distant ditch and olive trees. "Hurry!" the officer screamed. With the resignation of the doomed Mick climbed over the side.

"That way," the officer pointed, "the border."

The truck rumbled away. Mick felt exuberant with relief and torn with guilt for the two men in the rear. The girl sat in the dirt, arms clenched round her legs, weeping into her knees. He crouched beside her. "What happened?" She swung an arm hitting his face with the back of her wrist, crying and talking.

"*Ochi*," she kept weeping, "*Ochi*".

He remembered it meant no. "*Ochi?*" he said stupidly. "What, *ochi?*"

Again she swung at him, burst anew into tears. As he stood he saw a line of blood down her thigh and calf, till she wrapped her skirts closer and shouted angrily, waving her hand eastward, down the road.

He walked the rest of the day and slept that night in a crevice at the bottom of a limestone cliff. The next day there were trucks again on the road, and by late afternoon he was drinking gin and tonics with Johann in the bar of the Istanbul Hilton and watching the sun set over the Hellespont through the filthy air.

"Sent *Life* photos once, like I said. On Indonesia. Fockers refused them."

"When were you in Indonesia?"

"The Coup in sixty-five. Same shit as this. It's a perfect CIA deal: Operation Gladio. Just like Indonesia, the Generals ward off an imaginary leftist coup while planning a right-wing takeover, the entire process organized by the good old USA."

Johann motioned to the barman. "What they did in Iraq in sixty-three. CIA overthrew Kassem because he wasn't friendly enough to western oil companies, then gave Saddam Hussein's Ba'ath Party the names of thousands of people to execute – teachers, doctors, scientists, nurses, the country's entire well-educated people, then the Pentagon sent Hussein weapons to use against the Kurds. All for oil. Holy oil."

Mick told him what he'd seen in Bali. "You were stuck there with this white chick?" Johann sputtered. "And made it out alive – Holy crap!"

"The same thing. They killed off the teachers, union members, doctors, nurses, anyone with a brain. Apparently *we* gave them the names."

"Again, my boy, it was all about oil. Indonesia has enormous offshore reserves, almost a tenth of the world's supply. Sukarno wanted to release them slowly, use the money to modernize the country, but the US oil companies wanted it all *now*, didn't want to pay what Sukarno wanted." He sighed. "Now with a US puppet in office, in twenty years that oil'll be all gone, down the mouths of Esso, Standard Oil, Mobil and all those big cars you Americans fancy –"

You're gonna be sorry you were ever born, the Istanbul Hilton radio was singing,

Hey la, hey la, my boyfriend's back,
Cause he's kind of big and he's awful strong,

"Christ," Mick snorted, "we even poison the world with bad music."

Johann glanced over the smoky isthmus at the darkening sea. "Poor bloddy Greece. How many thousand years fighting off invaders? Look what good it's done."

Mick sucked icy gin across his broken tooth. "We're taking down these countries one by one, Indonesia, Vietnam, Cambodia, now Greece. And people don't even know."

"And the Russkies are taking down others – Eastern Europe, all those worthless places in Africa." Johann belched. "And the folks who live in these places just get kicked around, don't they?"

With shame Mick thought of the raped girl in the truck. "I freed a wolf in Salonika. From a tiny cage. Only good thing I've done for months."

"Good for you. All these people." Johann swung his head indicating the hotel, Istanbul, the world. "All in cages, what?" He drained his drink and held up two fingers for another. "Arabs're about to attack Israel. 'S next on the agenda. *Need* to be there."

Mick munched pistachios, avoiding the broken tooth. "*You* have a death wish."

"Can sell pix to British papers." Johann leaned forward. "But I can't write the stories in English. I take the pictures, you do the words, we make enough money to go back to Amsterdam and fuck beautiful Dutch girls till the Amstel freezes over."

"You want to go to Israel?"

"Nah. This bloody war will *not* start in Israel."

"Invaded from three sides? How can they hold out against Egypt, Jordan, and Syria?" Mick affected a nonchalance he didn't feel.

"Pray for Israel, so soon to be destroyed? All the other journalists are going to Israel," Johann shrugged. "So we go to Egypt, ride with the victors into Tel Aviv?"

18

WAITING FOR WAR

TROY STEPPED ON A SNAKE and as it bit he kicked it into the trees. Holding his rifle so it wouldn't clink on his belt he knelt to make sure the bite hadn't pierced his boot, eased up and looked round through the trees.

Sheets of brightness, waves of green. Lianas hanging everywhere. If somebody in this place wants to shoot you you'll never see them. Throb of forest, stink of soil, rotting leaves. Call of a macaw. Rustle of wind downhill through undergrowth. Who?

It's when you think you're good at this they get you.

How can you hate me? He asked Su Li. *What have I done to you? I just want you to be safe. I'm going crazy because there's no one like you and now you're gone too.*

He knelt peering between tree trunks for leg motion, squinted against the light for a flash of metal, hint of moving shadow, searched the ground for trip wires, darker soil that could be where a mine had been dug, took a step, stopped to check the ground again.

I'm being transferred, he'd told her. *Up north.* She'd jerked her head: So what?

Things are a bit hot up there, he'd added stupidly, glanced at her eyes.

Her eyes were blank. *I don't care.*

Mosquitoes coated him. But if you wore lotion Charlie smelled you.

A huge-leafed plant ahead, size of a waiter's tray. He started to go around it then thought maybe that was what they'd wanted, ducked under the leaf and moved on, dew down his neck.

It didn't make sense how at first she'd been so friendly, asking questions, but over time had become quiet and sad and withdrawn and stopped asking questions and now didn't want to see him. *How could she hate him? What had he done?*

Was it because he'd asked her to marry him? But why?

Fallen bough ahead, mushrooms underneath. On instinct he turned uphill ten feet through the soaked brush and turned back the direction he'd been going. This felt better, less likely. Glancing back he saw Outlaw through the leaves twenty feet behind.

He caught Outlaw's eye and pointed to the bough with the mush-rooms. *Come up here,* he motioned, turned and moved on, scanning the ground, the trunks ahead beside and behind, the windows of light through the leaves.

Over two thousand years ago, Su Li once said, a Chinese warlord had married his son to the daughter of the king of Vietnam so that his son would spy on the Vietnamese. In the ensuing war the son's wife was killed and he committed suicide out of heartbreak for what he'd done. "You see," Su Li added, "even those who betray us die of sorrow." *But how had he betrayed her? Was she talking about herself?*

Gun oil smell. On the downhill breeze, from the upper right. Two o'clock.

Chill emptiness in his chest. He dropped to the ground and elbowed his way backward trying not to budge the plants and stems, seeing the leaf shadows waver across the green ground. He could feel between his neck and shoulder where the bullet would hit. Smashing through his collarbone and ripping out his lung and liver and blowing open his side. He squirmed round and crouched up to the level of the leaf tops but couldn't see Outlaw or anyone.

Ambush. He'd nearly walked into an ambush, because he hadn't been paying attention. Because he'd been thinking about her.

He eased down the hill and there was Outlaw big as the Michelin man in his pack and flak jacket taking a piss on the huge-leafed plant.

"Charlie, two o'clock!" he whispered. Outlaw's eyes went wide and he stopped pissing and stuffed himself into his pants.

They pulled back across a stream and up a low hill.

"So we call it in," Colley said, scared.

"No," Troy said. "We set up a perimeter and wait. Let Charlie come to us."

"You're short, Troy," Outlaw said. "Why you wanna die now?"

Because I don't care, Troy thought. *I don't care without her.*

THE FECULENT STREETS OF CAIRO resounded with boisterous people egging the government on to war. They waved banners, shouted imprecations against Israel and America, and glorified Allah and his coming victory over the infidels. Little boys waved plastic guns and screamed death to the Jews, men prayed and women ululated. In their raging threats the women seemed even more blood-thirsty than the men. "I pity anyone," Johann snickered, "with God on their side."

Distrustful, mendacious, ill-willed, hostile, and larcenous, the denizens of Cairo scorned foreigners but extracted every piaster they could. Those with something to gain by dealing with infidels were insidiously polite, but in the streets mothers tautened their grip on children's arms when Mick and Johann passed, young girls turned from the windows, and old men watched them with ironic eyes. The air was a fetid miasma of incense, hydrocarbons, burning plastic, sewage and broiled meat, the traffic ruthless, the prostitutes garish and reeking of bad perfume.

"Our basic objective is the total destruction of Israel," President Nasser announced. Egypt had forced the UN out of the Sinai. There was nothing to do but wait for war, like a film where from the begin-ning you know that the hero and heroine are going to bed but it takes the whole movie to get them there.

Mick and Johann rented a green Fiat with bald tires and drove across the Nile into the Sinai on a very dusty road across measureless wastes and endless dunes to the filthy bedraggled town of Bir Gifgafa.

Wind was blowing sand everywhere, into their eyes and mouths, down shirts and up sleeves. The water tasted of potash; camel dung littered the streets. Egyptian Army trucks moved northeast all day toward Israel trailing mile-long plumes of dust. "What I need," Johann said, "is a triple gin'n tonic."

The night of June 3 Mick couldn't sleep in his bunk in the narrow-walled hovel he shared with Johann. The wind rustled sand across the bare concrete floor. Johann snored unevenly, as if he couldn't find the right rhythm, or like a train that goes behind a hill and reappears. All night the sky rattled with celebratory gunfire.

Mick's legs itched. Lighting a match he raised the soiled cotton blanket and found a mass of red welts. Bedbugs again. He moved to the floor and huddled in his clothes and coat but the concrete's chill ate through them. He lit a match and burned the line of bedbugs that had come down the leg of the bed and were crossing toward him. The smell woke Johann who muttered Dutch imprecations but was soon snoring again.

Would the US let Israel fall? Either way, did he really want to be in an Egyptian Army convoy in the middle of the Sinai?

Once again the Jews had been deserted. No country offered support; everyone looked the other way, as they had in 1940. The Vatican said nothing, just like before. Before then no one could have imagined Europe without Jews. But it had happened.

And happened again in fifty-six. A hundred million Arabs converging on six million Jews. While the world watched and the Soviets urged the Arabs on.

Next morning the Fiat coughed a great belch of black smoke and died. A man called Abdul, who was changing his name to Mohammed to glorify the coming battle, said for twenty-five dollars he'd drive them in his ancient Peugeot 403 to a dry oasis named Al-Behed where they could join an Egyptian convoy heading for Gaza. "There," Abdul-Mohammed said, drawing a map in the sand, "we will *crush* them."

He was perhaps thirty, thinly-bearded, dressed in a frayed djellaba and plastic sandals. "If yer so bloody hot for it," Johann asked him, "how come you are not fightin?"

"Me?" Abdul grinned bad teeth. "I'm too *old* for the Army –"

The morning breeze was clean and cool, dampened by desert dew. In many places sand had drifted over the road. A larger road came in from the southeast, rutted with fresh truck tracks. Abdul got into fourth gear and bounced along it, shocks clanging, engine stinking of charred oil. "Don't bloody kill us!" Johann yelled, "before the war starts."

"God protects us!" Abdul yelled exultantly. "God wants us to kill the Jews!"

In early afternoon they rolled over a rise and before them stretched a city of trucks and tanks, of thousands of men and khaki tents burnished by the sun. Abdul found an officer who glanced at Johann's press credentials and nodded. With a worrying heart Mick watched Abdul's Peugeot vanish southwest in the dust.

The officer brought them to two Egyptian journalists. They were excited and asked how soon they thought the battle would be over. "It'll take months," Johann said.

"You'll see," one journalist, a short tubby man named Al-Sharif, patted Mick's arm amiably. "In two days, Tel Aviv."

With the two Egyptians they were consigned to Lieutenant Karim Saleh. He had a fattish face, elastic smile, small oval glasses, a roundish torso, and spoke some English. He laughed a lot and rubbed chubby hands and made a blubbering lip noise when someone mentioned the Israelis. "We will *slaughter* them. Burn them *alive*. We will chase their children into the sea and *drown* them."

All day they rode with ten soldiers in a Russian troop carrier under the scathing sun. The canvas roof just made it hotter; dust roiled and scurried into the back and covered everyone like golden snow. The stink of half-combusted diesel from the hundreds of trucks ahead made Mick's head ache. He sucked at his broken tooth, unhappy and sick to his stomach from bad food.

The soldiers sat silently over their weapons, some staring through the cracks in the canvas sides or out the rear at the slowly passing desert, others facing the rattling floor, one caressing his rifle. Most of them were small and skinny and had bad teeth and dirty faces. Above the boiling dust the sky was so blue it seemed almost white.

At evening prayers they stopped in a dry wash between high sandstone cliffs. The two Egyptian journalists, Johann, and Mick were given cots in a tent with Lieutenant Saleh and three other officers. The mood of the camp was tense yet strangely passive. Voices chanted prayers and sayings of Mohammed, mantra-like, over and over.

Lieutenant Saleh was shadow boxing with imaginary Israelis on the side of the tent in the light of a petrol lantern. "How do you tell the difference," he panted, "between a live Jew and a dead Jew?"

"Tell us," one of the Egyptian journalists chuckled.

"One is today. One is tomorrow."

Johann took a sip of putrid desert water and gave Mick a bleak look. Wind rustled the canvas. "The sand," Johann said, "is getting in my bloody lenses."

"Ah, you need at minimum a four hundred millimeter," the journalist named Hamid said. "Very strong telephoto. This is desert war. The action far away."

Mick had hardly slept the last three nights but now a grainy nervous weariness kept him awake. With Hamid he wandered among the trucks spread out across the desert like tethered horses. A few of the soldiers were sleeping, but most sat in little clumps round petrol lanterns or battery-powered radios emitting singsong Arab music. They seemed pensive, but a few boastful and aggressive souls were stomping round from group to group, chanting slogans and trying to get the others to repeat them. "I'm afraid this will be a stalemate," Hamid sighed. "We will sit here months in this desert."

Bone-tired and wary Mick returned to his cot, worrying that the previous night's bedbugs might have come along for the ride. By midnight he was scratching all over and gave up sleeping, went outside. There was the smell of hash; someone was sitting with his back against a truck tire smoking. "*Salaam*," Mick whispered.

"*Sa-laam*," Johann snickered.

Mick took the pipe. "Maybe this'll help me sleep."

"Whole place's a bloody bedbug hotel. Hot as a furnace in the day, cold as a nun's tits at night, sand in your lenses, goddamn bloody scorpions everywhere –"

"Shook two out of my boots this morning."

"Like Hamid says, this war's going nowhere. Stuck here for months."

In the setting moon the rock walls above them gleamed like pewter. "From up there on that cliff," Mick said, "you could see a long way."

"How far you think we're from the border?"

"Israel? Karim says fifty klicks but I don't believe him."

"At least he's consistent. Everything he says is a lie." Johann stretched. "I had a girl like that once, she was consistent too – everything she did was sexy. Didn matter – eating a piece of cake, waiting for the bus, brushing her teeth – everything she did made me want to jump her."

"I can't get stuck here for months. Have to be back in New York soon, the draft board."

"Ugh."

"Can't figure out how to get free."

"This's about as close as it gets, mate. You hang out at home, boffin girls till something like this happens, then you race off to some bloody forkin corner of the universe, take a few pictures of people dyin in horror'n misery."

Mick looked at the cliffs. In an hour it would start to get light. "What day it is?"

"Monday, June five. Yawm-al-Ithnain, 26 Safar – 1387 in the Muslim calendar, if you prefer."

"Going to take a quick climb up that mountain, see what I can see."

Johann looked up the cliff, sighed, took a last drag from the pipe. "Might's well go too. Stay down here I'll get the runs from the food or the clap from Karim's breath, or be run over by some bloody raghead doesn't know how to drive."

"Shhh," Mick cautioned. "Some of them speak English –"

"I'm not speaking English; it's bloody Dunglish. A secret language. Wait a minute goddamn it, I said I'm coming too –"

They climbed the side canyon, away from the convoy. It was sandy and they kept sliding back down, Johann gasping and swearing. From the sheer edge at the top they could see to the far horizons. The scimitar moon hung low in the west, the east pale aqua, the stars still sharp and bright.

Mick sat on the wind-cut stone, sweaty from the climb, the wind cold on his neck.

"Bloody fool I am," Johann sat beside him, "follow you up here."

A thin red line widened in the east. In the valley below flashlights flickered, a few generators had started, now the shadows of men flitted before lanterns and truck headlights. Soon came the cadence of prayers.

"Religion," Johann said, settling his breath, "is for losers."

Far-off was a rumble of planes, very high.

"From a distance humans look almost peace-like. Sort of industrious, if you know what I mean. Nearly intelligent."

Johann chuckled. "An illusion."

"But we have so much . . . *possibility*. We don't have to be like this," Mick nodded at the convoy.

"We *are* industrious. Like ants. Compulsively active. They kill each other too."

"Maybe how it's supposed to be? Darwinian – how we evolve." There seemed a rumble far away but Mick could see nothing. "Kant said as individuals we should act the way we want all people to act. A categorical imperative."

"Sounds like cant to me. Maybe the reason those poor blighters down there're so ready to give away their lives – *Allahu akhbar*, God is greater than any human comprehension – is because they don't have bloody *anything* anyway. Now you take us creature-comfort Westerners –"

"So we can end war by making people prosperous?"

"What if we were all *one*?" Johann looked up, "One huge single thing? The same way our own bodies've been created, over time, by symbiosis of simpler organisms? As if the earth, the whole world, was one organism?"

The sounds were closer though still faraway, high and deep-throated. Now and again a star winked. "Planes," Mick whispered. "Headed toward Cairo."

"Jesus 'ey just bombed Tel Aviv and 'ey're going home! Bloody war's already over. *Fuck!* We won't get any pix. *Fuck!*" Johann stamped around yelling, "*Fuck!*" and kicking rocks and sand, raged his fist at the sky. "Damn you were right, we should've gone to Israel."

"Careful, you're going to fall off this cliff."

A lovely dawn was blooming like a rose, reds and oranges and yellows melting across the crystal desert. It was light enough to see men moving in the camp below, the dark glimmer of artillery, tents coming down like a circus leaving town. Mick thought with sorrow of the people dead and dying in Tel Aviv. "We should go down."

From a pocket of his malodorous shirt Johann pulled out his hash pipe and Zippo. "Forkin war went somewhere else, and we've got nothing but all day rumblin around the desert. *Fuck!*"

Mick checked his watch. "In ten minutes we go down. Karim'll be worried."

"'*E* doesn't give a bloody shit –"

"They'll leave without us."

Johann took a deep puff. "That they would."

Mick thought of his endless days in the Sahara. "It's a long walk back to Cairo."

"There'll be traffic." Johann stood brushing sand off his pants. "Must say, mate, I'm very depressed about this. You were right, we should've gone to Israel."

Mick felt sudden gladness they hadn't, wanted to go home. Camus' words came to him: *the body recoils before annihilation.*

"Whoah!" Johann jumped up. "What's *that*!"

Bright as diamonds three delta-winged jets screamed over the ridge down at them.

19

LIVING IS EASY

THE JETS RAKED the convoy, machine guns flashing, delta wings spitting rockets that blew the trucks, tents and scrambling men into seething red and white flames, their thunder shaking the cliffs. More jets raged over the ridge dropping silver pods that sluiced pillars of flame through the convoy, hemming the men in, driving them under the guns. Men on fire ran colliding with each other and the blazing trucks.

The Israeli Mirages had gone but the exploding ammunition and arms and fuel and hiss of blazing vehicles, the screams of burning men, all amplified by the valley walls, was deafening. A horrible stink and pall of gray greasy smoke came boiling up the valley. "My cameras!" Johann said quietly. "Bastards blew up my cameras."

"I'm going down," Mick said.

"For *what?*"

"To help."

"*Help?*" Johann grabbed him. "Those jets are coming back you idiot!"

An arc of sun appeared, hot as napalm. Up from the valley came continuous explosions. A desert sparrow flitted past, veered away. Three Mirages dropped over the ridge and howled down the valley spitting fire and smoke, tilting wings like the sparrow as they darted left and right then were dots on the horizon then nothing.

The staccato of explosions went on. Mick ran along the ridge wanting to go down, thinking of Hamid and Al-Sharif, the soldiers, boys from villages in the south, stone-age farmers or penniless city kids with no knowledge of the world beyond the desperate ghettos of Alexandra and Cairo and the brain-numbing rants of the Koran. Even Lieutenant Saleh, with his ridiculous posturing and dissembling flatteries seemed larger than life, immaculately tragic.

"If we go down now the surviving soldiers'll kill us." Johann caught up to him. "Because we're westerners. And with no bloody cameras we've nowhere to go."

In the piercing blue sky above them vapor trails heading south. "Going to Cairo," Mick said. "Israeli –"

"So I was right, after all. We were here and the war came to us."

"If we'd been down there we'd be dead now."

"Aye." Johann scratched at his nose. "That we would."

The sun had risen splendid and yellow-red above the desert. After no more planes came they went down. Men stumbled, dazed, tending to others who lay moaning or screaming. Others lugged stretchers of wounded toward a few undamaged trucks. Bloody men with clothes half-blown away lay scattered over the ground, crying, praying, silent.

He and Johann helped as best they could, lugging stretchers, dragging bodies to the semi-shelter of the cliffs, leaving long red-brown stains in the sand. There seemed to be no officers, no one in control. Holding a dead man's still-warm hand with its dirty nails and callused fingertips it was impossible to believe he wasn't alive till Mick looked at the fist-wide hole in his chest or the brain hanging from his skull.

All day Israeli jets laced the sky with contrails. To Mick it seemed the soldiers and the two journalists had been dead a long time, perhaps forever.

Before dark they started for Cairo, watching for Mirages. The smoky sky glowed. Smashed troop carriers and sun-swollen stinking corpses clustered along the track they had driven so jauntily the day before. Wounded men kept calling out; soon Mick and Johann had given away all their water.

Into the night they kept at a slow trot that became a nervous stumble along the slippery sands. Soldiers alone and in small groups were shuffling along the same track. Mick tried to remember the landmarks from before but there had been nothing to remember, just sand and bare ridges. After midnight they came on a destroyed convoy. Voices sobbed out of the darkness that stank of burnt tires and metal, oil and flesh. One fender Mick brushed was still too hot to touch.

They searched everywhere among the burst vehicles and contorted bodies but found no water. At the edge of the convoy, half under a tipped troop carrier, was a motorcycle with a burst front tire. Mick cut off the tube and tire and spliced the starter wires. Johann came back from rummaging for water among the corpses.

"Take this." Johann handed him a heavy cold object. "It's loaded. I've got one too. Makarovs. Eight shots in the handle and none in the breech. You'll have to cock it, like this. And here's the safety. It's on, just push down to release it, cock and fire."

Mick drove the motorcycle with Johann on the back southeast along the starlit rutted road past ruined vehicles, jettisoned weapons, packs, helmets, a radio that was still squawking, out of the ether a thin voice urgently repeating something. The motorcycle's bare front rim clanged over the ruts, vibrating the handlebars. Without the front tire there was no front brake. The bike's light was shattered but he would not have used it anyway, fearing soldiers as much as planes.

The bike's speedometer was broken but they were going about fifteen miles an hour. In eight hours maybe they could reach Al-Behed. But all they had was five hours, maybe, before the Mirages came back.

Hours later three soldiers with leveled rifles loomed out of the darkness blocking the road. Mick almost swung round them but feared they'd shoot, pulled up.

"Journalists!" Johann cried. One soldier shoved his bayonet at

Mick's stomach and he jumped off the bike thinking *what a lousy way to die*. How stupid he'd been to stick to the road, trying to make time.

Out of the corner of his eye something flittering down, a bird's wing, then another. Paper, sheets of it. A soldier snatched one out of the air. They handed it around but seemed unable to read it. There was large black lettering in Arabic script. Johann pulled a small flashlight from his vest and gave it to the soldier with the bayonet, gestured for him to keep it. The soldier turned it on but they did not try to read the paper.

They backed slowly away but one soldier swung his gun to motion them nearer. He pointed at Mick's feet; for an instant Mick feared he'd seen some western movie and was going to shoot at his feet. But he wanted his boots – though his feet were larger –Mick pulled them off and gave them to him. Johann took his off too.

The three soldiers climbed on the bike, the one with the bayonet driving, rifle slung across his chest, the other two on the back, boots slung over their shoulders, rifles still trained on Mick and Johann. The driver didn't understand the clutch and the bike kept stalling till another elbowed him aside and got it going and the three wavered away down the rutted road into the first light of day.

"Alright," Johann said. "Now where do we hide?"

The sand felt cold and damp through Mick's socks. "We're going to fry our fucking feet." It felt good to swear and he kept at it.

"They took our last water."

"Mirages'll get them." Mick had been too busy driving to stop to drink, now realized how thirsty he was. From high up came the hiss and rustle of planes.

Out here in the flats there was nowhere to hide. They ran stocking-footed from the road as behind them came the crunching thump of explosions and deeper roar of jets. After maybe forty-five minutes of running and stumbling over the sand they came on a shallow *wadi*. Their feet burned, their lungs full of dust, throats afire. They burrowed into the sand along a rocky west-facing ridge. "If the planes see one bloody thing," Johann grunted, "they'll blow us to forkin hell."

Mick remembered in the Sahara how his tongue had swelled from thirst. By midmorning the sand grew very hot from the sun and they dug in deeper, but that made the sand above slide down, cutting their air.

All day jets thundered over. By late afternoon the thirst was intolerable. "If we go back to the road," Johann mumbled, "someone'll kill us."

"So we use these pistols."

"Should've on those soldiers."

"They had us. There wasn't time." Mick realized how ready now he was to kill to protect himself. How he hated the Egyptians for their bellicose cowardice, their effeminate machismo, their anti-Semitism, their willingness to kill if they had a safe advantage. "If we get out of here I'll never come back. Never."

"Like I said," Johann dug deeper into the sand. "If we want to get out of here, we have to think. How to survive."

"I've *been* thinking all day but all I can think is keep going till Al-Behed or whatever it is." The tacky hotel room they had had days ago in that dry and dusty oasis now seemed a palace of safety and comfort. "Maybe Abdul-Mohammed, the guy who drove us, in that 403?"

"Place's probably leveled."

"They wouldn't bomb the town, the Israelis. Would they?" Mick realized he assumed a higher level of humanity from the Israelis, a lesser evil.

At dusk they tore up their shirts and tied them round their feet and walked all night, reaching Al-Behed before dawn, dizzy with exhaustion, thirst and hunger. The town had escaped damage, though a group of trucks on the road outside lay in charred hulks.

Before sunup they knocked on Abdul-Mohammed's door. He looked haggard and frightened, didn't want to open the door, to be seen near them. "We have a hundred dollars," Johann said. "It's yours if you drive us to Cairo."

Abdul shook his head. Four days earlier he'd seemed a comical, even farcical being; now he was larger than life, a deep and feeling soul who alone could rescue them. "Jews coming," he whispered through the cracked door.

"It's safe traveling now," Mick said. "We've been fine."

"Other guys here have cars." Johann said purposefully. "If you won't, they will."

"The war'll end soon," Mick urged. "Think how good this hundred dollars'll be."

On the road to Cairo there were no checkpoints, just the litter of an army on the run. The city's streets were deserted but for leaflets writhing in the wind. Gone were the mobs of chanting bloodthirsty people with God egging them on.

Mick walked the craven streets, knew he was a fool to be grieving for people he'd barely met – Hamid with his disputatious gregarious grin, the thousands of other unnecessary dead, the Israelis on the other side fighting their way out of Dachau, Ravensbruck, all the other death camps, all the pogroms back through time – why?

The first commercial flight to Paris was full of journalists and minor French and Arab diplomats acting mysterious and significant, all stunned the Israelis had won. "The great archetype of *David und Goliath*," said a *Die Welt* stringer, "has been proved true."

At Orly Johann left for Amsterdam. Mick stayed one night in Paris, not caring if the cops found him, hungering for Lily, to tell her what had happened, to hold her, smell her, touch her, taste her.

After midnight he ended up in a café on Rue du Commerce killing cognacs and shoving one-franc pieces into the juke box, "Strawberry Fields" over and over – *Nothing is real and nothing to get hung about* – till the words and melody became his mind and he did not hear them any longer.

An imaginary world where anything could shatter of its own immanence. And there was no one, anywhere, he could explain this to. Or who could explain it to him.

Living is easy with eyes closed,
Misunderstanding all you see

FLYING HOME FROM DANANG Troy felt elation, guilt and sorrow. In the green haze behind him were the men he'd commanded, the woman who hated him. And ahead the huge rich country that had sent him there to kill and die.

All around him guys laughing, singing in the joy of having escaped. The short-timers who'd made it. The cheer when the 707 lifted free of the runway and out across the China Sea, beyond machine gun range. Going home, they thought. They'd see.

He tried to settle into the hard seat. Hours to go, the sea turning gunmetal gray below the window. When he got back to the world he'd stay drunk for weeks. That's what the second tour guys said. You have to drink your way through it.

You will forget Su Li. She was part of the dream called Vietnam, she and his men who had died, the people he'd killed. He dropped his face into his folded arms on the seat tray as if sleeping. How could he go home when his men were facing death?

When Mick had written saying *come stay with me when you get out,* Troy had nearly cried. They might heal their old separation over the War. And Tara'd be there too in a few days. After some tour, she'd said.

But the faces of his dead friends – their bloody crumpled bodies, their young laughter and their hope they'd make it home all smashed now – kept rising before him as the image of a fatal cliff before the eyes of doomed climbers. He could tell himself they died for something, but Mick was right – they'd died for fucking nothing. Or *did* they? Liar.

He and Mick would argue. *Maybe I won't go see him, Tara either, when I get home.*

Why call it home?

Still an orphan, aren't you?

Twice.

· · ·

"I REMEMBER JIMI HENDRIX," Luis said. "Tall black dude plays left-handed. All over the neck guy very fast. Name used to be Maurice somebody –"

"Maurice Jones," Blade said, hands loose on the piano. "Yeah, Maurice Jones."

"– toured with Little Richard."

"Maurice James," Sybil said. "Played with the Isley Brothers too, you know 'Testify'?"

"*I'm a freak for music,*" Blade falsettoed, rolling it out on the keys,

"I'm a freak for music, it's in my soul,
Can't help if it moves me, down to my toes,
'Cause I'm a witness, I'm here to testify –"

"He the one burn his guitar," Luis said. "You hear that – he *burn* his guitar?"

"At Monterey," Blade said, tickling the keys.

"We shoulda gone there," Tiny said. "I was wrong. It was bigger than I thought, woulda been good publicity for us, the new single."

"We were on tour," Blade said. "You don't cancel tours and stay alive."

"Nobody should never burn a guitar," Luis said. "When some poor kid could use it." He swung his head side to side to loosen it, slid Benicia's sling up over his shoulder, ran through a lick faster than machine gun, a lovely blues rush. "If Hendrix, or whatever his name he change it to, if he's so goddamn good how come he don' sound pretty? Anybody can do tricks on a guitar. Anybody can make a guitar sound like war."

Tara smiled at him happily. There were lots of guitarists out there prettier than Jimi. Luis was prettier than Jimi. And almost as fast. As if that mattered.

I'm like Luis, she thought. For him and me, beauty is everything; you don't play to show off. You play because you love it so much you can't stop.

Because you love life and don't want to die.

And the music that came out of her, out of her lungs and up her throat into the raving world, was better than heroin.

But the heroin eased the terror that hit before every show. The screaming dread of seeing all those thousands of people out there.

And they all want you. They want to carve you up and eat you.

We are free, Voltaire said, *the moment we wish to be.*

What about me?

SUMMER IN THE CITY, The Lovin' Spoonful on the airwaves, the War on every front page, girls in miniskirts with nothing under, New York pulsing like a cancerous lung, the gritty cauldron of its streets and anonymous crowds,

> *All around people looking half-dead,*
> *Walking on the sidewalk hotter than a matchhead,*

while ten thousand Soviet ICBMs took aim at it and its rulers sent death to far-off places.

From a windy girder high over other skyscrapers Mick glanced down at the tiny car-jammed streets and mobbed sidewalks,

> *But at night it's a different world*
> *Go out and find a girl,*

nights sweaty naked on sweltering rooftops, soaring guitars and fabulous weed, tarnished bricks and filthy streets – nothing was forbidden because nothing lasted.

At six-thirty a.m., sleepless and fulfilled, he rode the construction elevator to the thirty-seventh floor of Dinofrio's latest job off Wall Street, a few blocks from Whitehall. A different foreman, another dance with death on the slippery skeleton of a future box full of people who would stare through glass walls at the people behind the glass walls of other boxes.

Despite the moments of true fear the pay was good; in a couple of weeks he paid $75 down on a '63 blue VW with a cloth sunroof and white seats, and drove it out of the city every weekend to go climbing.

But no matter how high he climbed his Sinai nightmares wouldn't die. *It was a just war* he told people: Israel's life had been endangered. It had no choice if it wished to survive. But for the emaciated *fellahin* and ghetto untouchables sent by their government and religion to die under the Mirages it had been pointless sorrow and agony.

Why die for a goal so irrelevant to their lives? Was this a delusion of soldiers everywhere? How had these threadbare hungry Egyptians become Barbusse's soldier? Why had they traded their freedom for the mirage of defending it?

The more he thought, the simpler the answer: they already had no freedom. They were poor without hope of a better future. Their religion, which they believed because they were ignorant, told them this was their fate. Their government, over which they had no control, totally controlled them. To the point of ordering, as would some ancient despot, their purposeless deaths.

But how was America different? The ghetto blacks and rural rednecks dying by the thousands in Vietnam had no stake in a small backward Asian country's civil war. Even they, like everyone hounded by the Draft Board, had not the freedom to refuse.

World boxing champion Muhammed Ali had just refused, saying, "I ain't got no quarrel with those Vietcong," and been convicted of draft evasion, sentenced to five years in prison, fined ten thousand dollars and barred from boxing for three years.

The same sentence, or worse, that everyone would face, if they refused.

Insane. If each person's awareness was the only way they could see the world, then they'd never know whether the world was illusion or reality. For an individual there could be, philosophically, no reality beyond his or her perceptions. The idea of "country" might be entirely an illusion, like a bad movie.

If one died defending the illusion, of course that illusion, the thing being imagined, died too, for it existed only in the mind of the one who died. So to die for what also ceases to exist when we die, because it is nothing but a projection of our own needy awareness, seemed ludicrous as dying in some war game played by children.

Back at work early Monday he wrapped his legs round a cold wet girder forty-six stories above a tiny street, the cars like ants, the people dots. If we owe our lives to the group, to be sacrificed whenever *it* chooses, then we're slaves, and the illusion of freedom just another shackle in our chain.

DAISY'S WORK WAS SO EXCITING she had time for little else, grabbing food at a student café, up past midnight till her eyes blurred, checking footnotes and running numbers on an adding machine. Sometimes she was surprised when her period came, she hadn't thought the time had passed so quickly since the last one, there'd been so much to do.

Slowly, a halting step at a time, she was closing in on how the brain works, how knowledge and emotion might be tied to specific neural substrates, could be therefore treated there, altered there, perhaps by a chemical.

If so, can experience alter DNA?

If it can, what is memory?

If brain areas differ, are multiple memories the same?

She was getting carried away by her own mind, she realized, chasing it down the rabbit hole to Wonderland.

And none of the men she slept with seemed to understand. The other grad students, deeply intellectual, mentally overstimulated and exhausted, could not see beyond the classes, the subjects, the tests and other dangers. *What are we doing this for?* she kept asking them.

Her lab partner Jason was rugged and smart and she told him she wanted to sleep with him and so they did, on her creaky-springed bed in the women's dorm. He fell asleep and she kept waking him to do it again till he complained and she lay there with arms crossed over her breasts, staring at the ceiling. *You aren't Mick,* she told him silently. *You silly prick you aren't Mick.*

A month later she spent a night with a visiting professor from

Spain. He was delicate and intense and it was great fun for hours. He woke with a lurch at six. "Oh my God in only two hours I have to be in class."

"Only two hours?" She grabbed his prick. "We better not waste them."

No doubt about it, sex was fun. She'd never had one fuck that wasn't. And lots of guys. In bed one night she lay back with her hands behind her head and tried to count them, got to thirty-one and fell asleep, woke and tried to remember what she'd been thinking about, it had been so much fun, whatever it was.

Now she remembered. You sleep with all these guys and each one is exciting, lustful, different, achingly fulfilling. But there's more, a deeper fire, she'd had it years ago with Mick.

But that was because with Mick it was so new, she was only fifteen and having more sex than most married women, she and Mick every instant they could find, on the way home from school, in the car, once in the football lockers when no one was there . . .

Oh God that was fun.

Why was it so different?

Mick had been a part of herself – the deepest part, the most honest and true. Since third grade. Since before he fell off the Sparkill Creek bridge showing off to her. Since they were eleven and he wanted to get married because she was moving away. Two times she'd moved away, the first to Nyack and the second to Iowa, and both times it had been as if someone wrenched out part of herself. The best part.

As if they shared the same bones, the same skin. How could that be?

Or that she'd always been more important to him than himself, and made her feel it. As he had been for her.

Or maybe it was just different because it was the first time. That's all.

TIMOTHY LEARY lived in Millbrook, a ninety-minute drive up the Taconic. "Some rich guy loaned him the place," Amy Feinglass said, tipping her sunglasses up on her head as she scanned the passing traffic.

Mick bent open the VW's wing window to let in more breeze. "So how you know him?"

"We're doing the appeal on his arrest last year in Laredo. We're arguing that the weed the cops found on him was for free exercise of religion. It's a little improbable, but we had to hang the appeal on something. Anyway it's probably going all the way to the Supremes."

"What's he like? The real guy?"

"Mellow, but often his mind moves so fast you can't keep up. He's trying to understand how acid can heal people, but also be enjoyed by normal people to expand their lives."

The mansion was a rambling late Victorian of turrets and pillared porches on vast sloping lawns. "Tim!" she called, pushing through the wide double doors. "Tim!"

Leary came out of an upstairs room, of middle height, slender and ascetic but solid with a sunny smile and thinning hair. "Sorry," he said, "a citation I can't find, brain chemistry . . ." He beamed at her. "So, how's our suit?"

"We didn't get a great choice on judges, but you know that. This's Mick," Amy brightened. "He wants to talk about acid."

"Acid?" Leary gave him a fake-astonished smile. "*Every*body wants to talk about acid."

They sat at a wooden table in a little room off the kitchen. "LSD's stunning," Mick said. "I want to understand the research, how it does what it does –"

"The first time I took it," Leary said, "I learned more about the brain than I had in twenty years of brain research. I could watch my brain at work. *From the inside.*" He leaned forward. "Is that an answer?"

"But how?"

"Think of it this way: over millennia we humans've learned evolutionarily to ignore a lot of sensory perception – what's out there in the real world – if it doesn't fit into our list of dangers and opportunities. A kind of tunnel vision." He leaned forward. "But all this sensory reality *is* out there – it's *all* real, *alive*, part of the world, but we're just not seeing it, experiencing it." He shrugged. "But it's an awareness we need, to live a good life."

He leaned forward again, full of volcanic activity. "*Life* did an article way back in fifty-seven on the religious use of psilocybin by Mexican Indians. So another guy from Harvard and I went down to Cuernavaca in 1960 to study it.

"At that time the CIA was doing research on LSD, a synthetic version of psilocybin being produced by Sandoz, the Swiss pharmaceutical company. And a lot of scientists at Harvard, Stanford, Chicago and other places became interested in its regenerative effects on the soul, if you wish. So Dick Alpert and some other Harvard researchers and I started the Harvard Psilocybin Project. In carefully controlled experiments we gave it to hundreds of volunteers – students and faculty – with very positive effects. Almost eighty percent said it was a major or *the* major religious experience of their lives. Then we did the Concord Prison Experiment, found that a combination of psilocybin and psychology cut recidivism eighty percent. After psilocybin had taught me so much, I was ready to see if LSD could also teach people to be happier, freer, lose a bit of the egocentrism that drives us all crazy.

"There have been over six thousand very positive studies on LSD, mescaline and psilocybin," Leary added, "covering over forty thousand people. Many of these studies have been done at Harvard. All done by top universities, top scientists. Potentially wonderful remedies for serious illnesses that have caused great tragedies of history, the sexual trauma that leads to fascism, the raging ambition and alcoholism that destroyed Rome and so many other cultures, the worship of money and power instead of the spirit and love that's ruined so many lives."

NIMH, the National Institute of Mental Health, he added, supported by the Food and Drug Administration, in hundreds of their own research projects had found LSD a valuable therapeutic tool, perhaps the most valuable yet discovered for problems like alcoholism, autism, and depression.

But under pressure from the CIA, the FDA began to restrict its use in 1962, and by 1965, he said, LSD could no longer be used either in research or in individual therapy. Without explanation the FDA halted progress on hundreds of its own promising research projects as well as those of the NIMH. In Senate hearings Robert Kennedy challenged this, asking why had they suddenly without explanation reversed course, but no answer was given.

Thus despite extensive scientific evidence of LSD's therapeutic and socially beneficial impacts, soon its possession was a federal crime. Why? What had the CIA found in this marvelous drug that threatened the power structure of America?

"The answer's easy," Leary smiled. "LSD teaches you to think independently. To feel. To realize you're going to die, maybe soon, and this may be the only life you have, so you better live it deeply and honestly."

So after a few LSD experiences you were unlikely to waste five hours a day being brainwashed by television, to work at a job you hated, to indebt yourself to buy what you didn't need but the culture and advertisers told you to buy, to obey the government when it told you to die, or to choose money and power over love and happiness. LSD had already freed you from all that.

Instead it made you intensely aware of the beauty and fragility of the earth, of other people, of animals and trees and the grass blowing in the wind. You understood that if you built a big house, a grove of redwoods or firs somewhere would die. You understood that if you paid taxes you were responsible if the government used that money to kill people on the other side of the world.

"But nothing," Leary added, "threatens the group more than individual freedom. Once you've seen the wonders of this mystical magical universe, how can you be a bank clerk for thirty years, a soldier, a secretary, anyone who commits half their waking life to repetitive drudgery?"

Mick thought of the steel and glass tower he was helping to build. "A wage slave in corporate America?"

Leary shrugged. "One of the first things LSD teaches is that if you're not excited when you get up in the morning then you need to change what you do."

Obviously, LSD *had* to be outlawed.

LEARY DIDN'T UNDERSTAND, Mick told Amy as they drove down the wide driveway and across the farm fields away from the house, how his ardent endorsement of LSD brought all the enemies of human awareness down on the research he and others did.

The enemies of human awareness didn't like it that LSD took you out of yourself and gave you the world. That it intensified life, that you saw, felt, heard, tasted everything so much deeper. That it showed what was important and what was bullshit. And like someone who'd been shut in a monastery all your life you were now free to go out and enjoy the world.

True, you walked an edge. You could fall into terror or despair or insane hilarity, but LSD also *taught you the way out*. And for the rest of your life you knew how to survive terror and grief, how to understand and avoid human insanities.

And it was *good* to face fear, the vast unknown, the void of meaning, the awareness of death with nothing after. It made you stronger and more sure, because you'd seen the darkness and could find your way out. And you had seen the light.

Amy switched on WOR-FM,

Remember, what the dormouse said,
Feed your head! Feed your head!

"I've got the munchies." She passed him the joint. "How about Ratner's on the way home? For chocolate cream pie?"

20

BACK IN THE WORLD

"WHAT A SHITHOLE!" Troy dropped his duffel on Mick's floor. "I can't believe you live here." He moved tentatively, not wanting to sit. "Worse'n some hutch in Hué."

Mick glanced at the Charles Street apartment it had taken him weeks to find after his trip overseas, and had cost a third of his month's steelworking wages. "Don't stay if you don't want."

Troy gave him a sharp look. "Where the fuck else'm I going to stay? This fucking country!" He crossed to the smog-stained window, looked down the lightwell. "This country is *fucked*, do you know that? Totally *fucked!*"

Troy never swore like this. "How so?" Mick said.

"Where I been my friends're getting killed every day, some of them we pull pieces of their bodies down from the trees, we're killing people – that beautiful country we're destroying it, I come back here, and nobody even *knows* there's a war, people driving round, going shopping, getting laid, fatheads talking on television . . . *Jesus!*"

"We know there's a war. We're trying to stop it. I think of it every day, all the time."

Troy turned on him. "You're wasting your time. All of you."

"You probably don't believe the Bertrand Russell Tribunal findings in Stockholm either."

With his buzzcut reddish hair, wiry frame and bulging biceps, Troy still looked like a soldier in civilian clothes. "No I don't."

Mick took two beers from the fridge. It hummed irritatedly; the door wouldn't shut. He handed Troy a beer. "A group of Nobel Prize winners and other international authorities finds the US guilty of war crimes, and you don't believe it?" He shuffled papers on the table, took out a newspaper article. "Sit down for Chrisssake."

"This couch is filthy."

"*We find the government and armed forces of the United States,*" Mick read, "*are guilty of the deliberate, systematic, and large-scale bombardment of civilian targets, including civilian populations, dwellings, villages, dams, dikes, medical establishments, schools, churches* – and you don't believe it?"

"Left-wing lies."

"The woman whose Senate campaign I worked on in Paris, Gisèle Halimi, she's the chairman of the Tribunal. She would never lie, not about anything." Mick leaned toward him. "Anyway, why would they *lie*? Why would a renowned philosopher and mathematician, and some of the greatest thinkers in the human race – why would they *lie*?"

Troy shrugged. "You tell me."

Mick sipped his beer, waiting as always for Troy's hostility to diminish so they could talk. Troy sat with his long legs crossed, his beer unopened in his lap. "If the War's immoral and we shouldn't be there – what are all these young Americans dying for?"

Mick shrugged. "You tell me."

Troy stared out the dirty window at the dirty fire escape and the filthy building across the lightwell, the filthy air. "That first day," he said finally, "when we met in the barracks –"

"Yeah?"

"What if we hadn't? I've had three lives: before your family, in your family, Vietnam. None of them relate, makes sense to the other two."

"When I think of how life was before you came, it seems two-dimensional. Like black and white instead of color. They have that now, did you see? Color TV."

A half-smile softened the muscles of Troy's jaw. "Riding the freight train south? The loneliness, knowing you've cut off everything in the past and can't ever go back, and that maybe going forward there'll be nothing?"

"I didn't have that. I returned to the past but everything was changed. Because of the trip, because of you. I've always wondered how I would've grown up. Tara too."

"She's going to be in New York – she tell you?"

Mick felt strange that she'd told Troy and not him. "When?"

"Next week, some concert –"

"They're getting big, that band. Imagine."

"Yeah but she doesn't like it, she says. The lifestyle. I don't blame her."

Again Mick felt displaced that Troy should know his sister better than he. "Why?"

"All the goddamn drugs." A volcanic intensity seemed to simmer just below Troy's surface. "I had to nail Marines all the time for smoking that shit."

"Marijuana? It's good, helps break down the walls between people."

"You sound like a fag –"

Mick grinned. "I get laid more in a week than most Marines in a year."

Troy clenched his fist, a red scar standing out. "My friends are dying so you can."

"Your friends aren't dying for my freedom. They're dying for Lyndon Johnson's ego, to keep our war machine going –"

Troy smashed his fist into Mick's mouth and they fell rolling on the floor and Mick flipped Troy up and banged his head against the brick wall, pounding his face with both fists in hatred of the War, for all the idiots who wanted people to die, for the sorrow of American boys dying and the hundreds of Vietnamese dying for each American, sorrow for Egyptians and Israelis, hatred for the evil inside people that could not be scraped out. Fists slippery with blood he hit harder, not minding Troy's punches into his own face because the pain just made him hit harder.

They pulled apart. "Asshole!" Mick yelled. *"I never should've asked you here!"*

"Coward." Troy wiped blood from his mouth. "Won't fight for your country."

"Are you so fucking dumb you can't see it's *wrong*? Don't you think I'd fight if it was right? If we weren't murdering millions of people for nothing?"

"Gooks? Life means nothing to them."

Mick grabbed another beer not knowing if he'd drink or throw it at Troy. "The person for whom life means nothing, Troy, is *you!*"

Troy's footsteps thudded down the stairs. Mick paced, massaging a torn fist. He started to call after Troy, stopped. *Fuck him.*

Even that first day in the old barracks there'd been an unreachable well of anger in Troy, a wound too ancient to heal. And all his life since then was just scar tissue over it. Mick had wanted to tell Troy about the Sinai's thousands who'd died for nothing. The Greek coup – Troy had studied the Spartans at the Air Force Academy. Indonesia: how could Troy condone slaughtering two million people? But what was Vietnam if not that?

He washed his fists in the sink but the blood kept spattering from his knuckles onto the porcelain. "Roaches gonna have a feast," he mumbled, aware of a great emptiness that could not be filled by drugs or sex or happiness, could not be filled at all.

KNOCKING PEOPLE ASIDE, Troy shoved his way up Fifth Avenue scowling back at their shocked faces, not caring. The store windows were psychotic – who could want clothes or things so fraudulent and pretentious? – the polished women in furs and leather, the sleek cars. Weirder than the moon, these weren't people like Corey Dillon,

Sergeant Boone, Saul Finkelstein. *Help me, take me back*, he called but there was no way they could help him. This was his solitary mission: *Find a way to live back in the world.*

Women's stiletto shoes forty-nine dollars, hundred-dollar handbags so inane they'd debase anyone who touched them, fatuous hats with little white and yellow plastic flowers – these were what his friends were dying for? For useless kitchen goods – things you bought because you were bored and wanted to show off to others? Did anyone really need that huge Eldorado idling at the curb? What was all this leather and chrome an atonement for? Was *this* what Marines were dying for? What he'd *killed* people for?

He switched shoulders with the duffle. Everything hurt, his shoulders, his eyes from the city light, the noise and stench, his lips and jaw that Mick had hit. Never met a Marine tough as Mick. Fuckin coward.

Even if the War *was* wrong, Troy hated everyone against it.

No way to understand peaceniks, Captain Cross said. *Your job's to kill gooks.* He did that. He did that good. But what was he going to do here?

A car screeched to a stop, horn braying. He was in the middle of a street, cars whizzing past, raised his fist at them. "Fuck you!" he screamed. "Fuck you all!"

A man got out of the car, big and black. "Hey soldier!" He took Troy's arm. "You git on over here to the sidewalk 'fore you git hit."

Troy swung on him. "Not a soldier. I'm a Marine!"

The big man grinned. "It's okay, still don't want you hit." He shoved Troy onto the curb, flashed a quick salute, "Glad you made it home," and drove off.

Troy's knees buckled; he wanted to kneel on the concrete and weep, instead continued uptown, duffle heavy, walking, walking. He was on patrol. Had to forget everything else.

The sidewalks narrowed, dirtier, nothing fancy in the windows now. He went into a bar stinking of moldy carpets and old beer, ordered a double Jack and a Schlitz chaser, another and another. His back to the bar he watched the hippies playing pool and pinball. *Maggots in their hair.* Hippie music on the juke box,

> *When the truth is found to be lies*
> *And all the joy within you dies,*
> *Don't you want somebody to love –*

some long-haired chick screaming, and what the hell was Tara doing in a band? Taking drugs, sleeping around? Su Li sleeping around too, maybe. Fuck her. Had to be some reason why she didn't love him. Hell, there were plenty reasons.

Goddamn long-hair was slapping the side of the pinball machine to make the ball dance back up. Without thinking Troy crossed the room and slapped him across the head like he was slapping the machine and the guy dropped, rolled over and came up in a crouch uncoiling a fist into Troy's face and slammed him face first into a shelf of trophies clattering down, agony of kidney punches, two guys trying to stop them, pinning him to a wall and he kicked one in the nuts and the other in the knee and threw someone into the pool table that cracked and fell on its side, a woman swearing, glasses smashing, he grabbed a bottle and broke off the end, liking the safe feeling of its sharp neck in his palm, ready to smash it into the face of any long-haired hippie motherfucker who killed his friends.

They backed away, the bartender came round the bar raising a lead pipe and Troy thought bizarrely of Uncle Hal, felt horrendous shame, grabbed his duffle, threw the broken bottle into the plate glass window and ran down the street, kidneys hurting, pain everywhere, around the corner out of sight, bent down gasping, spitting blood on the sidewalk, goddamn hippie music in his brain, *don't you want some-body to love?*

He missed his M16, the lovely spurt of bullets. How could he live without it?

Nobody needs anybody to love. Nobody.

He shouldered the duffle and headed toward Central Park. Some vets said you could sleep there, like the bums did. Just till Tara came next week. She'd know what to do. She always did.

HARMONICS – God, it was all there, all our secrets, in simple harmonics, the sounds we can't hear behind the sounds we hear, but when we separate them out they're Godlike.

Tara eased back in the big soft chair, her flame-red Gibson SG light atop her belly. *What we are*, harmonics, *visions of each other.*

They obsessed her, harmonics. That under each note so many deeper ones, unheard. So many people inside each person, so many meanings in each word, so many illusions behind what we believe. Like if she had many different lives.

She plucked that lovely transition from C major to G, so sweet and irrevocable, such promise, such hope.

But the problem with this promise, as you slide from perfect C into heartwarming G, is that then there's nowhere to go, there's no further promise, no hope. You can go to D, but that's tragic and sharp, settles nothing. You can of course take the easy road to Dm and then slip into Em, covering your tracks, but what a copout.

The only escape is back from G to C again and then up to F which allows you to take that lovely F-C drop, ecstatic in its beauty. How it, this one chord change, captures so much of human aspiration.

Like Mozart.

Or *Moonlight*. That perfect piece that Beethoven called *almost a fantasy*. How many months had she had been trying to recreate it on the electric guitar? How it starts quietly in the first movement, almost *pianissimo* at times, laying out the framework of the entire piece, then a growing yet calmed second movement to set things in place. Then *oh my God* the thunderous final, this wild descent into arpeggios and sforzandos that cut into your heart just like Luis's guitar solos, these magnificent stories he builds on the sweetest of our melodies.

Oh my God then it's over and you're spent, your heart and mind still up there, with that magnificent music that's still coursing through your body.

Orgasm.

After sex you can feel the man's sperm leaking out of your body, it slides down your crack and gets on the sheets. So does music slowly slide away and we lose it. Unless we keep doing it.

Over and over.

Oh my God music.

BOBBY MIGHT RUN FOR PRESIDENT. He hated being the center of attention but was driven by the daily deaths in Vietnam, the need to stop the killing, not by desire to *be* something. Though he feared a Democratic rupture that would let Nixon win, he seemed to say it was the Democrats' duty to do what was best for the country even if it lost them the election. But wouldn't any Democrat be better for the country than Nixon?

It was a late-night meeting at Bela Abzug's house – Bobby, Al, some of Bobby's advisers and several antiwar leaders as they debated options for the coming elections.

"The American people have had their president stolen from them and want him back," Mick started to say but halted, for Bobby was still too shattered by Jack's death.

Hubert Humphrey's sniveling opportunistic support for the War disgusted most traditional Dems but they were wary of antiwar groups, and the unions worried about jobs and redneck backlash. "If the Christian Democrats in Germany had stood against Hitler in 1933," Al Lowenstein argued, "they could have stopped him. That was just thirty-four years ago."

By organizing the campuses and the cities, Lowenstein insisted, they could expand the movement, bring out campaign workers and new voters. And no one else, not Eugene McCarthy or George McGovern, could beat Johnson. He faced Bobby. "Only *you* can."

Bobby saw right through this. "Last time we had barely fifty percent."

There were journalists on the phone and more meetings to sit through. Exhausted, sleepless, Bobby was full of energy. "If the antiwar groups come in behind you," Lowenstein said, "we can dump Johnson."

"Most of them will," Mick added. "Not the radicals like SDS. They want a whole new society, not just to influence a vote."

"We don't want them anyway. But will the others commit, work for it?"

"The church groups, the students, the returned vets, other groups like former Peace Corps volunteers – they all will."

"Just in New York? California?"

"The War's getting worse, more and more people across the country are against it."

Lowenstein smiled as if Mick had shown his naiveté by imagining a government run in accordance with the people's will. "But they won't *vote* against it –"

"They will when their kids come home in boxes. Their neighbors' kids."

Bobby winced. "That just hardens them."

"Pain teaches," Mick said, embarrassed. *You if anyone should know.*

Weeks later, they met again at Al's West Side mansion, a knot of long-haired radicals out of place in its vast rooms of inlaid floors, ornate mahogany, ancient rugs and tapestries, Renoirs and Van Goghs.

Al had recently become engaged to a brilliant and beautiful woman in Boston, but it didn't appear to divert him. He seemed no happier, but this was because he was always happy, had a sunny, outgoing and lovable personality. Combined with great kindness and honesty it made him someone it was impossible not to care for.

"You're coming to the wedding?" Al said.

To Mick a high-class society wedding in Boston was no way to spend a weekend when he could be rock climbing in the Shawangunks or making love with somebody lovely and exciting. Plus how could he show up, without a suit or even a sports coat?

"I'll try to come," he said, not wanting to appear impolite. But knew he would not.

"You should," Al patted his shoulder, turned away. "You might get lucky like me, and meet somebody you can't live without."

That was Al, one hundred percent. Sometimes you never even knew what he felt most deeply about. But his incessant work schedule worried everyone. "You're too wired," Mick said one night. "You don't sleep, you're going all the time. What're you running from?"

Al cocked one eye, grinned. "Whatever it is, I don't mind it."

"What did your parents do to you, anyways? You should smoke some weed, relax, stop thinking."

"Never have."

"Stopped thinking?"

"Smoked grass. I'm nearly 40, and I've never taken any drug."

"And you're the one who keeps saying to accomplish anything we have to give up our fear of consequences –"

They drove in Mick's VW downtown to Mick's apartment. Spare and barely furnished, it could not have contrasted more with Al's huge, tall-ceilinged and deep-carpeted rooms. Instead of silk-upholstered, leather chairs, they sat on the pine floor; Al took off his shoes and tried to sit cross-legged; they smoked some grass and Mick put *Rubber Soul* on the record player, but neither the grass nor the Beatles' sad joyous visions seemed to calm Al. In the racing frenzy of his mind he seemed not even to hear these lovely Elizabethan ballads, the Shakespearean purity of their lines, the elegantly understated yet indelible melodies.

"The Dems know they can't stay with Johnson," Al said over the music. "But they don't dare switch."

"And what're *your* fears?"

Al looked surprised. *I once had a girl,* the Beatles were singing, *Or should I say, she once had me –*

"What consequences *are* you running from?" Mick added.

"That we might fail. To dump Johnson. That we might make things worse."

"How can we?"

"And more than losing a shot at Congress I'll be banished to the outer Siberia of the Democratic Party. Be able to do no more good at all. Things I could have helped."

"Like Bobby says, letting Nixon in."

"Nixon's the only truly evil human being I've ever met. The worst." Al made some phone calls and grabbed a taxi uptown. Was Al right, Mick wondered, that a few thousand determined people could force a president from office? The huge demonstrations like the one coming this weekend at the Pentagon – could they make a difference?

He finished the joint, watching the night sky above the lightwell, thinking of the girl who'd undressed each night across from his Lower East side window, of fear and lies and consequences, the coming march on the Pentagon, while the Beatles sang,

Think for yourself if you can,
Hide your head in the sand

A letter from Johann was in his box the next day with an international money order for two hundred seventeen dollars. "I sold your Sinai War stories six times. Everybody likes them. You should be a journalist. Somebody has to tell the truth!"

You're foolish, Mick wanted to tell him, *if you think telling the truth makes a difference.*

FOURTH OF JULY WAS HORROR. The constant explosions drove Troy near mad. After the first few firecrackers he forced himself to stop diving for cover each time one went off. But they went off inside his head. In the paddies a bullet zipped past his head and blew off half the head of the man behind him. Hit another in the gut and he doubled up and you knew there was no pain worse than what he was feeling. Mortars shredding them. Guts on your face, chunks of blood. And he hated the facilely patriotic people who had never fought but set off these fireworks. Who did not even know what they did.

. . .

"YOU JEWS, *YOU'RE* THE PROBLEM!" Clancy Martin shook a fist at the microphone. "You Jews and white liberals with your nice houses and cars and you wake up in the morning and there's food on the table and money in your pocket and you think you can buy us off with white liberal shit. That you can buy us off with a nice convention here about a unified left."

He glared at the vast auditorium of dark and white faces. "Buy us off with these hotel rooms here in Chicago and three days of white hotel food in our bellies. Then *you* go back to Scarsdale or Alexandria or Hinsdale to your fancy house with three bathrooms and we go back to the ghetto. You can feel good, you done your duty."

He paced. "You got all the answers on the black people's problems. A little more welfare and food stamps – that's all it takes. Well, I'll tell you the black man's problem: it's the Jews who run this economy. It's the white man. It's white education and white bread and white rice and white money and white faces on the television telling us the white news, and the only time you see black faces on television is when we burn down another city. Well, just hold on, white folks," he smiled, "we gonna burn 'em *all* down."

With a black power salute he added, "Like Brother Malcolm told us, *the Negro revolution is controlled by foxy white liberals, by the Government itself.* It's time to end all that!" He stomped from the podium, scowling as Mick took his place.

The microphone hissed and boomed as Mick slid it higher. "We've come here from all over America," he said softly. "Right here in Chicago, this is *the largest conference in history* of antiwar, civil rights and other liberal groups. We're here to plan *a unified campaign* to change our country. But we're not going to make change by attacking each other.

"Now Clancy here says white liberals are the black man's problem. The Jews. Well, Clancy, it's the Jews and the white liberals who paid for this conference. Who give enormous amounts of money to SNCC and SDS and NAACP and all the other black groups trying to make change. A lot of black people have been killed in the south, but some white guys have been too. And *they* were Jews."

Rumbles of agreement and anger rose from the crowd. "Another person who talked like Clancy about Jews was Hitler," he looked out at them, "and I don't intend to join forces with Hitler or anyone like him."

People were leaning forward now, paying attention.

"Clancy, you'd be the first to tell us how many black men are dying in Vietnam. How many get drafted because they don't have college deferments. White liberals are trying to stop that War. Trying to stop young black people, young white people, from getting killed, Vietnamese people getting killed. The murder of a whole country."

He let this sink in. Even now, in the middle of a speech, when he'd already thought of it a hundred times today, it still brought tears to his eyes. When you'd heard the stories and seen the pictures.

"We all know that power only respects power." He coughed to clear the tears from his throat, felt suddenly naked before these thousands of people. "What I'm here to tell you is that it's *we* who have the greatest power!" He looked out not seeing them, just a pattern of white and black and gray through the tears, trying to think what to say next. "If we can come together, against the war in Vietnam and the war in our cities."

He tried to see the audience that swam before his eyes. "What if, Brother Clancy, instead of preaching hate and violence you tell black men to refuse induction? Tell them to join the Resistance? So they stop getting killed? War has a tremendous appetite; it feeds on young men. You stop feeding the War young men and it will die of hunger."

When he was done he didn't care if the audience agreed or not. There was no way to bridge the gap; there would be no unified left. He'd met black men here in Chicago who boasted how many whites they'd killed, black men who thought if they planted the seed of black revolution in the ghetto it would bloom all over America. They could divide America and get ten or twelve all-black states, a separate country.

He argued till he could barely speak but between black radicals and liberal whites there was no common ground. Like the divide between those who wanted the War and those who didn't, between Troy and himself, it was emotional, not subject to reason.

"YOU'VE GOT TO UNDERSTAND where Clancy's coming from," the girl named Diana Oughton said as they sat in an empty hallway. "You and I," and she scanned Mick momentarily, "we had parents who took good care of us and had enough money to put food on the table and keep the roaches off the walls and the bedbugs out of the beds – if there *are* beds –"

"Don't give me that noble poverty shit," Mick said, instantly ashamed to have said it, for this girl seemed too real, too honest, for that.

Surprisingly, she laughed. "Oh it sounds like that, I know." She tugged back a strand of long slim hair, not a sexual gesture, but wanting to get distractions out of the way. "I grew up with such comforts, a good Midwestern home."

"I grew up on a family farm. No shortage of milk and eggs. Or hard work, either."

She laughed again, silvery and light. "I grew up in an Illinois farm town, did 4-H, rode horses, Daddy took me hunting, Mother saw that I was a good musician, that I got into a fine college –"

"Which one?"

"Bryn Mawr. I was a good Republican middle-class girl. But then I went to Germany for junior year abroad, met some students who were socialists, they had questions I had no answers to, got me thinking about human equality. So my senior year I tutored kids in a Philadelphia ghetto. And I saw the other side of America."

"Which is?"

"Inner city poverty. Black kids in junior high who can't read or write. Who may have never seen their father, and whose mother won't be there when they get home. Who don't have the faintest idea what a healthy meal or decent job is, what familial love is –"

"Excuse me for being a prick, but how is that our country's fault?"

She nodded. "That's a fair question: does this social disaster result from the hideous aftermath of slavery? Or from black culture, or poverty, exclusion, no access to good education? I think the poverty and lack of options causes the breakdown of the family, then welfare just reinforces that breakdown, because the parents don't need to provide, there's enough to scrape by on, provided you're willing to live in a hellhole. And most of these people have never known anything else."

"So what's the answer?"

"Education, so kids understand there's another way to live. Keeping families together by replacing welfare with decent jobs –"

"To have a decent job you've got to know how to do something. If you can't read or write . . ."

"Exactly. It's an immensely complex problem. I've thought a lot about it and I believe the best start is with the young kids, to teach them well, with commitment and caring. After college I went to northern Guatemala for two years as a VISA teacher, and I'd sit at night in my mud hut and try to figure it out. Have you been to Central America? It's beyond description, the poverty and misery of families whose only income comes from working for American fruit companies, their lives constantly threatened by military death squads that murder anyone suspected of wanting to unionize or educate people with the hope of offering them fairer wages and a better way of life. Death squads funded by US military aid, of course."

"I've seen US military aid in action. Got caught up in the Indonesian coup, the Greek takeover."

"So you know. The people in rural Guatemala have literally no way out. They have no education, there *is* no education because teachers are routinely killed by the death squads. They're stuck working for United Fruit for a dollar a day of back-breaking labor, trying to support their families when the basic foods down there are almost as expensive as here. Think of it the next time you buy a banana, the misery that went into producing it –"

She was captivating, beautiful, intelligent, caring, and he wanted to go with her up to his room and make love all night. But she seemed distant, as if already committed. "All this wealth in America, all the poverty elsewhere," he said, "what's the connection?"

"The reason I'm here, at a radical conference in Chicago instead of a Saturday night dinner at the country club is that I've grown to realize how we – *our* country – makes *their* situation worse." She looked at him with direct amber eyes. "How else do we live honestly?"

"I'm here for . . ." He wondered. "I'm here because the War's wrong."

"How do you know?"

He smiled. "Thank you."

"Thank you?"

"For not just accepting the cant. I believe it's wrong to kill people on the other side of the globe because they aren't doing what we want. You know that –"

She nodded. "Of course. But it's surprising how many people don't know why they're against the War, just the same tired clichés."

"It's a visceral decision, the War."

"Of course, again." He had the sense of being appraised by someone far wiser and more caring than he, and liked her for it. "I've been doing research on napalm," she said.

"Napalm?" He averted his eyes from her slender long legs and the lovely bevel of her hips in the short skirt.

"If you want a good reason to hate the War, just think napalm. We're dropping nearly a million napalm canisters a week in Vietnam. On villages, rice paddies, farms –"

"What's new about that?" he'd said rather irritatedly.

"When they hit they spread out in an area the size of a football field and incinerate everything at three thousand degrees and cover everyone with this seething black tar you can't rub off. People near the flame area are instantly poisoned by carbon monoxide, they're paralyzed, can't escape. The burns are atrocious, people get burned right down to their bones. The agony is incomprehensible." She looked at him. "So what do we do?"

He turned away, sickened. "I know all this. Not about the temperatures, all that. But that we *do* it."

"And we're doing it to hundreds of thousands of people. Some of them are soldiers trying to protect their country from us. Most of them are just women, old people and kids."

She looked at him steadily. "So what do *we* do? That's my dilemma, the dilemma that we all here at this conference face. If that's the reality of what we're doing, we Americans, how far do *we* have to go – you and I and anyone who cares?" Her eyes transfixed him. *"How far do we have to go to stop it?"*

21

———

MOTOWN

BROWN SUGAR WAS JUST what Tara needed for the shakes, so a half hour before the concert she tuned up with Luis' needle. Sitting on the can in the backstage ladies', the needle trembling in her fingers, her body all quivery, gut queasy and wrists shivery, the worst butterflies she'd ever had and Detroit wasn't even a big show.

Lovely brown sugar how your body eases back and everything's golden sweet and you see that the show's nothing, you could do it eyes closed and *wow* this *was* good stuff, the warm feeling in her crotch melting up through her body. Holy sweet Jesus so much fun. *"Holy sweet Jesus,"* she sotto-voiced, *"Holy Jesus this is fun,"* took a nice hit of Benedictine.

Whack whack on the door and Sybil bust in saying *Get your pretty little ass off'n that hopper Honey, the damn hall is packed and Blade wants to start* – funny how my good sweet dyke Sybil was so uptight when everybody *knew* Tara'd sing her fucking heart out and everything'd be fine. Didn't she always? "Where's Benny?"

"On the floor beside you Honey. Where you put it. But no more now. Lots more at intermission, Honey. C'mon, let's get out there!"

"Fuck them," she pranced along the floor that was shaking from the crowd stomping and cheering, so Luis and Blade and Tiny must've

265

just gone on stage. "They don't want my music my way they don't get me." She fumbled in her shoulder bag past Tampax and kerchiefs and lipstick and found the cosmetic kit full of joints, lit one, sucked it in and knocked it back with more Benedictine as Sybil yanked her down the corridor toward the doorway's cruciform light. Growing thunder of the crowd out there, Luis tossing them a riff, the whole goddamn concert hall vibrating. Some night, she thought wildly, we're gonna rock someplace down to the ground.

"I'm gonna sing," she sang toward the light, knees shivering, *"gonna sing right outta my blues. Gonna sing, Lord, gonna sing right outta my blues,"* a hit on the joint and gulping down more Benny, *"So tell that man, Lord, put on his walkin shoes . . ."*

"Oh you got it to*night*, Honey," Sybil yelled over the roaring crowd. "You *got* it *tonight!*"

A HOTEL SUITE AFTERWARDS, peace and contentment, no concerts for a week. Tonight's crowd full of love and peace, giving back the intensity the band gave them. "I love Detroit," she said to no one. "It's so peaceful."

Luis sitting on a couch playing acoustic, "Stop in the Name of Love" then sliding into "Dancin in the Street." He looked at her. "Motown *is* America."

The suite full of strangers somebody'd invited after the show, her throat so sore, her voice hoarse. "Jesus I'm tired."

"Hold on till Kansas City, Baby. Then a whole month home."

A strange idea, home. Was it with Luis or Blade, or alone in Berkeley? She imagined sitting on the back porch in the sun, stroking Onya the cat in her lap, no need to worry about money or anything. Just the peace to stretch out and be.

"Callin out around the world," Luis sang. *"Are you ready for a brand new beat?"*

"Summer's here," she harmonized, *"and the time is right, for dancin in the streets."*

"Yeah," somebody kicked in, *"in Motor City too."*

Damn label, Motown. They'd met with Motown founder Berry Gordy the afternoon before the concert. Hard to believe that someone could be so kindly yet rapacious, wanting to help you and seemingly concerned about you as a person, then bleeds you dry.

That was Berry. How he was. Yet there was real pride in the label. You signed with Motown you were in the same dressing room as the Supremes, Martha and the Vandellas, Marvin Gaye. In that way Berry was a gift from God. He made it happen. Gentle, kind, and deadly, he was the best thing they'd ever get. "Set up like you is, Brother," Berry had said, "you just ain't Motown sound."

"Set up like we is?" Blade had answered.

"White woman vocalist, a white woman drummer, PR lead guitar."

Blade grinned at Luis. "He ain't Puerto Rican, he's American. And they ain't white, they're musicians."

"– and the only other black in the band, asides you, is this bass player, what's your name?"

Tiny straightened his huge bulk, voice soft. "Tiny."

"Motown is *black* music, Brother."

Blade had chuckled, slid his white hat forward. "That just too bad for Motown."

"You can keep her," Berry nodded at Tara. "But you gotta ditch these other two."

Blade tipped back his head, looking down on Berry. "We're not five people, Berry. We're *one*. You gonna ask me which leg to pull off? Which arm? Maybe I's the arm, you can pull me off and keep the res'."

"Hold down, Blade. Hold down. I ain't pushin you. I'm just suggesting how we might be a better match, you and we."

Blade glanced at Luis, Sybil and Tiny, turned back to Berry. "Don' you see, man? Without them there's no *us*!" Sadly he shook his head. "You just don't see it."

Berry smiled. "You're the one don't see it, Blade."

"Fuck it," Blade had grinned at the others. "We'll go with RCA."

Tara shook from her reverie. Sirens were moaning outside. And the heavy clang of fire engines. "Hey!" a tall black dude said, "was that guns?"

"Sure weren't firecrackers," a white guy said.

"How *you* know?"

"Hundred'n Seventy-Third Airborne." The white guy pulled back a sleeve to show an ugly red scar across his biceps. "Phuoc Long Province, May '65 to May '66 – You hear *that* – *that's* guns!"

Through the hot open windows a stench of burning tar. "Fire," someone said portentously. "Big one."

The black dude leaned out the window. "Over by Twelfth somewheres." He ducked back in. "Whoa Momma! The whole sky's red!"

Tara felt sleepy; time for a brown sugar nightcap. She went looking for Luis who wasn't sitting on the couch anymore. "He went downstairs," somebody said. "To see the fire."

"What fire?"

He nodded at the window. "That fire."

"Oh yeah," she remembered, wandered into the kitchen but Luis wasn't there. Blade would have some brown sugar but he was with some chicks somewhere and she couldn't find him. Angry at Luis for abandoning her she pushed through the kitchen door bumping into the Airborne guy with the blue tattoo. "Got any scag?" she said.

He scanned her. "So if I do?"

"Give me a hit you can fuck me all night."

A MAN STICKS HIS PRICK in you it feels wonderful, but when smack sticks its lovely tongue inside you it's even better. You know that someday it'll spit you out but you don't care cause what it gives you is better'n whatever else you had.

Acrid smoke singed her eyes. She shook herself from a lovely heroin dream, shoved the inert Airborne guy aside to shut the window, surprised it was daytime already, a lurid orange sky against boiling black clouds. Heat hit her face with a molten slap. There were yelling voices, crashing glass, gurgling sirens and gnashing engines, another *rat-tat-tat-tat* somebody had said was guns but maybe that was part of the heroin dream. She yanked Airborne's ankle, "Wake up, Asshole!"

He didn't move and she feared he'd OD'd, leaned down and felt his rotten breath on her cheek. "Get up you *asshole!*" She grabbed one cowboy boot thinking *Fucker fucked me with his boots on* and the boot slipped off clunking on the floor; she yanked him off the bed and *thump thump thumped* him down the stairs and out the front where the heat nearly knocked her over.

"Help!" she yelled at a man clutching a television but he kept running. She tried to carry Airborne over one shoulder but fell ripping her knee, got him over her shoulder again and staggered down the street in a mob of people as he barfed steadily down her neck.

People were smashing through store windows and leaping back out with arms full of things that fell on the sidewalk and other people grabbed them, radios, fur coats, teapots and TVs, a fat lady wobbling away with a vacuum cleaner, a man laughing as he drank a carton of chocolate milk, five guys running out of a gun shop with rifles, fire engines moaning, police cars screeching, helicopters overhead jabbing searchlights through the smoke. With a great *whoosh* a gas station on the corner blew up spurting fire on the next houses that crackled like paper, their windows blowing out; a child ran toward one screaming *Mama Mama* but someone grabbed him, the thunder of flames, the screams, sirens and clashing glass deafening. She dropped Airborne and knelt gasping for breath. "What's wrong with him?" yelled a young black woman in a nurse's uniform.

"OD'd."

"What?" the nurse cupped her ears.

"Overdose!" Tara shouted. The nurse waved at a police car that pulled over, three handcuffed black men in the back. The cops threw Airborne across the prisoners' laps and howled away.

The crowd was stampeding from the fires springing up everywhere, old women scuffling in slippers, one holding a lamp with its cord dragging, a weeping man carrying a wooden rocking horse, in the middle of the street a tall black man in the back of an open convertible speaking earnestly on a bullhorn as rocks whacked the car. Behind her the whole street afire, asphalt bubbling, houses writhing in flames, telephone poles crackling down, wires pinging.

"I need you!" the nurse yelled. "Three people in there. One ain't breathin."

It was a skinny gabled house, roof blazing, oily smoke writhing from second floor windows. Tara raced after her up the stairs into choking smoke, her hair seething. The nurse dragged a fat old man off a bed but he jammed in the door, she kicked it off the hinges and they pulled him downstairs, a little girl at the front door jumping up and down and screaming from the heat. "Who else?" Tara yelled. The little girl pointed to the back. They ran into the kitchen. On the floor was a thin woman, who Tara dizzily grabbed under the arms, the nurse her legs, and Tara began to pass out. "Get on the floor!" the nurse shook her. "Crawl!"

On hands and knees they dragged the woman into the street beside the old man; the nurse thumped the old man's chest and clamped her mouth over his. *The kiss of death*, Tara thought as she hugged the little girl saying, "It's okay, Honey. It's okay."

A black hearse pushed through the streaming people, a man in a baseball cap lifted the old man into it then the woman and girl. "Where they going?" Tara yelled.

"Ford Hospital," the nurse yelled back. "Hurry – next house!"

As they ran up the front stairs a huge boom knocked them onto the sidewalk; the front of the house fell outward framed in flames; they rolled aside as it crashed onto the sidewalk. Tara got to her feet, ears buzzing. *I need smack*, she thought. *Smack to sort this out.* "C'mon, Honey," the nurse shook her arm. "See that house? Nobody's checked it!"

Hours later they stood blackened and weary in a street of broken glass and milling people, the early sun a yellow pinhole in the smoky sky. "It's over," Tara said.

"Just ketchin its breath," the nurse said. "Gonna get worse."

"Christ. What started it?"

"The police, they raided some bar on Twelfth Street. A whole lot of people was there, partying over two local boys come home from Vietnam. Not in a black bag, you know, like lotsa boys come home. So everybody starts smashing windows, and now the police who started it they can't control it."

The Salvation Army had set up a shelter in a church, people sleeping on pews and the floor between them and on the altar, women in clusters of stunned and wordless children. "It's a war zone," Tara said. "Vietnam."

"They shoot my husband," a woman was weeping, rocking back and forth, hands over her eyes, tears running through her fingers. "They shoot him comin out the door."

Tara didn't know what to do. She sat with an arm round the woman's shoulder as she rocked back and forth weeping, "They just shoot him. Comin out the door. They just shoot him. Our house is burnin and he runs in to get my best coat and they shoot him comin out the door –"

"Who shot him?" Tara said.

"Them po-*lice*. Right in his own front door."

Beyond exhaustion, she slept holding the weeping woman, the nurse's head on her lap, the song bouncing back and forth inside her benumbed brain,

Are you ready for a brand new day?

A tall elderly man in a starched collar moved among the people holding their hands, speaking softly. "He the Reverent," the nurse said. "This his church."

He knelt beside the sobbing woman. "*Don't* you tell me," she said," that my Clarence is in heaven –"

"Ain't no heaven," he said wearily. "Just what we got down here."

"You tell me," Tara said angrily, "why they do this? Burn their homes, their own neighborhood?"

He stood, rubbed his near-bald scalp with a cindery hand. "*You* live here you burn *your* house too, *your* whole neighborhood. These good people living in shit and crime and danger and poverty with no way to get out, they just want to *cleanse* it, the Bible's *cleansing* fire." He inhaled like a man about to lift a great weight. "What they're saying is *this* life isn't enough. Better to have nothing. This is worse than nothing."

"Life is always better than death."

He smiled at her innocence. "The simple delight of burning the enemy. The roaches crawling the walls and the neighbors who won't let you sleep and the guns and drugs and danger . . . And the white man who owns the building and the street and government and banks and everything else that makes your life so hard –"

"Isn't that what Vietnam's all about?"

"Just what I'm saying. You live in a peaceful beautiful valley with a lovely forest and happy family and enough food, you don't burn it up."

"You don't have to," Tara said. "The US Air Force will do it for you."

"Detroit *is* Vietnam," the nurse said. "And Watts and Chicago and Newark and Toledo and Cleveland and the hundreds of burning cities of America. They're *all* war zones. The white power structure against people. Here in America and all over the world."

Tara realized she'd never thought of it this way. "But other countries, they don't have the opportunities –"

"Opportunities to do *what*, Sweetheart?"

"We can refuse –"

"Black boy from Woodward Avenue, he hire rich man's lawyer?"

Tara nodded, beginning to understand. "I never expected this."

"These people been down so long – what *did* you expect?"

"Didn't *know*, maybe. Or what I've been expecting. Nothing, maybe."

"We *got* to expect, Honey. What do *you* want?"

It shocked Tara she didn't know. A new cough sandpapered her throat. "Less you expect, less you lose?"

"My Daddy fought in France in forty-four. Think how far away that is now –"

"Twenty-three years –"

"Yeah, to almost this day. They fight all across France, and he goes by where this famous girl named Joan of Arc was from. This poor farm girl that spent her days minding the sheep and goats, gets a vision she can save her country. So she goes to the king and proves it by telling him things only *he* knows – it's her vision, see? – and he gives her a few soldiers and she wins these amazin battles – this skinny litt'l farm girl. Soon she's chasin the English out of France after they been there a hundred years." She chuckled. "So the English burn her at the stake."

"Just like Detroit."

"And Daddy said if he got home alive – my Momma was pregnant with me – and if I was a girl he was gonna name me for her."

"And so he did?"

"No, he wrote my Momma a letter. Before he was kilt. She named me after that skinny farm girl."

Tara couldn't speak, couldn't breathe. Couldn't think for a while then only sorrow. *Awful to never know your father. How lucky I've been.* "I have an adopted brother. Never knew his dad or ma."

"Your folks took him in?"

"When he was twelve."

"Wow you got wonderful folks –"

"He just got back from Vietnam."

"Your brother? You're lucky – mine's still there."

"I've been so worried, all this time." She felt an urge to share, confess. "Maybe that's why I drink so much. Shoot smack."

"Smack?" Joan glared. "Honey you *can't* do that. Ain't no way out but dead."

"Just to get me through these concerts. We do these concerts . . ." Tears rushed to Tara's eyes. "I get *so* fearful, beforehand."

Joan's eyes widened. "Oh my good Jesus! I *know* who you are now. You're Tara O'Brien! You're the *best*, Honey." She hugged her. "And you helped me save those people and risked your life and I never *knew* who you *were*."

Tara's eyes brimmed over. "Oh shit."

Holding each other they watched the charred and rubbled street, the dazed passersby, the armored vehicle grunting through the trash, the frightened white boys with guns and helmets staring down from it. "So what would Joan of Arc do now?"

"She'd save every house and building she could," Joan said. "And build it up again, more beautiful than before. A new day, Make it the best city in America."

They sat in the warm kinship of living souls, pain and joy flowing in and out of them, smelling each other's singed skin and hair and acrid sweat, their seared blouses with dried blood down Joan's and vomit on Tara's, in the full stink and glory of life.

I've never had a sister, Tara realized. *And always wanted one.*

THE NEW DAY was smoky and cloudy. She stumbled back to the hotel wondering where the band was, and fell asleep clothed on the bed.

It seemed afternoon when she woke. Her throat hurt horribly, her breath rasped. Her knee where she had fallen burned unmercifully. She staggered into the bathroom, shocked by her black-faced, singed-hair reflection. She tried to drink water but it stung her throat. She sat on the toilet but couldn't pee.

She called Luis' room but there was no answer, then Sybil's. "Christ, I was worried about you!" Sybil almost yelled. "You sound terrible."

"Where's Luis? Blade?"

"Don't know, Honey. There's a riot –"

"I know."

"Lots of people dead. Maybe they holed up somewhere, to wait it out?"

Night fell. The riot grew louder, wailing police cars and blaring fire trucks, rumbling tanks and armored vehicles, the steady crack of guns. Tara stared out the window of her expensive hotel at the burning city, worrying where Blade and Tiny and Luis were. *Knowing them*, she kept telling herself, *they're just partying. Found some girls.* But it wasn't like them to vanish, not hook up with Sybil and her.

All night she and Sybil waited. The National Guard and the 82nd Airborne had been called in to fight the people in the streets. "The vast majority of negroes and whites are shocked and outraged,"

Lyndon Johnson drawled on television. "Pillage, looting, murder and arson have nothing to do with civil rights."

She tried to drink Benedictine but didn't want it, smoked a joint that didn't hit, wondered where Joan was, if she was busy saving people. The Army was in gun battles with snipers, the news said. *Stay inside, don't go anywhere unless you have to.*

Early next morning she called Motown but Berry wasn't there. Everyone's gone, a secretary said, no one could help find a couple of missing musicians. She called the police but the line was busy, kept at it till an angry, short-tempered man answered, "No, we don't have any records of missing people," and shut down.

She called again and again but the line stayed busy. She walked two miles to Ford Hospital through battered streets where lonely chimneys teetered over smoking rubble. There was no information on the hundreds of new patients nor on those who had left. She walked the corridors looking in all the rooms but didn't find either Luis or Blade.

She went back to the hotel through streets where flames tossed garish shadows on facades, firemen wearing flak jackets fought fires while policemen crouched beside cruisers shooting at windows and other policemen held guns on young men leaning with hands spread against the walls.

Luis and Blade hadn't returned. She lay face-down on her bed trying not to cry. Everything she'd ever done was wrong. She shouldn't have joined the band, should've stayed in college. Without smack, depression overwhelmed her yet she felt it was right that she was punished, that she suffered. Unable to sleep she got up, went downstairs and asked the nervous desk clerk how to find the police station.

He gave her a guest map of Motor City with parks and museums marked by little icons. He put a red X for each nearby police station. "You can try these, but there's lots more too."

The police stations were clichés of Hell, jammed with handcuffed bleeding men, policemen with guns and nightsticks and gas masks, soldiers in combat gear. All night she wandered through seething crowds, ducking the armored cars and tanks and the soldiers with wide fearful eyes and pointing rifles. Once she stepped over a man on a bloody sidewalk and went back to him but he was dead, his white eyes locked on nothing.

LUIS SHOWED UP next morning, head bandaged, a huge cut down one cheek. "We were riding in a taxi, Blade and me. It got caught in the crowd." He sat holding his head. "The cops. They yanked us out beating us with damn nightsticks –" He raised his hands as if to ward them off. "They threw us in some jail, hundreds of guys in there. Hey, got a cigarette? I ain't seen Blade since. They were beating shit out of everybody, even white tourists caught up in it. What's this country coming to?"

"Same place it's always been," Sybil answered.

Tara made him clean up and go back with her to the Park Avenue police station, where handcuffed men lay and sat in the corridors, many in ankle chains. "Please help," they kept calling, "I haven't done anything. Help me call a lawyer –"

"You can't go back there," a cop said when Tara wanted to look for Blade. "You give me a description."

"He's black, about six feet, long curly black hair, a moustache."

"I got a thousand niggers like that," he snickered. "Get out of here."

SHE FOUND BLADE three days later at Ford Hospital. He had been admitted from jail with a concussion, broken arm, three missing teeth and five broken ribs. He had been kicked so hard and repeatedly in the balls he could not walk or sit, lying on his side on a cot while she held him gently as she could. "Only reason I got out," he whispered, "is somebody recognize me. That made them afraid."

Down the corridor a radio was playing *And she'll have fun fun fun 'til her daddy takes the T-Bird away.* "But why," she wept, "why'd they do this?"

"Hey," he almost cracked a smile, "I'm a nigger, remember?"

When it was over, forty-three people had died and thousands more were injured. Two thousand buildings had been burned and over seven thousand people arrested. Detroit looked like pictures of Dresden after the Allied bombings.

They were all burning – Chicago, Los Angeles, New York, Philadelphia, San Francisco, Newark, Cleveland, Boston, Atlanta, Tampa, Jersey City, Buffalo, Minneapolis, Rochester, Memphis. And places nobody had heard of: Waukegan, Benton Harbor, Elizabeth, Durham, Cairo, Patterson. Thousands of dead and injured, billions of dollars turned to ashes.

The cleansing fire. The start of the new American Revolution.

2 2

———

THE PENTAGON WALLS

AS TV CAMERAS HISSED and people cheered, Mick and fifteen other Resistance founders on October 16 dropped their draft cards into a box at Whitehall for delivery to the Justice Department, as did twelve hundred other resisters across the country.

Just by appearing he'd risked arrest. And refusal to carry a draft card meant five years in prison plus a ten thousand dollar fine. He had hated doing this, felt furious with himself for destroying his future. But if The Resistance could dry up the supply of draftees could it stop this War?

"It's far too radical," Al Lowenstein said that night.

"I can't *say* I support it," Bobby Kennedy smiled cryptically, "but I do."

"We want to make it acceptable to refuse the draft. Nobody wants to go to Vietnam; when nobody does then the War will end."

"You're a dreamer, Mick," Bobby said. "Most people don't have the courage."

He'd thought more and more about what the young woman, Diana Oughton, had said to him in Chicago, looking at him with those unblinking amber eyes: We know the War is very evil. *So how far do we have to go to stop it?*

279

Was it enough, this commitment he'd just made by turning in his draft card? Or did he have to do more? What was *more*?

Five years in prison seemed a suffocating evil darkness: no girls, no mountains, no wilderness, no drugs, no music. As with Barbusse's soldier, no freedom.

He couldn't imagine what to do, hated himself for being in this situation. *Go, and beat your crazy head against the sky,* sang the group whose name meant sex, and only sex could save your soul, sex and drugs and the all-embracing power of rock 'n roll.

But they wouldn't keep you out of Leavenworth.

How far do we have to go to stop it?

"THE STONES ARE REVOLUTIONARIES," Tiny said. "The Beatles write about revolution, but they don't mean it: *"Don't you know that you can count me out."*

"The funniest lines," Luis added, "is *But if you go carrying pictures of Chairman Mao, you ain't gonna make it with anyone anyhow –"*

"Compare all that," Tiny went on, "to *Everywhere I hear the sound of marching charging feet."* He raised his palms. "Now ain't that where we are today? *Cause summer's here and the time is right, for violent revolution!* – Now ain't that exactly where we're *going?"*

Blade sucked on a missing tooth. "Thing is, nobody wants anybody hurt."

"That's what my brother's trying to do," Tara said.

"What's that line," Blade paused, "the Dylan one, *And I just said good luck?"*

THE LINCOLN MEMORIAL on October 21 looked down in silent witness on the huge Washington rally to protest the War. The Reflecting Pool mirrored the tawny sky and the red-leafed trees along its edge. At its far end the Washington Monument looked like the giant obelisk Napoleon had stolen from Egypt and raised over the Place de la Concorde, a great phallus, symbol of male power.

Mick stood among the others on the podium with a sickening lurch in his stomach at the size of the crowd. *This is what a hundred thousand people looks like.* He felt skinny and small, naked. What could he say they didn't already know, that could have value?

What would Lincoln have thought to see this? But hadn't he led the country into the most horrible, destructive and deadly war in its history? Hadn't he killed and maimed hundreds of thousands of young men, burnt half the southern cities to the ground, for a principle? For the stated idea that no state had the right to leave the union. That's why all those young men died?

"I'm ashamed," Dr. Benjamin Spock said to the crowd, "that I campaigned for Lyndon Johnson in sixty-four, because he promised he wouldn't escalate in Vietnam. Lyndon Johnson betrayed me. Lyndon Johnson has betrayed America!"

He waited for the applause to die. "Our real enemy is not the Vietcong," he went on, "but Lyndon Johnson, whom we elected as a peace candidate in 1964, and who betrayed us within three months, and who has stubbornly led us deeper and deeper into a bloody quagmire."

"Peace now!" the crowd roared. "Peace now!" It seemed angry, powerful, destructive. *But how can you fight for peace?*

Speaker after speaker castigated the War, Phil Ochs sang and Vietnam vets threw their medals in a pile and Malcolm X's sister promised, "You want peace, you'll get it!" The announcer called Mick's name; another screamed, "The Re*sistance*!"

Numbly he climbed the podium, gripped the microphone like a cable that might save him from falling twenty stories. What could he say that could make a difference?

"One lone gunman," he said into the buzzy black microphone, "like in that tower in Austin, Texas, can terrorize a crowd. Two can terrorize thousands. And it only takes a few politicians and generals to terrorize millions of people and destroy the world. But what *right* do they have to invade another country, kill and injure people, burn homes and schools and churches and cause enormous suffering and then move on?"

The crowd grew silent. "Caesar in Gaul, the Germans in Poland, what we're doing to Vietnam now. What right do we have to destroy that beautiful country simply because they won't do what we want? As our beloved Martin Luther King has said, if America's soul dies of poison, the autopsy will read Vietnam. Do we want our country's soul to die? *No!* Do we want America's soul to die? *No!*"

The crowd roared; in the dizzy glare thousands of hands reached up. "What *we* have to do here in DC, *all* of us who care about America, is stop the Pentagon and Lyndon Johnson and all the other cowards who never faced bullets, from expanding this War they love so much."

He was yelling now over the exultant crowd. "And how we stop this War is to stop sending our young men to die in it!"

He waited for them to quiet. Over the steady rumble of the crowd distant sirens wailed; a helicopter flew over low; somewhere a police dog was barking; he shivered with nervousness. "And that's why I turned my draft card into the Justice Department, and why I ask all you guys to do the same –"

He smiled down at a long-haired woman in front. "And you sisters out there, please, love these brave guys who turn in their cards, and tell the other guys . . . well, you can tell them to ask Lyndon Johnson to bend over, 'cause that's all they'll get!"

The crowd roared and cheered and laughed. He raised his hands, feeling tiny and insignificant. Quickly he described the simple mathematics of it: "With no soldiers the Pentagon can't fight this War. And these young men, do they want to die perpetrating this horrible crime?

Tears choked him. "We want to keep our brothers alive, not dying in a rice paddy for some dictator. Think of the long lives and children they can have, years of work and love, grandchildren. Are we going to let them lose all that?"

The crowd quieted. "So if you're a man turn in your card. And if you're a woman, make sure every man you know does the same. Without any young men to die for them, the cowards in the White House might have to go and risk their own lives!" He raised his fists. "Now it's on to the Pentagon! We *can* stop this War! We *will* stop this War! We will stop this War *now!*"

Tears flooding his eyes he turned from the podium and stumbled blindly down the stairs, hands gripping him, people shaking his hand, women kissing him, hugging him.

Glancing around he wiped his eyes, realized he was looking for Troy.

"*Take your place on the great mandala,*" somebody was singing, the Peter Paul and Mary song, *while it turns through your brief moment of time,*"

Win or lose now, you must choose now,
And if you lose you're only losing your life.

THE PENTAGON'S HUGE WALLS loomed above them like a medieval fortress. Lines of soldiers massed before them, bayoneted rifles at the ready, lines of Federal Marshals behind the soldiers. Lights tossed garish shadows, the crowd rumbled and chanted. Tear gas hissed as canisters whispered through the air and clunked down among the demonstrators, who hurled them back among the soldiers and marshals.

Mick led a charge up the steps and the marshals beat them back, clubs thudding into soft flesh, blood spattering gray concrete. He faced a marshal a foot away, the man's black-helmeted face full of hate. Mick punched him and the man went down, others swinging their clubs as he ducked away, swung back and punched another, a club cracking Mick's arm as he pulled back again but now his arm was dead so he swung with his left till the pain knocked him to his knees and others drove forward.

Music came moving over the crowd, growing and growing as thousands of voices joined in, drowning out the whack of clubs and the sizzle of tear gas, everyone singing

O beautiful for spacious skies,
For amber waves of grain

For purple mountain majesties
Above the fruited plain

Again and again the crowd surged forward, pushing the soldiers and marshals back, the marshals' clubs flailing, women screaming as the marshals grabbed their hair, clubbing and clubbing, rifle butts rising and falling, the tear gas spreading like mist, as people sang on,

O beautiful for heroes proved
In liberating strife.
Who more than self their country loved
And mercy more than life

Cradling his broken arm he stared up at the tall implacable walls. The demonstrators were powerless as pea-shooters firing at a castle. "No way we can break in," he yelled over the singing. "Don't get hurt for nothing!"

People moved aside to let him pass; others were coming back bloody and swearing. "We need guns!" someone shouted. "Fight war with war!"

He was a big bearded pot-bellied guy in a green Pendleton shirt. "Get over there," Mick pointed at the marshals, "with your own kind."

"Gonna kill 'em," the man yelled. "Let's kill the bastards!"

"This guy's an FBI agitator!" Mick yelled. "Get him out of here!" He turned to grab the man but he'd vanished into the crowd.

As night fell it turned even colder; rank after rank of unarmed protesters had been beaten back from the Pentagon walls, hundreds more arrested. Mick's arm ached unbearably; people kept bumping it making him cry out with pain. You should leave, he told himself, but that was like an officer jumping from a sinking ship.

That afternoon a bunch of silly hippies led by Allen Ginsburg had made a pretense of trying to "levitate" the Pentagon with chants. To most Americans they must have seemed worse than inane, effeminate and totally irrelevant. And because the media focused on them, they became a misleading image of the antiwar movement: Ginsburg in his outlandish robes limp-wristedly clicking his bells – pranksters, not the serious, committed, dangerous revolutionaries who could frighten the power makers into changing their course. How can we change them, Mick wondered, if they don't fear us?

Protestors in clumps were lighting fires of their peace signs – he smiled to think how the body will always sacrifice its ideals to stay warm. But in truth the body had no ideals. Depression sank into him with the night chill.

It seemed to fit that Che Guevara was dead. Doctor, revolutionary, legendary war hero, strategist, philosopher, economist and writer, he'd just been executed by the CIA in the Bolivian jungle. For the crime of trying to give people a level playing field, the equal opportunities listed in the Constitution. He who had been so tormented by Vietnam he tried to open a second front against the US in Latin America. And had made the mistake of obeying the words of Christ.

Maybe Che and Christ were wrong. Maybe this is how things were supposed to be – slaughter, sorrow, destruction. Maybe we murderous humans were only doing what we were supposed to do.

"I seen you up there speakin," a black kid said. "You tryin hard, man, but all the speeches in the worl' won' do it."

"Just turn in your card," Mick said, too tired and full of pain.

"My brother dead in Vietnam. Ain't nothin I can turn in to git him back."

Mick sat on the cold ground. The kid crouched beside him. "You okay?"

"Arm's broken."

"Marshals done it?"

"Yeah."

"Sorry, man. But hey, *we* know how to burn things down. Maybe it's time?"

What was it Lily had said about the French Revolution so long ago, on another planet maybe? "Easy to light a fire. But how do you put it out?"

"We got plenty to burn down 'fore we have to worry bout that."

So much had failed, with more failure to come. It made Mick sick at heart. *All the speeches in the worl' won' do it.* Revolution was just another form of hate and killing.

"I saw you too, up there," a tall young man, crew cut, medals on his chest. "Have to thank you."

"It's okay," Mick said, holding his aching shoulder. The tall young man had only one arm. "You were in Nam?"

"Just got back. And I came here to add my voice, to say it's wrong."

Mick's arm hurt so bad he almost wished it was gone. "I'm sorry."

"Better than coming home in a body bag, like my friends." The soldier knelt beside him. "What you said up there, about killing civilians? I was in a campaign called Operation Wheeler, in the Song Ve Valley. We killed thousands of civilians, wasted all these villages, tortured so many people. Old people, you know, women raped, our guys wearing necklaces of human ears." He shrugged. "I was almost happy when I lost this arm. Just to get out of there." He stood. "You should talk about it, let it be known," and slipped into the crowd.

The Pentagon Wall rose darkly overhead, a vast colossus, the way people really were, the United States really was. It would crush any resistance. The Pentagon just a metaphor for America. To stop the War you had to change America. The American people.

Mick laughed at the futility of it all, got to his feet, and walked toward the ambulances filling with the wounded from the Wall.

DAISY GOT A TV GLIMPSE of a young man handsome, tall and alone, like a shepherd with arms raised in supplication for a truth no one will hear: that if everyone refuses the draft the War will end. That you can't kill soldiers if there are no soldiers to kill.

She knelt before the TV to see closer. Could've sworn it was Mick. The way he stood, tall and alert. Kind and friendly but ready for danger. The way he always had.

"Mick O'Brien," the stern newsman's voice said. "A leader of the anti-American group The Resistance, the one that's sending their draft cards back to the government and endangering the lives of our boys overseas."

"Mick." Her belly quivered, her legs felt weak, her mouth wanting. But there was no more, just pictures of the waves of protesters assaulting the Pentagon walls and being beaten back, to the tune of God Bless America.

It occurred to her with shock to wonder, *Is this America?*

Mick – where are you?

She could send him a letter. *Oh my God I've been so missing you all these years.*

My heart aches for you.

That means my heart inside my chest actually hurts when I think of you.

No, she couldn't write that.

Compared to what she was doing now, he was a hero. Risking his life, facing jail. Her work was too academic and too personal, motivated by her own needs and not that of others.

I'm going to switch, she decided. Like Mick, to take some risk. Do more research on LSD and peyote. That's where the real brain knowledge is.

But I won't get in touch with Mick. Knowing him, he probably has someone now. Lots of someones.

Do your research, girl. But keep your desires to yourself.

THE CHELSEA HOTEL was full of long-hairs whom Troy scowled at as he crossed the worn lobby rug to the desk, feeling disheveled and dirty from nights of sleeping in Central Park. In the mirror behind the desk he appeared out of place with his short hair, scarred face and rangy hard features.

When Tara came down the long twisting stairway he did not know her – skinny and drawn with bruise-like circles under her eyes, smaller than her long-sleeved tie-dyed blouse and worn Levis, the scuffed sandals with her red-painted toes sticking out. "Hey," she smiled.

Her body was thin and hard; she smelled of cigarettes and patchouli. Her hair once so sleek and fine felt rough against his cheek. "Christ," he muttered, "what's happened to you?"

They sat in a coffee house around the corner, Tara downing espressos and smoking Chesterfields while he drank water, feeling out of place. "You look like shit," she countered. "Taken a beating or two?"

With shame he thought of Mick. "This concert?"

"Tomorrow and the next night at The Bitter End. You can come? I'll comp your tickets . . . There'll be groupies for the guys – they'll give you some if you want."

He took her hand, thin and hard. "Christ, Tara –"

She lit a cigarette, waved out the match. "*Christ?* Don't give me that shit. You've been over there killing farmers –"

She looked older, without peace or illusions. Where was the vivacious, aggressive, lovely pianist who did calculus in her head and stole his slide rule? He slid his fingertips down the back of her hand and between the narrow fingers. "You doing drugs?"

She laughed, hoarse, weary. "Have *I* been doing drugs?" she mimicked. "Who are you, the parson's son?"

"I'm nobody's son."

She looked at him hard then softened. "Dad treated you like one."

"Treated ain't the same as being, you know that. Hard as he tried. And your Ma too. Bless her soul. Bless both their souls."

Tara sat silent, then brightened. "I saw Mick last night, after he got back."

Troy felt shame. "I saw him too, last week. We got in a fight."

"Idiots!" She looked at Troy. "He got a broken arm. At the Pentagon."

"I probably still couldn't beat him."

She caressed his cheek. "I'm happy you're back."

"I'm not." He shrugged. "I don't know where I am, Tara. Not here, not over there."

"*We're* just very happy you're *here*."

He smiled. "So what's with this band?"

"Our single just hit the Billboard top hundred. Our first album went nowhere, this's the second. So now we're touring, backing it up. After here we head to Boston, then Providence, Hartford, Buffalo, all over the map. Our agent, he's big-time, says we can make it."

"Make what?" He felt her going beyond him, to a dimension he couldn't enter. "What are you really *making*, if you end up looking like this?"

"*This?*" She took his hand; her palm felt rough, cold. "This is just normal shit. It's so hard to make a record. So hard to tour. Wears you down to the bone." She smiled, radiant an instant. "I remember when you and I used to *make* it."

He felt himself blush. "That was long ago."

"In the barn, down on the straw? Out in the woods? Jesus that was fun."

"And look where it got us."

"Yeah." She inhaled. "A dead child."

"And it killed *us*."

She gave him a sad smile. "We weren't going to make it anyway."

"Why?"

She shrugged. "Too much like incest. Inside us."

He turned away, back to her. "You still with that guitar god?"

She laughed. "Luis? On and off." She scanned him. "And you, no love life anymore? No lovely Annamite Mata Hari?" She tickled his palm. "I'm joking, Honey. Nobody over there but prostitutes, from what I hear. Unless you found some nice American nurse somewhere."

"I fell in love, Tara. With a teacher – I started to say *with a native girl* – can you imagine, *thinking* that? I really loved her. Still do."

Tara took his hand, her eyes warm. "And?"

He shrugged. "She won't have me."

She said nothing, then, "And now that you're back in the land of the free and the home of the brave?"

"Don't make fun."

"It *needs* to be made fun of, because it's *evil*. You know better than anyone."

He wanted to argue, strike back. Even if the War was wrong he still hated the people who put it down, who put down all the guys who'd died. The ones who *would* die. But why did they have to die? "I don't know any more."

She stroked his arm. "You free this afternoon?"

He snickered. "What would I be doing?"

"We'll drive out to Tappan, see the old place?" She squeezed his fingers. "I'll call Mick, see if he can come."

He felt empty, knowing it was her attempt to reach out, to rebuild the past. "Sure."

She went to the phone booth in the corner, came back. "No answer."

"Probably at some peacenik meeting."

"Let's go back to the hotel, I'll get my coat."

"Hell, it's warm out."

She grinned. "Not with the top down."

It was a silver XKE with red leather. "This *yours?*"

"I always rent one on tour. Won't fly or ride in helicopters like the rest of the band."

Traffic on the bridge had jammed. As they crossed it she sang *George Washington Bridge* like they'd sung years ago, but he stared silently through the windshield. *You're like Su Li*, he told her. *Enigma.* "I never could figure," he said, "how the revolutionaries made it through that last bitter winter on the high ridge above Shanks Village. The whole winter through hunger and terrible cold, in their rags and torn tents, then they came down from those hills and forests to defeat the British. And we don't value it, what they did."

"It's Vietnam – *that's* what you're saying?" She inched the car forward. The cars ahead and the bridge cables wobbled in exhaust-thick air. He imagined the lovely sloping field down from their old home to Lafayette's house – how many times had they walked it, he, she and Mick? The thought of Mick bothered him like a sore tooth, something left undone. He pulled a scab from the cuts on his face.

"That ridge where Washington's soldiers camped?" she said. "The elms where Dad hung the hammock? The valley with pastures and beech forest and that lovely stream with willows down the middle and that tall-steepled church at the end?"

"Maybe the hammock's still hanging there?" She did not answer. "Imagine," he added, "a hundred square miles, ridges and valleys and swamps and hillocks, streams and ponds and deer, bear, otter, raccoon, cottonmouths, water moccasins. Wow, how come we haven't gone back?"

The traffic loosened like a sewer pipe that finally unblocks. They were across the Hudson now, the Palisades on the left. The wind combed loose Tara's chestnut hair, freeing her high cheekbones. The highway had six lanes each way, on each side blocks and blocks of little boxes. *Little boxes,* she sang. Malvina Reynolds' song, wondering would it upset him,

There's a green one and a pink one
And a blue one and a yellow one,
And they're all made out of ticky tacky
And they all look just the same.

There was no sign for Shanks Village. "We must've made a wrong turn."

A sea of roofs expanded to the horizons. An exit dumped them into a vast tract where each house looked like the others, each tiny shorn lawn falsely bright with fertilizer and herbicides, the people on the narrow sidewalk looking, as in the song, all the same. The streets had tree names – Beech Road, Hawthorne Way, Birch Lane – but there were no trees. Instead of wild animals there was Badger Place, Fox Lane and Partridge Court. *No Trespassing* said the metal signs on the little picket fences.

"This can't be it –"

There was truly nowhere else. The unending forest was gone. The hill where their farmhouse had stood for two centuries had been bull-dozed into the valley where the stream once wandered past the white-steepled church, but the valley and stream and church were gone. There were no elms, no meadow, only unending mazes of streets with pert identical houses. On one corner a small blue steel sign tacked to a telephone pole said, "General Lafayette lived here in a house on the Bogart farm in 1780. Opposite is a spring used by the Continental Army camped on the West Ridge."

There was still a slight rise where for millennia the West Ridge had once risen to a lovely crown of beeches and oaks, where the American Revolutionary Army had spent that last savage winter. Now where Washington's spring had once flowed a concrete culvert ran under the highway.

The year Troy had started living with them Mick had taken him the first day of fishing season deep into the woods to his favorite stream. They dropped worms on hooks through snow-covered ice into pools where small trout struck like lightning. Around a curve in the stream they'd come to a dead doe chased down by dogs, her belly ripped open, her unborn fawn dead beside her, and he wanted to tell Tara that it had presaged the death of everything they'd loved, would ever love.

But there was no way to talk about it. They drove back into Tappan, down the long road they'd walked so many times together, she, Mick and Troy, along the convent fence where the white horse had grazed, past the huge oak and the 1776 House.

"I think of them so often," Tara said.

"Hal and Sylvia? It sounds nice, Florida."

"Grampy went with them, and that woman Sadie went with him, some place called Boca Raton. He says there's miles of beaches with nothing but palm trees. No houses, nothing."

"We tried to go there once," Troy said. "Me and Mick."

She laughed. "You think I don't remember?" She turned left on Washington Street over Sparkill Creek and it felt for a moment as if they were kids going to school again and the whole world was natural and young and pure.

She stopped to put the top up on the XKE and they crossed the bridge in a cold fog. Vietnam was far away but everything seemed like Vietnam. The place where they had lived and loved was gone. The children dead in the hooches and the child he and she had once killed were one and the same. Just as Vietnam was an addiction to evil that America could not relinquish, their killed child had kept them intolerably closer, a poisonous link of guilt.

As so many times he tried to reach across the barrier of hostility between them. The connection was almost there, then she retreated to some analgesic place where neither he nor she could reach her. They could connect, he realized, only enough to suffer from knowing they wanted to be together and could not.

"I'm wondering, like about going back. The guys I left there –"

"*Vietnam*? Are you *nuts*?"

"Once you've been in it – the terror and *rage*, the *depth*, when you come back to this world, you're empty. There's nothing here for you. Absolutely nothing."

"It's for that girl, that teacher – you'd go back?"

"She says she loves me, but . . ." He looked up at Manhattan's grim towers. He had wanted to protect his country. Protect Su Li. If he got posted back to Hué? The MACV compound on the south side of the Perfume River, you could almost see it from Chez Henri . . .

No Direction Home on the radio made him wonder *is that me?*

That night for hours they argued in the big soft bed in her creaky room at the Chelsea Hotel, their young bodies distorted by the stained Victorian mirror over the dresser; he wanted to make love to heal the rift between them, but she refused, wanting first to heal the rift with words. Finally they slept, exhausted, alone and emptily loving.

At breakfast his face reflected in the crystal water glass was misshapen, aged, and sad, and he wondered how many people had passed their lives in marriages long on frustration and short on joy. *Seek the untrodden*, he told himself. *Or go mad*. "We have to learn," he said, "to ignore each other."

She stuck out her tongue. "I'm not the one who started it."

"*We* are the ones who started it."

"It's the War. It kills everything."

In dead Shanks Village the tree names on the new street signs where the farms and forest had been were just replacing the real with a lie – wasn't that America?

If he was going take a fresh memory of his roots back to Nam, this would be it.

23

PERFUME RIVER

"**THE ENTIRE HISTORY OF THIS WAR,**" said Minnesota Senator Eugene McCarthy, announcing his challenge of President Johnson for the 1968 Democratic nomination, "has been one of continued error and misjudgment leading to the physical destruction of a small weak nation by the military of the world's most powerful, a hundred fifty thousand civilian deaths in South Vietnam alone, a third of its population refugees, vast loss of life in North Vietnam, over fifteen thousand American dead and nearly a hundred thousand wounded..."

"They'll shoot him." Tucker shut off the TV.

"Who?" Lucius Brown, another antiwar vet, said.

"McCarthy, if he starts to win."

"No, I mean *who* will shoot him?" Lucius had an aggravated, lazy way of talking, leaning back in his chair with his black beret tipped forward over his afro.

"Same ones got Kennedy."

"What do they get out of it?"

"Nixon."

"Nah," Lucius snickered. "You're too pessimistic. Nixon's a horrible man – who would vote for him?"

"Think about it," Mick said, "McNamara, Ball, Bundy, Moyers – all of Johnson's close people are leaving him because of the War. He's getting isolated, listening to generals and sycophants. The polls're shifting against him and the War. McCarthy could take him down."

"If that were so," Tucker said, "then the real question is, do we stay inside the system? Work for McCarthy, or build on these protests that are turning the nation against the War. Or both?"

"Confucius says revolution is good," Lucius added, "when the man is equal to the task. Even if a different senator in the White House don't mean revolution, it still might stop this War."

"If it's peaceful," Dave Dellinger said. "Not a revolution."

"It's not the protests that are turning the country," Lucius said. "It's the body bags. When people see these kids are dyin for no reason –"

"The hard thing," Tucker said, "is to believe McCarthy has a chance, it's worth fighting for. That these American idiots who think the War is justified will come around. That the democratic system can heal itself."

"If we just keep pushing," Mick said. "More riots in the streets, more draft card burnings, it makes people like McCarthy seem reasonable. But we have to unite the antiwar movement behind him too."

"Five hundred and eighty-five people've been arrested in the last four days in New York," Lucius said. "Including Ben Spock –"

"*Every*body's baby doctor."

"People believe in him," Tucker said. "He spent a lifetime bringing forth life, and thinking how best to grow it."

"He isn't some technician in the Pentagon counting bodies."

"And what I'm saying," Lucius snapped, "is that all those arrests and all the other poor people got their heads busted? It don't change a thing."

"Gene can't win," Dave Dellinger said. Once an ambulance driver in the Spanish Civil War, he had been a long-time pacifist, had spent three years in jail for refusing induction, and had organized the previous October's Pentagon March. "Lyndon has the unions, the regular Dems, the retirees, the Southern Christians. What'll Gene have, the peace folks, the good Christians, some returned vets," he smiled, "us leftist long-haired rabble –"

"Heck, David," Lucius said, "You don't have hardly no hair at all –"

"Gene'll have the students," Mick argued. "Al Lowenstein's organizing them through student body presidents nationwide. David Harris, who was the Stanford student body president, he's pulling them all together. Linking every campus against the War."

"The one who married Baez –"

"Johnson'll crush us," Dellinger said. "It'll drive the peace movement out of the Democratic Party, make us powerless."

Mick stared round the room of organizers, trying to look everyone in the eyes. "We all have to decide: are we with Gene or not?"

"What we want is return on our investment," Lucius said. "If we back McCarthy, he has to win and stop this War. If we're sure he can't do that we don't go with him."

"The first primary's March 12 in New Hampshire," Mick said. "Three and a half months from now. Gene's putting together a team – who wants to be on it?"

"Are we sliding toward some horrible revolution?" Reverend Coffin tented long fingers before his face. "If so, then Gene's just a Kerensky puffing out his chest till Lenin brings him down."

"Remember your *I Ching*," Lucius said, "the hexagram on revolution? When an influential man of inner strength and truth wants to change the government, it brings good fortune. That's Gene McCarthy –"

"Maybe," Dellinger shrugged. "But doesn't the following line say something about *a great man changes like a tiger* – at the very start he is believed and wins the support of the people? That's Bobby."

"Bobby's on the edge," Mick said, "but Ethel doesn't want him to. Fears he'll get killed. His brother united the Democratic Party and Bobby doesn't want to be the one to tear it apart. Anyway, now Gene's in first."

"Sad thing is," Coffin said, "Bobby can beat Nixon. McCarthy can't."

"You never know with poets," Lucius quipped, half-heartedly.

Mick watched them, worn down with arguing, with convincing, with trying to see things in his head first, what each person would say and how to influence them. To do what? To unite against this War that to him was becoming an obsession, that poisoned every desire, hope, or thought. While you're having dinner, a Vietnamese village full of people is being hit by phosphorous bombs. While you're fucking, or taking a shower, or walking down the sidewalk looking up at the blue sky.

What do we have to do to stop it?

LSD HAD UNLEASHED a scientific revolution. Nearly five thousand research studies done by Harvard, Stanford and other major universities had shown that LSD, mescaline and psilocybin had very positive results not only on spiritual growth but also in treating alcoholism, sexual trauma, autism, depression, and other maladies.

To do mind research was one of the reasons Daisy had gone to Stanford, and hallucinogens had been a promising new technique. Nearly a thousand FDA-approved scientific studies for the National Institute of Mental Health had proven LSD to be also very beneficial for compulsive disorders, fear of death in cancer patients, and general psychological issues. It even had a better cure rate for alcoholism than Alchoholics Anonymous.

Among more than fifty thousand people who had taken LSD in research situations, eighty percent said it was a major or *the* major religious experience of their lives. In prisons, recidivism dropped seventy-five percent among parolees who had taken LSD in research projects. Harvard and Stanford scientists were studying whether LSD could help people to lead happier, more constructive lives.

But the CIA, due perhaps to its own tarnished past with LSD, had pressured the FDA to make LSD illegal in both research and individual use.

"We've all spent years analyzing this, me and all my colleagues, have had superb results, and now it's a federal offense?" Dr. Vargas, the head of the Stanford neuroscience department, growled at Daisy. "*Acch!* What kind of crazy is that?"

"I've never met a person who had a bad trip," she said. "But the media says it happens all the time. Why are they lying?"

"It's the CIA. They developed LSD, them and Sandoz Labs in Switzerland, and now they want to shut it down. And they control lots of media, like *Time* and *Life* for instance, they keep running articles about how bad is LSD. But they were the ones started all this LSD, with their Project MKUltra, their LSD experiments in the 1950s and still ongoing today, though they deny that. CIA experiments in mind control, psychological torture, interrogation techniques using LSD and other hallucinogens . . . *Acch* – that kind of thing."

"It's creepy," she shivered, "we don't even know how much media they control. Or who they really are."

"LSD teaches you to think for yourself. Free yourself. And nothing threatens the group more than individual freedom. So of course it has to be illegal."

RIDING SHOTGUN INTO HUÉ in a shiny MACV jeep, Troy felt an astounded happiness. *I love this place,* he repeated silently to the iridescent paddies, the grass huts copsed in bamboos with their smooth green truncated bark, the concrete and stone memorials in graveyards, the explosions of color and scent, the patient water buffaloes with egrets on their backs, the pigs snorting and squealing in their bamboo pens, the slow undulant line of egrets over the Perfume River, *I forgot how much I love it.*

He could not tell why he loved it but knew he did. That it was more important to him now than any other place on earth.

Every white lotus blossom seemed impeccably lovely, every call of mynah in the tall cool-shadowed trees, every taste of breeze and smell of meat on charcoal and the thousand different trees and shrubs. He saw a woman in a snowy *ao dai* and remembered Su Li leaning to take a child's hand, her black hair cascading down her shoulder. Saw her writhing naked beneath him, then fifteen minutes later grinning at him over noodle soup, a tender chunk of meat in her chopsticks. Pushing her Vespa that first day. That last day outside her school when she said she hated him more than the VC.

The wide sheen of paddies gave way to bright market gardens then streets overarched by thick-trunked ancient trees, avenues of elegant French-style homes with wide verandas and red-tiled roofs, their wide lawns parted by tall stone walls. The world was a riot of reds, yellows, orange, persimmon and blues against a tumult of greens and a white-blue sky. Red, purple and yellow lotuses bloomed in canal backwaters spanned by delicate stone bridges, forests of orchids down their banks. Sampans, some with rounded roofs of wooden slats or canvas, slid silently along them.

In the markets women in conical hats sat crosslegged behind palm-leaf baskets piled with small bright pineapples and bananas, carmine strawberries, green grapefruits and orange mangoes, bowls of raw purple-white squid and yellow star-shaped carambolas, tan and pink yams, watercress and wild onions and gleaming red toma-toes. Women on bicycles were selling ripe limes, dragon fruit and tamarinds from wide wicker baskets suspended over their back wheels, others with their bicycles piled high with conical hats and baskets or cooking pans or lanterns.

He turned left by the Joan of Arc Church and crossed the Nguyen Hoang Bridge and turned north along the River toward Bach Dang through streets mobbed with people and bicycles, little boys with trays of Coca Cola and Budweiser hung from their necks.

The clickclack of bicycles coming up behind him – all so familiar – fragrances of a thousand flowers, of ripe fruits and grilled meat, of tea, incense, cooking oil and charcoal, and even the odors of fermented fish and the stolid canals now seemed nostalgic. How strange such a haven in a country crushed by war. In a way he'd become it, or it he; he couldn't tell and didn't care, just to *be* here, smiling at the betel-toothed mamasans offering trays of decapitated roses, candies, lychees and tamarinds, one calling, "Want nice girl, Maline?"

SU LI stared at him aghast. "What *you* doing here? I tell you go away for*ever*!"

"I came back for you."

"You crazy. I *no* want you!" But her eyes made everything she said a lie – or *was* he crazy? She took his face in her slim cool hands. "We both get kill," she said softly, "see each other anymore."

Her tenderness filled him with joy and hope. "Tell your mother I'll pay right now for you all – a plane to the States. If you're my fiancée the Marines can get you all a visa, you can get out."

Lacing fingers round his neck she kissed him. "You lovely man. I not mean it when I say I hate you. I try make you go away."

He laughed at the joy of it, kissing and kissing her, holding her delicate strength in the warm circle of his arms. "Why, you silly? *Why?*"

She took a slow breath, looked round the humble house, the low divan and table with the bowl of yellow lychees bright in late sun. "We not talk here. You go Chez Henri and I come there?"

"When, silly? When?"

"After dark." Again she glanced round, almost furtive. "Not safe here. Not you *ever* come back here. Take room hotel down from Chez Henri." She bit her lip, watchful. "I keep with you tonight. We talk."

"I CAME BACK TO NAM," Troy said, "because I couldn't stay back in the world knowing you guys were here." He looked out at the forty Marines of Advisory Team 3 sitting in the shade of the commandeered hotel in the MACV compound. "That *any* Americans were here."

"You don't think we *should* be here?" said a skinny black kid with glasses.

"I don't get into politics. I'm here to keep you safe. Much as I can."

"Wanna keep us safe?" A tall tough white kid, machine gunner. "Send us home."

Troy sat on his duffle. The guy I'm replacing, Lieutenant Asche?"

"He was bringing in a wounded guy and the medevac gets hit and the rotor cuts him in half." The black kid shrugged. "Trouble is, he was short. Three weeks."

"He a lot shorter," somebody snickered, "after that rotor get him –"

Troy scanned their young dirty faces aged by the terror of combat. "I want to talk with each of you. Want to know your thoughts, what you can do, how I can help you."

The machine gunner grinned. "Help us?"

Troy stood looking him in the eye. "To get you home alive. Unwounded."

"Too late," someone countered. "Most of us been wounded, few times."

"Right on," someone chuckled.

"And I want no bravado. The smallest injury – a leech pulled off wrong, razor grass, the skin of your feet worn rotten by wet boots – and you're less effective, less able to run fast, to duck, to walk light-footed out there in that jungle of death."

HE HAD NEVER known such joy, such hope. Su Li would come soon and he would convince her. Soon she would be safe back in the States and all he had to do was finish out his tour to be with her forever.

Sloshing his gin and tonic he glanced round Chez Henri's patio. The other clients, CIA types, ARVN officers from their HQ in the Citadel, merchants and businessmen, a few with women, all talked in low voices. The Perfume River gurgled softly beyond the rail, motor-bikes and buses clattered in the distance. Once a water bird cried, startled by a sampan hissing upriver, its outboard chugging. The lonely piano player from Vichy was singing *Summertime, and the livin's so easy, fish are jumpin and the cotton is fine,* gently running fingers down the keys, and everything was quiet and good and hopeful, even the two ARVN soldiers standing guard with M16s in the narrow street. *And some day,* the Vichy man sang, *you're gonna rise up into the sky,*

But till that morning
There's nothin can harm you

and it felt good and true and perhaps the War would end soon and people would see how silly it had been to hate and kill each other.

She appeared from nowhere and sat across from him. She wore a blue gown now and the blue and gold silk scarf he'd given her, the gold crucifix dangling in the hollow between her breasts. "My God," he smiled, "you are so lovely –"

"American soldier always tell Vietnam girl she is beautiful," she laughed. "So he can make her do *làm tình*."

He took her hand. "I want to do *làm tình* with you, for the rest of my life."

Her face clouded. "Don't talk bad luck."

"Why did you try to make me go away? Why?"

She looked at him thoughtfully. "When I first meet you, I think you funny. You are making faces, pushing my scooter, acting so important when you say there is water in petrol. I think you big stuffy bird."

He smiled, a little discomfited. "I liked you from the start. That instant."

"Then I not like you, just another American come destroy my country."

"I thought you were happy we're here –"

She glanced across the river at the ragged godowns on the far muddy bank. "You see what is happening to Vietnam?"

"That's why I want you to leave!"

"If this was happening to America, would *you* leave your country?"

He said nothing. She was right. "I want to bring your whole family."

"My mother sells vegetables and medicine plants. What she can do in America?"

It was true. He felt the despair of one who knows his deepest hopes are fantasy. He was here to kill people, not fall in love.

"You Americans not understand for thousands of years we fight everyone who come here. We fight and fight and never give up. Soon or late, all invaders leave. Someday Americans give up and leave too."

"We came to help you make a democratic country."

"Even you not believe that."

It was true. After a thousand years of domination, she'd told him, the Vietnamese had defeated the Chinese, only to be invaded by the Mongols, and defeated them too. How after five centuries of independence the French had finally conquered them in the eighteen-sixties, leading to the next fierce struggle for independence. Then in nineteen forty the Japanese had invaded, defeating the French, and the independence movement, called Viet Minh, was renewed. In the Japanese occupation "millions of people killed or starved, but we never stop fighting," and Ho Chi Minh and his troops, often aided by the United States, inflicted major losses on the Japanese.

When the Second World War ended "we thought we would be free, but the British attack us, nobody know why. Then come back the French –"

This he had studied at the Air Force Academy – the seven-year revolution against the French leading to the stunning Vietnamese victory at Dien Bien Phu, despite billions in US military aid to the French. At that point a democratic election was set to unify the south and the north, but the United States refused to allow it.

"Vietnam people never stop fighting outsiders," she had added intently. "Even for thousand more years. Like that General Giap say, *You will kill ten of our soldiers, and we will kill only one of yours, but we will still win.*"

And this was confusing: how did someone who so hated the Communists want the Americans to leave too?

They were silent as the rotund stolid patron brought their *steak frites* – American sirloins and Idaho fries traded at the PX for Vietnamese hash. *"Bon appetit,"* the man said and slippered away. Troy took her hand. "Forget history. Some day you and I will die and rot in the ground and some day the ground will blow away and eventually the earth will fall into the sun and the universe die, *so these few years are all we've got –"*

"That is most words I ever hear you say one time!" She squeezed his hand. "Food getting cold."

"Goddamn it Su Li don't make fun!"

Her black eyes caught his. "Any time grenade can blow, they sweep us in pieces into river. Don't talk of years!"

"You go to the States we *can* have years!"

She cut a piece of steak, extended it to him on the end of her fork. "Eat."

He batted it aside. "Answer me!"

She glanced at the chunk of steak on the floor, scowled. *"Never* waste food!"

Again he took her hand. "Never waste *life* –"

"You should talk!" She shook her head fiercely. "What do Marines do?"

"Yeah," he said softly. "We *waste* people." He looked down, wanting to weep, to understand, saw the CIA types watching from another table. "I came back for you. All that matters is love. And I love you –"

She bit her lip. He was shocked to see a tear wander down her cheek. She who never showed things. How much did she hold inside? How many tears fell every day from this War? "I'm learning, Su Li, that I don't want to fight any more. My brother is right to oppose this War." He shook his head, stared away, too upset to think.

She smiled tightly. "Unless this War, you no meet me, right? You no love me anymore?"

Great waves of emotion filled him; he could see her as they grew old together, sharing the years, children, acres of happiness, learning the meaning of life and death. He smiled. "Eat, darling. Food's getting cold."

After she had eaten her *steak frites* then another, making Troy wonder where she put it in her willowy frame, after he had emptied the last of the patron's rancid Beaujolais into their glasses and she had eaten her chocolate cake and his and had sat back wiping her lips primly on her paper napkin, they went down Tran Hung Dao Street and up the creaky stairs of the Elysées Hotel to the room he had rented on the second floor. He took the little padded box from his utilities' side pocket. "Can I look at your hand?"

She extended her right hand. "No," he said. "The other one."

She gave him her left. "To see am I getting fat? Then you no want me?"

He took the sapphire ring and slid it on her finger. "Oh!" she gasped. "No!"

"It looks good with your gown," he said, breathless, stomach tight.

She pulled away her hand, staring shocked at the ring. "Oh no oh no!" She tugged it off. "I get kill to wear this! You no understand?"

He took a breath. "Understand what?"

"You Americans no run Vietnam. *VC* run Vietnam. I wear this ring they kill me!"

"So don't wear it, just keep it. But please marry me?"

Biting her lips she stared at him, black eyes glistening, unsteady. "Okay. Someday I marry you. If we live through this war."

"You know we won't. Unless you leave."

"We no talk more." She took his hand, her fingers smooth as silk, and led him to the bed, pulled the long blue gown up over her shoulders and stood before him, the crucifix glistening between her small breasts, her body copper in the lantern light, a slender golden goddess. "We make love like it is last time ever."

His voice went hollow. "Don't say that."

She slipped into his arms. "One time will be."

HIS NIGHTS WITH SU LI consumed him. When he left the MACV Hué compound to go out on patrol he forced himself not to think of her but to focus on danger and death. Standing in a charred smoking field where North Vietnamese regulars torched by napalm lay screaming in death throes while his Marines went from one to the next firing bullets into their heads, he no longer could see them as inhuman enemies, sickened by their horrible suffering and needless deaths, by the pictures of girlfriends and wives and children in their wallets. No longer, he realized, was he a hardened combatant, enraged and vengeful over the loss of his friends, blind to the right or wrong, the damage that is done.

"In the end," one Marine laughed, "they're going to make heroes of us. They want us to die, so they can use us as heroes. To make more war."

His Vietnamese was getting better; every night back at the MACV compound he studied under a weak and stuttering light instead of playing poker or watching out-of-date movies like *Singin' in the Rain* – he and his men had spent a lot of time in the rain but never sang, and *Bridge on the River Kwai* – it was so easy to win battles in the movies. And the actors only pretended to die.

Then after Christmas and New Year's of 1968 she grew distant again. "You not good for Vietnam girl. All you G.I. bring cunt sickness."

It no longer astonished him that for a conservative Catholic girl how crude she could be, as if the body were so natural it could be spoken of vulgarly without diminishing its sanctity. "I don't sleep with whores, Su Li. Not with anyone but you."

He'd never wondered if she was sleeping with another man; he saw her so rarely; she certainly hadn't been a virgin, but made love with a lissome grace, loved to ride atop him with her slender perfect body tilted back. "Oh, you so much bigger from Vietnam man," she once had moaned.

"Maybe you'll get *cunt sickness*," he said, "from someone else?"

She giggled. "I not *làm tình* any man but you. Not long time."

"Who *did* you fuck?"

She stared at him angrily. "Not you business."

Jealousy made his prick ache. "I want to know."

She shrugged as if his wanting to know was his fault. "I love once. He dead."

His voice got husky. "How?"

"You bad man." She slapped him, half-playfully but it stung. Tears wet his eyes. "You ask more question," she snapped, "I never *làm tình* again you."

It drove him crazy, her mysterious mix of eroticism and shyness. "Yes I love you," she would answer when he asked. "I love you too much." One time after making love she said, "Oh how much I wish I didn't love you so much! It make me very unhappy to love you! But when I am with you I am so happy."

Their affair became more tempestuous and she more fatalistic. "We have tonight. Do not ask more."

At the inevitable sounds of gunfire she would tense, sit up in bed and listen. "Ah, over by Tay Loc Airfield, that."

He asked himself how had this happened, why was he so entranced? Was it her delicate beauty, her way of touching the world, her honeyed throaty voice, her light sure walk, stepping so straight on long slender feet she seemed almost pigeon-toed? Yes, all of that but above all it was her beautiful kindness, the caring she gave her students, her mother and little brothers, her neighbors. Her furtive smile that broke out like sunshine from behind the cloud of her shyness when she saw him. The gold crucifix dangling from her slender neck seemed to him to sum up her goodness, the best of that faith based on caring for the poor, the disadvantaged, the children and the meek.

At times she seemed distracted, torn, divided, so much that he wondered does she have another lover, yet she seemed so faithful, so deeply in love with him, that that was fantastical. He remembered the teacher Captain Cross had shot at the start of his first tour; was he in love with Su Li as penance for the girl who had been killed?

One day in mid-January she told him goodbye. Again the mystery of it enraged him. "Goddamnit I know you love me Su Li! What kind of foolishness is this?"

He sat beside her holding her, soothing her, his heart aching and confused. She pulled back, his reflection tiny in her huge dark eyes. "Can you get moved?" she said quickly. "Away from Hué, someplace safe?"

"Hué *is* safe."

"You tell the Marines send you away Hué *nanh chong,* soon after that I marry you. After Tet. In Year of Monkey." She stared long into his eyes. "And I go with you then. Very far, very far from here."

THE END

———

TET

THREE SAMPANS piled with long canvas bundles slid out of the darkness down the Perfume River and vanished into the Bach Dang mist. Standing on the bank by the sports complex Troy joyfully inhaled the river's musky rotten fertile dampness of fish and sewage and mud and almonds and bougainvillea, happily listening to the city quieting into night, its putputting motors, grumbling buses and bedlam voices silent, St. Xavier's melancholy bell tolling midnight through the thickening fog.

Su Li was here and the War faraway, almost an illusion, Hué eternal, the spirit of man, too ancient and sacred to destroy. Even in the World War they didn't bomb the cathedrals. But in the morning he'd tell the ARVN commander, Colonel Trang, that Bach Danh needed more Marines. Just to keep it this quiet. Apart from the War.

Severe yet friendly, Colonel Trang was short, round-faced, slightly bent forward. He had a frequent smile, a mix of gracious courtesy and natural good nature. He seemed to understand right away where you were coming from, and smiling in a kindly fashion, nodding, arms crossed, he would wait for you to get to your point. Troy worried as he crossed Tran Cao Vanh Street and nodded to the sentries as he entered the MACV compound gate, did Colonel Trang know about Su Li?

In his squad's main room a woman was screaming on the TV. Guys were laughing, drinking beer and smoking cigars, *Well don't go around tonight* on somebody's Sanyo,

It's bound to take your life.

He climbed the wooden stairs to his room. His roommate had pulled a week in Saigon and Troy was happy for the privacy, in his warm bunk in the narrow little room in the far sleepy din of radios and songs, loving the drift into sleep and thinking of Su Li.

HE WOKE UNEASY from a dream of superstition and sorrow, sat up rubbing sleep from his face and wondering what was wrong. Barefoot on the cool floorboards he checked his rifle and the three spare clips and two grenades beside it.

The city was quiet. *Dead of night.* Why call it that?

An AB-40 rocket screamed into the courtyard and blew apart, shrapnel ripping through the walls as he hit the floor. He rolled up and snatched his gun and ammo, yanked on a grenade vest as another rocket howled in knocking him down. He grabbed his boots, jammed the mattress against the outside wall and ran to his battle station on the northwest wall facing the Citadel. Flares dark-lit the sky, rifles and machine guns were firing from the gate. A third rocket smashed into the courtyard, men screaming. Three shadows flitted across the street below, he fired too late.

"They're hitting the front gate," someone yelled. He ran for it, untied boots flapping, in the horrible wail and spatter of bullets, took cover with other Marines behind the gate wall, and fired over it at the incoming tracers from a machine gun in the street. The machine gun stumbled, stopped, then suddenly blasted at him knocking chunks from the wall as he dove for shelter, other Marines firing at it and it stopped and a barefoot kid with a blooper dropped a couple of grenades on it. When the grenades blew, Troy ran with others up the street leaping flare-lit bodies and rubble and downed branches and crippled cars, green tracers leaping at them from everywhere, there was no cover but the corners of houses and tree trunks and cars and any indent in the terrain they could find as they pushed foot by foot toward Le Loi Street, dead Marines littering the road.

They fought their way behind two Ontos anti-personnel vehicles up Le Loi Street, VC hammering them with converging machine guns from streetside trenches, windows and roofs, guys falling, others running for the wounded, piling them on the Ontos, a Marine sobbing and holding his torn belly as he died, another trying to staunch the blood as bullets snapped around him.

At An Cuu Bridge he led a fire team around the abutments into a hail of machine gun bullets and rockets, dead Marines clumped on the pavement. A mortar hit twenty feet ahead with a hail of shrapnel and ripping girders, two Marines falling, metal screaming as the bridge began to slip into the river. He dashed from one pylon to the next, bullets zipping past, the bridge still shivering from the hit, and another mortar whispered down and hit the river with a great *oomph*.

Fearing a bullet through his helmet he inched his head round the pylon. From the far bank green tracers were converging on them, a constant *rat-ta-tat* of death against the girders, a wall of bullets they could not push through. On the River below the Citadel, Chez Henri was burning.

They were naked here. Through the hiss and crack of bullets Marines were trying to reach each other. From the stilt houses all up and down the far bank of the river and from the streets beyond green tracers were focused on them; to wait here was to die.

He ran for the next pylon; bullets tugged at his sleeve and smashed the rifle from his hand and as he dove for it one creased his skull. The rifle was smashed at the breech; he rolled to a dead Marine and grabbed his and three clips slippery with hot blood.

Five Marines ran across the bridge, two falling halfway, three reaching the pylons behind him. He dragged a wounded Marine back, waving at them to stop advancing then dashed for the far bank with a few others and took up a position firing carefully, defensively, to stretch out ammo. But there was no way to bring up more ammo or meds for the four wounded; before dawn they pulled back bringing five dead Marines.

Back on the south bank near Le Loi Street he ran out into the street to grab an AK-47 from a dead NVA and worked his way back to C Company, just as they were inserted into the house-by-house, street-by-street slaughter in the old city, block by block of death, toward the Citadel.

. . .

TET WAS EVERYWHERE on TV. All the time. Newsmen, politicians and generals spoke of the offensive as if it were an inanimate event where you felt good because progress was being made. As if thousands of people weren't being torn apart and dying.

In the Duchess Suite at the Crown Royal Hotel in Vancouver, Tara knelt by the bed and tried to pray. Bring him home safe, Lord, and I'll do anything. What would be the hardest thing to do? I'll do it. Bring him home, Lord, and I'll quit smack.

The floor hurt her knees. She was so skinny these days. It didn't use to be like this. Then it hit her like lightning that she was like this *because* of Troy. Because he was lost to her, and she still ached for him, and she bent down her head and told herself *Don't think about it.*

Just bring him back, Lord. Just bring him home.

ABOUT THE AUTHOR

MIKE BOND is the author of nearly a dozen best-selling novels, a war and human rights journalist, ecologist, international energy expert and award-winning poet. He has been called *"the master of the existential thriller"* (BBC), *"one of America's best thriller writers"* (Culture Buzz), *"a nature writer of the caliber of Matthiessen"* (WordDreams), and *"one of the 21st century's most exciting authors"* (Washington Times).

He has covered wars, revolutions, terrorism, military dictatorships and death squads in the Middle East, Latin America, Asia and Africa, and environmental issues including elephant poaching, habitat loss, wilderness survival, whales, wolves and many other endangered species.

His novels place the reader in intense experiences in the world's most perilous places, in dangerous liaisons, political and corporate conspiracies, wars and revolutions, making *"readers sweat with [their] relentless pace"* (Kirkus) "in that fatalistic margin where life and death are one and the existential reality leaves one caring only to survive." (Sunday Oregonian).

He has climbed mountains on every continent and trekked more than 50,000 miles in the Himalayas, Mongolia, Russia, Europe, New Zealand, North and South America, and Africa.

Website for Mike Bond: mikebondbooks.com

AMERICA

America is the first of Mike Bond's seven-volume historical novel series, capturing the victories and heartbreaks of the last 70 years and of our nation's most profound upheavals since the Civil War – a time that defined the end of the 20th Century and where we are today. Through the wild, joyous, heartbroken and visionary lives of four young people and many others, the Sixties come alive again. *"An extraordinary and deftly crafted novel."* – MIDWEST BOOK REVIEW

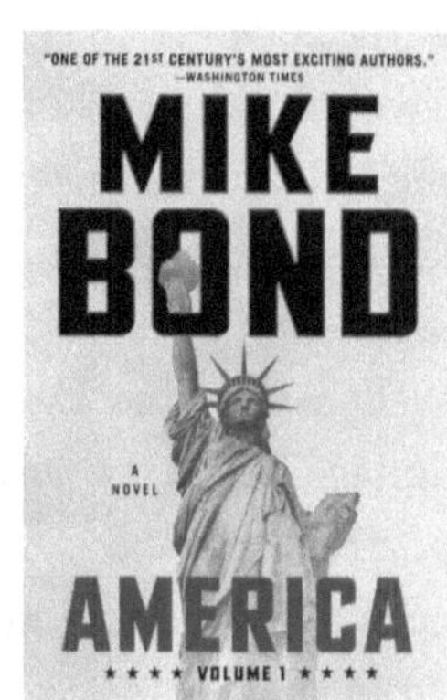

GOODBYE PARIS

Special Forces veteran Pono Hawkins races from Tahiti to France when a terrorist he'd thought was dead has a nuclear weapon to destroy Paris. Joining allies from US and French intelligence, Pono faces impossible odds to save the most beautiful city on earth. Alive with covert action and insider details from the war against terrorism, Goodbye Paris is a hallmark Mike Bond thriller: tense, exciting, and full of real places, and that will keep you up all night. *"A rip-roaring page-turner."* – CULTURE BUZZ

SNOW

Three hunters find a crashed plane filled with cocaine in the Montana wilderness. Two steal the cocaine and are soon hunted by the Mexican cartel, the DEA, Las Vegas killers, and the police of several states. From the frozen peaks of Montana to the heights of Wall Street, the Denver slums and million-dollar Vegas tables, Snow is an electric portrait of today's America, the invisible line between good and evil, and what people will do in their frantic search for love and freedom. *"Action-packed adventure."* – DENVER POST

ASSASSINS

From its terrifying start in the night skies over Afghanistan to its stunning end in the Paris terrorist attacks, Assassins is an insider's thriller of the last 30 years of war between Islam and the West. A US commando, an Afghani warlord, a French woman doctor, a Russian major, a top CIA operator, and a British woman journalist fight for their lives and loves in the deadly streets and lethal deserts of the Middle East. *"An epic spy story."* – HONOLULU STAR-ADVERTISER

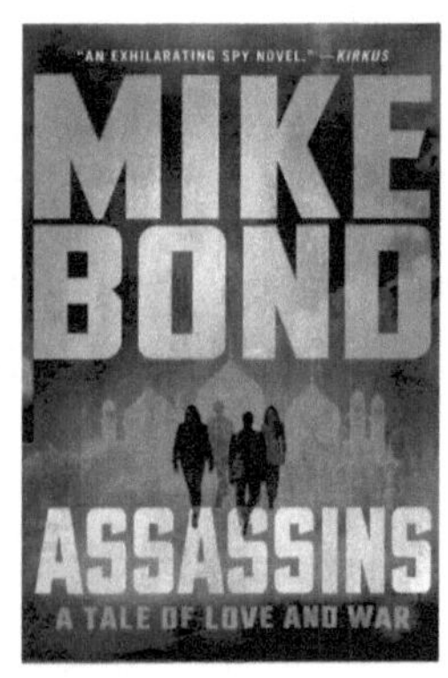

KILLING MAINE

Surfer and Special Forces veteran Pono Hawkins quits sunny Hawaii for Maine's brutal winter to help a former SF buddy beat a murder rap and fight the state's rampant political corruption. *"A gripping tale of murders, manhunts and other crimes set amidst today's dirty politics and corporate graft, an unforgettable hero facing enormous dangers as he tries to save a friend, protect the women he loves, and defend a beautiful, endangered place."* – FIRST PRIZE FOR FICTION, NEW ENGLAND BOOK FESTIVAL

———

SAVING PARADISE

When Special Forces veteran Pono Hawkins finds a beautiful journalist drowned off Waikiki, he is caught in a web of murder and political corruption. Hunting her killers, he soon finds them hunting him, and blamed for her death. A relentless thriller of politics, sex, and murder, *"an action-packed, must read novel ... taking readers behind the alluring façade of Hawaii's pristine beaches and tourist traps into a festering underworld of murder, intrigue and corruption."* – WASHINGTON TIMES

———

THE LAST SAVANNA

An intense memoir of humanity's ancient heartland, its people, wildlife, deserts and jungles, and the deep, abiding power of love. *"One of the best books yet on Africa, a stunning tale of love and loss amid a magnificent wilderness and its myriad animals, and a deadly manhunt through savage jungles, steep mountains and fierce deserts as an SAS commando tries to save the elephants, the woman he loves and the soul of Africa itself."* – FIRST PRIZE FOR FICTION, LOS ANGELES BOOK FESTIVAL

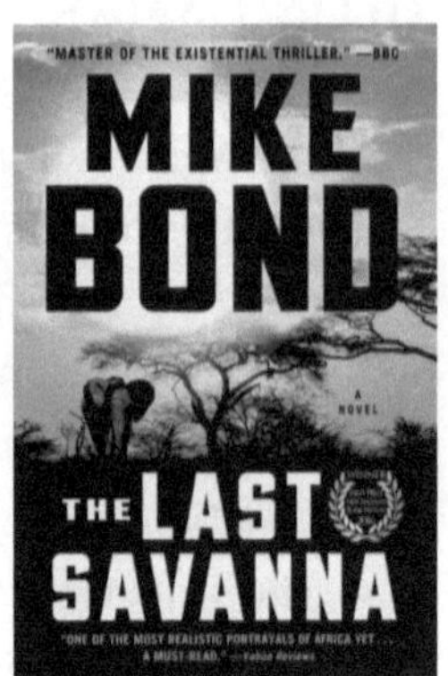

———

HOLY WAR

Based on the author's experiences in Middle East conflicts, Holy War is the story of the battle of Beirut, of implacable hatreds and frantic love affairs, of explosions, betrayals, assassinations, snipers and ambushes. An American spy, a French commando, a Hezbollah terrorist and a Palestinian woman guerrilla all cross paths on the deadly streets and fierce deserts of the Middle East. *"A profound tale of war... Impossible to stop reading."* – BRITISH ARMED FORCES BROADCASTING

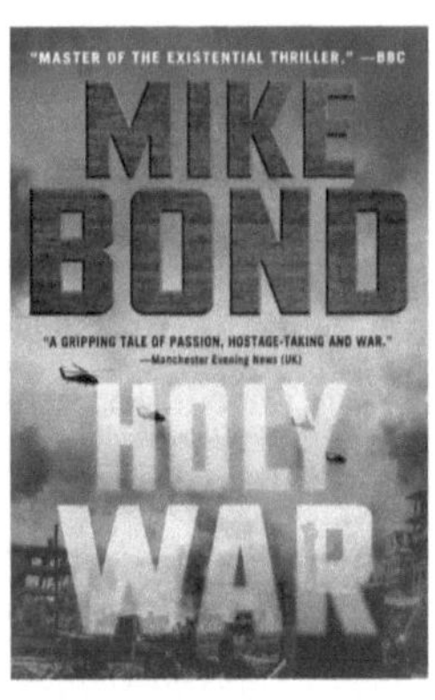

———

HOUSE OF JAGUAR

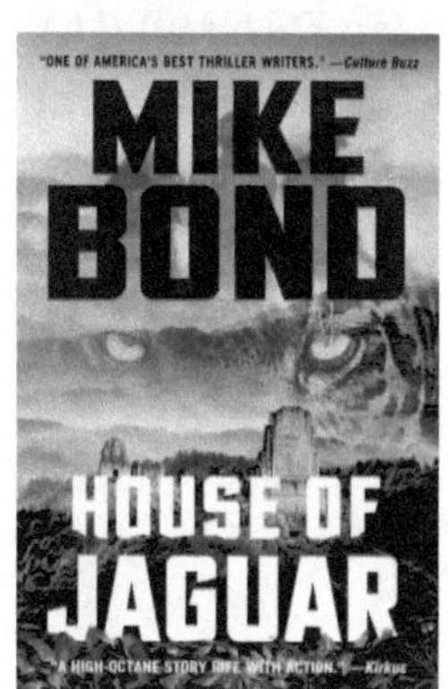

A stunning thriller of CIA operations in Latin America, guerrilla wars, drug flights, military dictatorships, and genocides, based on the author's experiences as as one of the last foreign journalists left alive in Guatemala after over 150 journalists had been killed by Army death squads. *"An extraordinary story that speaks from and to the heart. And a terrifying description of one man's battle against the CIA and Latin American death squads."* – BBC

———

TIBETAN CROSS

An exciting international manhunt and stunning love story. An American climber in the Himalayas stumbles on a shipment of nuclear weapons headed into Tibet for use against China. Pursued by spy agencies and other killers across Asia, Africa, Europe and the US, he is captured then rescued by a beautiful woman with whom he forms a deadly liaison. They escape, are captured and escape again, death always at their heels. *"Grips the reader from the opening chapter and never lets go."* – MIAMI HERALD

———

THE DRUM THAT BEATS WITHIN US

The tradition of the poet warrior endures throughout human history, from our Stone Age ancestors to the Bible's King David, the Vikings of Iceland, Japan's Samurai, the Shambhala teachings of Tibet, the ancient Greeks and medieval knights. Initially published by Lawrence Ferlinghetti in City Lights Books, Mike Bond has won multiple prizes for his poetry and prose. *"Passionately felt emotional connections, particularly to Western landscapes and Native American culture."* – KIRKUS